RICHER TANKERSLEY CUSICK

THE
UNSEEN

IT BEGINS · REST IN PEACE

speak

An Imprint of Penguin Group (USA) Inc.

THE UNSEEN

To Audrey, Suzie, B.J., Lynn, Michele, Victoria, and
the whole special gang—for your fun, your
faith and your friendship. I love you all.

SPEAK

Published by the Penguin Group

Penguin Group (USA) Inc., 345 Hudson Street, New York, New York 10014, U.S.A.

Penguin Group (Canada), 90 Eglinton Avenue East, Suite 700, Toronto, Ontario, Canada M4P 2Y3
(a division of Pearson Penguin Canada Inc.)

Penguin Books Ltd, 80 Strand, London WC2R 0RL, England

Penguin Ireland, 25 St Stephen's Green, Dublin 2, Ireland (a division of Penguin Books Ltd)

Penguin Group (Australia), 250 Camberwell Road, Camberwell, Victoria 3124, Australia
(a division of Pearson Australia Group Pty Ltd)

Penguin Books India Pvt Ltd, 11 Community Centre, Panchsheel Park, New Delhi - 110 017, India

Penguin Group (NZ), 67 Apollo Drive, Rosedale, Auckland 0632, New Zealand
(a division of Pearson New Zealand Ltd)

Penguin Books (South Africa) (Pty) Ltd, 24 Sturdee Avenue, Rosebank, Johannesburg 2196, South Africa

Penguin Books Ltd, Registered Offices: 80 Strand, London WC2R 0RL, England

First published in the UK by Scholastic Ltd, 2003

First published in the United States of America by Speak, an imprint of Penguin Group (USA) Inc., 2005

This omnibus edition published by Speak, an imprint of Penguin Group (USA) Inc., 2012

1 3 5 7 9 10 8 6 4 2

Copyright © Richie Tankersley Cusick, 2003

All rights reserved

LIBRARY OF CONGRESS CATALOGING-IN-PUBLICATION DATA

Cusick, Richie Tankersley.

It begins / Richie Tankersley Cusick.

p. cm.—(The unseen ; pt. 1)

First published in the UK by Scholastic Ltd., 2003.

Summary: After a horrifying encounter in a graveyard, Lucy cannot get over feeling
that she is being watched, but is unwilling to trust the one person who might be able to help her.

ISBN 0-14-240463-2 (pbk.)

[1. Supernatural—Fiction. 2. Psychic ability—Fiction. 3. Grief—Fiction.

4. Orphans—Fiction. 5. Family problems—Fiction.] I. Title.

PZ7.C9646Itab 2005 [Fic]—dc22 2005043446

Speak ISBN 978-0-14-242336-3

Set in Perpetua Regular

Printed in the United States of America

Prologue

She had deceived him!

He realized now with a terrible certainty that she'd deceived him from the beginning—planned this whole thing from the very start.

And she knew everything about him—*everything!*—what he was and what he'd done and all he was capable of doing . . .

She'd sought him out and gained his trust, for one purpose and one purpose only.

To see him destroyed.

After he'd been so careful . . . so cunning all these years . . . concealing the very nature of his soul . . . the ageless secrets of his kind . . .

And he'd trusted her. Taken her. Loved her more than he'd ever loved anyone.

Tears clouded his vision.

As though he were seeing the future through a dark red haze, a veil of blood.

He glanced down at his hands.

His strong, gentle fingers, wielding the power of life and death.

He hadn't even realized he was gripping the dagger, the dagger of his ancestors, nor did he remember even drawing it from its sheath.

He was gripping the blade so tightly that a stream of his own blood seeped from his fist. He watched it, strangely mesmerized, as it dripped onto the cold stone floor and pooled around his feet.

He hadn't thought he could feel such pain.

Not from the knife, for he had borne far worse injuries than this in his lifetime, had suffered the ravages of a thousand tortures. But those scars had faded quickly, like shadows swallowed by night, and the few that remained were points of honor to him now, sacred testimonies to his very survival.

No, this pain was different.

This pain burned from deep within, filling him with rage and a craving for revenge.

A craving so intense, he could almost taste it.

1

She should never have come here.

Not into this deep, dark place, not in this miserable weather . . . and *especially* not at night.

"A graveyard," Lucy murmured. "What was I thinking?"

But that was just it—she *hadn't* been thinking, she hadn't had *time* to think, she'd only felt that sudden surge of fear through her veins, and then she'd started running.

Someone was following her.

Not at first, not when she'd first left the house and started walking, but blocks afterward, six or seven maybe, when the storm had suddenly broken and she'd cut through an alley behind a church and tried to find a shortcut home.

No, not home! The words exploded inside her head, angry and defensive. *Aunt Irene's house isn't home, it won't ever be home. I don't have a home anymore.*

The rain was cold. Even with her jacket Lucy felt chilled, and she hunched her shoulders against the downpour, pulled her hood close around her face. She hadn't even realized where she was going; there was no sign posted, no gate to mark the boundaries of this cemetery, just an unexpected gap through the trees. She'd heard the footsteps and she'd panicked, she'd bolted instinctively into the first cover of darkness she could find.

But this was a terrible darkness.

Almost as dark as her own pain.

She crouched down between two headstones, straining her ears through the night. It had taken her several minutes to become aware of those footsteps back there on the sidewalk, and at first she'd thought she was imagining them. She'd thought it was only the rain plopping down, big soft drops, faint at first, but then louder and faster, sharper and clearer. Until suddenly they seemed to be echoing. Until suddenly they

seemed to have some awful purpose, and she realized they were coming closer.

She'd stopped beneath a streetlamp, and the footsteps had stopped, too. She'd forced herself to look back, back along the pavement, across the shadowy lawns and thick, tangled hedges, but there hadn't been anyone behind her.

No one she could see, anyway.

But *someone* was there.

Someone . . .

She was sure of it.

And that's when she'd run . . .

"I'm afraid you'll find Pine Ridge very different from what you're used to." How many times had Irene told her that, just in the one agonizing week Lucy had been here? "We're right on the lake, of course, and the university's here, so there's plenty to do. And we're only a half-hour drive to the city. But our neighborhood is quiet . . . rather exclusive, actually. Peaceful and private, just the way residents like it. Not at all like that old apartment of yours in the middle of downtown."

But Lucy had loved her old apartment, the tiny, third-floor walk-up that she and her

mother had filled with all their favorite things. And the sorrow she'd felt at leaving it only grew worse with each passing day.

She'd been too depressed on their ride from the airport that day to notice much about Pine Ridge; she had only the vaguest recollections of Aunt Irene pointing things out to her as they'd ridden through town. The college campus with its weathered brick buildings and stately oaks. The renovated historical district with its town square and gazebo; its bars, coffee shops and open-air cafés; its bookstores and art galleries and booths selling local crafts. They'd passed farms and fields to get here, and she'd caught occasional glimpses of the lake through dense, shadowy forests. And there'd been frost sheening the hillsides, and she remembered thinking that she'd never seen so many trees, so many vibrant autumn colors . . .

"And it's safe here in Pine Ridge," her aunt had assured her. "Unpleasant things don't happen."

You're wrong, Aunt Irene . . .

Lucy pressed a hand to her temple. That all-too-familiar pain was starting again, throbbing behind

her eyes, stabbing through her head, that agony of unshed tears, of inconsolable sorrow . . .

You're wrong, because unpleasant things do happen—anywhere—horrible, bad things—and just when you think they couldn't possibly ever happen to you—

"Oh, Mom," Lucy whispered. "Why'd you have to die?"

For a split second reality threatened to crush her. Closing her eyes, she bent forward and clamped her knees tight against her chest. She willed herself to take deep, even breaths, but the smell of stagnant earth and rotting leaves sent a deep shiver of nausea through her.

Don't think about that now, you can't think about that now, Mom's gone and you have to get out of here!

Very slowly she lifted her head. Maybe the footsteps had followed her in here—maybe someone was waiting close by, hiding in the shadows, waiting for her to make the slightest move. Or maybe someone was coming closer and closer this very second, searching methodically behind every tombstone, and she'd never hear the footsteps now, not on the soggy ground, not with the sound of the rain, not until it was too late—

Come on, move! Run!

But where? Where could she go? She wasn't even sure where she was, much less which direction to run in.

"Unpleasant things don't happen . . ."

Lucy's heart hammered in her chest. She clung desperately to her aunt's words; she ordered herself to *believe* them. Maybe she really *had* imagined those footsteps back there. Maybe it *had* just been the rain and she'd panicked for nothing. After all, she hadn't really been herself since Mom's funeral. As mechanical as a robot and just as hollow inside, moving in slow motion through an endless gray fog of days and nights, confused by the long, empty lapses in her memory. But shock did that to a person, Aunt Irene had informed her, in that cool, detached tone Lucy was beginning to get used to—*shock and grief and the unbearable pain of losing someone you love . . .*

I can do this . . . I have to do this . . .

Lucy got to her feet. Steadying herself against one of the headstones, she pushed her long wet hair back from her face, then turned slowly, blue eyes squinting hard into the gloom. High above her the limbs of a giant elm flailed wildly in the wind, sending down a soggy shower of leaves. The sky gushed like a waterfall. As the moon flickered briefly through churning clouds, she saw nothing but graves in every direction.

Just dead people, Lucy.

And dead people can't hurt you.

The storm clouds shifted, swallowing the moonlight once more. Swearing softly, Lucy ducked her head and ran.

She didn't have a clue where she was going. She'd never had any real talent for directions, and now she ran blindly, stumbling across uneven ground, weaving between headstones, falling over half-buried markers on forgotten graves. She wondered if Aunt Irene or Angela would be missing her about now—or if they even realized she was gone.

"Or care," Lucy muttered to herself.

The truth was, she'd hardly seen Angela since their initial—and totally awkward—

introduction. Angela—with her perfectly flowing waves of jet-black hair and tall, willowy model's figure—had been slumped in the doorway of her walk-in closet, smoking a cigarette and surveying her extensive wardrobe with a petulant frown.

"Angela, for heaven's sake!" Irene had promptly shut off the CD player that was blasting rock music through the room. "This is your cousin Lucy!"

Angela's eyes had barely even glanced in Lucy's direction—huge, dark eyes ringed with even darker layers of mascara. "So?"

It hadn't been said in a rude way, exactly—more apathetic if anything—but Lucy had felt hurt all the same.

"And get rid of that disgusting cigarette," Irene had ordered, shoving an ashtray toward her daughter. "You know how I feel about smoke in the house. And would it kill you to be civil just once? On Lucy's first night here? After all, you two are the same age; you probably have a lot in common."

Angela hadn't flinched. "You're kidding, right?"

"Fine, then. Very fine, Angela. From now on, I don't care *how* the two of you handle it—you girls will have to work things out between yourselves."

A careless shrug. "Whatever."

"Honestly, Angela, you never think about anyone but yourself," Irene had persisted.

Angela had reached over then . . . mashed out her cigarette in the ashtray her mom was still holding. She'd raised her arms above her head, stood on tiptoes, and stretched like a long, lean cat.

And then she'd walked very slowly, very deliberately, out of the room . . .

"Of course they won't care," Lucy muttered again.

She hadn't told either of them she was leaving earlier—she doubted if they'd have understood her desperate need to escape the house where she still felt so lonely and unwelcome. All Lucy had thought about was getting away, and so the darkness of empty streets had felt comforting to her then. But now she felt stupid for being so scared, for getting so lost. She should have gone back the way she'd come; she shouldn't have listened to her overactive imagination.

"Damnit!"

Without warning she stubbed her toe and pitched forward, landing facedown in the mud. For a second she lay there, too surprised to move, then slowly, carefully, she reached forward to push herself up.

Her hands met only air.

Gasping, she lifted her head and stared in horror. Even in this downpour, she could see the deep, rectangular hole yawning below her, and she realized it was an open grave. She was sprawled on the very edge of it, and as she clawed frantically for something to hold on to, she felt the ground melting away beneath her fingers.

With one last effort, she twisted sideways, just as a huge chunk of earth dissolved and slid to the bottom of the chasm.

And that's when she heard the cry.

Soft at first . . . like the low moan of wind through branches . . . or the whimper of a frightened animal . . . faint and muffled . . . drowned by the rush of the rain.

An abandoned cat, maybe? A stray dog? Some poor outcast just as lost as she was, wandering alone out here in the dark? Lucy's heart broke at the thought of it.

"Here, baby!" Stumbling to her feet, she cupped her hands around her mouth and tried to shout over the tremor in her voice. "Come to me! Don't be afraid!"

A rumble of thunder snaked its way through the cemetery.

As Lucy paused to listen, she felt a sudden chill up her spine.

Yes . . . there was the sound again.

Coming from the empty grave.

2

As if trapped in a nightmare, Lucy forced herself to peer down into the gaping hole. She was sure she hadn't imagined the sound this time, certain now that it wasn't an animal.

The voice was all too frighteningly human.

"Please!" it was begging her. *"Please . . ."*

Pressing both hands to her mouth, Lucy tried not to scream. For she could see now that the grave wasn't empty at all, that there was something lying at the very bottom, camouflaged by layers of mudslide and rising rainwater.

As a sliver of lightning split the clouds, she saw the girl's head strain upward, lips gasping for air. And then the girl's arm, lifting slowly . . . reaching out to her . . .

"Please . . . is someone there . . ."

Lucy stood paralyzed. She watched in horror as the girl's head fell back again into the mire, as water closed over the anguished face.

"Oh my God!"

She didn't remember jumping in. From some hazy part of her brain came vague sensations of sliding, of falling, of being buried alive, as the earth crumbled in around her and the ground sucked her down. She lunged for the body beneath the water. She tried to brace herself, but her feet kept slipping in the mud. Dropping to her knees, she managed to raise the girl's head and cradle it in her arms.

"Help!" she screamed. "*Somebody help us!*"

Was the girl dead? Lucy couldn't tell, but the body was limp and heavy and motionless now, the eyes and lips closed. She could hardly see anything in this darkness—only brief flashes of the livid face as lightning flickered over the girl's delicate features. Ghostly white cheeks. Dark swollen bruises. A scarf wound tight around her neck—

"Somebody! *Somebody help us!*"

Yet even as she shouted, Lucy knew no one would hear her. Not through this wind and rain, not in this place of the dead. With numb fingers, she worked feverishly at the scarf, but the wet material was knotted and wouldn't budge. In desperation, she smoothed the girl's matted hair and leaned closer to comfort her.

"Hang on, okay? I'm going to get you out of here, but I have to leave—just for a little while—and get help. I'll be back as quick as I—"

Something clamped onto her wrist.

As Lucy's words choked off, she could see the thin, pale hand clinging to her own . . . the muddy fingers lacing slowly between her own fingertips . . .

They began to squeeze.

"Oh, God," Lucy whimpered, "stop . . ."

Pain shot through the palm of her hand.

Pain like she'd never felt before.

Waves like fire, burning, scalding through every nerve and muscle, throbbing the length of her fingers, pulsing upward through her hand, her wrist, along her arm, piercing her heart and her head. Pain so intense she couldn't even scream. Her body began to shake uncontrollably. Her strength drained in a dizzying rush. Through a blur of strange blue light she saw the girl's head turn toward her . . . saw the scarf slip easily from the fragile neck. She saw the jagged gash across the girl's throat . . . the raw, stringy flesh . . . the glimmer of bone . . .

Lucy pitched forward. The girl's body was soft beneath her, cushioning her fall, and from some great distance she heard her own voice crying out at last, though she understood somehow that this was only in her mind.

"Who did this to you? What's happening?"

Listen, the girl whispered. Had her lips moved? Had she spoken aloud? Lucy didn't think so, yet she could *hear* this girl, could hear her just as clearly as two best friends sharing secrets.

Dazed and weak, she managed to lift herself onto one elbow. The girl was staring at her now, wide eyes boring into hers with an intensity both chilling and compelling. Lucy was helpless to look away.

Tell no one, the girl said, and her lips did *not* move, and Lucy could only gaze into those huge dark eyes and listen to the silence. *Do you understand? Promise me you understand . . .*

Lucy felt herself nod. Tears ran down her cheeks and streamed with the rain over the girl's cold skin. The hand holding hers slid away; the dark eyes shifted from her face, to something far beyond her, something Lucy couldn't see.

If you want to live, the girl murmured, *you mustn't tell anyone . . . not anyone . . . what you've seen here tonight.*

"Don't die," Lucy begged. "Please don't die—"

Promise me.

"Yes . . . yes . . . I promise."

The girl's eyelids slowly closed.

But for one split second, Lucy could have sworn that she smiled.

3

She didn't remember climbing out of the grave.

She didn't remember running or even finding her way out of the cemetery—but suddenly there were lights in the distance and muffled voices and the wild pounding of her own heartbeat in her ears.

Lucy stopped, gasping for breath.

She realized she was standing on a low rise, with a sidewalk about thirty yards below her. She could see streetlights glowing fuzzy through the rain, and beyond that, the watery reflections of headlights from passing cars.

Oh God, what should I do?

She couldn't stop shaking. She couldn't get warm, couldn't think. Her knees felt like rubber, and it was all she could do to force herself the rest of the way down the hill.

Maybe it didn't really happen. Maybe I fell into a hole back there and knocked myself out and started hallucinating.

She wanted to believe that. Wanted to believe that with every fiber of her being, because to accept what she'd just seen in the cemetery was too horrifying to deal with. Nothing seemed real anymore, not the rain beating down on her or even the nice solid feel of the pavement as she finally reached the curb and peered to the opposite side of the street. There was a gas station on the corner, lights on but pumps deserted, and the voices she'd heard were actually coming from loudspeakers playing country music.

Again Lucy stopped. She glanced behind her into the darkness, into the hidden secrets of the graveyard, and her mind whirled in an agony of indecision.

I promised. I promised her.

And yes, it *had* been real, and there was a girl, a girl maybe her own age lying dead, and no matter how sacred a promise, Lucy knew she couldn't just leave her there all alone in the rain . . .

"If you want to live . . . you won't tell anyone."

The girl's words echoed back to her, chilling her to the bone. Maybe it wasn't really a warning, she argued to herself, maybe it didn't mean anything at all. She knew people often said strange things when they were dying, when they were out of their heads from pain and confusion and that final slipping-away from the world. *Like Mom was at the end. Like Mom was—*

"No," Lucy whispered to herself. "Not now."

She took a deep breath and shut her eyes, but she couldn't shut out the image of those *other* eyes, those pleading, desperate eyes gazing up at her from the girl's bloodless face. Without even realizing it, she flexed her hand inside her jacket pocket. There was a vague sensation of pain, but she was too preoccupied to give it attention. As she stared over at the gas station, she suddenly noticed a drive-by telephone at one end of the parking area, and she knew what she had to do.

Keeping her head down, Lucy hurried across the street. Someone was working under the hood of a car inside the garage, but the lot was still deserted and the phone was far enough away that she didn't think she'd be noticed. She grabbed up the receiver and punched in 911, telling herself she wasn't *really* breaking her promise. It was only a compromise.

"911. What is your emergency?"

Lucy froze.

"You won't tell anyone . . ."

"911. What is your emergency, please?"

"Promise me . . ."

"Hello? Please state your emergency."

"Yes," Lucy whispered. "Yes . . . I—"

Without warning a horn blared behind her. Lucy slammed down the receiver and whirled around as a red Corvette screeched to a stop about three feet away. Then one of the windows slid down.

"You picked a hell of a night to run away," Angela greeted her blandly.

Lucy shook her head. Despite the fact that it was Angela, she felt an immense sense of relief. "I'm not running away."

"Oh."

She was sure her cousin sounded disappointed. The thought actually occurred to her to just turn and leave, but then she saw Angela nod toward the passenger door.

"So get in, already. Don't you know enough to come in out of the rain?"

With a last glance at the phone, Lucy hurried around the car and climbed into the front seat. *What am I going to do now?* Anxiously she wiped one sleeve over her wet face, then held out both hands to the heater.

"Look at this mess." Angela rolled her eyes. "You're dripping all over everything."

"Sorry." Scooting back, Lucy angled herself into the corner. She clamped her arms tightly around her chest, but the shivering wouldn't stop. "Do you have a towel or something?"

"No, I haven't got a towel. God, look at my floor."

"I got lost," was all Lucy could think of to say.

Angela grumbled something under her breath. She plucked a lighted cigarette from the ashtray, took a long drag, then blew a thin stream of smoke out through her nose.

"Irene's freaking out," she said at last.

"I'm sorry. I just wanted to take a walk, but then I got all turned around in the storm. I didn't mean to worry anybody—"

"Oh, she's not *worried* about you," Angela

seemed mildly amused. "She's freaking out 'cause you've made her late for a meeting."

Lucy bit hard on her bottom lip. She could feel a lump burning in her throat, anger and tears mixed bitterly together, but she was determined not to cry.

"Well," she managed to whisper. "Of course she would be."

"You should've known better."

"What?"

Angela rolled her eyes. "If you think wandering off like this is gonna get you *any* attention or sympathy from Irene, then forget it. You don't know her."

But I want to, Lucy thought miserably, *and I want her to know me, too . . .*

Right after she'd moved here, Lucy had made a habit of studying her aunt's face whenever Irene wasn't watching, longing for just a glimpse of the mother she'd lost. As if somehow her mother's spirit would be reflected in Irene's eyes or in her clothes or in the way she did things—living proof to Lucy that her mom was still with her.

But there'd been no similarities—no similarities whatsoever between the two women—and as the days passed, Lucy only felt more and more abandoned. No matter that Aunt Irene was her only living relative; Irene and Mom were as different as night and day.

Mom had been so . . . well . . . so *alive*. Fun and free-spirited, spontaneous and creative, with the wildest imagination and the most contagious laugh and the most stubborn determination when her mind was made up about something. Lucy had always admired her mother's disregard for rules and routines; there'd always been new things to try and new adventures to share on the spur of the moment. And she'd always loved hearing how much alike the two of them looked—the same blue-gray eyes and long, thick lashes, the same silky blond hair.

Mom had been a source of pride to her. A role model, an ideal she'd always aspired to. She'd never known her father, but Mom had been the best of *both* parents, not to mention her very best friend. Her whole world, really.

But now there was Aunt Irene.

Just Irene, who didn't seem anything like the sister she'd completely shut out of her life. Irene, who barely spoke to Lucy—barely even *looked* at her if she could help it. Who always acted tense and watchful and guarded, as though she expected something bad or dangerous to sneak up on her at any second. Irene and her high-profile job at the university . . . Irene and her endless very important meetings.

"She's self-absorbed," Mom had always told Lucy in those rare moments she ever mentioned Irene's name. "She's always been self-absorbed; she's never thought about anyone but herself. The only thing that makes her happy is getting her own way."

Lucy had never understood the estrangement between her mother and her aunt; Mom had always refused to talk about it. All she knew was that the women hadn't spoken for years, but when Mom was dying, trapped in the last throes of cancer, she'd requested—finally—that Irene be told.

And Irene had come.

To Lucy's shock, Irene had come and stayed— she'd doled out medications, stocked the refrigerator with takeout food, obsessively cleaned and tidied, and remained aloof while Lucy kept constant vigil in Mom's bedroom. And then something had happened one night. Something behind the closed door of Mom's room, something between Mom and Irene alone, something never discussed with Lucy. All Lucy knew was that Mom had suddenly seemed calm and strangely resolved, and the next morning, while Lucy sat beside her holding both her hands, Mom had slipped peacefully away.

Lucy didn't remember much after that.

Over the next few days the funeral had been arranged; over the next few weeks the apartment had been cleared out and rerented, her things had been systematically discarded, packed, or put into storage—all by Aunt Irene, she supposed, for she'd been too numb with grief even to function. And then Irene had brought her here.

"We're your family now, Lucy," Irene had announced in her cool, businesslike way. "This is your home."

And *some home*, Lucy had thought in awe,

laying eyes on the house for the very first time. Compared to the size and comfortable shabbiness of her old apartment, this new place seemed like a mansion, with its white brick walls and tall front columns, its circular driveway, its swimming pool in back. Yet surrounded as it was by thick woods, and only a short walk to the lake, Lucy would have sworn they were in the middle of a vast, lonely wilderness if Irene hadn't assured her that town was only a few blocks away.

Lucy had decided immediately that her life— and her happiness—were over . . .

"Looking for you is *not* how I planned to spend my evening."

With a jolt, Lucy came back to herself. She had no idea how long she'd been buried in her thoughts or how long Angela had been talking. She glanced at her cousin, but those dark-ringed eyes were focused on the rhythmic movement of the windshield wipers.

"I talked her out of calling the police, you know," Angela added.

"The police?" Lucy's tone was grim. "I

thought nothing unpleasant ever happened in Pine Ridge."

"Who told you that?"

"Your mother," Lucy mumbled, wishing they could just leave. She didn't want to sit here any more, here where she could see the cemetery right across the street. She didn't want to sit here knowing what she knew, and she didn't want to remember anything that had happened tonight because she was cold and hungry and exhausted, and if her 911 call *had* been traced, then she *especially* didn't want to be here when the police showed up.

But Angela took another long puff and glanced at Lucy with a tight smile. "How funny."

"What?"

"Nothing unpleasant ever happening here. And Irene—of *all* people—saying so."

Lucy frowned. "What do you—" she began, but Angela cut her off, gesturing vaguely toward the parking lot.

"So what were you doing just now? Trying to call somebody?"

Lucy stole a quick look at the phone box outside the car. How long did someone have to stay on the line for a call to be traced? How long did it take the police to find someone in Pine Ridge?

"Yes." Her mind was racing; the smoke was making her feel claustrophobic. "I was trying to call your house, but . . . but I couldn't remember the number."

"Well, I don't know where you were walking," Angela said matter-of-factly, "but you look like a zombie."

Lucy cringed. She thought of the girl in the grave. A sick taste of guilt welled up inside her, and she swallowed hard, forcing it down. "Can we please go?"

"Oh, great. You're not gonna get sick in my car, are you?"

"I hope not."

To Lucy's relief, Angela instantly buzzed down the driver's window and flicked her half-smoked cigarette out into the rain. Then she rolled the window up again, sat back, and turned up the heater full blast.

"Thanks," Lucy said. "I appreciate it."

"I didn't do it for you. I did it for my car."

Of course you did. What was I thinking? Lucy

tensed, listening. Was that a siren she'd just heard in the distance? Or only a muted sound from the radio? *Please . . . please . . . let's just leave . . .*

"Look, let's get this straight. If you came here expecting money, Irene's not gonna change her will. You're not gonna get one bit of the inheritance." Angela's voice was stony. "Just so you know."

Lucy faced her in surprise. "I didn't come here for your money. I didn't come here for anything, Angela. I didn't even *want* to come here—it wasn't *my* idea. Your mother *made* me come here." She hesitated, then said, "Just so *you* know."

"She's not my mother," Angela muttered.

"What?"

"I said, she's not my mother. She's my stepmother." Reaching over, Angela readjusted the heater again, then leaned back with an exasperated sigh. "My father married her when I was ten. And then he died two years later, and I was *stuck* with her. We've *never* gotten along, Irene and me—we've *always* hated each other. And I'm *leaving* here just as soon as—"

Abruptly Angela broke off. She reached for a

fresh cigarette, and Lucy could see how she trembled with anger.

"As soon as I turn eighteen," Angela finished defiantly. She held a lighter to the tip of her cigarette, the tiny spark glowing orange in the dark. "As soon as I'm eighteen, I'm taking off for New Orleans," she murmured again. "That's when I inherit my money, and I can do what I want. Till then I'm a goddamn hostage."

Lucy gave a distracted nod. *No . . . no . . . it's not a siren. It's going away now, in another direction . . .*

Taking a deep breath, she tried to focus once more on the girl beside her.

"I didn't know anything about you," Lucy admitted, unsure what else to say. "Not about you *or* Irene. My mom barely mentioned Irene the whole time I was growing up. I'm really sorry."

Angela's eyes widened, almost mockingly. "Sorry? Don't be sorry for me. Don't *ever* be sorry for me—I can take care of myself just fine."

"Angela, I didn't mean—"

"Just forget it. Who the hell do you think you are?"

I don't know anymore, Lucy thought miserably. *I used to know, but everything's different now . . . I'm different now . . .*

She was beginning to feel sick again. She wanted to leave, wanted Angela to stop talking and start driving. She could feel the girl's eyes upon her, and she could still see the eyes of that dead girl, and there was too *much* death, death in her past, and death tonight, she was drowning in it, drowning in all this death, and *if we don't leave right this minute I'm going to totally lose it and start screaming—*

"God, what'd you touch?" Angela asked suddenly.

"Touch?" A chill crawled up Lucy's spine, though she managed to keep her voice steady. "What do you mean?"

And Angela was leaning closer now, staring harder, her eyes like big black hollows in the shadows of the car.

"There," Angela told her. "There on your hand."

Startled, Lucy looked down.

She stared at the narrow black welts on the back of her right hand and between her fingers, at the misshapen black stain on the skin of her palm. In one more quicksilver flash, she saw the girl in the open grave, remembered the girl's hand closing around her own . . .

"I . . . I don't know," she heard herself whisper. "When I fell, maybe. That's what happened . . . I tripped . . . and I must have bruised myself when I fell."

For an endless moment there was silence.

"That's no bruise," Angela said at last.

She pulled the Corvette back onto the street and peeled away, but Lucy scarcely noticed.

Because the thing on her hand really *didn't* look like a bruise.

It looked like a burn.

Like something had burned itself right into her skin.

4

He'd come back one last time.

Just to make sure she was dead.

Some killers didn't like to come back, he realized, for fear of being seen, being connected in some way, being caught—these dangers, of course, were of no concern to him.

But after he'd done what he had to do, he couldn't get her out of his mind. He'd stood at his window watching the rain, replaying her voice over and over again in his head—her pleas for mercy, her screams of pain. And suddenly he'd begun to grow restless. Restless in a way he couldn't understand, a strange uneasiness in his veins that made him pace in the dark and jump at small sounds and warily watch the shadows.

And so he'd come back.

One last time.

She was just as he'd left her, naturally, and this soothed him a little. He'd stood over the crumbling grave and he'd stared down at her, and he'd stood for such a long, long time, waiting to see if she'd speak, if she'd move, if her eyes would open, if she'd look at him in the old familiar way he'd so loved being looked at.

But she didn't move.

And she didn't say his name.

The water and the mud were over her face, from the walls of the grave caving in, and if he hadn't put her there himself, he'd never have known she was there at all, he'd have thought she was just a pathetic mound of soggy earth at the bottom of the yawning hole.

He really was so amazingly clever.

The old graveyard. A violent storm. No one in Pine Ridge would even consider venturing into this place tonight.

So he'd thrown his arms wide to the rain, and his hair had blown wild in the wind, and he'd sucked in the darkness, until it filled him and sated him and consumed him and—

And then that restlessness again.

That vague, creeping uneasiness, gnawing in the pit of his soul.

He'd actually felt a moment of doubt.

And so he'd lowered himself into her grave.

He'd knelt down beside her and wiped the mud from her face, and he'd studied her in death, all the while wondering about her final moments of life.

She would have lingered awhile. Been aware of the warm blood pumping from her throat, leaking out between the torn chunks of her flesh, spurting with every heartbeat, then growing weaker . . . weaker . . . until it became merely a thin trickle, melting into the soggy earth.

The thought made him smile.

She was no threat to him now.

She was dead, and he was free.

And so he'd leaned over, oh so gently, and he'd put his mouth upon hers . . . cold lips together . . .

And then he'd kissed her.

One last time.

5

God, it was freezing in here.

It must be me, Lucy thought, as she slid lower in the claw-footed tub, closing her eyes, trying to relax beneath the bubbles. The bathroom was large and luxurious just like the rest of the house, but even with central heating, and even with the water as hot as she could stand it, she couldn't seem to get warm.

What am I going to do?

She could smell takeout pizza wafting up from the kitchen, and her stomach gave a queasy lurch. She could hear the muffled sound of the TV downstairs, and Angela's rock music blaring from the next room. And though Aunt Irene was now en route to yet another very important meeting, Lucy could still picture that formidable frown waiting for them when she and Angela had gotten home. Lucy had been relieved when Irene ordered her straight upstairs and into a hot bath. She hadn't felt like explaining any more details about her evening.

So what am I going to do?

She felt drained and bone-tired. Like her whole body had gone comatose and her brain had fizzled out. The cemetery . . . the girl . . . the warning . . . everything seemed like a distant dream now, or something she'd seen in a horror movie. An out-of-body experience that had happened to someone else's body . . .

"Hey!" Angela banged on the door. "Don't use up all the hot water!"

It was almost too much effort to answer. Groaning, Lucy roused herself and called back, "I'm not."

"And don't go to sleep and die in my bathtub."

"I wouldn't dream of it."

"Dinner's ready."

"I'm not hungry."

"Don't you like pizza?"

"Not three nights in a row."

Gently she massaged her forehead. She could imagine Angela leaning against the other side of the door, filing her fingernails and admiring the shape of her hands. No wonder her cousin looked practically anorexic, she thought— there hadn't been a single healthy or home-cooked meal in this kitchen since Lucy had been here.

The music abruptly shut off.

"If you die in there, you'll bloat and be all wrinkled," Angela informed her.

Lucy sighed. She listened to Angela's footsteps fading down the stairs, then she closed her eyes and drifted lower into the water.

I have to do something.

I have to tell somebody.

She couldn't call from here, that was certain. She didn't have a cell phone, and it would be too risky trying to call the police from a phone inside the house—too easy to be traced.

But besides that, something else was bothering her.

And even though she'd forced herself not to think about the obvious truth of the matter, she couldn't avoid it any longer. It had been lurking there in the farthest reaches of her mind, a mocking shadow keeping just beyond consciousness, ever since she'd made her gruesome discovery.

But now she had to face it.

Someone killed that poor girl.

Someone had *murdered* that girl, and not mercifully.

The death wound hadn't been clean or swift; someone had hacked at her throat, leaving her alone and helpless and frightened, leaving her to bleed to death in the rain.

Which meant the murderer was still out there.

And if I tell, he might find out.

And if he finds out it was me, then he'll kill me, *too.*

Trembling, Lucy readjusted the loose coils of hair she'd pinned on top of her head. She wrung out her washcloth, molded it to her face, and eased farther down into the water, resting her head against the back of the tub.

Could he have seen me? Could he have followed me?

Again she thought back, trying to convince herself she was safe: it had been so dark, storming so hard, she'd had the hood of her jacket pulled down around her face. And if the murderer really *had* been close by, wouldn't he have stopped her *then*? Done whatever he had to do to keep her from leaving?

No, something told Lucy that she and the girl had been the only ones out there in the cemetery. At least for those brief, terrifying moments.

Still . . .

A gust of wind rattled the bathroom window. Lucy jerked the washcloth from her face and sat up straight, her heart pounding.

At least you were with her at the end . . . at least she wasn't alone . . .

As the overhead light flickered, Lucy grabbed for her towel on the rack. Holding her breath, she waited. Within several minutes the lights slowly regained brightness, so she dried off quickly, pulled on her nightgown, and hurried through the connecting door into her bedroom.

Not my bedroom, she reminded herself grimly. *My prison.*

For the first two days after she'd come here, she'd simply stayed in bed, sleeping and crying, then sleeping again, missing her mother so much that her soul felt raw. The containers of takeout food that Irene regularly left on her dresser went virtually untouched. She hated the stark white walls and carpeting. She hated the sleek white furniture that looked like something straight out of a decorating magazine. She'd been so depressed, she hadn't even bothered to put out any of her favorite personal things. What she'd brought with her was still packed in boxes and suitcases, stored upstairs in the attic, all of them painful reminders of her happy life that had died.

"I'm sure you'll love your room, Lucy," Irene had assured her on the plane ride here. But Lucy had hated it at first sight, hated everything about it, including the sheer-curtained sliding doors that opened side by side out onto a little wrought-iron balcony, making her feel both exposed and accessible. She even hated the giant mulberry tree that grew beside it, the one that scraped and clawed at the railing and eaves and made it sound as though someone were trying to break in and kill her every single night.

God, Mom, what were you thinking, sending me here?

Sighing, Lucy shut off the overhead light and left just the lamp burning on the nightstand by her bed. She could hear Angela slamming cupboard doors in the kitchen and then tromping back up the staircase.

Lucy gritted her teeth and counted to five.

Angela's CD player blasted through the upstairs, vibrating the floors, rattling the windowpanes. Ten ear-shattering seconds of rage and defiance—Lucy knew it was ten, for she'd clocked it many times—before the volume cut off and silence reigned again, everywhere but in Angela's headphones.

It's a miracle she hasn't gone deaf by now, Lucy thought glumly. Rubbing her ears, she walked over and stood in front of the sliding doors.

Her room was at the back of the house, separated from Angela's by their adjoining bathroom, and at the opposite end of the hallway from Aunt Irene. From here she could look down onto the manicured lawn; the brick patio and terraced wooden deck; the glassed-in hot tub; the swimming pool, covered now for the winter; the landscaped flower beds and mulched pathways and discreetly camouflaged woodpile, all coated with a thin layer of frost. At the rear of the lawn stood a low stone wall with a gate, and beyond that, a narrow pathway led through dense woods to a private stretch of lake. Despite the heavy rain, a pale gray fog had begun to ooze through the trees. Lucy watched it, strangely fascinated, as it wound its way toward the house, smooth and silent as a snake. There was no moonlight. Only an occasional burst of lightning managed to rip the storm clouds and illuminate the landscape below.

Shivering, Lucy started to turn away.

And then she saw something.

What is *that?*

Frowning, she leaned closer, squinting hard through the glass.

Had she imagined it? That very slight movement just beyond the wall? As though one shadow had separated itself from all the others . . . as though it were hovering there, like a wisp of pale smoke, just on the other side of the gate . . .

Come on, Lucy, get a grip.

Of *course* there were shadows out there— *millions* of shadows out there—and of *course* things were moving. *Fog and wind and rain and—*

"Some animal," Lucy whispered. *A deer,*

probably. She'd spotted an occasional deer in the yard since she'd been here. Irene hated them, said they caused major damage to her expensive shrubs; she'd forbidden Angela to leave out food of any kind.

"Just a deer," Lucy told herself again, more firmly this time.

And yet . . .

Frowning, she pressed closer to the doors, lamplight soft behind her. *"Peaceful and private"* —isn't that what Irene had said about this neighborhood? Yet Lucy could feel a vague sense of unease prickling up her spine. As though something far more ominous than a deer was out there in the woods . . . watching her.

Don't be ridiculous . . . it's because of what happened tonight . . . you're only imagining things.

She thought of the girl. Of her own promise. She wondered again what she should do. She didn't want to stand here looking out anymore, but she couldn't seem to turn away from the dark.

Her breath quickened. She could feel her heart fluttering in her chest. Only moments ago she'd been freezing, but now a peculiar warmth was spreading through her, hot liquid in her veins. Her favorite nightgown, much too thin for these unforeseen autumn nights, now seemed unusually constricting. She opened the first three buttons down the front and leaned forward, resting her forehead against the glass.

Something moved on the corner of her balcony.

Gasping, Lucy's head came up, and she peered anxiously out into the night. *Just the tree . . . that stupid tree hitting the railing . . . nothing more!* But even as she tried to reason with herself, she was already tugging at the doors, sliding them open to the wind.

Rain swept savagely into the room. With a cry, Lucy grabbed both doors and after a brief struggle, managed to lock them in place. Then she backed away and sat on the edge of her bed, soaking wet.

What on earth were you thinking?

She was cold again—cold to the bone—and besides that, she felt unbelievably stupid.

"And paranoid," she reminded herself glumly. "Don't forget paranoid."

As her mind flashed back to the cemetery, she tried to block it out. No wonder she was seeing watchers in the woods now, and lurkers on the balcony, and danger in every shadow. And thank God Angela was buried in her headphones right now, completely oblivious to the rest of the world—Lucy wasn't up for any more confrontations or excuses.

Leaving her gown in the bathroom to dry, Lucy toweled off and changed into a warm pair of sweats. Then she shut off the lamp and tried to cocoon herself deep inside her blankets.

She lay there, wide-eyed, too exhausted to sleep.

She lay there feeling numb, and each time a vision of the dead girl floated into her mind, she tried to think of other things. *Home before. Mom before. My perfect and wonderful life before.* She'd had friends . . . she'd been popular . . . she'd had fun, and she'd had ambitions. What were her friends doing now, she wondered sadly. She'd withdrawn from them more and more during Mom's illness, and since she'd come here to live, she'd scarcely thought about them at all—hadn't written, hadn't even called. She'd promised a few of them to keep in touch, to send them her address—why hadn't she?

Because I hate it here so much. Because I'm so miserable, and I don't want them to know how horrible my life is now . . .

Her thoughts swirled and faded. The storm continued to rage outside her windows, and after a very long time she finally drifted off.

She wasn't sure what woke her.

It was a feeling rather than a sound.

A slow, cold chilling at the back of her neck . . . a vague sense that she wasn't quite alone.

Lucy struggled to open her eyes. She was lying on her side facing the sliding glass doors, and as lightning flashed beyond the rain-streaked panes, the room went in and out of shadow.

"Lucy," a voice said softly.

Raising herself on one elbow, Lucy stared. She could see the curtains blowing in, billowing like lacy feathers, though she knew it was *impossible*, that she'd already shut those doors, already bolted them tight against the wind—

"Lucy . . ."

Her eyes widened in alarm. A sob caught in her throat.

"Mom?"

She tried to struggle up in bed, strained her eyes to see. And yes, the curtains *were* moving, fanning out like delicate wings, only there was something *else* there, too—a hazy figure silhouetted against the glass—she could *see* it now, though it was flimsy and formless, as sheer as those fine gauzy curtains . . .

"*Mom!*" Tears streamed down Lucy's cheeks. "Mom, is that you?"

"Listen to me, sweetheart."

And it *was* her mother's voice, but so sad, so sad. *Why does she sound like that, so terribly sad and hopeless . . .*

"Mom—"

"Be careful, Lucy," the voice whispered, and it was already fading, scarcely more than a breath. "You're going to a place where I can't help you . . ."

"What do you mean, Mom? No, *wait*! Don't leave! *Please* don't leave me!"

Lucy flung out her arms, reaching . . . reaching . . .

But the mournful shadow was gone now . . .

And the curtains hung pale and soft and deathly still.

6

A knock.

Two loud knocks, and then another, firm and persistent, hammering their way into her warm, cozy dream.

"Go away," Lucy mumbled.

She was decorating the Christmas tree in their apartment. Mom was baking gingerbread men for all her fourth-grade students, and they were both singing carols at the top of their lungs, and Mrs. Manetti from downstairs was bringing up homemade soup later for all of them to share . . .

"Wake up, Lucy. You'll be late."

"Go away," Lucy said again, only this time the dream faded down a dark tunnel, and her eyes opened to hazy light and someone standing in the open doorway to the hall.

"We've already discussed this," Irene said firmly. "I said I'd give you one week to settle in. Today you're going to school."

"Today?" She was wide awake now, the announcement finally sinking in, along with a feeling of panic. "But it's Friday—why can't I wait till next week?"

"Because one day will be difficult enough to get through. And you'll have the entire weekend to recover before you start fresh on Monday."

"But it's too soon! I'm not ready!"

"You can ride with Angela, so hurry up."

Irene didn't wait for a response, and this time Lucy didn't give one. She lay there with her face buried in the pillow, too stunned to move. Her eyes felt swollen, as though she'd been crying . . . her whole body felt achy and stiff. She wondered if maybe she was catching the flu, yet there was a vague sense of uneasiness nagging far back in her mind.

No, not the flu. Something else . . .

Something dark and suffocating . . . something gnawing at the distant edges of her mind . . . something bad that she couldn't quite place . . .

Something horrible. But what?

Groaning softly, she turned onto her side. Her right hand was aching, as though she might have wrenched it in her sleep, so she propped herself on one elbow and leaned over to examine her palm.

Memory slammed her full force.

As every horror of last night came back to her in shocking, grisly detail, Lucy let out a cry and felt the room spin around her. How could she have forgotten—even for a moment! *The girl— the grave—my promise—*

She'd hoped so much to be wrong. That somehow she'd only imagined it in her mind, that it had only been a nightmare, that she'd wake up this morning and realize the whole thing had never happened!

But it *had* happened.

And now, as Lucy stared down at her hand, she could see the evidence all too clearly, the truth etched deeply into her skin.

It was a strange marking.

Not at all as it had looked last night, for the ugly welts and discolorations had practically faded away. Now there was only the smallest reminder—the pale, puckered flesh of a tiny scar—stamped into the exact center of her right palm. It looked like a sliver of something. Like a sliver of moon. *That's it . . . a crescent moon.* So perfectly formed, it seemed neither random nor accidental. As if some miniature branding iron had been used to sear a pattern into her flesh.

No. No, that's crazy.

Grabbing the blanket, Lucy rubbed it vigorously against her palm. These were crazy thoughts she was having, thoughts that didn't make sense, because this scar on her hand was just that—a *scar*—a *wound*—nothing more. She'd tried to help, and in their struggle the poor girl had scratched her, and eventually this little scar would fade, too . . .

But how did it heal so fast?

Lucy let go of the blanket. Despite the fact that she'd been rubbing so hard, her scar wasn't even red. She stared at it in disbelief, remembering how gruesome her hand had looked last night, remembering the excruciating pain she'd felt when the girl had grabbed her in the cemetery.

What's happening to me? Am I having some kind of nervous breakdown?

"Lucy!"

Angela's voice shocked her back to attention. The door from the bathroom flew open, and Lucy saw her cousin scowling at her from the threshold.

"What am I, your private chauffeur?" Angela's miniskirt barely covered her crotch. Her designer sweater looked as if she'd spray-painted it over her chest. She looked like an expensive hooker. "You're not even up yet, and I am *so* not waiting for you."

"Yes," Lucy nodded, throwing off the covers. "Yes, I'm hurrying."

The door slammed shut. As Lucy sat up in bed, she tried to ignore the sick feeling in the pit of her stomach. When had she eaten last— sometime yesterday? So much had happened since then . . . so much confusion in her head. She couldn't think straight. She couldn't think at all.

She closed her eyes, then opened them. Her gaze traveled slowly around the room. She could see the windows . . . the sliding doors . . . the slow dawn of an autumn morning struggling to break through.

Mom . . . I saw Mom . . .

Lucy's heart caught in her chest. *Yes . . . Mom was here . . . she said something to me . . .*

Her mind tried frantically to remember. She could almost hear the tone of her mother's voice . . . could almost see her mother's face . . . but the words she'd spoken were completely gone.

Frustrated, Lucy got up. She padded barefoot to the sliding doors and squinted down at the carpet, as if she expected to see a footprint or a distinctive clue, some confirmation of her mother's visit. She ran a tentative hand down the length of the curtains, and her eyes misted with tears.

Of course she wasn't really here. It was just a dream. She wasn't here, and she wasn't a ghost either, because ghosts don't exist . . .

Lucy opened the curtains and peered out. A watery sun was spreading across the backyard, and she could see Angela recklessly scooping seeds into all the bird feeders. The rain had stopped, but beneath a cold November sky lay the widespread destruction from last night's storm—piles of wet leaves, splintered tree branches, strewn garbage, uprooted plants, even a few wood shingles and a broken shutter— and as Lucy's gaze shifted to the stone wall in back, she saw that the gate was standing open.

Her heart clenched in her chest. She forced herself to take a deep breath.

It doesn't mean anything. It was just the storm.

"Just the storm," Lucy repeated to herself. Of *course* nobody would have been out there watching her window in the middle of a storm—she'd just been feeling overly paranoid last night. As fierce as the wind had been, it was a miracle the gate was even still there at all.

She let the curtains fall back into place.

"*Lucy!*" Irene shouted.

"Coming!" Lucy shouted back.

She hurried to the bathroom, but couldn't resist checking the clothes hamper first. There were her clothes, right where she'd tossed them last night, totally covered in mud. *What did you expect—isn't that scar proof enough for you? Are you still hoping last night didn't happen?* She picked up her toothbrush, squeezed toothpaste across the bristles. *Think, Lucy, think!* Why was it so hard to focus this morning? Why couldn't she brush her teeth without trembling? *Maybe I can sneak out of school and find another pay phone . . . maybe I can pretend I have an emergency and borrow someone's cell phone—cell phones can't be traced, can they?*

Lucy frowned at herself in the bathroom mirror.

I'll have to go back to the cemetery on my own. I'll have to go back there and find her. It's the only thing I can do.

Yet she knew in her heart it was pointless. She was certain the girl was dead—*had* been dead now, for nearly twelve hours. Not only that, but she'd been lost last night, panicky and disoriented—she didn't have a *clue* where the cemetery was. *And even if you do manage to find the cemetery, even if you do manage to find the grave—what then?*

What if the killer had come back, what if the killer were *there*? What if he really *did* recognize her from last night—she'd be as good as dead.

Sighing, Lucy leaned closer to her reflection. She had dark bruises under her eyes, and her normally tan complexion was pale. She'd never worn much makeup—Mom had always insisted that Lucy had a natural sort of beauty—but today she added a touch of blush and lipstick. Just for color, she told herself. *Just for confidence, you mean.*

"Angela's right," she sighed. "I *do* look like a zombie."

She didn't even know what outfit to put on— what did kids in Pine Ridge wear, anyway? She wasn't prepared for the chilly autumn weather here, and she'd never needed warm clothes at home—no matter what she picked out this morning, she was sure to look stupid. She made a face at the mirror and tied her hair back in a ponytail. Then she went to her room, took jeans and a pale blue sweater from her dresser drawer, and pulled on thick socks and sneakers.

"Lucy! Angela is waiting!"

"I'm coming!"

God, this was going to be an awful day. As if everything else weren't bad enough already, just thinking of going into a new school, and being introduced and having everyone stare at her, made her feel sicker than ever.

She could hear the TV as she came downstairs. Pausing on the bottom step, Lucy listened nervously to a brief review of the local news. Nothing about a murder. No body discovered anywhere. Not knowing whether to feel relieved or not, she started into the kitchen when the sound of voices stopped her just outside the door.

"You can't do this to me!" Angela cried angrily. "It's not fair!"

Then Aunt Irene, cold and utterly calm. "I told you if you got one more speeding ticket, you'd be grounded. You had plenty of warning."

"But the Festival's this weekend!"

"Keep your voice down. You're acting so high-strung—are you coming down with something?"

"Yes. Dreams. I'm coming down with dreams, Irene. Weird, sexy ones, all night long. Send me to the hospital."

"Angela, will you please be mature this morning? Must we go through this—"

"Every single day?" Angela finished. "I *have* to go to the Festival. *Everyone's* going! I *have* to be there!"

"You should have thought of that before. And you should have known better than to think I wouldn't find out about this latest ticket."

"Oh, right, I forgot. Your personal friends on the police force. Or was it the judge this time?"

"This discussion is over. You can use your car to drive to and from school, but nowhere else. There will be no social events of any kind until I say so."

"It's not even about me, is it?" Despite Angela's sarcasm, Lucy could hear the threat of tears. "It's just about you looking bad in front of your important friends—"

"That's quite enough, Angela."

"If it was Lucy, you wouldn't ground *her*."

"If it was *Lucy*, I wouldn't be *having* these problems."

"Right." Angela's tone was suddenly as cold as her mother's. "Right, I forgot. 'Cause Lucy's so goddamn perfect."

Lucy pressed a hand to her mouth. She heard the kitchen door fly open.

"Angela, come back here," Irene ordered. "You have to take Lucy to school."

"*You* take her," Angela threw back. "It was *your* idea to bring her here—*you* take her!"

The door slammed shut with a bang. As tears sprang to her eyes, Lucy flattened herself against the wall and fought down her own wave of anger. *Thanks a lot, Irene. Do you think you can get Angela to hate me just a little bit more?*

"Lucy!" Irene fairly shrieked.

Quickly Lucy went back to the stairs, then came noisily down the hall again, as though she'd just arrived.

"Yes, here I am. Sorry."

"Get in the car. We're already late."

"I thought you said Angela—"

"I forgot she had some errands to run before school. I'll be taking you. Where's your jacket?"

"I . . . it got so wet last night, I—"

"Here. Take this jacket of Angela's. She'll never miss it."

"But—"

"Just put it on, Lucy. I can promise you she will *never* wear it, simply because *I* gave it to her. And Angela would rather *die* than be seen in *anything* I pick out for her. I'm sure it will fit you nicely."

"If you say so."

Irene was silent for the whole drive. It wasn't until they pulled up in front of the high school that she finally graced Lucy with a comment.

"I know classes have already started this morning, but as you know, I've spoken with Principal Howser several times. He's assured me that everything's been taken care of, so all you need to do is go straight to his office. He'll be expecting you."

"Thanks. I'll be fine."

"I'm sure you will be. Have a nice day, Lucy."

As her aunt drove off, Lucy stood there on the pavement and made a quick assessment of the school: two-story buildings of ivy-covered brick; stone benches placed strategically around the wide, sweeping campus; a covered courtyard with tables and chairs; an outdoor stage; rows of bleachers and an athletic field in the distance. Lots of trees, lots of windows, lots of cars in the parking spaces, *lots of students to face . . .*

Taking a deep breath, Lucy took one hesitant step toward the gate. Then she stopped.

You don't have to do this now. You can wait and go Monday. You can tell Irene you got sick and had to go home, and it's not really a lie, and it's not like one more day will make that much difference . . .

Lucy turned slowly, her eyes scanning the sidewalk and street beyond. A quiet, residential area; nothing but houses as far as she could see. But she'd noticed a post office and a grocery store on their drive here—someone was sure to know where the cemetery was.

She glanced over her shoulder at Pine Ridge High.

Then she ducked her head and hurried away from the school.

7

It didn't take long to find what she wanted.

But then, standing beneath the weathered sign of PINE RIDGE CEMETERY, she realized it didn't look anything like she remembered.

There hadn't been gates where she'd come in before; there hadn't been a fence or a sign. *Maybe this isn't the right cemetery, maybe Pine Ridge has more than one.* But the old man she'd asked outside the post office hadn't even hesitated—he'd pointed her straight in this direction. The old part and the new part, he'd explained to her, with the empty old church still standing guard at one end. *You were disoriented last night, you were terrified, of course nothing's going to look the same today.*

Lucy glanced up and down the narrow, deserted street. Directly across from her was an empty lot; a block away, the street suddenly ended, giving way to an overgrown field and a rickety, boarded-up house set far back beneath some trees. There was no traffic here. Not a single pedestrian in sight.

Well, what are you waiting for? Just go in and get it over with.

Lucy began walking. She hadn't expected the place to be so big—much bigger than it looked from the sidewalk—with row upon row of perfectly aligned headstones and carefully placed markers. The grass was spongy, littered with remnants of last night's storm. Plastic flowers lay everywhere, along with shredded plants and broken vases, toppled wreaths and even some soggy toys.

As Lucy walked farther, she began to notice a distinct difference in her surroundings. How the ground seemed to be actually sinking, rainwater standing in shallow pools . . . how the trees seemed to be pressing closer, weaving their branches more tightly overhead. And *yes*, she thought suddenly, fear and hope beating together, fluttering in her chest—*yes, this all seems familiar . . .*

Back here, so far from the cemetery's entrance, these graves had been forgotten. Patches of dead weeds pushed against tombstones; piles of dead leaves obliterated names. It was colder here, and piercingly damp. Locks hung rusted from mausoleum doors, heavily shrouded in spiderwebs. Stone angels and sleeping children, once meant to be comforting, now gazed back at Lucy with hollow eyes and moldy faces, their tender smiles rotted away. As though weary of their burden, many headstones had slipped quietly beneath the ivy; others were crumbled to dust.

Lucy stopped beside an unmarked grave and lowered her face into her hands.

What am I doing here, Mom? Can you even believe this?

Suddenly she was furious with herself. She must have been insane to come here, wandering around alone in this isolated place instead of being in school! *Did you really think you'd find her—some dead girl in an open grave?* There were *hundreds* of burial plots in here—*thousands*, probably!—how long could she possibly keep searching? Not to mention how enraged Irene would be when she found out Lucy had skipped school.

"Bad idea," Lucy whispered to herself. "*Very bad idea.*"

Forget good intentions—she'd leave this place now and find a pay phone. Promise or no promise, she'd make an anonymous call to the police, and then she'd get back to the house. She'd go straight to bed, and when Irene came home, she'd swear she really *had* been sick all day, but next Monday she'd be—*miraculously!*—recovered and more than ready to begin her new life.

Resolved, Lucy raised her head. She hunched her shoulders against the cold, dank breeze and turned back the way she'd come.

She was scarcely aware of his shadow.

There were so many of them, really, surrounding her in deep, dark pools . . . soft and black like liquid, oozing between the graves, seeping beneath the low-sweeping branches of the trees . . .

And later she would wonder how he got there—appearing without a word or a sound—just suddenly *there*, his tall shadow figure blocking her path, one arm extended in front of her to prevent her escape.

She saw him gazing down at her—eyes without light, face without features—or was it her own fear distorting his image, blurring everything into an indistinct mask? She wanted to run, but she was frozen in place; she heard his voice, but it seemed like some strange, faraway echo.

"She's not here," he said. "The one you're looking for."

Lucy could barely choke out a whisper. "What? What are you talking about?"

And the angels were watching—all around her, Lucy could see their blank, empty stares . . . their dead, decaying eyes . . .

The stranger was above her now.

Leaning over . . . reaching out . . . a sharp black silhouette against pale, pale light.

"She's not here," the stranger said again. "He's taken her away."

8

Someone had ahold of her shoulders.

As Lucy fell back a step, she realized that strong hands were trying to steady her, to keep her facing forward. She willed herself to scream, but all that came out was a frightened whimper.

"Take it easy," a voice said. "Just breathe."

Breathe? Struck by a fresh wave of panic, Lucy began to struggle. The hands holding her immediately tightened their grip, and before she realized what was happening, she felt herself being pulled tight against her captor's chest.

"Stop it! I'm not going to hurt you."

Lucy stopped. With her arms pinned securely to her sides, she looked up to see a pair of dark eyes gazing back at her with calm, cool intensity. In a split-second appraisal, she guessed him to be a little over six feet tall, with a strong, lean build, probably about her own age, possibly a year or two older. High cheek-bones accentuated the angles of his face; a faint shadow of beard ran along his chin and jawline and upper lip. His hair was thick and as black as his eyes, falling in loose, tousled waves to his shoulders. And he held himself very straight—though not so much a formal posture, she sensed, as a wary and watchful one.

Lucy realized she was staring. As fear and confusion coursed through her, her mind scrambled for some self-defense tactic, but the rest of her still felt too stunned to cooperate.

"I'm not going to hurt you," he said again. "I just want to talk."

He released her so unexpectedly that she nearly fell over. Recovering herself as best she could, Lucy watched as he took three steps back, then he raised his hands into the air where she could see them.

"You ran away," he stated. His eyes narrowed slightly, yet the piercing stare never wavered, even when Lucy began to back up.

"What do you mean?" she demanded. "I don't know what you're talking about. Who are you?"

Her heart was racing like a trip-hammer, her thoughts spinning in all directions. *He knows about the girl—how could he know? The only way he could possibly know anything is if he was* here—*if he was the one who—*

"You tried to help her, but it was too late. And if you tell anyone—anyone at all—you could die." His tone was so even, so matter of fact—which somehow made it all the more frightening.

Lucy's voice rose. "You don't know *anything*! You don't know—"

"And they wouldn't believe you anyway—"

"*Who are you?*"

"I'm Byron. I want to help you."

"I don't know you! And I don't need your help! Why are you doing this? Why are you saying these things?"

"Because they're true."

Slowly he lowered his arms. He slid his hands into the pockets of his jacket, and he turned his eyes to the ground, and when he spoke, Lucy could hear the cold contempt in his voice.

"It's not your fault, you know. You couldn't have saved her. Nobody could."

Tears blurred Lucy's vision. Wheeling around, she was finally able to run.

This is insane! This can't be happening!

She realized she was crying, crying so hard she couldn't see, and her chest was hurting, and her lungs were aching from the cold. She slid on wet leaves and sank ankle-deep in mud. Every breath she took was a knife blade between her ribs.

God, why had she ever come here this morning? How could she be so stupid, what could she possibly have been thinking?

And now, on top of everything else, here was some psycho lurking in the graveyard, acting like he *knew* her, acting like he knew about what had *happened* here last night—*some psycho who must be the murderer, who else could he be?—he saw me and he knows who I am and now it's a game—cat and mouse—he's taunting me and now he's going to kill me, too—*

"You're in danger," the voice warned.

Lucy screamed. She hadn't heard him following, hadn't seen him coming, but now her back was flat against a tree, and he was *standing* there, just inches away, gazing at her with those dark, dark eyes.

"People know I'm here!" she babbled. "They'll be looking for me—they'll be worried if—"

"I told you, you don't have to be afraid of me. I'm a friend."

"Leave me alone! I don't have any friends!"

"But you need one. Someone you love is gone now . . . you need one."

Lucy gaped at him. A wave of nausea rose up from her stomach, lodged in the middle of her throat. *I'm going to be sick . . . Oh God, I'm—*

"Sorry about your mother," he whispered.

As Lucy drew an incredulous breath, all feelings of nausea vanished. She simply stood there with her mouth open, staring at him in utter disbelief.

"Someone told you." At last her words choked out, tight with fury. "Someone *had* to tell you! My aunt or—or—my cousin—or someone at school—"

"No one had to tell me. I see it in your eyes."

She was vaguely aware of a rushing in her

head—a churning mixture of shock and rage and despair—and the tears that wouldn't stop, still pouring down her cheeks. For a moment she couldn't think, didn't even realize that she'd moved toward him, or that her hands had clenched into fists or that she'd shoved them hard against his chest.

"You really expect me to *believe* that?" she cried.

She saw him shake his head. Saw his hands close firmly over her fists, though he made no move to push her away.

"Some things take time to believe in," he said solemnly. "And right now . . . we don't have a lot of time."

As Lucy stared at him in bewilderment, he eased her hands from the front of his jacket. Then, still holding her wrists, he leaned down toward her, his voice low and urgent.

"Something happened here last night. Something important."

Yes, she thought desperately, *a murder. A cold-blooded murder and*—

"I think something touched you."

"You don't know anything," Lucy whispered.

But *"What'd you touch?" Angela had asked . . . and the dying girl's hand, squeezing so hard . . . the pain, the horrible pain, the excruciating pain . . . and "That's no bruise," Angela had said . . . That's no bruise . . .*

"I think something was . . . passed on to you," Byron murmured.

Lucy's eyes widened. As she tried to pull free, Byron's grip tightened, forcing her closer. With one smooth movement, he turned both her hands palms-up and gazed down at the tiny, crescent-shaped scar.

"Let go!"

Jerking from his grasp, Lucy stumbled back out of reach. She could feel her right hand beginning to tingle—ice-hot needle pricks spreading out from the center, out to her fingertips—and she clamped it shut and thrust it deep into her pocket. She told herself it was just the cold, told herself Byron had just held her too tight, shut off her circulation, but her hand was stinging . . . feeling so strange . . . and it was starting to tremble, just like her knees were trembling, just like her voice was trembling . . .

"Stay away from me!" she burst out. "I don't know why you're here, and I don't have a *clue* what you're talking about, and I'm *not* afraid of you!"

For a long moment Byron stared at her. "It's not me you need to be afraid of," he said at last.

It took every ounce of courage to turn her back on him. Holding her head high, Lucy made her way determinedly back through the graves, and she told herself that she wouldn't look back.

But when she did, he was still standing there, and she couldn't help thinking how very much he resembled some dark angel, some ominous messenger in the midst of all that death . . .

"Be careful," he called to her then, his voice as heavy as the shadows around him. "Someone won't be glad you're here."

9

The whole morning had been a disaster.

A complete, miserable, and utter disaster.

Lucy stood in the doorway of the cafeteria, clutching her books to her chest. She let her eyes wander over the laughing, chattering mass of students, then turned and walked slowly down the hall. She hadn't planned on coming to school this morning after her visit to the graveyard; she'd wanted to find a way back to the house and hide there and try to make sense of things—until she suddenly remembered she didn't even have a key.

She hadn't tried to find a pay phone. *"You tried to help her . . . it was too late . . ."* She hadn't reported last night's murder. *"You can't tell anyone . . . you could die . . . they wouldn't believe you anyway . . ."* She'd been so frightened, so thoroughly shaken by her encounter with Byron, that she didn't even realize she'd retraced her steps back to school. She'd simply looked up and found herself standing outside Pine Ridge High, wondering how she'd gotten there.

Oh, God. What's happening to my life?

She'd stared at the school, and she'd weighed her options—*Could I spend the day hiding out in some coffee shop? The library? How about the bus depot?*—but she hadn't been able to come to a single decision.

He knew *things! Byron* knew *things about last night, he knew things about* me *he couldn't possibly know!*

She'd rested her head against the fence while the world passed in a blur. He was a total stranger, but he'd known about her mother. He was a total stranger, yet it was almost as if he'd been *waiting* for her there, as if he'd *expected* her to show up there this morning . . .

Maybe he really *was* the murderer, Lucy thought again. And maybe he really *had* been taunting her, playing with her, trying to see how much she really knew. *So why didn't he kill me? Why didn't he kill me right then, when he had the perfect chance?*

She hadn't been able to shut out his words: *"She's not here . . . the one you're looking for . . . he took her away . . ."*

His words . . . those frightening, fateful words playing over and over and over again, relentlessly through her brain—

"We don't have a lot of time . . ."

"Be careful . . ."

"Someone won't be glad you're here."

She'd stood outside Pine Ridge High, afraid to go in, afraid to go anywhere, until a teacher hurrying into the building had spotted her and ushered her to Principal Howser's office. To Lucy's relief, the man had actually believed her story about being sick that morning. He'd welcomed her warmly and offered deep condolences for her loss; he'd praised her high grades from her former school, and he'd talked about how wonderful Aunt Irene was. He'd gone on and on about some Festival the school was having, and how he hoped she'd enjoy living in Pine Ridge. Then he'd handed her a schedule, assigned her a locker, given her a tour, and escorted her to class.

"Here we are, Lucy. I believe your cousin Angela has Miss Calloway this hour, too."

Wonderful. My morning's complete.

He'd interrupted a pop history quiz to introduce her, leaving her to stand like an idiot at the front of the room while Miss Calloway tried not to look annoyed and all the kids had stared. She'd felt flushed and panicky and embarrassed. Some of the kids were laughing, she'd noticed—some of the girls whispering to each other, some of the guys whistling loudly. And then she'd spotted Angela, sitting in the very back row, snickering loudest of all.

It wasn't till she'd run to the bathroom afterward that Lucy realized she had dead leaves stuck in her hair and mud spattered over her clothes. She'd stared at her sorry reflection in the mirror and felt so mortified, she'd actually considered hiding in there the rest of the day.

Wonderful, Lucy, just wonderful. Leave it to you to make a great first impression.

But at least the humiliation had distracted her.

At least it had kept her from dwelling on the cemetery . . . the murdered girl . . . *Byron* . . .

Thank God lunch was over now; she had only a few more hours to get through.

By the time Lucy found her next class, her head was pounding. Dull ribbons of pain crept down one side of her face and unfurled behind her eyes. She was achy and stiff, her shoes and socks were damp, and she still hadn't had anything to eat. Her mind was worn out from worrying; her brain had turned to mush. She didn't have a clue how she was going to make it through math. Like a robot, she slid into her assigned desk and saw Angela sitting right beside her. The dark raccoon eyes fixed on her accusingly.

"I've been thinking about that jacket of yours," Angela frowned, leaning toward her.

Lucy braced herself. "What about it?"

"It looks really familiar to me. In fact, I have one exactly like it."

"I know." Lucy kept her gaze lowered. "Irene said I could borrow it."

"And you didn't even *ask* me?"

"You were already gone. And she said you never wear it anyway, because she gave it to you."

"I can't *believe* this!" Angela pulled back as several kids squeezed between them, book bags swinging dangerously. "*Look* at it! It's totally *ruined!*"

Someone bumped Lucy's desk and murmured an apology. She glanced up to see the back of his faded jacket as he leaned over the desk in front of hers. Then Angela snapped her back to attention.

"Did you hear what I said?"

"I heard you," Lucy sighed. "I'll pay to have it cleaned, okay?"

"You'll pay to buy me another one, is what you mean. God, who do you think you are?"

To Lucy's relief, Mrs. Lowenthal called the class to order and instructed them to take out their books. Then, while the woman droned on and on about numbers that made no sense, Lucy tried to ignore the venomous looks Angela kept shooting at her from across the aisle. *Don't let her get to you . . . right now Angela's the least of your worries . . .*

"—announcements regarding the Fall Festival," Mrs. Lowenthal was saying. Fall Festival? When had they finished with math? When had they stopped working problems on the chalkboard? Lucy didn't know . . . hadn't been paying attention.

Something soft hit her foot. Glancing down, she saw what looked like a necklace lying there on the floor, but she had no idea where it had come from. Her eyes did a quick sweep of the class, but everyone was focused on the front of the room. Lucy scooted the necklace closer with the toe of her shoe, then picked it up to examine it.

It was a simple piece of jewelry—nothing expensive, elaborate, or even professional, she thought. Just a single strand of tiny beads, dark green glass, that looked rather childishly handmade. *Pretty, though, in a plain sort of way . . .*

"—want all of you there early if you're working a booth," Mrs. Lowenthal continued.

Lucy put her left hand to her forehead. Was it just her, or was the room getting hotter by the second?

"—big fund-raiser of the year, as you all know," Mrs. Lowenthal said.

It *was* getting hotter in here, Lucy was sure of it. She could feel drops of sweat along her hairline; she shifted uncomfortably in her chair.

"—those volunteers will meet this afternoon in the library—"

Maybe I'm coming down with something—getting a fever—God, I'm burning up—

"—be sure to check the schedule to see which shifts you're working—"

Lucy slid lower in her desk. Her head was way past throbbing now—it felt like it was going to burst. She wound the necklace around her wrist, twined it between her fingers; she could feel the tiny beads cutting into the tender flesh of her palm—

"—can use my car to transport some of the food—"

For a brief second the room shimmered around her. A tingling pain shot through her hand, and Lucy tried to brace herself against the desktop, tried to prop herself up, but her wrists were so limp, so useless . . .

What's happening?

She couldn't hold her head up anymore. She couldn't hear . . . couldn't see—yet at the same time she could see *everything*, *hear* everything, everything all at once, every single sense wide open—

What's . . . happening?

The classroom vanished. The warmth building steadily inside her now burst into scalding heat, searing through nerves and muscles, throbbing the length of her fingers and upward through her hand, along her arm, exploding inside her head.

I've felt this before—oh God—just like last night—

And then they came.

Lightning fast and just as merciless—images so vivid, so sharp, her body reeled with the force of them—

Hands—such powerful hands—eyes glowing through shadows—lips on her neck, her throat, and blood flowing, life flowing, "Could have been different . . . could have been perfect . . ."

Wind! Ah, the cold, sweet rush of it, taste of it, caress of it—night smells night sounds damp and cold! And fog so thick . . . woods so black . . . black and deep as—

"Death," Lucy murmured. "I'm not afraid to die . . ."

And "Lucy?" . . . someone saying her name, over and over again, "Lucy . . . Lucy . . ."

"Lucy?" Mrs. Lowenthal's voice, anxious and loud. "Lucy, are you all right?"

Lucy's eyes flew open.

She was slumped on her desk, both arms pillowing her head. She was clutching something in her right hand, and her whole arm felt numb and prickly, as if she'd been shot full of novocaine.

"Lucy?" Mrs. Lowenthal said again.

Very slowly Lucy lifted her head. She could see that the classroom was there again, along with the faces of the students, all of them staring, and Angela smirking beside her, and Mrs. Lowenthal leaning over her with a worried frown.

"You're so pale, Lucy, are you ill? Do you need to be excused?"

Lucy tried to answer, but couldn't. Instead she opened her fingers and stared down at the necklace in her hand.

"I'll have someone take you to the nurse," Mrs. Lowenthal decided. "Angela can help you. Here, Angela, let me write you a pass."

But Lucy wasn't paying attention anymore to Mrs. Lowenthal or Angela or the curious stares of her classmates.

As the guy in front of her turned around, she saw that he'd taken off his jacket. She saw the thick black hair falling soft to his shoulders, and the calm gaze of his midnight eyes. And then she saw him reach back and slide the necklace from her hand.

"Thanks," Byron said quietly. "I must have dropped this."

10

She knew she was going to be sick.

As Byron faced forward again, Lucy got to her feet and rushed up the aisle to the door. Then, ignoring an alarmed Mrs. Lowenthal, she hurried down the hall in search of a bathroom.

She finally found one near the stairs, barely making it inside before dry heaves took over. She left the stall door open and fell to her knees, sweat pouring down her face, her insides like jelly. She dreaded Mrs. Lowenthal coming to check on her—or even worse, sending Angela.

"This might help," a voice said softly.

Lucy was too weak to lift her head. She felt a cold, wet paper towel on the back of her neck . . . a gentle hand smoothing her hair back from each side of her face.

She heaved again, but there was nothing in her stomach but pain.

"Thank you," she managed to whisper.

"No need," the voice whispered back to her. "The first time's always the worst."

Lucy lifted her head.

Turning around, she stared out at the bare floor, at the row of sinks and the dingy mirror stretching over them, reflecting nothing.

"Hello?" she called shakily. "Who's there?"

Her voice echoed back to her from the bathroom walls. With trembling fingers, she took the paper towel from the back of her neck and got slowly to her feet. One by one, she moved down the row of stalls and opened each door, but they were all empty.

"The first time's always the worst . . ."

Without warning a group of girls came giggling in from the hallway. Was one of them the kind-hearted stranger? But none of the girls even glanced her way, so Lucy ran fresh water onto the paper towel and blotted it over her face. Mrs. Lowenthal was right—she *was* pale— *frighteningly* pale. *Think, Lucy, think! Try and calm down . . . try to put things in perspective . . .*

Perspective? How could she possibly be calm or rational about all the things that had happened to her in the last twenty-four hours? She was way past confusion now—way beyond frightened. Something had taken hold of her back there in the classroom—something had *consumed* her back there in the classroom—something she didn't understand and certainly hadn't been able to control. Something had crept over her and through her, transporting her to another place and time—she'd *seen* things, *felt* things—*horrible* things, intense and painful and terrifyingly real, and yet . . .

And yet there'd been no *complete* picture, Lucy realized. Nothing like a carefully posed photograph or neatly framed painting or smooth sequence of movie scenes running logically through her mind.

No, this had been different.

Just flashes of things, glimpses of things, puzzle pieces spilled helter-skelter from a box. Things without order, things that made no sense, though she felt they *should make sense*, and *did* make sense somehow, if only she could put them together . . .

Frowning, she stared down at her hand. The strange crescent scar stood out sharply against her palm, and there was a faint, lingering ache along her fingertips.

The necklace.

Lucy shut her eyes . . . opened them again . . . drew a slow intake of breath.

There was darkness . . . and death . . . and it started when I picked up that necklace . . .

The bathroom door swung shut. As Lucy turned in surprise, she realized that all the girls had left, and that Angela was now standing beside her.

"I've been looking all over for you." Angela gave an exasperated sigh. "What the hell happened back there?"

Lucy couldn't answer. She watched dully as her cousin leaned toward the mirror and primped at her hair.

"Well?" Angela demanded.

"I . . . felt like I was going to pass out," Lucy murmured.

"I've never seen anyone shake like that before they passed out," Angela said, casting Lucy a critical glance. "God, you look even worse now than you did last night. Whatever you've got, you better not be contagious."

"Who's the guy in class?" Lucy asked tersely.

"*What* are you talking about?"

"The dark-haired guy sitting in front of me."

"Byron?"

Lucy nodded, tight-lipped.

"Well, what about him?" Tilting her head, Angela gave her hair one more fluff. "Oh, please. Don't tell me you're *interested*."

Lucy merely shrugged.

"Right. Another smitten female falls under the spell of the mysterious Byron Wetherly," Angela announced. Then her lips curled in a dry smile. "Well, yeah, he's gorgeous. *And* sexy. *And* so very, *very* cool. But . . . you know . . . every girl in school is after him."

She paused a moment, as if considering a matter of great importance. Then she lifted one eyebrow, amused.

"Frankly, Lucy, I wouldn't bet on your chances."

Ignoring the remark, Lucy pulled a fresh paper towel from the dispenser. "What do you mean, mysterious? Why is he mysterious?"

"Well, who knows *anything* about him, really? He keeps pretty much to himself."

"Maybe he's shy."

"He doesn't talk much. But with a face and body like that . . . why would he need to?"

"I see." Lucy played along. "The quiet, secretive type. *That's* what makes him mysterious."

"Not just that. His family, too."

"So his *family's* mysterious."

"They're poor." Tilting her head sideways, Angela studied her profile in the glass. "And extremely weird. I mean, the word is that Byron must be adopted or something—he's the only normal one in the whole bunch. He lives with his grandmother—well, takes *care* of his grandmother; she's an invalid. His mother's been locked up for years."

Lucy looked startled. "Locked up?"

"As in *loony bin*? As in *institution*?" Angela pointed to the side of her head and made wide circles with her finger. "As in *psychopathic maniac*?"

"Yes, Angela, I get it. What's wrong with her?"

"She murdered her kids."

"Come on . . . you're not serious."

"Burned down the house with them in it. Oh, for God's sake, it happened years ago. I'm not sure anyone around here even remembers the woman *personally*—it's just something everyone knows about." Angela paused, thought for a second, then once again faced the mirror. "You know. Like a campfire story. Or one of those urban legends."

"But what about Byron?" Lucy asked.

"Well, *obviously* he got out, didn't he? Him and his crazy sister. Are you finished in here?"

Lucy nodded. She ran some water over the towel, squeezed it out, then pressed it against her cheeks, stalling for a little more time.

"So . . . is the mom in prison?" she asked.

Angela rolled her eyes. "No, just in a straightjacket for the rest of her life. Poor Byron. I mean, can you even imagine? Everyone knowing your mother's a cold-blooded killer? And, like *that's* not bad enough, that sister of his was turning out just as bad—it was only a matter of time before *she* got carted off to the funny farm. Lucky for everybody, she ended up leaving town before anything really horrible happened."

"I guess that *was* lucky," Lucy agreed quietly. "So tell me about the sister."

"She *saw* things." Another dramatic sigh. "Well . . . at least that's what she wanted people to believe. She *saw* things."

"You mean . . . like hallucinations?"

"Call them whatever you want—*she* called them *visions*."

Lucy's heart caught in her chest. She was feeling colder by the second. "What kinds of visions?"

"How would *I* know? *I* never saw her have one." Angela sounded impatient. "Telling-the-future-and-talking-to-the-dead kinds of visions, I guess. I mean, the girl was *way* creepy."

"So she never had a vision in school?" Lucy's voice was scarcely a whisper.

"She didn't go to school. She didn't go anywhere, really. I mean, nobody ever saw her."

"Then if nobody ever saw her . . . how do you know she even existed?"

Angela gave a sniff of disdain. "Well . . . nobody *normal* ever saw her. Nobody *I* know ever saw her. But there were stories, you know?" Leaning closer to her reflection, she rubbed at a tiny smudge of lipstick on her tooth. "Sometimes people would drive past the Wetherly place at night, and they'd see her watching from an upstairs window with bars on it. And sometimes, people just going down that road at night would hear screams coming from inside the house. That's why they never let her out. She was totally dangerous."

Despite her uneasiness, Lucy frowned. "Sounds like old wives' tales to me."

"Whatever. But she ran away last year, so that was a big relief to everybody. *Especially* to Byron, I imagine. I mean, God, how humiliating—so *not* cool for his social life. Now there's only him and his grandmother." She paused, her brow creasing in thought. "Good thing he's so gorgeous—he certainly doesn't have good breeding going for him."

"Then how can you really know him?" Lucy asked tightly. "How can you be so sure he's *not* like his mother? *Or* his sister?" *How can you be sure he doesn't stalk unsuspecting victims, or murder girls in cemeteries, or see into a person's mind . . .*

"Well . . ." Angela's look was blank. "That's just silly."

"*Why* is it silly? You said he keeps to himself . . . that no one really knows him—"

"God, what is this whole *obsessing* thing?"

"What about his life away from school? What about his private thoughts? What about his feelings?"

Angela made no effort to hide her amusement. "His feelings? Oh, I'd like to feel him, all right—in places *besides* my fantasies. Just like every other female around here."

She stepped back from the mirror. She ran a slow gaze over Lucy, then shook her head in mock disappointment.

"Poor Lucy . . . take my advice, okay? Forget about Byron. As a matter of fact, forget about *anybody*. You look like you've been run over by a bus. And you just had some kind of weird fit—not to mention nearly throwing up—in the middle of class. I mean, it's so *embarrassing*. Everyone already thinks you're a freak, and it's only your first day."

It took all Lucy's effort to compose herself. She wadded up her paper towel, tossed it into the trash, and carefully smoothed the front of her sweater. "You know what? I'm actually feeling much better. In fact, I don't think I even need to see the nurse now."

"Then why'd I waste my time trying to find you?"

Biting back a reply, Lucy followed Angela back to class. Byron didn't even glance at her as she slid into her seat, didn't seem to feel her eyes boring into him as she tried to ignore the stares and whispers around her. He was out of his chair as soon as the bell rang, and though Lucy hurried to catch up with him, he'd already disappeared into the crowded hallway by the time she reached the door.

She didn't see him again the rest of the afternoon, neither in class nor on campus. As though he'd vanished from her life just as quickly as he'd appeared.

By the time the final bell rang, Lucy was never so glad to have a day end—it took every last effort just to drag herself to her locker. Everywhere she turned, there was talk about the big weekend ahead, exciting plans for the Fall Festival, but all *she* planned on doing was locking herself in her room and staying in bed. She was just rechecking her homework assignments when Angela showed up, greeting her with a sullen frown.

"Hurry up," Angela complained. "I have better things to do than stand around and wait for you all day."

"You just got here. You've been waiting for—what? Two whole seconds?"

"Do you want a ride or not?"

Lucy slammed her locker door. Lowering her head, she did a quick assessment of her books, oblivious to the kids shoving past her till she felt a quick, light pressure on her arm.

"What?" Startled, she looked up. Angela was standing several feet away, watching her with growing impatience.

"What?" Angela echoed.

"Did you just touch me?" Yet even as she asked, Lucy knew it hadn't been Angela. Somehow, in that precise moment, she *knew* it was the girl who'd come to her aid in the bathroom. *That's impossible . . . how could I know that?*

"What are you talking about?" Angela frowned.

Immediately Lucy stood on tiptoes, anxiously

scanning the corridor. It was packed with students eager to start the weekend, but none of them seemed to be paying any attention to her.

This is just crazy.

"Someone touched my arm," Lucy insisted. Puzzled, she turned to Angela, who was now making an exaggerated show of checking her watch.

"You *think?*" Angela threw back at her. "I mean, there're only about a *million* people around here bumping into each other."

"No, but . . ."

"But what?"

"This was different. It wasn't an accident. She . . ."

"She, who? She, *what?*"

She wanted me to know. The realization came to Lucy with warm, calm clarity. *She did it on purpose because she wanted me to know she was here, that she was* real, *that I* didn't *imagine her—*

"You're not gonna have another fit, are you?" Angela was regarding her warily. "Because if you are, I'm leaving."

"No," Lucy murmured, taking one last

puzzled look around. "No . . . I'm ready."

"Then let's go."

For once, Lucy didn't mind Angela's music blaring—in fact, she hardly even noticed it at all. While her cousin sang loudly off-key all the way home, Lucy leaned her head against the window and tried to sort out all the troubling events of the day. *Explanations? None. Logic? None. Worry factor? Definitely rising. And Byron . . .*

She could still see those dark, dark eyes searching hers . . . hear the edge in that low, deep voice . . . feel those strong hands on her shoulders. It was his ominous warning that had finally convinced her *not* to report the dead girl . . . at least not yet. She'd been frightened of him, still *was* frightened of him—only now that fear was tempered with an almost fascinated curiosity. He had answers—she was sure of it—but answers to things she *wasn't* sure she wanted to pursue. As the car pulled into the driveway, Lucy wished she could ask her cousin more about Byron—but she didn't dare. Her life was complicated enough already without having Angela any more involved.

The house was empty when they went in. As

Lucy shut herself in her room, she thought she heard Angela scrolling through the messages on the answering machine . . . thought there might be one from Irene, though she couldn't make it out. She stood for a moment with her back against the door, eyes closed, weary relief flooding through her body.

And then her eyes opened with a start.

What's that smell?

A very faint fragrance . . . and pleasantly sweet . . . yet nothing she recognized, nothing she could recall ever having smelled before . . .

Frowning, Lucy dropped her stuff on the desk and walked to the sliding glass doors. She opened them all the way, letting in crisp fall air, then she stepped out onto the balcony and stared off across the lengthening shadows over the lawn.

The woods still looked menacing, even in the last few hours of daylight. A slight breeze was blowing, and as Lucy gazed into the trees' shifting patterns of darkness and fading autumn colors, a shiver crept slowly up her spine.

That feeling again . . .

That feeling of being watched . . .

"Bad habit," Lucy muttered. "Get over it, for crying out loud."

Irritated with herself, she turned back into the room.

She took a few steps, then stopped abruptly by the bed.

That's strange . . .

Despite the fresh air blowing in, she could still smell that aroma . . . delicate . . . sweet . . . and . . . *something else . . .*

Lucy tilted her head. Breathed deeply and long.

The fragrance flowed down easy . . . soft and smooth as wine . . . velvet in her veins . . .

Intoxicating.

Yes . . . that's it. Intoxicating.

Light-headed, Lucy reached out a hand toward her bed. She sat down unsteadily, then lay back and closed her eyes.

The scent floated from the covers.

Like an exotic perfume, it rose up around her, enveloped her from every side—sheets, blankets, pillows, comforter—even her nightclothes, which she'd carelessly tossed across the headboard that morning in her hurry to dress. It seeped into the pores of her skin, and brushed softly across her eyelids, and tingled along the fingertips of her right hand . . .

And that's when Lucy realized.

That's when it hit her full force that someone had been in here today.

In her room . . .

And in her bed.

11

"Lucy! What the hell are you doing?"

Lucy could hear Angela shouting at her from the bathroom doorway, but she didn't care. She didn't care, and she didn't stop—she kept right on stripping the linens from her bed.

"Lucy! Did you hear me? You know we have a cleaning lady who does that!"

"I don't care about the cleaning lady—I don't want to *wait* for the cleaning lady. I want these off now. I want them washed. I want clean sheets. I want a new bedspread. I want—"

"Have you totally lost your mind?" Angela yelled. "Florence was here *today*! Everything already *is* clean!"

Lucy froze. She stood there like a statue, then very slowly turned around.

"Today?" she murmured. "You mean . . . the cleaning lady—"

"Florence, yes, our cleaning lady. She always comes on Fridays—"

"That's not true. My room's different. Someone was in my room."

"You've hardly come *out* of your room since the first day you got here," Angela reminded her sharply. "Irene told Florence not to go in there till you felt better. So today she cleaned it."

No . . . that's not right.

Lucy stared at her cousin with a puzzled frown. Of course it made perfect sense . . . of course it must be true . . .

"There's . . . a smell," she finished lamely.

Angela came farther into the room and sniffed.

"Well, *yeah*—probably air freshener. Or furniture polish. Or stuff she puts in the carpet. Florence always sprays *everything* around here. *Especially* when we've been sick or something."

No! That's not right!

"You are so weird." Angela glowered at her. "Didn't anybody ever use air freshener where you came from?"

Lucy didn't answer. She sank down on to the foot of the bed and gazed in bewilderment at the sheets and blankets piled around her on the floor.

"Put on something warm," Angela said then. "We're going to the Festival."

"What?" Lucy looked up just in time to see her cousin disappear into the bathroom. "We're doing . . . what?"

"Going to the Festival!" Angela's voice hollered back to her. "It's Friday night—I can't stand to be here one more second!"

"But you're not supposed—" Lucy began, then stopped. Not a good idea to let Angela know she'd eavesdropped this morning, that she'd heard Irene grounding the girl. But not a good idea either, aiding and abetting a criminal . . .

Your choice. Get out or stay in this creepy room.

She heard the shower running, so she went over and shut the door. Then she crossed her arms over her chest and leaned back against the wall, studying her bed as though it were some unwelcome alien dropped in her midst.

I don't believe you, Angela. Why don't I believe you?

Lucy was beginning to think Angela might be right—that maybe she truly *was* losing her mind. Some sweet-smelling air spray had sent her into a complete tailspin—she'd jumped to the most ridiculous conclusion. Someone in her room? Well, of *course* someone had been in her room—*Florence* had been in her room, simply doing her job!

And yet . . .

Lucy chewed mercilessly on a fingernail. Something inside her—*deep* inside her—still felt uneasy . . . uneasy and unconvinced. *Why?* She'd always been so sensible, so logical, always prided herself on her levelheadedness. But that was before the cemetery, she reminded herself now. Before the girl in the grave . . . before all the *other* crazy things that had happened to her, *before I started jumping at every shadow and letting my imagination spin entirely out of control—*

"Florence," Lucy said firmly to herself. "Florence, Florence, Florence. Florence the cleaning lady."

But, *no*, her mind answered her, without the slightest hesitation . . . *No, not Florence . . .*

Someone else.

"Lucy!"

Startled, Lucy looked up to see Angela glaring at her from the doorway again.

"Irene has a very important meeting tonight that'll last till at least eleven. If we leave now, we can beat her home."

Lucy couldn't resist. "And why would we want to do that?"

"I've been having some car trouble." Angela didn't miss a beat. "I promised her I wouldn't be out on those dirt roads after dark. Just, you know, in case something should happen."

"I see."

"So if we're back early, she won't have to know about it. I mean, I wouldn't want her to worry."

Lucy shook her head. "Of course not."

"So come on!"

The door slammed between them, and Lucy gazed at it for a few seconds, wrestling with her conscience. It *would* be better than staying here in this room right now. And since she wasn't supposed to know Angela was grounded, *she* certainly wouldn't be the one in trouble if Irene discovered they'd gone out. Besides, Lucy reasoned, doing this for Angela might help make a truce between them.

It was just the Fall Festival, after all.

And what could possibly happen to them at a Festival?

12

He'd been fascinated when he'd first seen her—
that beautiful girl at the window.

He hadn't been able to turn away, gazing at
her through the trees, through the rain—he
hadn't expected anyone to be there, hadn't
even realized there was a house at the edge of
the woods. Once his work was done at
the graveyard, he'd needed a safer, darker
sanctuary, and so instinct had driven him deep
into the moonless shelter of the forest.

He often prowled after he'd killed.

City streets . . . neighborhoods . . . country
roads . . . any convenient place to work off those
lingering effects of restlessness and release.

He hunted unhindered. Undetected.
Unseen . . .

It amused him to stand over people while

they slept . . . people who didn't know he was there, people unaware that their lives were in his power. With one quick decision he could determine if they awakened tomorrow, or if they languished for hours or days on end, or if their hearts stopped suddenly, midbeat, without the slightest warning.

Just as *his* heart had had no warning when he saw her there at the window.

He'd watched her curiously, the light glowing pale behind her, the outline of her soft, sweet curves beneath the flimsy fabric of her nightdress. At one point he thought she might have seen him, too, for she was peering at the woods, at the low stone wall . . . but he was always much quicker than a glance. He'd been a shadow for a while, and then a wisp of fog. He'd watched her unbuttoning her gown, the delicate swell of her breasts as she'd leaned forward against the glass, and then he'd been outside on her balcony as she'd slid open the doors and gotten drenched from the rain. He'd reached out and touched her cheek, but she hadn't known; he could have gone inside with her, but he'd waited.

He didn't need an invitation—not from her,

not from anyone—he went where he pleased, when he pleased.

How he pleased.

But her sorrow had stopped him.

Like a fragile aura, it surrounded her and flowed from her—he could feel the palpable grief, the vulnerability and despair, and though it would have been so easy, so pleasurable, to take her then, he'd decided against it.

He'd taken the other girl instead.

The other girl had left her window open just the tiniest crack, and he'd slipped through the screen, slipped right inside on the cold, wet breeze, and he'd stayed till nearly dawn. Even in slumber she'd reeked of anger and rebellion, and he'd found this exciting, this wild, defiant nature so very much like his own.

She'd thought she was dreaming, of course.

When he'd pulled down her covers without the slightest disturbance . . . when he'd caressed her naked body with his eyes, his hands, his mind . . .

Her thighs had parted, her back had arched, such a delicious nightmare, inviting him to join her.

He usually came as a dream.

At least the first time.

A dream that lingered long past waking . . . like a deep, slow burning that could not be satisfied.

And when he'd finally left her, languid and sated with his memory, he'd waited in the woods behind the house.

He'd waited for the sun to come up and the house to be empty, and then he'd willed himself onto that balcony and let himself in through the sliding glass doors.

Her name was Lucy, he discovered.

Lucy . . .

He'd found it stamped on an airline ticket that she'd tossed on her dresser; he'd seen it written on a luggage tag still attached to a suitcase full of clothes.

Lucy. Lucy Dennison.

He hadn't expected an interruption. He'd paused and listened, mildly annoyed, as the back door unlocked, as the kitchen cupboards banged open and shut, as the cleaning lady made her slow, labored journey up the stairs and down the hall.

But still, he'd had time to walk around Lucy's room.

To touch Lucy's things.

And, in those last few seconds before taking his leave, to lie down . . . smiling . . . in Lucy's bed.

13

"Why don't *you* drive?" Angela insisted as she opened the garage door.

Lucy paused beside the little red Corvette, her eyes wide with feigned innocence. *Good one, Angela—now you can honestly say you didn't drive your car anywhere except back and forth to school.* "Me? Oh, no, I'd rather *you* did. I mean, if you've been having trouble with it—"

"The thing is," Angela said quickly, "is that I'm sort of getting a headache."

"Oh. Well then, maybe we'd better stay home."

"I can't. I mean, I shouldn't. I mean, I promised my friends—you know, I'm supposed to be working one of the booths tonight at the fair, so I have to at least show up and help."

Was she telling the truth? Lucy doubted it, but told herself it didn't matter anyway. What was more important right now was just getting out of the house and getting along with her cousin.

"So what exactly is this Fall Festival?" she asked, as Angela guided her through the neighborhood and toward the opposite end of town.

Angela slumped down in her seat and sounded bored. "It's the school's biggest fundraiser, and they have it every year."

"That's it?"

"It's like a fair, okay?" The girl gave an exasperated sigh. "They do it every year. Anyone can participate, so the school rents space to set up booths and then we get to keep whatever money we make. Lots of people come in from other towns, and there's, like, this little carnival, and they have food and stupid crafts for sale, and dumb games and prizes and stuff."

Lucy was only half listening, driving with one hand, using the other to fiddle with the radio. "Sounds fascinating. So where do you work?"

"Hey, that's my favorite station!" Angela complained. "What do you think you're doing?"

"I just wanted to catch the news. Just for one second, okay?"

"*One.*"

"Thanks. Now . . . *where* do you work?"

"Pin the nose on the scarecrow."

"Really?" The announcer was highlighting the day's local headlines. Fall Festival . . . daycare facility closing . . . fender bender on the old highway. . . . "You make scarecrows?" No mention of dead bodies, no girls in open graves, no murders in Pine Ridge. *I couldn't have imagined it all, could I? Did I imagine Byron, too? And the necklace in class . . . and the girl in the bathroom . . . and the scar on my hand—*

"Watch out!" Angela yelped. "What is *wrong* with you?"

Startled, Lucy swung the car back to her own side of the road. "Sorry."

"Well, it might help if you stopped looking at your hand and kept both of them on the steering wheel, for God's sake."

"Sorry." Lucy's brain struggled to reengage. "What were you saying about scarecrows?"

"I *said*, of course I don't make scarecrows. It's a *game.* You blindfold people and spin them around, and then they have to stick this ridiculous nose on the scarecrow."

"Like pin the tail on the donkey?"

"Exactly. And if you get the nose in the right place, you win a prize. Except we use velcro, not pins."

"What kind of prize?"

Angela sighed. "A scarecrow doll, what do you think?"

"Well . . . it sounds kind of fun."

"Yeah, if you have no *life*. Turn here."

Lucy did as she was told. They followed a narrow strip of blacktop for about ten minutes, then turned off again onto an even narrower dirt road, this one winding off through thickly wooded countryside for several more miles.

"That's it up there," Angela finally announced.

To Lucy's relief she saw the fairgrounds up ahead, a noisy carnival bright with lights and busy with activity. Across the road and a good walk away stretched a large unlit field where kids with flashlights directed traffic and motioned them to their parking spot.

"Okay," Angela said, unstrapping her seat belt.

"Why don't we just meet back here about ten-thirty?"

Lucy looked doubtful. "You're sure that's enough time to . . . to not worry Irene?" she remembered to say. "I mean, how can you know for sure how long her meeting will be?"

"Trust me. It's a stupid disciplinary committee, and they never end before eleven. Night's the only time they can get everyone together without having *other* very important meetings to go to."

"What kind of discipline?" Lucy couldn't help asking.

"A bunch of stupid frat guys. They're always such jerks, and they're always in some kind of trouble. I mean, you'd think they'd learn by now that it's *not* cool to get drunk and act like total idiots in the cemetery."

Lucy's hand froze on the door handle. "What . . . about the cemetery?"

"Some guys went into the cemetery last night and got drunk and were messing around. And I guess somebody saw them and complained."

It was all Lucy could do to keep her voice casual. "What were they doing, do you know?"

"The usual stuff, probably. Breaking things . . . stealing things . . . spray-painting the headstones . . . just your usual damage to private property. Oh—and I always love this one—making out with their girlfriends on the graves."

"So . . ." Lucy could barely choke out the words, "it was just a . . . a joke?"

"Well, *they* thought it was. But they're gonna get suspended and their fraternity will get put on probation." Angela thought a minute, then gave a wry smile. "That's the part Irene really likes. The punishment part."

But Lucy wasn't listening anymore. As she got the door open and climbed out, her mind was spinning with rage and disbelief. *A joke! Kids drunk and playing pranks!* No wonder there hadn't been any news coverage . . . no murder investigations . . . no reports of missing girls . . . And all the agony she'd suffered . . . the terror . . . the guilt and regret and horror and—

"Are you coming?" Angela was waving at her from the other side of the car. "The Festival's *this* way. God, I can't believe they made us park way out here in all this mud!"

Yet that still didn't explain her encounter with Byron that morning, Lucy reminded herself, following Angela through the field. Still didn't explain the things he'd said . . . the things he'd known . . .

Unless he was part of the joke, too. Unless he was there last night with those other guys, and he guessed I might come back this morning, and he wanted to scare me into not saying anything . . .

"*If you tell anyone . . . you could die . . . they wouldn't believe you anyway . . .*"

"Did you hear me?" Angela snapped.

"What? Sorry—what?" *Still doesn't explain Byron . . . still doesn't explain a lot of things—*

"I *said*, let's just meet back here at the car. Are you *listening* to me?"

"Yes," Lucy murmured. "I'm listening. Ten-thirty. Here at the car."

She felt betrayed. Mortified and furious at being the butt of such a cruel, twisted joke. How those guys must be laughing at her right now—if, in fact, they even remembered the sick charade they'd carried out last night.

"Okay," Angela said. "See you later."

They parted at the main gate, but Lucy

stood on the sidelines for a moment, taking everything in. It was after six now, and the Fall Festival was in full swing. Angela was right about one thing, she noted—it seemed the whole town had turned out for the event—the whole town and a whole lot more. The place was packed with people in the mood for fun. Lines were already long at the concession stands, and the air throbbed with loud music and the wild rumble of rides, the carousel calliope, and barkers hawking games of various skills and staminas. Lucy could smell food from every direction—hot dogs, doughnuts, cotton candy, barbecue. For the first time in hours she actually realized how hungry she was; she'd barely eaten anything since yesterday.

She bought a greasy hamburger and a watered-down Coke and ate while she walked. It had been years since she'd been to anything like a carnival, and it brought back happy memories of her childhood, of her and Mom off together on their special adventures. Despite the tasteless food and poignant memories, she actually began to feel better. And despite the pain and embarrassment of her entire day, she felt herself almost smile.

She tossed her trash into a bin and kept walking, squeezing her way in and out through the crowds. The night was chilly, the breeze sharp but not unbearable in her flannel shirt and oversized parka. She was glad she'd opted to leave her purse at home tonight—with her money and ID tucked tightly into the pocket of her jeans, she felt a lot safer. *Safer . . . that's funny.* For some reason, the irony of that nearly brought another smile to her face.

She paused at a booth selling candy apples. She bought one and bit through the hard, sticky sweetness, and then she headed back into the crowd.

The slow, shivery prickle at the back of her neck had nothing to do with the cold.

Lucy stopped, and three people ran into her from behind. She felt a sharp burst of pain as her upper lip split between the candy apple and her two front teeth.

Mumbling apologies, she worked her way over to a booth and stood with her back to the wall. She could feel the blood swelling from the cut, and she wiped it carelessly with the back of her hand. Her eyes roamed anxiously over the teeming mobs of people.

Someone's following me. I feel it.

Just like last night . . . when she'd run from those footsteps . . . when she'd run from one nightmare, straight into another . . .

She didn't see anything suspicious, of course—in that solid mass of faces, how *would* she? And after all that had happened in the last two days, Lucy wasn't even sure how much she could trust her own instincts anymore.

She dabbed at the blood on her lip.

She took another survey of the crowd.

You're imagining things. Enough's enough. Pull yourself together, for crying out loud.

She was almost past the carousel when she saw him.

He was moving quickly, shoving his way toward her through the mob, and as she recognized his face, Lucy instantly turned and headed the opposite way.

"Lucy!" she heard him yell, but she didn't answer, didn't even acknowledge him, just kept walking.

"Lucy! Wait! We've got to talk!"

She thought she could outrun him, but Byron caught up with her easily, grabbing her arm and forcing her around. Dropping her apple, Lucy twisted furiously from his grasp.

"Haven't you done enough already?" she exploded.

The look he gave her was grim, his voice low and urgent. "Come on, we can't talk here—"

"You've had your fun, okay? Now leave me alone!"

"Fun? What *fun*? What is this—?"

"Those frat guys playing jokes at the cemetery—and you were there, too—that's how you knew I'd come back! Well, are you proud of yourself?"

"I don't have a clue what you're talking about, but please, just listen to me—"

"I've listened to you enough. Now I'm going."

With one smooth movement, Byron caught her shoulders and steered her over to a booth. Then, pinning her flat against the wall, he leaned down over her, his black eyes narrowed.

"There are things you need to understand."

"No, *you* need to understand!" Lucy tried to break free, but he only held her tighter. "If you don't leave me alone right now, I'm going to scream as loud as I can and have you arrested!"

"Look, I know you're scared—you have every right to be. What happened last night was horrible, and you have no reason in the world to trust me. But you *have* to. You *have* to meet me tomorrow—"

"I'm not meeting you anywhere—"

"—the old church—nine o'clock—"

She opened her mouth to scream. She felt his fingers dig into her shoulders as he gave her a firm, quick shake.

"You saw something today," he said. His lips moved soft against her ear; his voice dropped to a whisper. "When you touched the necklace, you saw something happen. *You* know it . . . and so do I."

This time when she struggled, he let her go. Lucy bolted into the crowd, frantically shoving her way through, not caring where she ran, only desperate to get away.

She looked back once and thought she saw him following.

Instinctively she veered from the midway, cut behind the Ferris wheel, and raced down a narrow path between two busy picnic shelters. It took her a minute to realize she'd lost him. Another minute to catch her breath and get her bearings. She bent over, hands on knees, and took deep gulps of air, waiting for her heartbeat to return to normal.

Then slowly she lifted her head.

That smell . . .

Frowning, Lucy glanced at her surroundings. It was darker back here, and though several groups of people had congregated nearby to socialize, the booths had thinned out, giving way to weeds and trash Dumpsters and a tall wire fence. *Great. I must be at the back of the fairgrounds.*

The night seemed colder. Without the insulation of the crowds, Lucy felt the sting of the wind and tugged her parka tight around her. Even the air felt different, she realized—softer and heavier and mysterious somehow, ripe with the scent of woods and fields and deep lake waters . . .

And that other smell . . .

She could feel her heart quickening again in her chest. Her throat constricting. The blood chilling in her veins . . .

That other, familiar smell . . .

That sweet, lingering smell that had filled her room and her bed.

14

She had to follow it.

Despite the sick fear coursing through her, Lucy knew she had no other choice.

She had to follow it, and she had to find it.

But where?

It didn't seem to be coming from one particular spot, or even from one specific direction, but rather permeated the air around her like a fine, invisible mist. Very deliberately this time, Lucy breathed it in . . . sweet like before . . . delicate like before . . . only this time stirring something deep within her, as though long-dulled senses were struggling to awake.

Several girls walked by and gave her strange looks. Didn't they smell it, Lucy wondered? *How can they not smell it?* Such an unusual fragrance . . . tantalizing . . . weaving its way through the festival, separate and distinct among the millions of other aromas hanging in the thick night air . . .

She didn't go back the way she'd come. Instead she passed bumper cars and a petting zoo, and then she began walking faster, making her way behind a barn where an auctioneer competed with enthusiastic bingo players. She could smell fried chicken and fried pies, popcorn and cotton candy, and still, *still*, that heavenly fragrance, wafting just out of reach . . .

She turned a corner and walked faster. Past country singers on makeshift stages. Games of darts. Tables of homemade pickles and jams. The smell was getting stronger now—she could feel that it was close. As she broke into a run, she suddenly spotted a big orange tent ahead of her, with a huge display of scarecrows around it.

Scarecrows . . .

She could see the whimsical sign over the entrance—PIN THE NOSE ON THE SCARECROW—and the boisterous line of kids waiting to take their turns. *Isn't this where Angela's supposed to be working?*

Mumbling apologies, Lucy pushed her way to the front. It didn't make sense, but the fragrance actually seemed *stronger* here, more tangible than any other place she'd been so far, almost as though she could reach out and touch it and hold it in her hand. If only she could find Angela, she was sure her cousin would confirm it—how could *anyone* forget that curious aroma once they'd breathed it in?

"Hey, get to the end of the line!" A solemn-faced girl stopped her at the door, holding up one hand while trying to blindfold two squirming kids with the other. "Aren't you a little old for this game?"

Lucy hurriedly identified herself. "Sorry, I'm Angela's cousin—Angela Foster? Do you know where she is?"

"I thought you looked familiar—you were in some of my classes today." The girl nodded, though her expression didn't change. "Angela's having a smoke."

"I really need to find her."

"Go around back. I just saw her talking to some guy out there a second ago."

What a surprise. "Thanks."

Lucy didn't waste any time. As she slipped around the side of the tent, she saw that it backed up to a fence, with just a narrow grassy space between. Thick woods pressed so closely from the other side that some of the trees hung over, their branches practically sweeping the ground. In spite of the festivities going on in front, it felt weirdly isolated here, shadowy and claustrophobic.

"Angela?"

Turning the corner, Lucy stopped. The light was dim at best . . . yet she thought she saw the glimmer of a cigarette at the opposite end of the tent.

"Angela? It's me . . . Lucy."

Without warning, something soft slid over her forehead . . . covered her eyes. With a startled cry, Lucy reached up and felt something like cloth—felt it being tied snugly at the back of her head—and realized it was a blindfold.

"Angela, cut it out! This isn't funny!"

"Did you come to play?" the voice whispered.

Lucy stiffened. She could *feel* someone now, a body standing close behind her, someone tall, someone strong, pressed lightly against her back.

Someone who *wasn't* Angela.

"This isn't funny," she managed to choke out. *Kids playing pranks! Friends of Angela maybe— or just a case of mistaken identity—that's it! They think I'm someone* else—*they must think I'm* Angela—

"I'm not Angela," she said, more forcefully this time. "You've got the wrong girl."

"On the contrary . . ." the voice murmured, "I've got *exactly* the girl I want."

Her body turned to ice. Her mind fought for calm. There were people only yards away, yet she was alone. She could scream, but she doubted anyone would hear her over the noise of the fair. Should she scream anyway? Try to run? She could feel his body, the lean, firm length of it, touching hers, yet not forcefully, *not threateningly*, she realized with slow surprise.

He wasn't even holding her.

He was only holding the blindfold at the back of her head, and as Lucy's heart hammered wildly in her chest, she tried to keep her voice even.

"I think you've made a mistake," she said. "I'm not from here, and I don't know anyone. I'm just trying to find my cousin."

"But you haven't. It seems you've found *me* instead."

Again her mind raced. Had she heard that voice before? Did she recognize it—*anything* about it? He was talking so softly, as though his lips barely moved . . . a low whisper from deep in his throat . . . warm and resonant . . . thick and smooth as . . . *what?*

Lucy's breath caught.

His hand slid leisurely down the back of her neck . . . lingered upon her left shoulder. Every instinct told her to break away—to tear off the blindfold and run—yet her body felt strangely paralyzed.

"Where's Angela?" she demanded. Her voice had begun to quiver, and she knew he could hear it, though she tried to disguise it with anger. "They said she was out here with someone—you must have seen her!"

Something brushed gently across her mouth.

"You're bleeding," he murmured.

She'd forgotten the cut on her upper lip, but

now she felt it swell . . . felt the tender skin split open. A warm drop of blood seeped out and began to trickle down.

Lips closed over hers.

A kiss so tender that time faded and stopped . . . so passionate, it sucked her breath away.

Lucy's senses reeled. Searing heat swept through her—pain and pleasure throbbing through her veins. With a helpless moan, she leaned into him and realized with a shock the kiss had ended.

At last she ripped the blindfold from her eyes.

The scent that had lured her here hung heavy in the night, though its fragile sweetness now held a trace of something more . . . something musky and faintly metallic . . .

Trembling violently, Lucy stared into the shadows.

But she was alone.

And she was cold.

15

It can't be ten-thirty.

As Lucy paused outside the scarecrow tent, she shook her wrist, tapped her watch, then held it to her ear and listened. Yes, it seemed to be working fine . . .

But there's no way it can be ten-thirty already!

"It's ten-thirty," the serious-faced girl said again. She was still trying to blindfold kids and maintain order at the same time, and as she frowned at Lucy, she added, "Did you have an accident or something?"

"Accident?" Lucy echoed. "No—what do you mean?"

"You're white as a sheet. And your lip's all swollen."

Lucy put a hand to her mouth and immediately winced. The skin on her lip felt pulpy and tender; she could feel a thin crust of dried blood.

"Are you sure Angela's not here?" she asked weakly.

"I told you, she left at ten-thirty. She said she had to meet her cousin—you—at the car."

"Right. Thanks anyway."

Her knees had turned to rubber. She wasn't sure she could walk three feet, much less the entire distance back to the parking lot. Her insides wouldn't stop shaking; she felt strangely disoriented. She'd stepped right into a dangerous situation with her eyes wide open, and she'd simply stayed in the middle of it, simply allowed the rest to happen. *What in God's name is wrong with me?*

She was probably lucky to be alive. The stranger—whoever he was—could have done a hundred horrible things to her—*and what did I do? I stood there and let him—I let him . . .*

Shame and confusion flushed through her. She could still feel his hand on her neck . . . on her shoulder . . . his body touching hers. And his kiss. That unexpected moment, senses reeling, his low whispery voice, intimate somehow, almost as though he knew her . . .

Her memory groped back—searching, searching. Trying to recall someone—*anyone*—he might have been. The guys from the cemetery last night? Had they followed her here, intent on more jokes? It seemed highly unlikely, given the disciplinary meeting tonight. Some guy at school she didn't know? *Byron?* Byron had a low, deep voice, but Byron had seemed agitated when she'd seen him earlier, he'd been tense and upset, and why follow her and frighten her when he'd already asked her to meet him secretly tomorrow?

And what about the smell?

Just thinking of that brought a fresh wave of panic. Because there *was* no explanation for it . . . none she could possibly think of . . . none that made any sort of sense. Before, she'd been almost willing to consider the air-freshener theory, but now . . .

As Lucy wandered out of the exit gates, she wished she had someone to leave with. The Festival was still in full swing, and only a handful of people were straggling toward the parking lot. Within minutes they'd located their cars, leaving her to walk the rest of the way alone.

The lights grew dim behind her. The noise began to fade. Out here in the field it was eerily quiet.

Now where exactly did we park?

Lucy stopped, cursing herself for her horrible sense of direction. It had gotten her in *major* trouble last night; she wasn't about to let it happen again. She glanced around, trying to find some sort of landmark, but all she could see was row after row of cars.

Why hadn't she thought of that earlier? Picked out a checkpoint to help her find her way back?

Frustrated, Lucy went on, trying to dodge puddles and sinkholes in the dark. Maybe Angela was in the car waiting for her—hadn't that girl at the tent said she'd already left?

"Angela!" Lucy called. "Angela! Are you out here?"

No answer. Just her own voice drifting back to her on the chilly breeze.

Lucy tried to walk faster. Why hadn't anyone thought to put temporary lighting out here? Why hadn't she thought to bring a flashlight?

Why hadn't she and Angela agreed to meet somewhere *inside* the Festival where it was bright and crowded and safe? *God, it's really, really spooky out here . . .*

She dug her hands in her pockets and felt the keyless entry to Angela's car. *Of course!*

Pulling it out, Lucy immediately hit a button. She could hear the blip of a horn in the distance, and she thought she saw the faraway flicker of headlights. *Well, at least I'm headed in the right direction.*

With the help of the mechanism, she finally spotted the Corvette, still about ten rows away, right on the end near the woods. The ground was even soggier out here, forcing her to walk close to the treeline. As she tramped her way through the weeds, she suddenly lifted her head to listen . . .

What was that?

She was sure she'd heard a sound just then . . . a faint scuffling off through those trees to her right. As though some animal were moving invisibly through the darkness . . .

A deer. Just like last night when I thought I saw something, just a deer in the woods. That's all it is.

Lucy stopped.

The noise stopped, too.

Very slowly she turned her head, eyes probing the bare, shifting branches of the trees . . . the deep, black underbelly of the forest . . .

Or maybe it's a bear—bears live close to lakes, don't they? Or a wolf? Or—

She broke into a run.

Because suddenly she didn't want to think what else it could be, this invisible presence keeping pace alongside her, skulking through the dark where she couldn't see.

It was last night's horror all over again.

With a burst of speed Lucy veered off between the cars, away from the woods, punching the entry over and over again, so the horn of the Corvette kept blasting and the headlights kept flashing on and off—on and off—

God—oh God—help me—

But it was *behind* her now—she could hear it thudding over the ground, *gaining* on her—coming closer—*closer*—

"Damnit, Lucy!" Angela yelled. "Wait up!"

With a cry, Lucy whirled around, just as her cousin closed the distance between them.

"Angela, you idiot! You scared the life out of me!"

"*I* did?" Braking to a stop, Angela tried to catch her breath. "*You're* the one running away—I thought something was *after* you!"

"Well, *I* thought something was, too!" Lucy exploded. "Were you in the woods just now?"

"What would I be doing in the woods?"

"I *heard* something in the woods."

"Oh, for God's sake—there's, like, about a *million* things you could've heard in the woods!" Angela gestured angrily toward the trees. "And where the hell have you been? I waited and waited by the car, but you never came. And *you* have the damn keys!"

Lucy thought quickly. There was no way she was going to mention what had happened back there at the tent. Not now . . . not ever.

"Sorry—I guess I lost track of time."

"I guess you did. Come on, let's get outta here."

Nodding, Lucy followed her to the car and got in, but not without a last anxious look at the woods. *Had* something really been there, following her? During the last few days, she'd lost so much faith in her instincts, she didn't know *what* to believe anymore.

She locked the doors and windows, but even after leaving the parking lot, Lucy still couldn't relax. The narrow, winding road was even harder to maneuver now that full night had fallen, and it took all her concentration to miss the endless potholes. Even Angela seemed edgier than usual, Lucy observed, watching the girl light up one cigarette after another, then mash them out half-smoked.

"Are you okay?" Lucy finally asked her.

Angela pointed to the clock on the dashboard. "I just want to get home before Irene does, that's all. Thank God she's going out of town tomorrow night, so I can have some peace. Lucy—hurry!"

"I'm hurrying."

"Well, hurry faster."

Glancing at her, Lucy sighed. "With all these stupid holes around here, if I hurry any faster, we're likely to bounce right off and—"

"*Look out!*"

As Lucy's eyes shot back to the road, she saw a quick streak of darkness in front of them. Jerking the wheel, she swerved the car sharply to the right, then slammed on the brakes as they slid dangerously along the shoulder. Angela gaped at her in alarm.

"Did you see that?"

"I saw *something*. But what was it?"

The Corvette had stopped now, and the two of them peered nervously out into the darkness. There was nothing on the road. Nothing moving in the beam of the headlights, nothing stirring at the sides of the car.

"We didn't hit anything, did we?" Angela finally asked.

"I don't think so. I didn't feel any sort of impact, did you?"

Angela shook her head. "It looked big. I mean, I only saw it for a second, but it was *big*."

"A deer, maybe?"

"No. It didn't seem like a deer. And it was so *fast*—just there and gone. I mean, what could move so fast that you can't even see it?"

"I don't know," Lucy answered uneasily. She

made a quick check in the rearview mirror. "Are you okay?"

"Yeah. I just hope my car is."

For my sake, I hope so, too. But the minute Lucy hit the accelerator, she heard the furious spinning of the tires. "Oh, great," she muttered.

"Oh, great, *what*?

"We're stuck."

"Stuck?" Angela seemed incredulous. "How can we be stuck?"

"Because there's about a foot of mud out there, and we drove right into it."

"No, *you* drove right into it." Shifting around, Angela unlocked her door. "If you've scratched anything out—"

"Stop," Lucy said. "Don't open it."

As Angela turned toward her in bewilderment, Lucy reached out slowly . . . put a hand on her arm.

"Lock your door," she whispered. "Now."

Even in the dim interior, she saw Angela go pale. She waited for the click of the lock, then leaned slowly toward the windshield.

"What is it?" Angela asked tightly.

"I saw something."

"Are you sure? Where?"

Lucy pointed. The car had skidded at a forty-five-degree angle, its headlights slicing off through the trees at the side of the road. As Lucy watched the illuminated pocket of woods, she felt a chill creep up her spine.

"Something's out there, Angela. It's watching us . . . don't you feel it?"

The girl's eyes widened slowly. Then she gave a forced laugh. "Come on, Lucy, you don't really expect me to fall for that, do you?"

But Lucy's tone was dead serious. "Do you have your phone with you?"

"Well, sure, but—"

"Call 911."

"Stop it. This isn't funny, and I don't believe you anyway."

"Well, you better believe me, because I'm telling you, there's something out there. And . . ."

As Lucy's sentence trailed off, Angela threw a quick, wary glance out her window. "Look. You're just shook up because of what happened. But I'm telling you, that thing was moving *fast*! Whatever it was, it's long gone by now—"

"Give me your phone," Lucy said tersely.

Before Angela could stop her, she grabbed the girl's purse and started rummaging through it, but Angela quickly snatched it back.

"What are you doing?" Angela snapped at her. "That's mine!"

"Your phone, Angela—your phone!" Lucy's voice was louder now, thin with rising panic. "Hurry up! Call 911! *Do* it, Angela, call for help!"

But she could see now that it was finally sinking in, Angela's eyes the size of saucers, her hands digging through her purse, tossing things out, searching for her cell phone. "This is sick, Lucy, do you hear me? This is *sick*!"

"It's coming closer! Make the call!"

Lucy's heart was racing. She could *feel* something out there—something furtive—something evil—a sense of danger so intense that every nerve vibrated with terror. It was standing just out of sight, standing just beyond the trees, one with the woods, one with the darkness, and it was waiting to strike . . . waiting to see what they would do . . .

"Oh, God," Lucy whispered, "Oh my God—"

"What is it!" Angela shouted, thoroughly frightened now. She dumped her purse upside down, the contents spilling everywhere, shaking it back and forth, helplessly close to tears. "I can't find it! I can't find my phone!"

"It's too late!" Lucy cried.

Something hit the side of the car. As both girls screamed, the Corvette rocked from the impact, and there was a frantic clawing at Angela's door.

"Get down!" Lucy yelled, even as she grabbed the girl and forced her to the floor.

"*What is it?*" Angela shrieked. "I can't see anything!"

Once more something lunged at the side. As the car swayed and slid, they heard a scratching at the door handle, as though something were trying to wrench it open. Terrified, Angela huddled beneath the dashboard, while Lucy whirled around just in time to see a dark shape dart behind the car. *Oh, God, it's coming to my side!* She leaned on the horn, the harsh sound splitting through the night, and then she gunned the motor.

The tires spun in the muck. Without even

thinking, Lucy shifted forward, then back, forward, then back—*tires whining, horn blasting, Angela screaming*—

The car lurched free.

Without warning, it popped from the mud and skidded sideways onto the road. Clutching the wheel for dear life, Lucy floored the accelerator, not stopping, not even slowing down till they'd reached the main highway once again.

"Stop it, Angela," she said then, quietly. "We're safe now."

"Safe?" The girl was practically hysterical. "*Safe?* How do you know we're safe? What *was* that thing?"

Lucy shook her head and said nothing.

"Then how do you know it didn't follow us? How do you know it's not sitting up there on the roof right now? Or—or—riding back there in the trunk?"

"Because it's not." Lucy's lips pressed into a tight line. "It's not. I just know."

As they paused at a stop sign, she shifted in her seat and took a long, deliberate look through every single window.

How do *I know?* she wondered. *How do I really know?*

There were houses around them now, and quiet, tree-lined streets.

And the peaceful silence of neighborhoods settled in for the night.

But Angela was crying.

And Lucy's heart was still beating wildly in her chest.

How did I know that thing was out there to begin with?

16

It was a miracle they got home before Irene.

The girls pulled into the garage with just minutes to spare, leaving no time to examine the car or discuss what had happened back there on that dark country road. Not that Angela would have wanted to anyway, Lucy figured—which was perfectly fine with her. Trying to rationalize it to herself was hard enough.

She stood in the shower, trembling beneath the hard spray of the water. Still badly shaken from the attack on the car . . . still badly frightened from her encounter with the stranger behind the tent. *Only frightened?* Again she berated herself for being so careless, for putting herself in such a dangerous situation . . . yet at the same time she could still hear that low, whispery voice . . . feel the gentle urgency of that kiss . . .

How could cold, stark fear be so alluring at the same time? She was furious with herself for even considering such a notion. *What's wrong with me?*

She turned the water as hot as she could stand it, washing her hair, her face, her lips, every inch of her body, as though she might be able to wash away every memory, every horror, every single event that had touched her in the last two days. All she wanted to do was crawl into bed and have a peaceful night of dreamless, uninterrupted sleep. So it surprised her when she heard a soft knock on her bedroom door about an hour later and saw Angela peek in.

"We need to talk," Angela said.

Lucy nodded and motioned her inside. She'd been sitting up, too, unable to relax; now she scooted over so Angela could plop down beside her. The girl's dark raccoon eyes had been wiped off for the night, her long hair braided down her back. She was wearing a polka-dot flannel nightshirt and looked almost normal.

"I can't stop thinking about what happened," Angela blurted out. Her expression seemed strained and almost embarrassed. Her hands twisted nervously in her lap. "What do you think that was? I mean . . . really?"

"I don't know. I've been thinking about it, too . . . and I honestly don't know."

"Well, it must have been a wolf," Angela announced flatly.

"Are there wolves around here?"

"Well . . . usually farther north, but sometimes they leave their territory, right? I mean, like if they're hungry, or certain areas get too populated, I've heard of animals doing that."

Lucy wanted to believe her. "It's possible, I guess."

"But . . . it could have been a bear, too, maybe," Angela mused. "I was thinking maybe it was wounded. When an animal's wounded, it makes them kind of crazy, and then they attack things they wouldn't normally attack, right? I mean, haven't you heard that?"

Lucy nodded. "It makes sense."

"So if something was hurt . . . and hungry . . . and smelled us in the car . . ."

Angela paused, her eyes almost pleading. "It *could've* happened that way. Right?"

"Sure. Sure it could."

"Great." Angela let out a huge sigh of relief. "And it's probably not a good idea to tell anyone else about it, do you think? Just so we don't cause a panic or something. And especially Irene. Because of her worrying, I mean."

"Absolutely. Our secret."

Another relieved sigh. Angela stretched her willowy limbs, then hopped off the bed.

"Great. Good night, then."

"Good night."

Mildly amazed, Lucy watched her go. How did Angela do it, she wondered? How could she make something go away so easily—or not even exist at all—just by refusing to accept it?

But isn't that what you're doing?

"No," Lucy mumbled to herself. "That's different."

Is it?

And in that very instant, razor-sharp images began strobing through her mind—images of Byron at the cemetery, Byron at the Festival, Byron trying to talk to her, to warn her about something: "I want to help you . . . some things take time to believe in . . . we don't have a lot of time . . . something happened . . . something important . . . touched you . . . was passed on to you . . . you need to understand . . ." As Lucy pressed her hands to her head, it was as if she could suddenly *feel* all those crazy puzzle pieces tumbling through her mind . . . falling into place . . . beginning to make a frightening kind of sense.

Could it possibly be true? Could there *honestly* be a connection between Byron's warnings and the bizarre events that had begun to darken her life?

"*. . . no reason in the world to trust me . . . have to meet me tomorrow . . .*"

"You're right," Lucy mumbled again. "I don't have the slightest reason to trust you."

"Did you say something?" Angela asked.

Lucy jumped and stared at the door. Angela was back again, propped in the threshold, smoking a cigarette and frowning at her.

"I didn't say anything," Lucy muttered.

Her cousin shrugged. "You'll need to get my car washed in the morning."

"*I* will?"

"Well . . . *yeah*. Irene didn't see it tonight 'cause someone picked her up and she didn't go in the garage. But tomorrow she'll probably be using her car—and if she sees the shape *my* car's in, she's bound to know we were out tonight."

"But what about the damage? How are you going to explain all those scratches?"

"Vandalism *happens* in the school parking lot, Lucy." Angela gazed down at the floor, her expression bland. "It happens all the time. So just take it to the car wash, okay?"

"And who was your servant this time last year?"

Angela rolled her eyes. "Very funny. Just do it?"

"No, I won't do it. If she sees your dirty car, too bad." Grumpily, Lucy stacked up her pillows and fell back on top of them. "And you can *stop* giving me all these excuses about Irene worrying—I heard you two this morning, and I know you're grounded."

Angela stared. A flush went over her face, though from anger or embarrassment, Lucy couldn't tell. She hesitated a moment, as if trying to decide what to do. Then with a sound of exasperation, she tossed her cigarette into the toilet, walked back to the bed, and flounced down on the edge.

"If you knew, then why'd you take me tonight?" she demanded.

"Because I thought it would help things between us. I wanted us to be friends."

"That's stupid. How could we ever be friends?"

"My point exactly. Which is why I'm not going to get your car washed tomorrow."

"If Irene finds out I left tonight, she'll cancel my credit cards!"

Lucy shrugged. She reached over and flipped off the lamp. Angela flipped it back on.

"Fine!" Angela pouted. "Look, if I tell you something *really* important and *really* secret about someone I met tonight, *then* will you wash my car?"

Lucy stared at her. Really *important*? Really *secret*? What could be more important than being stalked, than girls in graves, than hungry predators on lonely roads? What could be more secret than strangers with blindfolds, and painful visions, and disembodied voices in bathrooms?

She'd had enough. She switched off the light.

Angela switched it back on.

"Okay," Angela sighed. "I'll be your friend. Are you satisfied?"

"Angela, you don't know the meaning of the word."

The girl looked blank. "*Friend?* Or *satisfied?*"

"Neither one. Now get out of here and let me go to sleep."

This time when she reached for the lamp, Angela grabbed her arm. "I'll tell her *you* took my car. I'll tell her *you* stole my keys, and I didn't know anything about it. And if you deny it, I'll tell her you're lying . . . that you . . . that you . . . sneaked out to meet somebody!"

Lucy gave a humorless laugh. "Yeah, that's a good one, Angela, I'm sure she'll believe *that*. And while you're at it, be sure to tell her about the wild orgy I had out there behind the tents."

It slipped out before she even thought.

She saw Angela's eyes go wide, her face go red, saw her cheeks flinch as she drew in her breath.

"You bitch," she muttered. "You were *spying* on me!"

"What? Angela, no—I wasn't!"

161

Shocked at her cousin's reaction, Lucy tried to take her arm, but Angela was already halfway across the room.

"I was joking!" Lucy insisted. "I was joking about *myself*—I don't even know what you're talking about!"

"The hell you don't," Angela said furiously. "How long did you stand there watching, anyway? And it *wasn't* an orgy!"

"I wasn't watching anything! I was just making fun of myself!"

She saw Angela turn toward her then, a range of emotions flickering over the girl's face—indecision, guilt, embarrassment and the horrible realization that she'd just given herself away.

"Well . . . well . . . me, too!" she announced, with a forced little laugh. "*I* was just joking, too. I just wanted to see what you'd say."

Lucy stared at her as though she'd lost her mind. "Okay," she offered tentatively. "So we're even, right?"

"Right." The laugh again, almost brittle. "Okay, then. Great jokes. Good night."

"Good night." Lucy paused, then, "Angela?"

"What?"

"How late does Irene sleep on Saturdays?"

"Till around ten. Why?"

"I'll get your car washed. But I want to leave early, just in case she gets up."

"Like, how early?

"Like, before nine."

17

It was no problem slipping out of the house the next morning.

Everyone else was still asleep, and since Angela had already given her the keys and explicit directions to the car wash, Lucy was away in no time at all.

The car wash hadn't opened yet. Checking her watch, she saw that it was only eight-thirty, so she made a quick run through a fast-food drive-through, then sat in the parking lot, trying to digest both her food and her thoughts.

This is really stupid. Byron probably won't even be there. And if I do go, and it really is another joke, I'll never be able to show my face anywhere in Pine Ridge again.

But obviously he'd gotten there before her.

As Lucy drove slowly past the church, she noticed an old Jeep pulled alongside the curb in front, but not a soul to be seen. *Strange that Byron would park here in plain sight*, she found herself thinking. Especially since he'd made this meeting sound so secret and so mysterious . . .

Still, this *was* an abandoned church, and it *was* in an abandoned area—*not like there's going to be anyone around here watching us or wondering what we're up to*. Besides, seeing his Jeep out here in the open made her feel a whole lot safer.

Lucy parked, then made her way slowly up the crumbled walkway. The church had looked so spooky that night of the storm, and here in the daylight, it didn't look a whole lot better. Like the original section of the cemetery stretching off behind it, tall weeds had taken over, and shadows lurked beneath the gnarled branches of giant old trees. The steps to the door were rotted. The belltower didn't look at all sturdy. Several stained-glass windows were broken, and dead ivy crept over the walls.

It was very still. No breeze this morning, and frostily cold. Lucy's breath hung in the air as she glanced nervously back at her car. She'd parked close for a quick getaway. She told herself to go inside, then stopped with her hand on the door. *You're doing it again—walking right into an isolated, unknown place—have you completely lost your mind?*

When girls in *movies* did this, they always got killed, she reminded herself. But this wasn't a movie, this was real life—*my life!*—and she needed answers, and right now it seemed that Byron was her *only* chance at getting those answers.

She saw then that one of the large wooden doors was slightly open. That there were muddy footprints on the steps, leading inside.

Very slowly Lucy inched open the door. "Hello? Is anyone here?"

The silence was unnerving. Again she glanced back over her shoulder, but nothing moved within those calm, black shadows.

"Byron?" she called softly. "Hello?"

Lucy strained her ears through the quiet. Had the door creaked then, just ever so slightly? As though someone might be pushing it from the other side?

Instinctively she released it and stepped back. "Hello?"

Why wasn't he watching for her, why wasn't he out here waiting to see if she showed up? It had been *his* idea, after all—if he'd wanted her here so badly, why wasn't he coming out to meet her?

But it was very cold, she reasoned, and it made perfect sense that he'd probably go inside to wait. And these doors, made of such thick solid oak, surely muffled any sounds from outside. *Don't be so paranoid . . . Angela knows him . . . apparently all the girls at school are in love with him . . . it's not like he's some total creep that nobody's ever heard of . . .*

Still, Lucy suddenly wished she'd told somebody where she was headed this morning.

Just in case.

Okay . . . here goes.

She took a deep breath and yanked hard at the door. As it moved on rusty hinges, a low groan echoed back through the vast interior of the church.

She smelled dampness and old stone. Cold, stale air, long unbreathed, long undisturbed.

Shivering, Lucy stood there a moment, her eyes trying to adjust to the gloom. As the door swung shut with a dull thud, she moved farther into the vestibule.

"Byron?"

The church was still sadly, hauntingly beautiful. In the muted stained-glass light, Lucy could see saints gazing down at her from niches along the walls, their painted faces filled with loving concern. Wooden pews stood empty, sifted with dust, and high in the rafters of the arched ceiling, doves fluttered gently as she passed beneath them. Lucy walked slowly up the center aisle. She could see the main altar ahead of her, draped with a dingy white cloth, decorated with arrangements of long-dead flowers.

Despite the eerieness of the place, Lucy felt strangely fascinated. She stopped before the altar, trailing her fingers over the musty cloth, over faded droplets of candle wax, over brittle chrysanthemum petals. Even her heart seemed to echo in here; she could hear the faint beat of her pulse.

God, it's so cold . . .

Blowing on her hands, Lucy turned in a slow circle and glanced uneasily at her surroundings. Was it her imagination, or had the temperature dropped about ten degrees just since she'd walked through the door? *You are imagining things.* Yet as she blew once more on her hands, she could see her breath forming, a soft vapory cloud right in front of her face.

"Byron?"

Her own voice whispered back to her from the shadows.

The doves stirred restlessly with a muffled beating of wings.

"Come on, Byron, if you have something to say, you'd better say it—*now!*"

This is stupid. He's not here, and he's obviously not going to show up, and all you're doing is creeping yourself out.

With growing anxiety, Lucy gnawed on a fingernail. *Not again . . .* not again! *What did you expect, anyway? Haven't you learned your lesson by now?*

But she'd wanted this time to be different—she'd wanted so *much* to believe that Byron could help her. She'd wanted to *prove* to herself once and for all that it wasn't just her, that there were reasons and answers and explanations for the things that were happening, that she *wasn't* just making up dreams in her mind—

Something's here.

Lucy gasped as a sliver of dread snaked its way up her back and lodged at the base of her neck.

Something's here!

Instantly her eyes swept over the walls and ceiling, the massive wooden cross above the altar, the partially shattered glass of the crucifixion behind it, the confessionals in the darkened aisles along the side . . .

The confessionals . . .

A soft sound slithered through the church. A sound like . . . *what?* A sigh of wind? A flurry of feathers? Or . . .

Breathing.

Lucy's body stiffened, every nerve electrified. *No, it can't be . . . there's no one here . . . no one . . . no one . . .*

Yet she could feel herself moving across the cold stone floor, moving steadily toward the confessionals, almost as though something were *drawing* her forward, some force against her will.

She tried to stop, but she couldn't. Tried to resist, but the pull seemed only to grow stronger.

She stopped outside one of the doors.

Byron?

She tried to whisper, but the words stuck soundlessly in her throat. She could see the door cracked open, barely an inch, but she couldn't see what was inside. And yes—*yes!*—there was the sound again . . . like the faintest breath, the most feeble attempt at a sigh.

Steeling herself, Lucy jerked open the door.

The space was cramped and narrow, murky with shadows, and as she stepped tentatively across the threshold, she could see the small priest's window to the left, the bit of screen and gauzy curtain concealing it from the other side, the kneeler beneath it on the floor.

The compartment stank of mildew; it was covered thickly in dust.

No sins had been confessed here for a long, long time.

See? Nothing. Just your imagination.

Almost weak with relief, Lucy turned to walk out.

And saw the door slowly creak shut.

Startled, she stared at it a moment, then gave it a push. The door didn't move. She pushed harder, then leaned into it with her shoulder. It wouldn't so much as budge.

That's strange . . . She couldn't remember seeing a latch on the outside of the door, and it hadn't stuck when she'd yanked it open. Trying not to panic, Lucy tried it again, harder this time, then harder still, but the door refused to give. Dust swirled into the air, choking her, irritating her eyes. She yelled and pounded on the walls. The space seemed to be growing smaller, the dust thicker, the high walls closing in—*Oh God—let me out of here!*

The thought briefly shot through her mind that no one would find her, maybe not for days and days, maybe not ever—she'd simply die here in the dark, in this tiny dark space, trapped in an upright coffin.

"Byron!" Lucy screamed. There was a *car* parked outside, for God's sake, *somebody* must be around! "Please! Please, somebody, I'm stuck in here—*let me out!*"

"Have you come to seek God's forgiveness, my child?" the voice murmured.

Lucy went cold. Her fists froze upon the door, her mouth gaped in a silent scream.

Her eyes turned fearfully to the wall . . .

She could see the priest's window, only now it was open. The curtain had been pulled back, and beyond the small screen was the dim outline of a face.

A face . . . yet somehow . . . and even more terrifyingly . . . *not* a face.

"Who are you?" Lucy choked out. Her back was against the door now, her knees so shaky she could hardly stand. It took every ounce of willpower to focus on that window and the featureless profile beyond. *"Who are you?"*

"Your salvation."

And she *knew* the voice, and he seemed to be all around her now, in the air, in the dust, in the echo of her heartbeat, in the thoughts inside her head, in the ice flowing through her veins . . .

"You were at the Festival," she realized. "Behind the tent, you were the one—"

"Meant to save you," he whispered. "No more sorrow . . . no more pain. Reprieve from the lifetime of loneliness that awaits you. Redemption from yourself."

"Please—"

"I know how lost you've been without your mother."

Tears filled Lucy's eyes . . . trickled slowly down her cheeks. "Why? Why are you doing this?"

"It's no longer a matter of why. It's a matter of when. Of how."

"I don't understand. I don't know you . . . I haven't done anything to you. Why won't you just leave me alone?"

"But you *have* done something to me. We have a connection, you and I." The voice sounded mildly amused. "So let me ask you again . . . have you come to seek God's forgiveness?"

"Forgiveness for what?" she cried desperately.

"For the places your heart will take you . . . where your soul cannot go."

Without warning the door came open.

As Lucy stumbled out into the aisle, she grabbed the door of the priest's compartment and flung it open.

But the darkness inside was empty.

And the dust not even disturbed.

18

Lucy stood there, unable to move.

Like a distant observer, she watched herself staring into the confessional, felt her slow-motion shock and disbelief—yet at the same time, felt oddly detached from reality. As she wheeled around to run, a tall figure suddenly materialized from the shadows behind her, sending her back with a scream.

"Hey, sorry!" he laughed. "Didn't mean to scare you! Guess I should've yelled or something, right?"

Before she could even react, the young man stepped closer, right into a narrow beam of light angling down from an overhead window. He had a friendly, boyish, dirt-streaked face and an equally friendly smile. Mid-twenties, probably—broad, solid shoulders . . . slender build . . . thighs and arms leanly muscled beneath skintight jeans and the pushed-up sleeves of a grimy sweatshirt. His eyes were deep blue, fringed with long dark lashes. His thick brown hair, though dusted with cobwebs, still showed a few golden streaks of fading summer sun. He was slightly out of breath and carrying a large cardboard box, which he immediately wrestled down to the floor.

Lucy gazed at him with open—and hostile— suspicion.

The young man merely grinned. "Is there something I can help you with?"

Lucy's gaze hardened. The stranger seemed oblivious.

"Matt," he said, reaching toward her. "Oh, wait. Sorry." He swiped his hand across the back of his jeans, then offered it again. "Matt. Well . . . *Father* Matt, actually. Well . . . Father *Matthew*, really. But you can call me Matt."

Lucy was dumbfounded. "You're . . . a *priest?*"

"Hmmm . . ." He glanced around in mock concern. "Should I apologize?" And then, as she continued to stare at him, he added, "Hey, it's okay. I'm out of uniform. And you are—?"

Lucy said nothing. Matt gave a solemn nod.

"Speechless," he said.

"Lucy," she finally whispered.

"Nice to meet you, Lucy. But I hope you weren't planning on confessing anything today, because as you can see, we're slightly out of service at the moment. Have been, actually, for years."

Lucy's eyes narrowed. Was this guy for real? Was he telling the truth? She tried to concentrate on his voice . . . what would that voice sound like, low and deep and whispering?

"Listen, are you okay?" Matt's smile seemed genuinely concerned. "Would you like to sit down?"

"Where were you just now?" Lucy murmured.

She saw his smile falter, but only for a second. "Sorry?"

"Just now. Where were you?" Her voice was trembling from aftershock; she fought to keep it steady. She watched his glance flicker toward the confessionals . . . the altar . . . the empty pews behind him.

"Just now?" This time he gestured vaguely with one arm. "Going through some closets in back. Sorry, I didn't know you were here—otherwise I'd have been a lot more hospitable."

"You didn't hear me yelling?"

"Yelling?" Matt frowned. Then, as though a thought had just occurred to him, he pulled some headphones from the box and dangled them in front of her. "I've been lost in Mozart. Just pulled these off when I saw you standing here. What were you yelling about?"

"I was . . ." Lucy's mind raced. "I was yelling . . . to see . . . if anyone was here."

Matt's smile widened. "Well, now you know."

He must be telling the truth . . . he wouldn't have had time to run from the confessional and grab that big box from somewhere and come back without me seeing him or hearing him or—

"Is it my face?" Matt asked, deadpan. "Or are you having a religious experience?"

Lucy snapped back to attention. "What?"

"You're staring at me like I have horns growing out of my head or something."

Flustered, Lucy looked away. "Are you alone here?"

"Alone?"

"Is there someone else here with you?"

Matt's eyes made a quick survey of the church. "Not that I know of. Why?"

"Nothing . . . I . . . I just thought I heard something, that's all."

"Now you're making *me* nervous," he teased, though once more his eyes swept the room. "It was probably just me rummaging around back there. There's a major echo in this old place, and—"

"No. No, it . . . it wasn't like that. It was a voice."

"A voice? Well, what did it sound like?"

Lucy shook her head. He *seemed* sincere, but how could she know for sure? And if he really *was* who he said he was, then how could she explain something so totally unbelievable? For an instant she dug deep into her memory, trying to recall the exact sound, the exact tone of that voice in the confessional . . . that voice at the fair. It *could* be Matt's voice disguised . . . just like it could be *anybody's* voice disguised.

Or maybe it wasn't disguised at all . . .

Lucy wrapped her arms about herself, suppressing a shudder. "I must have imagined it. I thought I heard someone."

This time Matt turned and took a good hard look toward the entrance. "Well, I didn't lock the door behind me this morning. So I guess it's possible someone could've sneaked in. Kind of like you did."

This seemed to amuse him, especially when a slow flush crept over Lucy's cheeks. Quickly she stammered out an explanation.

"I was . . . *supposed* to be meeting someone."

"Ah. A clandestine rendezvous. How intriguing."

Flushing hotter, she mumbled, "It's not what you think."

"No? And how do you know what I think?" Matt's eyes sparkled with humor, and he ran one hand back through his hair. "Maybe it was this friend of yours you heard. Maybe he really did show up, but he thought you weren't here."

And maybe I was a total fool for believing what Byron said and for coming here to meet him. "I don't think so."

"Well, maybe it was burglars," Matt said practically. "And when they realized there wasn't anything to steal, they got disappointed and left."

Lucy was ready to change the subject. "What happened to this place, anyway?"

"Don't you know?"

"I'm not from here. I just came a few weeks ago, to live with my aunt."

"I see." Matt leaned back against the wall, crossing his long legs, folding his arms casually across his chest. For a second Lucy thought he was going to ask her some personal questions, but instead he said, "All I know is that a bigger, fancier church was built in the center of town, and that's when this place became . . . shall we say . . . a sort of ecclesiastical warehouse."

"So you must remember when this place was really beautiful."

Matt shook his head. "Actually, no—I'm not from Pine Ridge either. And in *theory*, I'm only supposed to be here temporarily."

"In theory?"

"Well, that's what Monsignor's telling Father

Paul at the moment. That I'm only here till he gets back on his feet."

"Who's Father Paul?"

"The priest at the *real* church," Matt explained. "He's *old*—no, let me rephrase that—he's *ancient*. And very set in his ways. He's been refusing to take on an assistant for years, but I guess you could say he finally got a dose of Divine Intervention."

"How's that?"

Matt chuckled. "He fell down a flight of stairs." Then, at Lucy's look of alarm, "No, no, he's *fine*—but now that he's got a broken leg, it's forced him to slow down and listen to reason."

"And how does he feel about *you* being here?"

Again Matt laughed. "Let's put it this way. Since he's been here for about a hundred years and has a very particular way of doing things, I *obviously* am a complete and total moron. And just trying to wade through his particular way of doing things is probably going to take me the rest of my natural life."

Pausing, he gave Lucy a helpless look

"*If* he doesn't kill me before then. Like right now, I'm supposed to be looking for some statues he *swears* are stored down here in one of the cellars. But I can't seem to find the right doors—*or* the right keys."

He looked so distressed that Lucy couldn't help smiling. But as she caught a sudden movement from the corner of her eye, she gasped and spun toward it.

"Hey, easy," Matt soothed her, "it's just one of the cats."

"Cats?"

"Yeah, there're a bunch of them in here—the cleaning lady's always bringing them in. Just call it environment-friendly rodent control."

As Lucy nodded uncertainly, he frowned and lifted a hand to her forehead.

"You know, Lucy, maybe it's just this bad light, but you sure don't look like you feel very well. Why don't you sit down, and I'll get you some water."

His touch was firm, but gentle. His fingertips skimmed lightly over her skin and carefully brushed a strand of hair from her eyes. With no warning, Lucy felt a strange, slow warmth pulse softly at her temples . . . flow like liquid to the back of her brain . . .

Flowing . . . flowing . . . blood flowing . . . a dark red pool of blood on . . . on . . . a floor and something—something—sharp!—cutting!—pain and blood and anger—

"You hurt yourself," Lucy said. She stepped back and saw a look of dismay on Matt's face. "You hurt yourself, and it was very painful, and you bled for a long time."

The throbbing in her head was gone now, but her body felt shaky and drained. She watched as Matt frowned at her, as he lowered his hand. As he stared at the long, narrow cut on his palm and cautiously flexed his fingers.

"Well, yeah, but it's okay now," he assured her. "I mean, it happened a few days ago . . . it's not infected or anything, if that's what you're worried about."

Lucy took another step back, her emotions whirling. *He thinks I saw it*, she realized, *only I didn't see it, not the way he thinks—not with my eyes, but somewhere inside my head—and not exactly what happened—just those flashes again—flashes and feelings and colors and—*

"—broken glass," Matt was saying, as she tried to quiet her mind, focus in, act normally. "From one of those windows . . . it sliced right through me. It hurt like hell."

"I'm . . . I'm sorry." Flustered, Lucy pointed to the front of the church. "I'm feeling better now. I need to go."

But she could tell Matt wasn't convinced, even as she began walking away from him.

"What about your friend?" he asked her. "Is he supposed to pick you up?"

Lucy shook her head.

"Well, how are you getting home?"

"I have a car."

Look," Matt said kindly, "I'd be more than happy to drive you. Someone can come back later for your car."

"No. I'm fine, really. But thanks."

She was almost outside when he stopped her. She heard him call her name, and she turned to see him running after her, waving something in his hand.

"Lucy," he said again, catching up with her at the door. "I think you must've dropped this."

Lucy stared down at the thing he was holding.

And felt her eyes widen in alarm.

"I don't know anything about it," she said quickly. *Too quickly?* Because she could see the way he was looking at her now, that quizzical expression on his face, as though he *knew* she was lying, as though he *knew* and was waiting for her to confess . . .

She backed away, trying to put distance between them. "Sorry. It's not mine."

"Oh, that's too bad." Matt shrugged. "I found it on the floor near the altar. I just assumed it must be yours."

He gazed down at the necklace he was holding.

A single strand of tiny green beads.

"No," Lucy said again breathlessly, "no, it's not mine."

"Well, I guess I'll just leave it, then. Just in case whoever lost it comes back."

"Yeah. Maybe."

She hurried down the walkway, and she didn't once look back.

But if she had, she would have seen him still standing there . . . watching . . .

Watching her . . . even as he slipped the necklace casually into his pocket.

19

Lucy couldn't get into the car fast enough.

She locked the doors and fumbled the key into the ignition, turning it, pumping the accelerator, but the engine only coughed uselessly.

"Damn!"

Leaning forward, she rested her head on the steering wheel and alternately struggled to catch her breath and not give in to tears.

So Byron *had* been at the church. He *must* have been; otherwise, how would the necklace have ended up there? Yet she couldn't imagine him leaving it behind. Even from her brief encounters with Byron, it was obvious the necklace was important to him, that it tied in somehow to that girl in the cemetery. And Lucy had definitely experienced something when she'd handled it yesterday—and Byron had definitely known.

What if something's happened to him?

A million thoughts ran through her mind. Could he have left it as a message to her? A warning? Or could it even have been some sort of trap? But a trap for what?

Like so many other things these last few days, it didn't make any sense to her, didn't fit into any concept of logic or reality.

Lucy groaned and lifted her head. As she reached out again for the key, she suddenly saw a movement in the rearview mirror. With a shocked cry, she spun around just as Byron clamped a hand down on her shoulder.

"Ssh . . . it's just me," he said tightly. "Look, I really need your help."

Furiously, Lucy flung his hand away, then fixed him with a glare.

"What the *hell* do you think you're doing!" she shouted. "You nearly gave me a heart attack!"

"Then lock your doors next time." He frowned back at her. "Are you listening to me? The necklace is gone."

"*What?*"

Byron's jaw stiffened. "It was gone when I got home last night."

"After the Festival?"

At Byron's nod, Lucy gave him a puzzled look. "But I just saw it."

"What do you mean you just saw it?"

"In there. Matt has it."

"Who?"

"Matt . . . uh . . . Father Matt," Lucy stammered.

"Who's that?"

"The priest. The new priest at the church."

"*What* new priest?"

Lucy bristled. "How should I know? Father Paul's new assistant—he's here helping out because Father Paul broke his leg."

"So that's who was in there," Byron muttered. "Well, did you get it from him?"

"No, I didn't get it from him. It's not my necklace. Why would I get it from him?"

Facing forward again, she redirected her glare to his reflection. She saw him rub a hand across his forehead; she saw the visible strain upon his face.

"Are you sure it was the same necklace?" He sounded almost accusing. "That just doesn't make sense."

"He said he found it on the floor."

"But that's impossible, I didn't even *have* it when I was in the church."

Lucy couldn't keep the sarcasm from her voice. "And speaking of that—why exactly *weren't* you in there? If you were supposed to be *meeting* me?"

"Because I heard someone come in. Because I didn't know who it was, and I wasn't sure it was safe."

"Well, you were right. It *wasn't* safe. But, hey, it wasn't *you* being scared to death, so why were you even worried about it?"

"What do you mean?" His glance was sharp. "What happened?"

"I don't *know* what happened!" Lucy could hear herself getting louder, could hear the edge of hysteria in her voice, but couldn't seem to stop herself. "I don't know why I even *came* here today! I don't know why I'm even *speaking* to you! Get out of my car!"

"Drive," he said.

"*What?*"

"Just drive. I'll tell you where."

"No, I'll tell *you* where! *No*where! I'm not moving one inch till you get out of this car."

"I'm not getting out until we talk." She felt his hand on her shoulder again. His voice softened, tired. "Please. You have to listen to me. You're the only one I can talk to."

Lucy lowered her head. She chewed anxiously on her thumbnail, then shot him another look in the mirror.

"I can't go. The car won't start."

Byron stared at her a long moment. Then a faint smile played at the corners of his mouth.

"You flooded the engine, that's all. Try it again."

This time when she tried to start it, the car sprang to life. Grumbling under her breath, Lucy headed off down the street.

"So what happened in the church?" Byron asked again. He'd scooted closer to her now, leaning in between the bucket seats, and Lucy could feel the faint pressure of his arm against hers.

"If I tell you," she answered wryly, "you won't believe me."

"I doubt that. Turn here."

"Where are we going?"

"Someplace private."

Lucy cast him a sidelong glance. "I can't believe I'm doing this. Why should I even trust you?"

"Because you have to trust somebody. Because I'm guessing your life's suddenly been turned upside down."

Lucy tried to keep her expression blank, tried to ignore her shiver of apprehension. "I'm not sure that's an answer."

"Okay. Then for the same reason I have to trust you," Byron replied flatly. "We're the only ones who know about the cemetery. The only ones who know that something happened."

Lucy gave a terse nod. "So you're telling me that what I saw *wasn't* the fraternity prank I heard about. That what I saw was—"

"Real. Yes."

"So that girl . . ."

"Was murdered."

"But . . . by *who?*"

"That's why we have to get the necklace back. So you can tell us."

"So *I* can tell us? Tell us *what?*"

"Who killed her."

"Oh, now, wait a minute—"

"Hey, watch the road," Byron warned, as the car veered sharply into the wrong lane. "I'll tell you everything when we get to where we're going. Even the stuff you won't want to hear."

Lucy gripped harder on the steering wheel. "And how do I know *you* didn't kill her?"

She hadn't known she was going to say it; the words burst out before she could stop them. She felt his steady gaze upon her, and her heartbeat quickened in her chest.

"Just drive," he said tersely.

Yet with a start, Lucy realized how very sad he sounded.

Following his directions, she drove several miles outside of town, then turned off onto an isolated road that followed the curve of the lake. After another half hour, they finally pulled up to a cabin nestled among tall green pines, with a breathtaking view of the water.

"This is so beautiful," Lucy murmured. "Is it yours?"

"No. Somebody's summer home."

"Somebody's?"

"It's locked up now for the winter, but I have the key."

"And how did you manage that?"

Byron turned and glanced out the back windshield. With a twinge of uneasiness, Lucy wondered if he was afraid they'd been followed.

"Just park the car," he told her. "Over there behind those trees."

It wasn't until they were inside—door securely locked and bolted—that Byron seemed to relax a little. The cabin was very cold, and as Lucy stood rubbing her hands together, Byron went into the adjoining room, returned with a quilt, then motioned her into a rocking chair beside the fireplace.

Lucy sat. "Will you please just tell me what's going on?"

"Do you promise to believe me?"

"Probably not."

She thought a reluctant smile might have tugged at his mouth. He tossed her the quilt, then waited while she snuggled beneath it.

This is insane, Lucy thought. *This is completely insane. With everything else that's happened to me, I can't believe I'm sitting here in a cabin in the woods with some stranger who's asking me to trust him. If he murders me right now in this rocking chair, then I guess I deserve it.*

As Byron leaned down over her, her breath caught in her throat. His stare held her for an endless moment and then he slowly straightened.

"You still don't trust me. I see it in your eyes."

Lucy didn't miss a beat. "I don't believe you can see anything in my eyes. When I first saw you in the cemetery, you knew my mother had died, that I was alone. But you go to school with Angela—anyone could have known that."

"You're right. Anyone could've known, because Angela told everyone you were coming. Except . . ."

"Except what?"

Byron stepped closer. "Except I didn't know what you looked like. I'd never seen any pictures of you . . . never heard any descriptions. And I didn't know when you came to the cemetery that morning, that you were Angela's cousin."

Again that tiny shiver of apprehension; again Lucy tried to ignore it. "So . . . what are you trying to prove? That you have some sort of supernatural power? That you can know things about people just by staring at them?"

She wanted to laugh, to make light of it, but she suddenly realized that Byron had taken her hand, her right hand, that he was lifting it toward him and placing it over his heart.

"What do you feel?" he murmured.

And without warning, a whole range of emotions surged through her—*warmth . . . gentleness . . . fear . . . pain . . . sorrow*—all in a split-second rush that made her numb, that made her dizzy—*anger . . . loss . . . love*—

With a cry, Lucy jerked her hand from his grasp and cradled it against her chest, staring at him with wide, shocked eyes.

"You've been given a gift," Byron said solemnly. "And your life will never be the same."

20

"Do you think this is easy for me either? Having to say all these things to you—somebody I just met? And knowing how crazy it all sounds? And knowing—*understanding*, even—that the last thing in the world *you* want to do is *believe* me?"

Byron stopped . . . shook his head. There was bitterness in his tone.

"And why *would* you believe me? I mean, why would anyone believe *any* of this?"

Lucy couldn't do anything but stare. She watched as he crossed to the other side of the room, as he began pacing, slowly, back and forth between the fireplace and the door.

"That night at the cemetery," Byron's voice was low. "Try to think, Lucy. Try to remember."

But still Lucy sat there, paralyzed.

"Remember when I told you that something had been *passed on?*" Byron asked her.

At last she managed a nod.

"This gift you have . . . I think it was passed on to you from the girl who died. I suspected it . . . but I wasn't really positive till you picked up the necklace in class yesterday."

As if from a distance, Lucy heard herself ask, "I don't understand. Not about any gift . . . not about the necklace—"

"It was *her* necklace. She never took it off. So I know the only possible reason she did was to leave a clue behind. To try and tell me who killed her. To tell *you* who killed her."

"No. No . . . wait a minute. This is too much, this is—"

"True." Byron paused and shot her a level glance. "It's *true*, and no matter how much you want to forget about it, you *can't.* You have a responsibility now. You have—"

"A responsibility to who?" Lucy's voice went shrill with anger. "I don't have any responsibility to *anybody*—not to *you*—not to—"

"She had powers," Byron insisted. "She had powers nobody understood—and most people didn't believe in. And she used them for good, and she used them to help others when she could. But at the same time, she suffered for them her whole life. And now—now she's given them to you."

Lucy's lips parted soundlessly. For a second, Byron seemed to recede into some black void, then reappear again at the side of her chair.

"She could sense things," he said urgently. "See things that had already happened—sometimes even things that *hadn't* happened yet. By touching. Do you understand?"

Lucy shook her head. She wished he would stop talking, would leave, would just go away, but he knelt on the floor in front of her, where she couldn't ignore him.

"It didn't happen every single time—that's not the way it worked. But when it *did* happen, it was very powerful. She could never anticipate when the visions might come—sometimes they came from a person, sometimes from an object, just some little thing you'd never even think about."

Again Lucy shook her head. "So these visions she'd have . . . what were they, exactly?"

He stared at a spot beyond her, deep in thought, choosing his words carefully. "When she tried to describe it to me, she always said there weren't complete pictures. More like . . . like quick images or feelings. Sometimes colors or smells or sounds. She said it was like all her five senses had been peeled open, and raw, and they just kept absorbing all these impulses, with nothing to protect them."

His focus shifted back to her. Lucy saw his face through a fine mist and realized that tears had filled her eyes.

"Oh my God," she whispered. "Yes . . . it *is* like that . . ."

"You mean . . . like when you held the necklace?"

Without answering, she began to rock . . . a slow, gentle rhythm of self-comfort.

"Why'd you go there that night?" Byron asked quietly.

Lucy shut her eyes . . . tried to will the pain away.

"Please tell me, Lucy."

And so she did . . . recounting every moment from the time she'd left the house till Angela picked her up and took her back to Irene's. She told him everything, still feeling as though this were all some strange, distorted nightmare . . . still wishing she'd wake up, safe and warm in her mother's home. Still wondering why she was taking a chance with this mysterious young man she didn't know . . . why she was here trusting him and believing him, and in some painful way, feeling so grateful for his company . . .

And when she'd finally told her story, she realized that he'd taken her hand . . . spread her fingers wide apart . . . was gazing down at the tiny crescent scar upon her palm.

"She had a scar just like this," he said, not meeting Lucy's eyes. "In the same spot . . . on the same hand."

"It hurt," Lucy acknowledged numbly. "When she grabbed me . . . the pain I felt was unbearable—not like anything I'd ever felt before."

Nodding slightly, Byron placed her hand on the arm of the rocking chair. "I was supposed to meet her that night. She'd been away, and I hadn't seen her in nearly a year. Then I got this message from her—just out of the blue. Something important, she said. She told me to come alone, she'd be waiting at the old church. I could tell from her note that she was really scared. Only . . . she never showed up."

"So . . . I just happened to be walking past there at the same time?"

"I think the person following you that night was me."

Byron rocked back on his heels, his expression thoughtful. "I'd just gotten to the church when I saw you running away. And it was storming so bad, I couldn't really see anything. For a minute I thought it might be her, so I went after you—but then you turned under the streetlight. And when I realized it wasn't her, I went back."

"And that's when I ran into the cemetery. Because I thought you were stalking me."

"I should have known it was something bad." Byron's eyes were as hard as his voice. "When she didn't show up on time, I should have left right away—I should have looked for her then. But I just kept thinking maybe it was the storm, she was having trouble getting there, but that she'd *be* there, just five more minutes, she'd *be* there . . ."

He paused. Drew a sharp breath.

"I don't think I wanted to believe it. Even when I got in my van and started driving around, looking for her. I didn't want to believe something had happened to her. And that's when I saw you again."

"Me?"

"You were coming out of the cemetery, and you ran across the street to use the phone. And you looked terrified."

Lucy's heart gave a sickening lurch. How easily those feelings of terror returned, just from talking, just from remembering. She watched as Byron stood up and walked to the window. He propped his hands upon the sill and leaned forward, his shoulders stiff with tension.

"I knew," he mumbled. "I mean, there you were, scared and muddy and soaking wet—and suddenly I just *knew*. I knew it had something to do with her."

For several long moments there was quiet between them. Only the patient creak of the rocking chair upon the wooden floor. The muted songs of birds outside the windows. Until at last Byron spoke again.

"I tried to get over to you . . . to see if you needed help. But by the time I got the van turned around, you were gone. So I went back to the cemetery. And I looked for her." Byron's head lowered. "I never found her."

Lucy stopped rocking. She stared at his back with a puzzled frown. "But when I saw you the next morning—the things you said—how could you have known those things if you never found her? If you weren't actually there?"

"Because she told me."

"She . . ." Lucy sat straight in her chair. The quilt slid down to her waist, and she impatiently pushed it aside. "What do you mean, she told you—what are you saying?"

"In a dream that night. She told me in a dream."

He turned around to face her. As Lucy held his steady gaze, she slowly shook her head.

"You know something, Byron . . . you're asking me to believe a *lot*."

"Haven't you ever had a dream so real, you knew it was *more* than a dream?"

"Yes, but . . ." Lucy's voice trailed off. Until that moment she'd almost forgotten her *own* dream of two nights ago . . . her mother at the window, sounding so sad . . .

"But what?" Byron persisted.

"I did have one like that," Lucy murmured. "That night, after I got home from the cemetery. My mother came back to me. It was like . . . like she was trying to warn me about something."

"What'd she say?"

Lucy's voice faltered. "She said . . . that I was going to a place where . . . where she couldn't help me."

Byron gave an almost imperceptible nod. His eyes shone even darker.

"So your mother shows up with a warning. On the very night a dying girl touches you and leaves this scar on your hand. Doesn't that seem a little more than coincidence?"

"Oh God . . ."

"When I finally went to sleep that night," Byron said tightly, "I dreamed she was in a grave. I saw the storm. I saw her covered in blood . . . and I saw her reaching out."

"But . . . you didn't see who killed her?"

"No. She was talking to me . . . she wanted me to know that she was gone. And that she hadn't been alone when she died. She told me I should go to the cemetery the next morning and wait for someone. And then she said, 'Help her . . . now *you* must help the one who helped *me*.'"

Lucy didn't know how to respond. As Byron fell silent, his sorrow seemed to fill the room, yet at the same time she sensed his own defenses struggling to pull it back.

"So . . . what you're saying," she stammered, "is that *I* have these . . . these powers now. And *I'm* going to start having visions . . . and . . . and *feeling* things I don't want to feel just because I *touch* something?"

But when Byron didn't answer, Lucy's tone grew almost pleading. "Are you absolutely sure? Are you positive it was her? I mean . . . maybe she didn't even show up that night. Maybe she was never here in town. Maybe it was just some girl you didn't know, who just happened to be in the wrong place at the wrong time—"

"Lucy, stop," he said tightly.

"But it could have been, right? I mean, it *could* have been a mistake and maybe she's still alive somewhere, maybe she—"

"She's not alive."

"Then where's her body? Where's the grave? If she's really dead, you would have *found* her— you would have found *something*—"

"Lucy, stop!" His voice struck out at her, cold and final. "There are just some things you *know*, because every part of you feels it, because you have a bond with somebody that's special and unique. And she and I had that kind of bond. So . . . no. *No.* It wasn't a mistake."

He raked a hand back through his hair. His face twisted in pain.

"She's dead, Lucy. She's dead."

Lucy's heart ached at the sight of him. "You really loved her, didn't you?" she whispered.

A muscle clenched in his jaw. He turned stiffly back to the window. "Yes."

"So . . . she was your girlfriend?"

"No. Katherine was my sister."

21

"Your sister?" Lucy echoed. "The one who—"

She broke off, flustered, as he shot her a cold glance over his shoulder.

"Was crazy?" he finished sarcastically.

"I was going to say . . . the one who went away."

"Well, you *have* been in Pine Ridge awhile. Time enough to have heard all the gruesome stories about my family, I'm sure."

"I'm sorry." Lucy's cheeks reddened. "I haven't heard that much."

"It doesn't matter. Actually, it's not so bad, being part of the local folklore. People tend to leave you alone."

"Is that what you want? To be left alone?"

He leaned back against the wall, folding his arms across his chest, fixing her with another intense stare. "I guess that depends on who it is."

Lucy dropped her eyes. She heard him move to the fireplace and sit down upon the hearth.

"Are you sure you want to hear the rest of it?" he asked pointedly.

"Can it get any worse?" She gave him a wan smile, and he almost—but not quite—returned it.

"These . . . powers . . . forces . . . psychic abilities . . . whatever you want to call them," he began tentatively, "they run in our family. At least that's what my grandmother says. When I was little, I thought she was magic. Sometimes she could tell us things before they actually happened."

"What kinds of things?"

"Well . . . like when a certain neighbor was going to knock on our door—and then they would. Or who'd be on the other end of the phone before she even picked it up. Just simple things like that. She could tell you where to find things you'd lost . . . or that a storm was coming when there wasn't a cloud in the sky. And I never thought it was strange. It was normal to me."

Intrigued, Lucy leaned forward. "So *all* of you had psychic talents?"

"It was always so obvious with Katherine. From the time we were little, she was already having visions and seeing things nobody else could see. It was just a part of who she was. But mine was different. I was older the first time it happened. Probably around ten or so. And a woman—someone I'd never met before—had come to see my grandmother, and I remember she was so sad."

He hesitated, as though reluctant to venture too far into the past.

"I remember she was sitting at our kitchen table, waiting for Gran to come downstairs. And I sat down across from her, and suddenly she just *looked* at me. Looked me full in the face, and her eyes were so big and so desperately unhappy."

Byron's voice lowered. A poignant blend of sorrow and awe.

"I stared right back at her. Right back into her eyes. Deep, deep into that terrible sadness. And I said, 'I'm sorry about your little girl; I'm sorry she drowned.' And I remember she tried to smile at me, but she *couldn't* smile—all she could do was cry—and I felt so bad for her."

Again he paused. Then he met Lucy's gaze with a level one of his own.

"There was no way I could have known about her *or* her daughter; she didn't even live around there. Gran told me later that I'd had a glimpse of her soul."

"Eyes," Lucy murmured. "Eyes are supposed to be windows to the soul."

"Some people say so," he agreed. "I couldn't explain it then, and I don't even try anymore. But if that's true—about windows to the soul— then the daughter she'd lost was the most important feeling in her soul that day. And I had a glimpse of it."

"Is it like"—Lucy struggled for words— "looking beyond pain? Or seeing something that's even deeper than grief?"

His shoulders moved in a shrug. "It's nothing like Katherine could do—nothing that clear or sharp. No smells or sounds or things like that. It's like . . . looking through a veil. There's fog . . . mist . . . no definite features or details. Yet somehow I'm able to pull something out of it."

"Like . . . through a curtain . . . or a screen?"

"Sort of, yeah. Lucy? What is it?"

But as the memory of the confessional flashed through her mind, Lucy hurriedly shook her head. *Not now. Not yet. This isn't the right time . . .*

"Nothing," she assured him. "Tell me more about Katherine. About this gift of hers."

"A gift sometimes. But also a curse."

The edge was back in his voice, and Lucy felt a prickle of apprehension as he continued with the explanation.

"As she got older, she didn't want to use it anymore, because it scared her too much. She'd get nervous and embarrassed because she never knew when the visions would hit her—how strong they'd be, or how frightening—and most people didn't understand. Most people didn't even *try* to. All they knew was that she was different, and that sometimes she acted strange. And so some people laughed at her, and some made fun of her. And others were just plain scared."

Byron pressed both hands to his forehead . . . gently massaged his temples.

"But of course, she *couldn't* just not use it

anymore—that was impossible. It's not like a switch she could just turn on and off whenever she wanted. It was *part* of her; part of who she was. So it got to where she wouldn't even leave the house. Gran and I were the only ones she trusted; home was the only place she felt safe."

Lucy frowned, taking everything in. "But if that's true," she asked carefully, "then why did she end up leaving?"

She saw him tense . . . saw the briefest flicker of indecision over his face. She sat up straighter in her chair as her voice grew suspicious.

"There's something else," she accused him. "Something you're not telling me."

Byron stood up from the hearth. He pulled her from the rocking chair, then turned and strode purposefully to the door.

"Come with me," he said. "And I'll tell you the rest of the story."

22

It was a relief to get out.

Despite the coziness of the cabin, Lucy was beginning to feel claustrophobic. As if every new revelation of Byron's cast a dark, uneasy shadow over her heart and her mind.

The crisp, cold air felt wonderful. As they walked together toward the lake, the pungent fragrance of pines swirled through her head, almost making her forget, almost sweeping the doubts and fears away.

"It's so beautiful out here," Lucy murmured. She followed him to the shore, to the wooden dock stretching out over the water. A boat was tied at the end, bobbing peacefully upon the barely rippled surface, and with one smooth movement, Byron helped her down into the bow and slipped the rope free.

Here I go again, Lucy thought ruefully, watching the dock glide farther and farther from view—*getting myself into another dangerous situation*. And yet, out here in this pristine wilderness, surrounded by such stillness, watching Byron rhythmically work the oars, she felt a sense of peace that she hadn't felt for days.

"Don't ruin it," she said suddenly, and felt her cheeks flush as Byron gave her a curious look.

"What?"

"The mood. The minute."

He cocked his head . . . lifted an eyebrow. A playful wind tugged at his hair, streaming it back from his face. "I'll just keep rowing, then."

"So much has happened," she tried to explain, her words tumbling out in a rush. "*Too* much— too much to comprehend and understand and try to believe. And from what you're telling me—and maybe from what you're *going* to be telling me—things might be getting worse."

He didn't answer, but still, she could see the seriousness in his eyes.

"So just give me this one minute, okay? To breathe? And be away from everything that's bad? And see the world in a way that makes some sense to me."

Lucy's voice caught. She turned from him abruptly and fixed her gaze on the distant shoreline . . . on the woods and the hills and the endless blue sky above. For a long time there was only the sound of the oars dipping water . . . the music of the birds . . . the soft sigh of pine-rich breezes. Lucy shut her eyes and pretended wishes came true, and she wished this could last forever.

But wishes never come true. At least not mine. At least not the good ones.

As she felt the boat jar, her eyes came open. A second later the dinghy was scraping up onto a narrow stretch of beach, and Byron was out of the boat, anchoring it securely between a small shelter of trees.

"Grab those blankets under your seat," he said, reaching for her hand. "We'll go this way—I think you'll like the scenery."

"What is this? Some kind of island?"

"No, just another side of the lake. We could have driven—there's a road off that way about half a mile—but I think the boat ride's much nicer."

"How do you know about these places?" Lucy asked, as he pulled her up a steep rise and on to a stretch of level ground.

"I grew up here, remember? And I take care of a lot of these cabins off-season. And in the summer I do some maintenance work."

"What kind of maintenance work?"

"Handyman stuff, mostly."

"So that's how you had that key."

"I have all the keys."

Taking the blankets, he led her along the beach for another five minutes, then suddenly veered off again toward the shore. After maneuvering several more rocky slopes, Lucy found herself in a small, wooded cove with a breathtaking view of the lake.

"You're right, it is beautiful," she said appreciatively, gazing out across the shimmering expanse of water.

"And private." Byron shook out a blanket and spread it over the ground. "Sit down . . . wrap this other one around you. It's pretty cold out here."

Lucy did so. She watched as he sat beside her, his eyes narrowed intently on the opposite horizon. She hugged her legs to her chest and rested her chin on her knees.

"Do you believe in evil?" Byron asked.

Lucy turned to him in surprise. Somehow, surrounded by all this peaceful beauty, his question seemed almost laughable . . . and far more than ominous.

"Evil?"

"An evil that can transcend time and space? An evil so obsessive that you can't escape it, no matter how hard you try?"

Her brow creased in a frown. She drew back from him and stared harder. "You're really serious."

"You told me you thought you were being stalked the other night, when you ran from the church. Do you remember how you felt?"

"Of course I remember. I was terrified."

"Well, that's how Katherine felt all the time . . . like she was being stalked by someone. Except she couldn't outrun him. And she couldn't hide. Because he was in her visions and in her dreams."

"Byron—*what* are you talking about?"

But he wouldn't look at her, just kept staring

out across the water, at the play of light and shadow off the woods across the lake.

"They started about three years ago," he said gravely. "When she was sixteen. And they weren't like the other visions she'd had her whole life. These were like the worst kind of nightmares. Nightmares she couldn't wake up from. Nightmares she couldn't escape. Things more horrible than you could ever imagine."

With an unconscious gesture, Lucy pulled the blanket closer around her. The breeze off the beach had nothing to do with the sudden chill in her veins.

"She said it was like looking at the world through the essence of evil . . . as though *she* were inside his head, thinking out through his thoughts and seeing things through his eyes."

"Sort of"—Lucy was struggling to understand— "like a camera taking pictures?"

"Yes, capturing every gory detail as it happens."

Despite the blanket, Lucy felt even colder. "Did she tell you what these things were?"

"Never. Only that they were inhuman. So violent and hideous, she couldn't bear them anymore. Never knowing when they'd come . . . or how long they'd last. And worst of all, never being able to stop them. Just having to stand by and watch, over and over again."

"So where were these visions coming from?"

"From the mind of a monster. From someone sick and twisted, who enjoyed causing pain and watching his victims suffer."

"My God . . . so you think . . . you think this person was *real*?"

Byron's expression turned grim. "Katherine did. And she was convinced he'd keep right on killing and brutalizing people, and that he'd never get caught. Because *she* was the only one who knew about him."

"And she didn't have any idea who he was?"

"None. She never saw his face. Because she was always seeing things from *his* perspective."

Lucy could feel goose bumps along her arms. Could feel a cold, stealthy uneasiness gnawing at the back of her mind. Determinedly she tried to force it away, tried to concentrate on what Byron was saying.

"—a connection," he continued. "But why? We never knew."

"You mean, a connection between their minds? Between their thoughts? Like the bond *you* had with Katherine?"

Byron's face went rigid. "How can you even compare the two? That's—"

"No, I'm sorry, that's not what I meant," she said quickly. "I'm just trying to understand this. So Katherine could see these . . . these *atrocities* this guy was committing. *As* he was committing them?"

"Yes. *Forced* to watch him. But *helpless* to stop him."

"Then . . . was it someone she knew?"

"Impossible."

"Someone she met just one time, maybe? Someone with psychic abilities as exceptional as hers, who was somehow able to lock into her mind?"

"You mean . . . sort of like a psychic parasite?"

"Exactly."

"She hardly left the house. And this is a small community—people tend to know each other around here. I can't think of anybody who fits into an evil mode like this one. And believe me . . . I've tried."

"But you said she sensed things—*saw* things—by touching. So maybe she bumped into him in a crowd . . . I mean, he could have just been passing through town, or visiting somebody here. Maybe he dropped something . . . or . . . or accidentally left something of his behind. And Katherine just happened to pick it up."

Byron sounded weary. "I've thought of that, too. And I guess it *is* possible . . . except I think she'd only have felt a connection to it when it was in her hands. Just when she touched it. *Not* on and on for three years."

"But maybe she kept it. Maybe she found something, and took it home with her and didn't realize."

"She'd have realized, Lucy, believe me."

Lucy went silent. She watched as he leaned back on the ground, propping himself on his elbows. He stared far out at the opposite bank, and his gaze narrowed, hard as steel.

"Katherine was such a gentle person. Probably the only truly good person I've ever known in my life. And that's what made it so much worse. The way she suffered . . . her fear and her pain . . . There were times she really thought she was losing her mind. And sometimes I think . . ." His voice faltered . . . softened. "I think maybe . . . finally . . . in a way . . ."

A shadow seemed to cross his face. After a moment of uncertain silence, Lucy gently touched his shoulder.

"Wasn't there anyone she could talk to? Someone who could help her?"

"And who would that have been? How do you explain something like that—especially in a town like this? Hell, everybody here *already* thought she was crazy."

"But maybe someone who has experience in—"

"Ssh!" Jerking upright, Byron grabbed her shoulder. "Did you hear something?"

Lucy's heart took a dive to her stomach. As she slowly followed the direction of his gaze, she listened hard through the quiet.

Wind sighing through trees . . . water lapping gently at the shore . . . her own pulse pounding in her ears . . .

"What?" she mouthed silently. "What is it?"

But she could feel his grip relaxing now . . . his body easing back down beside her. His hand slid away from her arm, though his expression remained wary.

"What?" she asked aloud, but Byron only frowned and turned his attention back to the view.

"Nothing. Just jumpy, I guess."

Lucy glanced nervously over her shoulder. Strange . . . she hadn't really heard anything, yet she could feel a tiny sliver of dread at the back of her neck.

"It's okay," Byron reassured her again. "This is one of my secret places . . . and nobody's around here this time of year anyway."

Lucy wasn't entirely convinced. She picked up a broken twig and nervously began scratching circles in the dirt.

"What about your grandmother?" she asked then. "Does she know about Katherine?"

His mouth twisted in a rueful smile. "There's not much Gran doesn't know. But I haven't told her, if that's what you mean."

"So . . . do you think *she* believes Katherine's dead?"

Byron fixed her with a calm stare. "When Katherine left home a year ago—that was before

224

Gran had her stroke—Gran told me I'd never see Katherine alive again. I didn't want to believe that, of course. I should have known better. Maybe if I'd tried harder to stop Katherine from going . . . or maybe if I'd gone with her, maybe she'd still be alive now. That's why you have to listen to me—maybe we can stop it this time— before you get hurt—"

"Before *I* get hurt?" Lucy shrank back in dismay. "What do you mean—"

"Because maybe he hasn't realized it yet—"

"Byron—"

"—hasn't realized yet who you are—"

"Stop it! You're scaring me!"

"You *should* be scared, Lucy—you *need* to be scared! It might be the only thing that keeps you alive if—"

He broke off abruptly, his body tensing, his glance shooting once more toward the trees. As Lucy followed the direction of his focus, she felt that fine prickle of fear again, though now it was creeping down the length of her arms.

Very slowly Byron got to his feet. As Lucy started to follow, he shook his head at her and held a finger to his lips.

"No," he whispered. "Wait here."

"Where are you going?" Thoroughly alarmed now, Lucy watched him disappear into the woods. She stood there, heart pounding, listening to the faint rustle of branches as Byron moved away from her. But even that sound faded within minutes.

All that remained was silence.

Dangerous silence.

Should she call his name? Ignore what he'd told her and go after him? Lucy didn't know what to do. With the lake on one side and the woods on all others, this spot that had seemed so idyllic just five minutes before, now seemed more like a . . .

Trap.

That's it. I'm going.

Lucy started toward the trees, toward the exact spot where Byron had gone in. Surely he couldn't be that far ahead of her—it should be easy to catch up. But what if she got lost? She'd be of no use to him then, and someone had to be able to go for help.

She wished she had a weapon. Quickly her eyes scanned the shore, coming to rest on a large branch dangling over the water. With some effort, she managed to wrestle it loose; she could use it as a club if she had to.

"*Lucy!*"

Lucy froze. She hadn't imagined it, had she? That voice calling through the trees . . .

"Byron?" she yelled back.

It had sounded so faint, that call—distant and muffled. *Oh God, maybe he really is hurt.* Why had he just gone off like that, anyway—what a stupid thing to do!

Lucy squinted off through the shifting shadows of the forest. Cupping her hands around her mouth, she shouted as loud as she could. "By-ron!"

No answer.

I didn't imagine it—I'm sure I didn't imagine it!

Yet at the same time the hairs lifted at the back of her neck, and her nerves went taut as wires. *Just like I didn't imagine that voice in the confessional, that voice behind the tent at the fair . . .*

She wished now that she'd told Byron about that voice—*why* hadn't she told Byron about it?

"*Byron!*" she called frantically. "Byron, where *are* you?"

The wind blew a long cold breeze in off the lake.

It wrapped around her like a damp caress.

"Lucy!" the voice seemed to echo, ghostly through the hills. "Please, Lucy! I need you!"

"Oh, God . . . oh God . . ." She knew then that something *must* have happened to him—something bad—something terrible—and it was all she could do to hold her panic in check.

"I'm coming!" Lucy shouted.

And ran headlong into the woods.

23

"Byron! Where are you?"

But she hadn't heard him call in several minutes now, and she knew she'd be hopelessly lost if she went much farther.

Frightened and frustrated, Lucy stopped and yelled one more time. "Byron! *Please!* Answer me!"

Even the breeze seemed to have stopped. Even the trees seemed to hold their breath around her.

Maybe he'd been injured so badly that he'd lost consciousness by now. Mauled by some animal. Lying broken at the bottom of some ravine. Slowly and steadily bleeding to death. *Oh God, what should I do?* If she ended up lost in these dark woods, it wouldn't do *either* of them any good.

Instinctively, Lucy turned and raced back to the beach. Had there been a radio in the boat? A cell phone? She didn't remember seeing any, but she hadn't been paying much attention. As she broke through the trees, she suddenly halted in her tracks and stared in shock at the lake.

A small boat was floating some distance from the shore.

An empty boat.

Our boat?

"No!"

Lucy couldn't believe it. A thousand menacing scenarios rushed through her head, muddling into a numbing darkness. Fearfully she spun around and peered off into the forest.

"Byron!"

Her shout echoed back to her, mocking.

She had to think . . . think what to do. Try to find help—but where? She didn't have a clue where to go—and what if Bryon roused again and called for her? Still, he was familiar with this place . . . perhaps even now he was on his way to safety . . .

The road!

Lucy suddenly remembered—hadn't Byron mentioned a road when they'd first gotten out of the boat? A road about half a mile from here?

Praying she could find her way back to the cove, Lucy tried to retrace the route they'd taken earlier. She'd noticed a pathway, a narrow trail leading back from the beach and angling off through the woods. As she finally reached the place where they'd originally docked, Lucy could see the path clearly, and she took it without hesitation.

The trail wound mostly uphill, and though she'd been chilly when she first started out she soon grew sweaty and out of breath. She was thankful she'd worn her sneakers. More than once she was forced to scale fallen logs and sharp boulders that blocked the rugged terrain.

She wasn't sure when she began to be aware of the quiet. It seemed to slip up on her gradually, like shadows stalking through underbrush. As she stopped to listen, Lucy realized that the birds had stopped singing, that there wasn't a breath of wind.

The forest filled with an eerie silence.

Just like it felt back there when I was looking for Byron . . .

Her heart fluttered beneath her jacket. She forced herself to keep walking, to keep her thoughts carefully focused on the emergency at hand. Find help. Find Byron. She couldn't let herself think of anything beyond that. She just hoped he wasn't hurt—

"Maybe we can stop it this time—before you get hurt—"

Lucy's eyes widened as his words sprang unexpectedly into her mind. *No. No. I won't think about that; I refuse to think about that . . .*

"Because maybe he hasn't realized it yet—hasn't realized yet who you are—"

And Byron had started to tell her something, something important, had been trying to warn her about something, when the sound had come, when he'd looked so startled and so wary, when he'd gone into the woods and never come out again . . .

"You should *be scared, Lucy—you* need *to be scared! It might be the only thing that keeps you alive if—"*

Lucy broke into a run.

And the silence was so loud, so dangerous, threatening her from every side, silence like shadows, silence like stalkers . . .

No—no—it's just my imagination—

Silence like evil . . .

No!

Silence like death—

Her feet slid off into nothingness; her body hurtled down through an endless black void . . .

She didn't even have time to scream.

Just fell farther and farther . . . down and down . . . into the silence . . .

And finally lay still.

24

She was so beautiful.

Beautiful in this brief spell of sleep . . . lost in her dreamless drifting . . .

Is this what peace looks like? he wondered.

The way *she'd* looked that night at her window, and the way she'd looked at the Festival . . . her face tilted, smiling, bathed in the glow of the lights, just so . . .

And now . . . as she lay here on her back, unconscious from falling, sprawled before him in innocent slumber . . .

He could do anything he wanted to her at this very moment, anything he pleased, for she'd be helpless and completely unaware . . .

But time enough for that later.

Right now all he wanted to do was look at her.

At her hair spread around her head like a halo, her lashes soft against her cheeks. Her fingers curled in upon her palms, like flower petals unopened, and her arms wide in an empty embrace, half buried beneath the leaves that had cushioned her fall.

She was still wearing red.

He loved her even more when she wore red.

It seared into his soul, this brand-new image, like the pink of that very first night . . . like the blue of the Festival . . . and oh, how he'd loved the deep bloodred of her panic and terror at the church just this morning . . .

He'd carried those sights of her, those smells of her, deep in his heart through every single hour since then.

Like a seductive dream, both sleeping and waking.

It was sheer luck that he'd tasted her, as well . . .

He'd picked up the apple she'd dropped at the fair, and she'd never suspected, never stopped to look back, never even realized he was near. And ah, how it tasted just the way he'd imagined . . . the blood from her lip still fresh on the fruit . . . so luscious, so sweet, with its red candy coating.

He'd savored the juice of it inside his mouth, and then he'd lured her to a dark, hidden place.

She'd caught his scent, and she'd come to him . . .

He *loved* how she loved the scent of him.

The way he *always* smelled after he killed.

For blood, as he'd come to learn through the years, was a very personal thing.

It mingled with one's own essence . . . and tempted . . . like expensive cologne or perfume.

She'd followed him there, and she'd found him there, and when he'd sucked the blood from her lip, her heart had beat wildly, as frantically as his own . . .

And after that—*especially* after that—he vowed that *nothing* would stop him from having her.

Only . . . not now.

Not now.

Now he would simply watch and admire . . .

For this was the sweetest torment of all.

The ache of her loneliness . . . the pain of her grief . . .

He *fed* off emotions such as these, they *called* to him like shining beacons in pitch-black rooms.

They made him dizzy with longing, and they made him want to possess her totally.

Soon, he told himself. *Soon . . .*

He had to be patient with this one.

Not arouse suspicion . . . gain her trust. That was how these things were done . . . slow and methodical . . . and he was nothing if not methodical.

It was a fine art he'd perfected through these many years—that when he desired something, he'd do *anything* to get it.

Say anything . . . *be* anything . . . no matter how deceitful, no matter how ruthless.

It was his nature.

And he could wait for however long it took.

No need to hurry, he reminded himself.

No need whatsoever to rush.

After all . . . he had eternity on his side.

25

"*Lu-cy . . .*"

"Mom?" Lucy mumbled.

She always sounded like that when she'd locked herself out of the apartment, standing down on the street corner, yelling up at Lucy's bedroom window . . .

"*Lu-cy . . .*"

It was ridiculous; she was always telling Mom how ridiculous it was, a grown woman forgetting her keys all the time, leaving them at work or at the grocery store or on the kitchen table: *I mean, one of these days I'm not going to be here, I won't be here to let you in, and then what are you going to do?*

"*Lucy!*"

"Hang on, I'm coming . . . I'm . . ."

Cobwebs drifted through her mind, but they

were getting thinner now, almost transparent, and there was light coming through . . .

"Coming . . ." she murmured.

Lucy sat up so quickly that the world spun around her and the cobwebs burst like bubbles.

She didn't realize at first what had happened.

Not until she shook herself out of the leaves and squinted up at the walls of the ravine and saw a shadowy blur of trees and sky high above her.

I was running just a minute ago . . . how'd I get down here?

She ached all over. Her clothes were twisted around her, and she was covered with dirt. *This is starting to feel normal*, she thought disgustedly, stretching out her arms and then her legs. At least nothing seemed to be broken or sprained. *So far, so good . . .*

Byron!

It all came back to her then—why she was out here in the middle of the woods, what must have happened. She should have been paying attention, watched where she was going—now what was she going to do? If Byron were still out there somewhere, wounded or even dying, she'd never get help back to him in time. Gazing up at the steep incline, she wasn't even sure she could help *herself*.

"Damnit," Lucy muttered, fighting down panic. "*Damnit!*" Her body winced with pain as she tried to stand up. She hobbled over to one side of the gorge, then suddenly noticed the outline of a head hanging over the ledge above her.

"Lucy!" Even from down here, she could hear Byron's sigh of relief. "Are you okay?"

"Am I okay?" her voice shot back to him, dangerously close to tears. "Do I *look* okay? My *God*, Byron—where have you *been*?"

"What are you doing down there?"

"Trying to save you!"

He leaned out farther over the edge. Lucy heard the sarcasm in his voice. "And a fine job you're doing, too."

"Get me out of here! You scared me to death!"

"I'll be right down."

Lucy sagged back against the wall of the escarpment, wiping furiously at her eyes. By the time Byron finally worked his way down beside her, her nerves were raw.

"I thought you were dead!" she exploded. "Where *were* you? Why didn't you answer me?"

Byron regarded her solemnly. "I could ask you the same question."

"What are you talking about? *I'm* not the one who was lost!"

"Then who have I been looking for? I heard you calling for help, but I couldn't find you anywhere."

"*I'm* not the one who called for help—*you're* the one who called for help! *You're* the one who disappeared!" Lucy was trembling now, with anger and relief. "You're the one who went off and *left* me! I called and called, and the boat floated away!"

Byron's eyes narrowed. "You mean, *you* didn't take the boat?"

"Why would I do that? It was out in the middle of the lake! Then I tried to find a road—so I could get someone to look for you! And then—"

"Lucy," he interrupted, taking her shoulders, giving her a gentle shake. "Lucy, listen to me, I'm telling you the truth. I heard your voice, but it was so deep in the woods—and you kept saying my name, calling for help. You sounded like you were crying, like you'd been hurt. But I looked and looked, and I couldn't find you. I've been searching for three hours!"

Lucy stared back at him, calmer now, but bewildered. "But . . . I heard *you*, too—and I thought *you* were hurt—"

"You heard *me*? When?"

"Right after you went into the woods! I was so scared and—" She broke off abruptly at the expression on his face. "What? What is it?"

"I didn't call you, Lucy. I *never* called you. I was . . ."

"*What?*"

"I was afraid for you." For a second he seemed almost angry. He clenched his jaw, and something dark flickered far back in his eyes. "I didn't want anyone to know you were here. So I didn't call you."

Lucy hadn't realized she was trembling again. Taking her arm, Byron sat her on the ground and knelt beside her.

"Then who did?" Lucy whispered. "Who did?"

Byron shook his head, his gaze lowered. Then

finally he said, "I was trying to tell you when I heard something in the woods."

"What's going on, Byron? I don't understand."

The lines of his face went hard. "The truth is, I brought you here to warn you."

"To . . . warn me? Why? About what?"

"Lucy, the night Katherine left home, she woke me up and told me she couldn't stand to see Gran and me hurting for her anymore. And that she was going to *go* wherever she had to, and *do* whatever she had to, to learn the truth about those evil visions. She swore that no matter what it took, she'd put them to rest, once and for all."

"So you think she actually tried to find that evil person who was connecting to her thoughts?"

"I think she *did* find him. And I think he killed her."

Lucy watched the carefully controlled rage in his expression . . . the muscle working tightly in his cheek.

"Katherine was wearing that green necklace when she went away. It was a present I'd given her years before, and she never took it off. But yesterday morning I found it in the cemetery, so I knew—*I knew then for certain*—that she was dead. She'd never have taken it off otherwise. Never."

"So you think it came off in the struggle?"

"I think she *took* it off *because* of the struggle. To leave a clue behind . . . and a warning."

He paused a second, chewing thoughtfully on his lower lip. Then he turned to Lucy with a grave frown.

"I think Katherine's murderer touched that necklace while she was fighting for her life. And I think she left it there on purpose *because* he'd touched it, and I think she passed her power on to you, so *someone* would know who killed her."

Lucy went pale. "So you're saying . . . that when I held the necklace, I was actually seeing her . . . her death?"

Without another word she jumped up and started pacing.

"Lucy!"

"No, I don't *want* this—I don't want any *part* of this—I didn't *ask* for this—I—"

"You don't have a choice." Byron was on his feet again, beside her in an instant. "You *are* part of it now, whether you like it or not. There's nothing you can do but accept it."

"And anyway, when I *did* hold the necklace, I didn't see anyone!" Lucy babbled, as though she hadn't heard a single word Bryon said. "I didn't see the face of any killer! I just felt wind and there were eyes and hands and blood and . . . and . . ."

He reached out for her and held her at arms length, forcing her to look at him. "I told you, sometimes it doesn't happen all at once. The next time you touch it, you might see something else, something more—"

"There won't *be* a next time! I'm *not* going to hold that necklace! I'm not going to touch *anything*!" Angrily, Lucy broke free from his grasp. "You don't even know if the guy in Katherine's visions and the guy who killed her are the same person! You don't even know for sure if the guy in her visions was real! I mean, maybe she truly was . . . was . . . sick, and she couldn't help it. I'm sorry, but it *is* possible—people can be sick—"

"Like my mother." Byron's tone was frosty. "I'm assuming that's who you mean?"

"I . . ." Lucy looked at him helplessly. Everything was wrong, everything was falling in on her, the *world* was falling in on her, and she was all alone, and she couldn't get away. "I didn't mean—"

"I want to show you something," Byron said.

Lucy watched him reach into his pocket and pull out a crumpled piece of paper, ragged and soiled around the edges, as though it had been folded and unfolded, read and reread many times.

"This is the last message I got from Katherine. She asks me to meet her at the church. She says she needs to talk to me about something important. And then she ends it with this."

He thrust it out to Lucy. Reluctantly she looked down at the note, where two words had been hastily scrawled at the bottom of the page.

HE LIVES

26

A feeling of numbness crept over her.

She handed the paper back.

"I'm going now, Byron. I'm going to climb out of here and find the road and go home. Even if I have to walk all the way back to town."

"Lucy—"

"No. Don't talk to me. I just want to go."

Somehow she made it up the embankment. As she reached the top, she was surprised to see cuts and scrapes all over her hands, and rips in the knees of her jeans. Dusting herself off as best she could, Lucy started walking. From somewhere behind her, she was vaguely aware that Byron was following. But it wasn't till he yelled after her that she stopped.

"But you can't ignore it, can you? Because things have been happening to you, haven't they? Other things besides the necklace? Things you can't explain? And they're scaring you, aren't they? They're scaring you to death!"

Lucy spun around, enraged. "Leave me alone! You don't know anything!"

"Then tell me! Why don't you tell me? I want to help!"

"How can you help?" Tears brimmed in her eyes and she fought to keep her voice steady. "You couldn't even help Katherine! You couldn't even keep her from dying, could you?"

She saw his face, the anger and grief in his tortured expression. "Don't you think I know that? Don't you think I've been tormented by that? Do you have any idea how horrible it was, watching her go through that? Watching somebody you love suffer like she did, with no explanations and no help?"

His voice quivered with rage. His dark eyes flashed with helpless frustration.

"And the same thing will happen to you. You'll try to warn people, but they won't believe you. You'll try to save people, but you'll fail. You'll see tragedies that you won't be able to prevent, and you'll feel every single human grief and suffering and sorrow like a knife thrust deep in your heart. I saw what it did to her. Day by day, and tragedy by tragedy, it wore her down, it poisoned her mind. I *know* in my heart she was happy to die in the end . . . she was *glad* to be free from that *gift* of hers."

Lucy stood there, unable to move, watching the anguish pour out of him. It was like watching a dam break in slow motion, and then, finally, wondering how it had ever held up for so long.

"Oh, God, Byron," Lucy whispered. "I'm so sorry."

She moved toward him at last. She reached out and gently touched his cheek, and for a brief moment, the walls remained down and unguarded.

"All right," she murmured. "I'll tell you everything."

With almost numb detachment, Lucy recounted every strange and frightening event of the past few days. They sat together on a low outcrop of rocks, facing each other while she admitted her doubts to him, questioned her reasoning and wild imagination, allowed for the possibility of coincidence.

Byron listened attentively . . . but it wasn't until she'd finished that he finally allowed himself to comment.

"You can't *really* believe you imagined all that." His tone was slightly incredulous. "You *can't* believe those are coincidences. And especially after what just happened now in the woods."

Lucy let out a weary sigh. "I don't know what I think anymore."

For an endless moment silence settled between them. Then Byron said quietly, "Katherine warned you not to tell anyone, didn't she? Because your life could be in danger."

"Yes." Reluctantly Lucy nodded. "So . . . why? Because she was afraid he'd kill me, too?"

"What did he say in the confessional? When you asked him who he was?"

She shuddered, merely thinking about it. "He told me he was my salvation."

Byron looked thoughtful. He ran his fingers slowly along his chin. "You said he wasn't there when you found Katherine. He may not even realize yet that she passed her powers on to you. In fact . . . he might not even know you were there at all."

"If that's true, then why is he suddenly so interested in me?"

"I'm not sure. But I think if we can figure out what his connection was to *Katherine*, that might help us figure out what his connection is to you."

Lucy's shoulders sagged. Lowering her head, she covered her face with her hands and groaned. "And what if we don't? What if we never do?"

"He could have been here today," Byron speculated, dodging her question. "Tricking us into getting separated. Untying the boat. Hoping you'd be alone . . ."

"So what you're telling me is, he could be anywhere. He could be anyone. Watching me. All the time."

"That's why we have to go back and get the necklace. I think we need to start there. It'll give us a clue to who killed Katherine. And why."

"I just hope it's still there at the church," Lucy said glumly.

"You said some priest had it?"

She nodded. "Matt. Father Matt."

"And what'd he do with it?"

"He just said he was going to put it back where he found it—by the altar. In case whoever dropped it came back for it. But if you want to talk to him, I think he's going to be there all day, going through storage closets and stuff."

Byron hesitated. "I don't think we should go back till he leaves."

"Why not? Why would he think anything about it?"

"You're the one who heard voices in the confessional. You tell me." Then, at Lucy's distressed look, he said quickly, "Look, I just think the less people who know about any of this, the better. Doesn't that make sense?"

"You're right," she agreed. "And by the way, how did you get into the church this morning, if Father Matt wasn't there yet?"

Bryon raised an eyebrow. "Gran used to be the cleaning lady at the church. I have a key."

"So you weren't lying. You *do* have all the keys. To just about everything."

She thought he almost smiled at that. He stood and pulled her to her feet.

"Do you really think the necklace is going to help me?" As Lucy gazed up into his face, her eyes were almost pleading.

Byron stared down at her, a faint frown creasing his brow. Then, with wary tenderness, he lifted his hand and lightly touched her cheek.

"Only if we find it before the killer does."

27

Luckily, they didn't have far to walk.

As they finally came out on the other side of the woods, Byron recognized the driver of a passing pickup truck and flagged him down for a ride.

"Well, Byron, what brings you up today?" The old man greeted Byron with a grin.

"Just checking some cabins, Ray." Byron introduced Lucy, then added, "Do you think you could help me out? I borrowed Mac's boat, and it came untied back there at the cove. I don't have time to look for it 'cause I need to get Lucy back to town."

Ray gave them a wink. "Don't you worry. I'll tow it back, and nobody'll ever know it was gone."

"Thanks, I appreciate it."

As they neared the cabin where Lucy had

left the car, Byron casually asked if anyone had noticed any suspicious activity around the area.

"Haven't seen anything like that," Ray said anxiously. "Why? Something wrong?"

Byron's answer was casual and calculated. "Just wondering. It looks like someone might have tried to break into the Millers' place."

"Well, I'll sure keep a lookout," Ray promised. "If I see any strangers, I'll be sure and report them right away."

Squeezed tightly together in the front seat, Lucy gave Byron a grateful smile. When Ray let them out at the cabin, they waited till he was out of sight, then locked up and headed back into town.

"How about I pick you up around seven?" Byron asked her. "The church should be locked up again by then."

"I think we should meet somewhere," Lucy suggested instead. "Angela's way too nosy, and Irene's been in a horrible mood. I'd rather not borrow more trouble."

Byron agreed. "What about the Festival, then?"

"Well . . . I'm pretty sure Angela will want to go back. But she's supposed to be grounded, so I'll have to see if we can sneak out again."

"Can you lose her once you get there?"

"No problem. The less she has to be with me, the more she likes it. Besides, I think she's been hanging out with some guy there she doesn't want her mom to know about."

"Perfect. I'll meet you at the carousel."

After letting Byron out at his house, Lucy went on to the car wash. She hadn't realized how exhausted she was, but now, with the turbulent morning behind her, she could feel all her emotions letting down at last. She drove through the car wash, relishing the blasts of water and churning brushes all around her, feeling in some strange way almost as cleansed as the Corvette.

It gave her time to collect her thoughts. Angela would demand an explanation when she got back; that much she could count on. She told herself she had to act normally, think clearly, come up with some logical excuses for being so late. She remembered the few times Irene had suggested that Lucy go shopping for new clothes, mentioning stores where she could use Irene's accounts.

Yes. Good cover. Glancing down at her stained jeans and jacket, Lucy thought how funny that was. On a whim, she stopped at the same fast-food restaurant she'd stopped at that morning, and slipped into the women's restroom. Using bunches of paper towels, she did her best at a hasty cleanup, then ran a comb through her hair. *Fine. That'll work.*

Driving home, her thoughts kept wandering, even though she tried to keep them in check. Thinking too much was dangerous to her now, she decided—the slightest little thing might send her over the edge. How could a day start off so innocently, then turn so deadly? How could your life change completely in a matter of seconds? And how could she and Katherine—a girl she'd never met and would never even know—become so tragically intertwined?

So much for fate, Lucy thought wearily.

How strange it was, the way events wove themselves together, pulling innocent people into the middle of darkness, into the middle of bad surprises. If only she hadn't gone for a walk the other night, none of this would have happened. *If only Mom hadn't died, I wouldn't be here in the first place. If only . . . if only . . .*

No use going there, she told herself sternly. There was nothing she could do about any of it till tonight. *Except drive yourself crazy with worrying.*

She heard the battle before she was even halfway in the back door. Irene and Angela in the kitchen, voices raised at fever pitch. Angela's furious tears, and Irene's unyielding authority.

"You were *seen* there last night, Angela!" Irene was livid. "I *told* you you were grounded, and you *deliberately* disobeyed me!"

"It wasn't my fault!" Angela whined.

"Did you actually think it wouldn't get back to me?" Irene countered. "In this town where I know so many people? I can't trust you for a minute, can I? But I *told* you what would happen, and now you have to accept the consequences. No car. Period. Not to school, not anywhere. And your credit cards—as of right now—are canceled."

"You can't do that!"

"I just did."

"I'm not giving them to you!"

"Angela, it doesn't matter. I have all the numbers right here in my briefcase, and it's as good as done. Now go upstairs."

"Daddy would *never* have treated me this way!"

"Well, he's not here. And if he *had* treated you a little more this way, you wouldn't be so selfish and self-indulgent."

"I'll run away!"

"Oh, Angela, don't be ridiculous. You couldn't survive for one night without all the comforts of home. Just once I'd like to be able to walk out this door and leave this house without having to go through all these theatrics."

"I swear I will! I'll run away where you'll never find me—"

"It was my fault," Lucy announced.

Irene and Angela both turned in surprise. Lucy took a deep breath and came boldly into the room.

"It was my fault," she said again. She could see Irene's mask of a face, her look of perpetual disapproval.

"Lucy?" Irene raised one suspicious eyebrow.

"I wanted to go to the Festival last night, and I didn't know how to get there." Lucy squared her shoulders. "And you know how horrible I am at directions. And Angela *told* me she was grounded, but . . . but I begged her."

Irene wasn't to be swayed. "That's no excuse. Angela should have known better."

"But it was my fault," Lucy insisted again. "Angela didn't even stay. She dropped me off there, and then she came back to pick me up later. And . . . I forgot where we were supposed to meet, so she had to come and look for me."

Irene gave an impassive nod. "I see."

Lucy glanced at Angela. Angela's expression was stubborn and defiant. Irene looked at one girl, and then at the other.

Finally she said, "Lucy, I also expect *you* to abide by house rules."

"I know." Lucy nodded contritely. "I'm sorry."

"Both of you go upstairs."

"What about my credit cards?" Angela demanded.

"I told you," Irene said. "Canceled."

With a cry of rage, Angela stomped up to her room. As Lucy stood by uncertainly, Irene gathered her overnight bag, briefcase, her purse and her coat.

"I've left the hotel number by the phone. I should be home early tomorrow afternoon."

Lucy nodded. As Irene passed through the door, she gave Lucy a frosty glare.

"That was very noble of you, Lucy. It's admirable of you to want to protect your cousin . . . but in the future, I won't tolerate lying. Even if you *are* trying to be noble."

Lucy made a hasty exit, bracing herself against the blast of Angela's music that shook her bedroom walls. After a while she heard Irene leaving and the music promptly shutting off.

She lay down across the bed and buried her face in her arms. She wanted to sleep. She wanted to sleep and sleep and just forget . . .

She drifted. She heard the kitchen door open and shut several times, Angela going up and down the stairs, but she was too tired to wonder about it. She wondered instead how she could rearrange the evening now, how she'd manage to get out of the house. Irene had not only issued orders, she'd confiscated Angela's car keys. It would be tricky now, getting back to the Festival.

She shouldn't have worried.

"Come on!" Angela announced several hours later, bursting through the door. Lucy nearly jumped out of her skin.

"What do you think you're doing?" she demanded.

"What do *you* think? Going to the Festival!"

"Angela, are you insane? After that major blowup with Irene?"

"Do I look like I care?"

"If someone saw you there *last* night, they're bound to see you again tonight! Irene's probably hired spies! She'll be furious!"

"Trust me . . ." Angela said mysteriously. "Irene will never know."

"Angela, what—"

"Don't ask questions. Just get in the car."

"But the keys—"

With a Cheshire cat grin, she dangled an extra set between her fingers. "Do I look that stupid to you?"

"Angela—"

"Do you wanna go or *not?*"

Lucy thought about how much trouble they'd be in. And then she thought about the necklace and all that was at stake.

And then she nodded and grabbed her jacket.

"Yes," she said. "I definitely want to go."

28

Despite Lucy's reluctance—and the fact that Irene had confiscated her license, as well—Angela insisted on driving. Lucy spent the whole ride slumped down in the seat, as though by making herself invisible, no police would dare to stop their car. Unfortunately, Angela wasn't in such a law-abiding mode—she couldn't wait to do every single reckless thing she could think of, now that Irene had left town.

"I have a bad feeling about tonight," Lucy said, but Angela just laughed.

"Trust me. I will *not* get grounded for this."

"Angela, you've lost your mind. You truly have."

"I will *not* get grounded or punished in any way, shape, or form, thank you very much."

"If you say so."

"Come on, Lucy—just have a little faith."

Lucy breathed a sigh of relief when they arrived at the Festival. As the two of them walked through the gates, she didn't even have to come up with an excuse. Angela flipped her a wave and headed straight into the crowd.

"Meet you same time same place," Lucy said.

Angela beamed at her. "Hey! Don't count on it!"

"Angela?" Lucy shouted, but the girl just ignored her. "Angela!"

What is she up to? Lucy didn't have time to worry about it, though. Byron was waiting for her, as promised, right by the carousel.

"Ready?" he asked.

"As I'll ever be."

Taking her arm, he steered her toward the exit. Lucy couldn't help noticing some of the looks they got on their way—girls eyeing them with a mixture of curiosity and blatant envy. When she was certain he wasn't looking, she stole a look up at Byron's face—the handsomely chiseled features set off by that guarded, mysterious stare. Now she found herself wondering if anyone else really understood that expression, the way she'd come to know it today. She doubted if he'd ever shown such vulnerability before; she doubted he'd ever be so willing again.

Still, seeing the wistful looks cast in their direction she couldn't help but get a warm feeling inside. She was only human, after all. *Nothing like calling attention to yourself, Lucy.* Her appearance with Byron Wetherly would be all over school by homeroom Monday morning.

The world lay shrouded in black. There were no stars tonight, only a bloodred moon, full and round. As they drove through town to the old church, Lucy watched it, fascinated, as it seemed to follow them through the pale tattered clouds.

"Full moon," Byron said, noting the focus of her stare. "No wonder things have been so strange around here."

Lucy suppressed a little shiver. "I've never seen the moon that color before—it's creepy."

He glanced at her sideways, but said nothing.

The church looked ominous as ever when they pulled up and parked. Byron cut the headlights, and they sat there a moment, listening to the muffled sounds of the night. The sky flowed like thick oil overhead . . . a light mist swirled through the graveyard.

"Nice horror movie," Byron commented dryly.

Lucy nodded. It was the only church she'd ever seen that made her feel so unsettled. And she didn't feel any *less* unsettled once they'd gone inside.

They stood side by side, their eyes readjusting to an almost stygian darkness. Byron took a flashlight from his jacket pocket and quietly flicked it on. They seemed to be alone. Their footfalls echoed hollowly as they walked up the aisle, and Lucy could hear the faint scurryings of mice darting beneath the pews. As they neared the altar, a fiendish howl suddenly rose up, disembodied, from the gloom. It echoed back from the damp stone walls . . . wafted through the shadows . . . shivered down along her spine.

Instinctively she grabbed for Byron's arm.

Then let out a nervous laugh.

"Cats," she mumbled. "Matt said they keep cats in here. For rodent control."

Even Byron seemed momentarily unnerved by the spectral howl. As a large black cat slipped around the end of the altar, he shone his flashlight on it, causing it to freeze instantly. It arched its back and hissed, then crouched down again and slunk away.

"Not very friendly," Byron murmured, putting one hand on her back, guiding her gently forward.

"Well, he sure didn't seem to like *you* much."

Byron ignored the remark. "Do you see it?" he asked her, squinting through the blackness.

Lucy, too, strained her eyes, running her hands over the dusty altar cloth. "No. But he said he'd leave it right here."

"Maybe he forgot."

Lucy sighed. "Then we'll never find it—he could have put it anywhere. He could have taken it with him, for that matter."

She turned to see Byron standing by the confessionals, and her heart gave a fearful twist.

"Is this where it happened?" he asked softly. "Where you saw . . . well . . . whoever he was you saw?"

Lucy nodded reluctantly. As if merely conjuring the memory might bring it back again in all its terror.

"He must have been in here already," Byron mused. "Before you showed up. From where I was sitting, I would have seen him go in."

"He could have come through some other way though. Matt mentioned some cellars. In these old places, there could be lots of entrances, right? Even secret ones."

"Possibly."

Byron's voice echoed, empty and toneless. Even the shadows seemed to slither away from it, skulking along the walls and ceiling, worse than any cats. She watched uneasily as he opened one of the confessional doors. As he shone the light in and skimmed it over the dark, cramped space.

"And when you came out from here . . . it was just the priest," he murmured.

Lucy wished they could talk about something else. "But it couldn't have been him," she said, almost defensively.

He lifted an eyebrow. "I didn't say it was."

He opened the priest's compartment, following the same slow ritual with his flashlight. He opened the door on the opposite side.

All of them, empty.

"Byron," Lucy said suddenly, "let's go."

He turned to her in wary surprise. "What's wrong?"

"I . . . I don't know. I just . . ."

Her voice trailed away. She cast a nervous look around them, down the center aisle, the intersecting pews, the dirty linen altar cloth.

"Please," she whispered. Was it getting colder in here? Just like the time before . . . just like the last time when she'd heard the whisper . . . followed the voice . . . seen that malevolent shadow behind the screen . . .

"Byron . . ."

And she could see *him* looking now, too, trying to follow the direction of her eyes, trying to see what was wrong. And somehow she knew what would come next . . . she was *expecting* it—was *ready* for it—and yes, she realized with a shock, *longing* for it, as well, like the scent of a favorite flower or the warmth of a favorite memory that transported the spirit back to sweeter times . . .

Without another word she turned and ran for the doors.

"Lucy! Wait!"

She could hear Byron shouting at her, but she didn't stop. She put her hands against the doors and pushed, but they wouldn't open.

"Oh, God!"

She struggled against them, pushing, pushing, and she could see the crazy arc of the flashlight sweeping the ceiling, over the faces of the saints, the broken shards of agonies and ecstasies and long-forgotten prayers . . .

"Lucy—for God's sake—"

With one last effort, her body fell against them, and the doors burst wide and welcomed the night in.

Screaming, Lucy toppled right into a strong pair of arms.

And a very shocked expression.

Shielding himself from her flailing limbs, Matt tried to steady Lucy and keep his balance at the same time. The next thing she knew, Byron had ahold of her, both his arms around her, restraining her and pulling her back.

"Lucy—what is *wrong* with you?"

She stopped struggling. She stared at Matt, who was staring back at her—tousled hair, easy grin, only now the grimy jeans and sweatshirt had been replaced with black pants, black shirt, and a priest's collar.

"Lucy!" He gave a relieved laugh. "I didn't expect to see you in here! I thought I saw a light—thought maybe someone was breaking in."

She clamped her arms across her chest. Byron had released her now, but she could feel him, the warm, lean strength of him, pressed against her back.

"So," Matt was trying to peer around them into the darkness. "Is there something wrong? Is there—"

"Byron," Byron said quickly. "Byron Wetherly."

The two stared into each other's eyes. Held each other's gazes for an extended moment. Exchanged handshakes, firm and slow.

"Oh, Byron, hello. Matt."

"The new priest," Byron said.

"Well, more of a gofer right now."

Their hands unclasped and slid away.

"Well," Byron said politely. "Welcome to Pine Ridge."

"The necklace," Lucy blurted out. "Do you still have it?"

For a second Matt looked puzzled. Then his grin relaxed.

"Right! That green necklace I found this morning. What happened—did you suddenly remember it was yours?" At Lucy's wan smile, he moved his shoulders in an apologetic shrug. "But . . . I'm so sorry . . . somebody else already came by for it."

Lucy and Byron traded glances. "Who?"

"Well . . . I don't know, actually." Another gesture of apology. "I left it by the altar like I said I would. But I had to leave for a while, and the cleaning lady was here. She said someone came by to claim it."

"But you don't know who it was?" Lucy persisted.

"I sure don't, sorry."

"What about the cleaning lady? Would *she* know who it was?" Byron asked casually.

"Well . . . from what I understand, she knows just about everybody around here. Do you know Mrs. Dempsey?"

"Sure. Come on then, Lucy." Byron nudged her from behind. "We better go."

Nodding, Lucy looked back over her shoulder,

making one last survey of the church. No cold now . . . no fragrance. But her heart was still racing, and her blood still had that chill . . .

"Sorry we worried you," Byron mumbled, pushing past Matt onto the steps.

"I wasn't worried," Matt said.

Lucy glanced up into his face as she passed him. His smile was still warm, still teasing. He gave her a conspiratorial wink, and she quickly glanced away.

As they reached the sidewalk, Matt suddenly called them back.

"Hey, wait a minute—I *do* remember something she said." At Lucy's perplexed look, he added, "The cleaning lady. When the guy came for that necklace."

He was quiet a moment, thinking. Byron's fingers dug sharply into Lucy's shoulder blade.

"Right." Matt nodded. "A guy. That's what she said, a good-looking guy . . . he said he'd gotten it as a present."

"A present?" Lucy echoed. "For what?"

"Not what . . . *who*. For a girl." Matt chuckled. "He said it was a present for a girl he'd met at the Fall Festival."

Lucy froze. A sick taste of fear rose slowly into her throat.

"Did he . . . did he say what her name was?"

Matt cocked his head and thought again. "Just . . . oh, now I remember. Something about New Orleans."

Lucy spun and stared up at Byron.

"Oh my God," she choked. "Angela."

29

"Wait—slow down! You're not making any sense."

"Hurry! We've got to get back to the Festival!"

"Lucy, calm *down*! Will you please tell me what's going on—"

"I don't *know* what's going on, okay? Just drive! All I know is that Angela's in some kind of trouble."

"*How* do you know that? And start from the beginning."

Lucy leaned toward him in the front seat, her voice tense with anxiety. "Remember when I told you she was hanging out at the fair with some guy Irene didn't know about? *He* must be the guy who picked up the necklace."

"That's impossible. The necklace doesn't have anything to do with Angela." Byron's hands tightened on the steering wheel. "What *possible* connection could Katherine's stalker have with Angela?"

"I don't know—I don't *know*! But that's why we have to find her!"

"You don't even know if it *is* Angela this guy picked up the necklace for."

"He said New Orleans! And Angela wants to go to New Orleans!"

"So? Lots of people want to go to New Orleans. *I* wouldn't mind going to New Orleans—"

"Call it a hunch then. Just please hurry."

They reached the Festival again in record time. Leaving Byron to follow, Lucy went immediately for the scarecrow-game tent and shoved her way to the front of the line amid irate kids and their equally irate parents. At the entrance she recognized the same girl who'd been there last night, the one with the serious face.

"Where's Angela?" Lucy asked breathlessly.

"Huh! Wouldn't *we* like to know! She left just the two of us here tonight with twice as many brats!"

"But have you seen her?"

"Yeah, a little earlier, but—"

"Please—it's important!"

The girl shrugged. "She said she was going with some guy."

"Going? Going where?"

"I don't know. Getting a ride? Or going away? Or—"

"Was it the same guy she was with last night?"

This time the girl rolled her eyes. "How would I know that? They were pretty busy, if you know what I mean. It's not like I could really see his face."

"Can't you remember anything about him? Anything at all?"

"I think he might have been tall. Maybe dark hair . . . but you know, they were back in the shadows."

As Byron caught up with her, Lucy spun to face him. "We have to go after her."

"After her *where*? How can we go after her if we don't know where she went?"

Lucy looked so desperate that the solemn-faced girl sighed sympathetically, then called out to her coworker. "Did Angela say where she was going tonight?"

"You mean, with that guy?" the other girl called back.

"Yeah."

"Uh . . . something about New Orleans, I think."

"Did they say how? Driving? Flying?"

"Maybe driving. I heard something about a bus."

Again Lucy whirled to face Byron. "We've got to stop her."

As Byron attempted to calm her down, they heard the second girl speak up.

"Oh, hey, wait a minute? Are you Lucy?"

Lucy nodded. "Yes."

"Well, somebody left this for you."

"Was it Angela?"

The girl planted herself in the tent doorway, grabbing some rowdy children, trying to establish some semblance of order. "You know, I'm not really sure, okay? Just somebody left it for you. See? It's got your name on it."

The girl handed her a small manila envelope. Lucy's name was printed across the front, and with trembling fingers, she slid open the flimsy seal across the back.

"It's the necklace," she murmured, her eyes going wide. "I know it is . . . oh, Byron, I can't do this . . . I can't—"

Byron grabbed it away from her and ripped open the flap.

Out fell Angela's car keys.

30

He hadn't meant for it to come to this.

At least not with this one . . . and especially not this soon.

He always enjoyed playing with them awhile . . . luring them . . . teasing them . . . manipulating them with praises and with promises . . .

And this one had been so easy, so predictable.

But sometimes, he simply grew tired of them.

Sometimes, after a day or a week or a lifetime, he simply discovered they no longer fit into the well-ordered chaos of his world.

She'd been shocked, of course.

That instant of disbelief—that depth of betrayal in her eyes.

"But don't you remember what you told me?"

she'd pleaded, as he'd tasted the tears of her sorrow. "Don't you remember what you said?"

"Of course," he'd soothed her, "of course I do . . ."

"Don't you remember you promised?"

And he'd pressed her against his heart, and plunged the dagger through her throat, and twisted it with cold, calm ease.

And then he'd smiled.

"Of course I remember, Angela . . . but I lied."

31

Lucy stared in disbelief.

As she glanced over at Byron, she saw him hold the envelope upside down and give it a shake. If she hadn't been so stunned, it would have been comical.

"I thought . . ." she stammered, "I really thought—"

"Me, too. But are you sensing anything?"

Trying to break the tension, Lucy bounced the keyless entry in the palm of her hand. "Yeah. I've got a sense these are keys."

"Your psychic abilities are impressive," he deadpanned. He balled up the envelope and tossed it into a trash can, then gave her a curt nod. "Come on."

"Where are we going?" Lucy asked, hurrying to match his long stride.

"You heard her. Let's try the bus depot."

They were there in ten minutes. Not only was the place small, but the waiting room was practically empty. While Byron checked the schedules for southern destinations, Lucy questioned the clerks at the ticket counter. No one remembered Irene Foster's daughter buying a bus ticket today, but after thinking a moment, one of the clerks remembered a young couple bundled in coats and hats and sunglasses who'd taken a southbound express about an hour before.

"I think it's worth a try," Byron decided. "They don't have that much of a head start, and they'll be making stops along the way. It should be easy to catch them."

Lucy felt sick. Sick to her stomach and sick at heart. As she climbed up beside him into the van, she shot him a look of desperation.

"What if you're right?"

"How so?"

"What if this whole thing with the necklace has *nothing* to do with Angela? I mean . . . what if she's really and truly found the love of her life, and they're going off to live happily ever after, and we're going after them and being stupid?"

Byron put the key in the ignition. He stared thoughtfully at the dashboard.

"Then," he said carefully, "at least we know. Then we turn around and come back home. And they have their lives . . . and we have ours."

Lucy sighed. "I can't help it, though. I just still *feel* something—just *here*." She clamped her arms around her midsection and fixed him with a worried frown. "I just feel like something about this isn't right. It's just this awful *nagging* feeling, and it won't go away."

"You're probably feeling a lot of things right now," Byron reminded her. "You thought you had the necklace, and you'd psyched yourself up to face it."

"So did you," she said quietly.

He shrugged. "Emotional roller coaster."

"You're right. I don't know whether to be scared now, or relieved."

"How about a little of both? It's okay, you know, to feel both."

She tried to smile at him, but her emotions were at full pitch. As they sailed along the highway, she leaned against her door and stared out the window of the van. Everything's flowing tonight, she thought vaguely . . . *flowing road . . . flowing van . . . flowing curves . . . flowing hills . . .*

She could still see that strange red moon watching her through the clouds. The color of rust . . . the color of decay. A stain of old dried blood on the wrinkled flesh of the sky.

Shivering, Lucy hunched her shoulders and burrowed deeper into her jacket. It felt like it was getting colder, both outside and in. And the moon . . . that eerie red moon . . . actually seemed to be growing. Growing and glowing among the tops of the trees, like some forgotten Christmas ornament.

Lucy frowned and burrowed deeper. Why did full moons like that make her feel so weird? Make her think of creepy things like . . . like . . .

Prey . . .

"What?" She sat up straight and looked at Byron, who looked back at her suspiciously.

"What?" he echoed.

"Did you just say something?"

"Yeah, I said, just pray my brakes hold out."

"Oh my God, don't tell me that—your brakes?"

"Well . . . all these curves sure aren't helping my van."

"Thank you, Byron. That definitely eases my mind, your sharing that with me."

She saw that slow half smile working at one corner of his mouth. She realized that she really loved it when he smiled like that. She wished he'd do it more often.

"Stop staring at me," he said, and, grinning, she turned back to her window.

She closed her eyes. The hum of the motor, the rocking motion of the van on the road . . . she could feel herself drifting off. That pleasant state between sleep and attention, when everything seemed soft and warm and safe. She forced her eyes open and searched for taillights up ahead of them, but the road was so twisted, she couldn't see a thing. There wasn't even traffic out tonight, she suddenly realized. But she could see the slow, pale curls of fog beginning to creep in over the highway . . . blurring the yellow line . . . swallowing the road ahead of them.

That feeling again. Gnawing at the pit of her stomach.

"Byron," she said uneasily, "be careful."

He cast her a sidelong glance. "Always."

"No, I mean it. Please."

"Are you okay?"

"Yes . . . just . . . I don't know. Restless. Nervous."

"If you want, we can stop for some coffee the first place we see. It might be a good idea."

She gave a distracted nod. She gazed out into the darkness . . . out at that bloody moon. She wished it would go behind a cloud for the rest of the night . . . she wished it would just go away.

She sensed something beside them on the road.

Something she couldn't actually see, something just out of sight off the shoulder, something moving swiftly through the tall weeds, keeping pace with the van.

Strange . . .

Lucy looked over at the speedometer. Sixty. Yet she was sure—she was *certain*—that something was out there running, running even faster than the van could go, running even faster than the wind could go . . .

"Byron," she mumbled.

"What?"

She saw him turn toward her.

Saw his hand slide across the seat and reach for her.

She looked into his eyes . . . deep and black as midnight . . . and in that moment she could see in their depths all the truths and emotions that she'd felt that morning with her hand upon his heart.

A sob went through her.

Byron opened his mouth and started to say her name.

But he never got the chance.

As the dark shape came out of the fog, Byron hit the brakes, the tires screeching, the van skidding, sliding, going into a spin. As they whirled around and around, Lucy could see it there—the huge, black shape silhouetted against the fog, standing on all fours, statuelike in the middle of the road. Watching them . . . *watching them . . .*

She tried to reach for Byron—reached *desperately* for Byron—

But her head slammed the window, and the

van careened off the hill, and all she could think in those last few seconds was *he never got to say it . . .*

Byron never said my name.

32

So this is what it's like to die . . .

Lying there on her back in the grass, all alone in the darkness, she could sense the wet, runny mask of her face—tears? blood?—she couldn't be sure, couldn't be sure she even *had* a face, couldn't be sure about anything except that her body screamed in pain each time she tried to draw even the shallowest of breaths.

I can't move . . . help . . . somebody, help me . . .

With a ragged cry, Lucy tried to lift her head, tried to peer through the thick, endless night surrounding her. As in a dream, she could see the faraway sky blazing bright, lit by a giant fire—and along with those sickening smells of pain and fear and despair that threatened to choke her, now there was the gasoline . . . burning rubber . . . white-hot metal . . . and something else . . . something dear to her heart . . .

Byron!

That's Byron's van!

She'd been sitting in the front seat beside him, and she'd been staring at the moon. That bloodred moon hovering there behind the trees and glowing out through the dark, shredded fabric of the clouds. She'd been staring at the moon, and then she'd jolted with the first sharp swerve of the van. Confused and groggy, she'd heard Byron's shout, the piercing shriek of brakes and tires; she'd felt the road give way to air beneath them as they dove off the shoulder and off the crest of the hill, and out through the foggy night, plummeting down and down into nothingness . . .

Byron? Can you hear me?

She knew somehow that she hadn't spoken aloud, knew somehow that her thoughts had burst free of her pain, only to fall silent among the shadows. It was so dark out here. So dark, so frighteningly still, except for those flames leaping and glowing against the distant horizon . . .

Something ran in front us.

With a moan, Lucy struggled to shut out the pain, struggled to focus her hazy thoughts.

Byron tried to swerve, he tried to miss hitting it, but something ran in front of us . . .

She wished she could remember. She wished she could remember what it was that had caused the accident. But there was only the briefest glimmer of memory in that last fatal second, only the briefest image of something caught in headlights as the car veered and left the road.

What was *that?*

It seemed so familiar somehow . . .

But her thoughts were fading . . . fading . . . and she knew she was slipping away. In desperation she stared up at the trees overhead, great gnarled branches etched thickly against the black dome of the sky. And then she noticed that moon.

So full and round. So red like blood. Caught in a web of tangled limbs, oozing out through the clouds, wine stains on velvet.

Byron, I'm so scared! Please help me!

And that's when she heard it.

The soft rustling sound, like wind sighing through grass. Except that she couldn't *feel* any wind, not even the faintest of breezes, in this heavy night air.

The sound was close by.

Coming even closer . . .

Oh God!

Once more she tried to lift herself, to call out for help. But the rustlings were in her head now, in her thoughts and in her pain, like so many urgent whispers, whispers of great importance.

As Lucy's head turned helplessly to one side, she saw shadows all around her, shadows slinking along the ground and through the trees, slivers of black, and pale, pale gray, and sparks of amber light . . .

Terror exploded within her. Even through the paralyzing numbness of pain and shock, she sensed that these were animals, and she sensed why they were here. Instinct told her that she was surrounded, though one stood closer than the others. She could hear the slow, calm rhythm of its breathing as it watched her from a place she couldn't see.

Oh, God, don't let me die like this!

She thought of Byron. The vision burst inside her brain with such force that she choked and gagged and vomited blood in the grass. In that one instant of agonizing clarity she saw his midnight eyes, heard his calm, deep voice, telling her not to be afraid. Now she remembered how he'd turned to her in that last split second of his life, his eyes desperate with helplessness and disbelief as he'd reached for her hand. *Did he touch me?* The thought drifted through her mind, light as a feather. *Did we touch one last time?*

But the whispers were louder now, and the fire was brighter than ever, and she was so weak . . . so tired.

Please . . . please . . . just let me die fast . . .

Night swayed around her. As tears ran silently down her cheeks, something huge and dark leaned in over her, blocking her view of the sky.

She steeled herself for the end. Felt hot breath caressing her throat . . . smelled the faint, familiar scent of something sweet . . .

Byron . . . I'm so sorry. . .

"Byron has gone," the voice murmured. "Only I can save you now."

Who are you? What *are you?*

Down . . . down she sank into the endlessness of time.

And that voice . . . fading far into nothingness . . .

"Oh, Lucy . . . There's no name for what we are."

THE
UNSEEN

PART TWO: REST IN PEACE

For Sandra, Barbara, Julie, Susan, Jenifer, Anna, Suzanne, Janice,
Ellen, Peggy, Richard, Pete, and Bill—I could never make it
through these writing days without you. Thanks with all my heart.

SPEAK
Published by the Penguin Group
Penguin Group (USA) Inc., 345 Hudson Street, New York, New York 10014, U.S.A.
Penguin Group (Canada), 90 Eglinton Avenue East, Suite 700, Toronto, Ontario, Canada M4P 2Y3
(a division of Pearson Penguin Canada Inc.)
Penguin Books Ltd, 80 Strand, London WC2R 0RL, England
Penguin Ireland, 25 St Stephen's Green, Dublin 2, Ireland (a division of Penguin Books Ltd)
Penguin Group (Australia), 250 Camberwell Road, Camberwell, Victoria 3124, Australia
(a division of Pearson Australia Group Pty Ltd)
Penguin Books India Pvt Ltd, 11 Community Centre, Panchsheel Park, New Delhi - 110 017, India
Penguin Group (NZ), 67 Apollo Drive, Rosedale, Auckland 0632, New Zealand
(a division of Pearson New Zealand Ltd)
Penguin Books (South Africa) (Pty) Ltd, 24 Sturdee Avenue,
Rosebank, Johannesburg 2196, South Africa

Penguin Books Ltd, Registered Offices: 80 Strand, London WC2R 0RL, England

First published in the UK by Scholastic Ltd, 2004
First published in the United States of America by Speak, an imprint of Penguin Group (USA) Inc., 2005
This omnibus edition published by Speak, an imprint of Penguin Group (USA) Inc., 2012

1 3 5 7 9 10 8 6 4 2

Copyright © Richie Tankersley Cusick, 2004
All rights reserved

LIBRARY OF CONGRESS CATALOGING-IN-PUBLICATION DATA
Cusick, Richie Tankersley.
Rest in peace / Richie Tankersley Cusick.
p.   cm.—(The unseen ; pt. 2)
First published in the UK by Scholastic Ltd., 2004.
Summary: Having survived the accident that killed her friend Byron, Lucy tries to cope
with her new powers and attempts to figure out who—or what—is stalking her.
ISBN 0-14-240464-0 (pbk.)
[1. Extrasensory perception—Fiction. 2. Horror stories—Fiction.] I. Title.
PZ7.C9646Res 2005 [Fic]—dc22 2005047435

Speak ISBN 978-0-14-242336-3

Set in Perpetua Regular

Printed in the United States of America

ALWAYS LEARNING   PEARSON

Prologue

He stood and he watched her.

Watched the frantic rolling of her eyes beneath her closed, bruised eyelids . . . the terrified heaving of her breasts beneath the torn, mangled material of her blouse. From time to time a whimper escaped her lips . . . or a gasp . . . or even a whispered plea for help, as she dreamed her terrible dream. And sometimes her hands would thrash against the darkness, clawing at shadows and bloodstained bandages, as she relived, over and over again, those last tragic moments of her waking nightmare . . .

He knew this dream well.

Knew every scene—every gory, meticulous detail—for he had been with her the night it began, and he had been with her every night since, feeling it replay endlessly, torturously, through her sleep . . .

So this is what it's like to die . . .

Lying there on her back in the grass, all alone in the darkness, Lucy could sense the wet, runny mask of her face. Tears? Blood? She couldn't be sure, couldn't be sure she even had a face, couldn't be sure about anything except that her body screamed in pain each time she tried to draw even the shallowest of breaths.

I can't move . . . Help . . . Somebody, help me . . .

With a ragged cry, Lucy tried to lift her head, tried to peer through the thick, endless night surrounding her. As in a dream, she could see the faraway sky blazing bright, lit by a giant fire—and along with those sickening smells of pain and fear and despair that threatened to choke her, now there was the gasoline . . . burning rubber . . . white-hot metal . . . and something else . . . something dear to her heart . . .

Byron!

That's Byron's van!

She'd been sitting in the front seat beside him, and she'd been staring at the moon. That blood red moon hovering there behind the trees and glowing out through the dark, shredded fabric of the clouds. She'd been staring at the moon, and then she'd jolted with the first sharp swerve of the van. Confused and groggy, she'd heard Byron's shout, the piercing shriek of brakes and tires, she'd felt the road give way to air beneath them as they dove off the shoulder and off the crest of the hill, and out through the foggy night, plummeting down and down into nothingness . . .

Byron? Can you hear me?

She knew somehow that she hadn't spoken aloud, knew somehow that her thoughts had burst free of her pain, only to fall silent among the shadows. It was so dark out here. So dark, so frighteningly still, except for those flames leaping and glowing against the distant horizon . . .

Something ran in front of us.

With a moan, Lucy struggled to shut out the pain, struggled to focus her hazy thoughts.

Byron tried to swerve, he tried to miss hitting it, but something ran in front of us . . .

She wished she could remember. She wished she could remember what it was that had caused the accident. But there was only the briefest glimmer of memory in that last fatal second, only the briefest image of something caught in the headlights as the car veered and left the road.

What was that?

It seemed so familiar somehow . . .

But her thoughts were fading . . . fading . . . and she knew she was slipping away. In desperation she stared up at the trees overhead, great gnarled branches etched thickly against the black dome of the sky. And then she noticed that moon.

So full and round. So red like blood. Caught in a web of tangled limbs, oozing out through the clouds, wine stains on velvet.

Byron, I'm so scared! Please help me!

And that's when she heard it.

The soft rustling sound, like wind sighing through grass. Except that she couldn't feel any wind, not even the faintest of breezes, in this heavy night air.

The sound was close by.

Coming even closer . . .

Oh God!

Once more she tried to lift herself, to call out for help. But the rustlings were in her head now, in her thoughts and in her pain, like so many urgent whispers, whispers of great importance.

As Lucy's head turned helplessly to one side, she saw

4

shadows all around her, shadows slinking along the ground and through the trees, slivers of black and pale pale gray, and sparks of amber light . . .

Terror exploded within her. Even through the paralyzing numbness of pain and shock, she sensed that these were animals, and she sensed why they were here. Instinct told her that she was surrounded, though one stood closer than the others. She could hear the slow, calm rhythm of its breathing as it watched her from a place she couldn't see.

Oh, God, don't let me die like this!

She thought of Byron. The vision burst inside her brain with such force that she choked and gagged and vomited blood in the grass. In that one instant of agonizing clarity she saw his midnight eyes, heard his calm, deep voice telling her not to be afraid. Now she remembered how he'd turned to her in that last split second of his life, his eyes desperate with helplessness and disbelief as he'd reached for her hand. Did he touch me? *The thought drifted through her mind, light as a feather.* Did we touch one last time?

But the whispers were louder now, and the fire was brighter than ever, and she was so weak . . . so tired.

Please . . . please . . . just let me die fast . . .

Night swayed around her. As tears ran silently

down her cheeks, something huge and dark leaned in over her, blocking her view of the sky.

She braced herself for the end. Felt hot breath caressing her throat . . . smelled the faint, familiar scent of something sweet . . .

Byron . . . I'm so sorry . . .

"Byron has gone," the voice murmured. "Only I can save you now."

Down, down, she sank . . . into the endlessness of time . . .

Who are you . . . ? What are you . . . ?

And that voice . . . fading far into nothingness. . .

"Oh, Lucy . . . there's no name for what we are . . ."

And so he stood, and he watched her.

How lovely she was . . . and how curious . . . so small and fragile, her pale skin nearly transparent, her expression as remote, as beautiful, as death.

But not quite.

Not quite dead yet.

Shock was just a stepping-stone. It would be so easy, he knew, to ease her across that tenuous threshold; just one swift, silent act on his part.

But there was something entrancing . . . mesmerizing . . . about the way she hovered there—just on the edge, between life and eternity—that was exciting to him.

There had been no time to take her before.

Before, as he dragged her to safety, and then as she lay there in the tall scorched grass, bruised and battered and drenched in blood, the others sweeping in silently around her, quivering with anticipation . . .

But "No," he had ordered them. "Stand away—this one is mine."

Damn those who had stopped to help!

And a firetruck, no less—a whole *convoy* of emergency vehicles, in fact—heading homeward from some tragedy, following a careful distance behind the van, yet still close enough to witness its fatal careen off the road, its hurtling descent down the rocky hillside, the bits and pieces of its broken shell raining like fireworks through the shattered night.

So many people! Sirens, lights, confusion!

The others of his kind had fled at once, but he alone had stayed.

He alone had stayed behind . . .

Hidden and silent . . .

Guarding his prize.

So there had been no time to take her then, in the panic, the chaos, of that hopeless rescue, the air stinking of futility and death even as he swept her away with him through the fog-shrouded woods, to this place of dark secrets and solitude. And every night afterward . . . including this late night . . . he had been here, watching over her, slinking through the terror of her dreams.

It was these dreams he feasted on in the meantime.

The loneliness, the heartache, the empty black holes of despair.

Hazy images of a mother who had died . . . a cozy home that was no more . . . and now this loss of someone new, this grievous, unexpected loss of Byron . . . such painful memories buried within her, buried deep, because to remember them would be far too much agony to endure.

"Cold . . . I'm so cold . . ."

He heard her whimper, a plea as faint as breath. And there was no hesitation as he leaned down over her, his lips drawn instinctively to that perfect, most sensitive spot.

Relief was instant and needle-sharp—teeth stabbing like fire, piercing hot through her skin, sinking deep through her flesh, clamping down and holding on, suspending her on boiling waves of panic and burning pleasure . . .

"*Lucy* . . ." His breath caressed her cheek, the delicate lids of her eyes, the tender flesh of her throat . . . "*No more cold . . . no more pain . . . no more loneliness . . .*"

Had she smiled? Ever so softly in her sleep?

He pondered this as he gazed upon her, as she stirred languidly in the aftermath of his kiss. Pondered this so intently that he failed to anticipate the slight, sudden movement of her hand as it groped through the shadows and brushed the side of his face, touching him with an innocence that caught him completely unaware.

He drew in his breath, every muscle tightening. His keen eyes narrowed, gleaming with annoyance and a hint of wonder. He had let his guard down—a weakness he could not afford—and yet for that one fleeting second, the gentle reward of her hand upon his cheek had been well worth his carelessness.

He drew back from her now, strangely unnerved, as her hand lowered once again to her side. As she lay weak and helpless, lost in the sorrow of her memories.

But little by little he would take those memories.

Devour them until the past, as she knew it, existed no more.

And then she would be filled with him . . . her mind, her body, her soul.

Like life's rich blood . . .

Filled with him and him alone.

1

Lucy's eyes flew open.

With a gasp of terror, she tried to scream, to fight her way free, but *free from what*, she wondered groggily, *I can't move, I can't see, something's holding me down* . . .

"Aunt Irene?"

She'd meant to call out, yet she couldn't hear her own voice. There was only silence, as still and deep as a grave, and the frantic pounding of her heartbeat.

"Aunt Irene, are you there?"

Slowly . . . hazily . . . her surroundings began shifting into focus. Lucy realized that she was lying on her back, and that the thing holding her down was a blanket—a blanket that should have been easy to push back, except that she didn't have the strength to kick it away. Beneath her the ground was cold and damp; beside her a candle flickered weakly, its melted stub drowning in a puddle of wax. As she gazed up at the curved ceiling, grotesque shadows leaped across in a macabre dance.

Where am I?

There were smells in here. Curious smells from every direction, smells she couldn't quite identify. Like the one lingering upon her blanket and in the tangled strands of her hair . . . an outdoors smell, wild and earthy, and not altogether unpleasant. It reminded her of frost and snowy moonlight, autumn wind and warm, wet fur . . .

A musky smell. A primitive smell.

Some sort of animal?

Moaning softly, Lucy struggled to sit up, totally unprepared for the wave of dizziness that pulled her down again. Her whole body reeled from the force of it; her nerves screamed in agony as pain ripped through every bone and muscle. Clutching her head with both hands, she felt a strip of wet, sticky cloth sagging low over her left eye.

"Aunt Irene!"

A spray of stars burst in her brain. It blurred behind her eyes, and memories began struggling to the surface of her mind, clawing their way through a sludge of fear and rising panic.

Byron! Oh, God, I remember . . . I remember everything. The accident . . . fire . . . and he didn't get out . . . Byron didn't get out—

"Can anyone hear me?" Lucy cried. "Please! Is anybody there?"

Oh my God, what's happening?

Trembling violently, she eased the blanket down from her shoulders. Her skin felt raw against the roughness of the fabric, raw and chilled and unusually sensitive. To her shock, she suddenly realized that all her clothes had been removed.

Lucy curled herself tightly beneath the blanket. *Please let this be a dream—please let me wake up!* Her mind was wild with terror, her heart pumped out of control. She couldn't breathe, couldn't stop shaking, couldn't stop the frantic spinning of her thoughts. Where was she, and how had she gotten here? How badly was she injured? How long had she been unconscious, and who had been here with her while she'd slept? She had to get away—*run away*—but from what? From whom? And where would she go? How could she possibly escape from one unknown to another?

And then a much more chilling thought crept in among all the others. Was someone here with her right now? Watching as she realized her hopeless predicament? Waiting for her to make a move? Cat and mouse, waiting to pounce?

Without warning, the ground gave a slow, deep shudder beneath her. As Lucy cried out in alarm, she felt another rumble of thunder resonating through the shadows; she heard the muffled, but unmistakable, downpouring of rain.

A storm. And it sounded close by.

Clenching her teeth against another onslaught of pain, Lucy reached out for the candle. She pried it from the glaze of dried wax, then held it at arm's length, moving it in a slow, deliberate arc.

She seemed to be in a cave. A small, denlike space with damp, water-stained walls and a low ceiling. About fifteen feet off to her left, the ceiling vanished completely into the pitch-blackness of a tunnel—while the same distance to her right, it sloped sharply upward before dead-ending.

No . . . not a dead end . . .

As Lucy's gaze followed the angle of the ceiling, she realized it led to an opening—a tiny opening scarcely big enough to squeeze through, an opening she hadn't recognized at first because it was covered up. But now she could see a hint of gray light around its edges, and a ragged hole near the bottom where part of the camouflage had blown away, and she realized that tree branches had been stacked up and wedged in from outside.

Someone had deliberately disguised the entrance to the cave.

To keep others out?

Or to keep me in?

A dank breeze snaked across the floor, threatening the candlelight and swathing Lucy in those strange and secret smells. But there was another odor she detected now—a much stronger odor than the one she'd noticed before. Something dead. Something spoiled.

Only bats, she tried to convince herself. Bats and rats and other creepy things that hid in dark places, shying away from the light. Or some wounded animal that had wandered in here once upon a time to die. Some poor creature, lost and trapped.

Trapped like me.

With sheer willpower, Lucy pulled herself to her knees. The feeble candlelight revealed several small puddles of water around her— black, shiny pools, shallow but thick. She could see dark splatters over the ground, and dark smears trailing back into the tunnel where her light couldn't reach.

She drew in her breath and closed her eyes. She opened them again and swallowed down a sick taste of fear.

Clutching the blanket, Lucy worked her way slowly to the nearest wall. It took several moments for her queasiness to pass, even longer to stand up. The gloom spun around her as she braced against the stone. She forced herself to take three halting steps.

There was no time to lose.

Moving toward the front of the cave, Lucy

spotted a pile of clothes lying directly in her path. She picked it up and ran her fingertips through the tangled shreds, relief giving way to disappointment. Her blouse—or rather, what was left of it—was completely useless. Her jacket was there, too—torn and stained, with one sleeve ripped away, but at least it was dry. Her jeans were missing. Also her socks. No shoes. No underwear.

Lucy eased her arms slowly, torturously, into her jacket. Then once again she wrapped the blanket around her shoulders and started walking.

Keep going. You can do it. One step at a time . . .

Her foot sank into something wet.

Wet and cold and slimy.

At once a stench rose into the air, the same foul odor she'd smelled before, except it was overpowering now, *suffocating* now. She jerked away, wiping her foot across the ground, and in the weakening candlelight saw one of the thick, black puddles she'd stepped in. She stumbled back, only to realize that the hem of her blanket had also trailed in the pool. Quickly she yanked it up again, losing her balance as her other foot slammed down on something small and furry.

She felt the sharp snap of tiny bones.

The gush of curdled liquid squishing between her toes.

Screaming, Lucy toppled over, landing hard on her stomach, fighting desperately not to pass out. As she lifted her head, she found herself staring into the dull, sightless eyes of a rabbit.

It had been dead for quite a while.

She could tell from the lolling posture of its neck, the jagged slash through its underbelly, the way it had been savagely gutted, leaving only a few strings of raw flesh and muscle and leftover entrails smeared across the bottom of her foot.

Lucy's mind went dark.

As her fingers dug into the ground, the whole world turned upside down, and her brain exploded in a kaleidoscope of panic:

Running—racing—right left zigzag path—paws thundering silently—shadow swift—scent of hopeless terror—screams—shrill screams—breath razor hot—sprays of red gurgling bubbling—

One last look at the sky . . . one last smell of the pines . . . sweet woodland home fading . . .

Lucy's eyes slowly opened. Shaking violently, she turned her head sideways and threw up.

The candle flared one last time.

As Lucy tried to reach it, to revive it for another second, the hot red wax dripped over her fingers, molding to her like a second skin.

As though her own hand was stained with the innocent blood of her vision.

2

It was madness, she knew.

Sheer madness to run, not knowing where she was or what lay outside the cave, not knowing where she could possibly go.

Sheer, utter madness.

Yet not nearly as crazy as staying here, Lucy reminded herself. Here in this place of death and darkness, not knowing when her captor might return. She knew now that those pools and splatters on the ground, those stains leading back into the tunnel, could be only one thing— and that much blood could never have come from one small rabbit.

What kind of person was she dealing with?

What kind of insanity?

Peeling the wax from her fingers, Lucy staggered to her feet and limped to the entrance of the cave. Her earlier suspicions had been right—someone had tried to cover it with brush and branches, but where some of the limbs had fallen away, she had a clear view of the world beyond.

Trees.

Trees as far as she could see. A leaden gray sky overhead. Ghostly gray mist . . . a solid downpour of cold gray rain. Lucy couldn't tell if it was dusk or early morning.

He could be out there right now. Hiding. Watching. Waiting to see if I'll try to escape. Waiting so he can catch me and bring me back again.

It was a chance she had to take.

Steeling herself, she began tearing at the barricade. The branches were heavy and cumbersome, most of them hopelessly entwined, and Lucy had to stop frequently to catch her breath, brace herself against the wall, will her dizziness away, and force herself not to cry out. The blanket slipped from her shoulders onto the wet ground. The few remaining buttons on her jacket were useless against the chill. Every simple movement was almost more than she could bear.

But at last she began to make headway. The opening grew larger; she could see more of the woods beyond. The rain fell harder, and as she stopped once more to catch her breath, she gathered the soggy blanket and shoved it through the opening. *Not much protection, but better than nothing.* She watched it land in a puddle on the other side, and then, gathering all the strength she could, Lucy squeezed through after it.

The ground was frozen. The wind was raw. Her whole body recoiled from the shock of the elements, and for several agonizing moments all she could do was lie there, sprawled in the mud where she'd fallen. Something slid down over her left eye, and she managed to pull it off. She remembered feeling a strip of cloth there earlier. Now she could see that it was a bandage, and that it was soaked with blood.

My blood? Oh God . . . how bad am I really hurt?

With cautious fingers she touched the swollen places on her forehead, the ragged edges of split skin, the crustiness in her hair. She choked down a fresh wave of horror and stumbled to her feet, then pulled the blanket around her and began to run.

She had no idea where she was going. She simply plunged into the woods, ignoring the dizziness in her head, the weakness in her knees. Her body felt like a stranger's body as she tried to drag it through the forest, tripping over the soggy blanket, crawling through the mud and underbrush, forcing herself up again. She could see her breath—short gasps of pain hanging frosty in the air—and her nose was running, and her tears seemed to freeze upon her cheeks. Her heart thudded in her ears, and every clumsy footstep seemed to echo around her, causing her to look back in terror, certain she was being followed.

Don't stop—run! Run faster, run harder! Run for your life!

But run *where*?

Lucy was completely lost. Like a liquid dream, minutes flowed into hours, and then into no time at all. The woods were endless. With so many twists and turns, she wondered if she might even be going in circles. It was definitely growing darker. She couldn't feel her feet anymore. As she glanced down to see if they were still at the end of her legs, she realized that the blanket had fallen off, though she didn't remember dropping it.

It doesn't matter! Keep running!

She tried to hold her jacket around her, but her arms had gone numb. Through the steady rush of rain, she was aware of trees like phantoms, and the dying brilliance of fallen leaves, thick cushions of pine needles, and the ups and downs of hills that went on and on.

She wanted to give up.

To collapse and simply lie there, to close her eyes and drift away.

Better to die out here than back in the cave. Better to die on her own terms than at the hands of some maniac.

She paused a moment, breath sharp in her ribs, trying to peer off through the dense maze of trees. Surely there was a house out here somewhere—a farm, a cabin? Surely there must be a pathway or a road? She thought about screaming for help, but decided against it. She doubted anyone could hear her above this rain, and if her captor had returned by now to find her missing, she couldn't take the chance of giving herself away.

Lucy turned slowly in all directions.

There must be a way out—there *had* to be a way out!

And then her body went rigid with fear.

A shadow?

Had she seen a shadow just now . . . off to the side of her . . . slipping through the woods?

Seconds crept by but she couldn't move, could scarcely even breathe. Of course she'd imagined it. The rain was playing tricks on her. It was just leaves swirling to the ground, branches swaying in the wind, some startled animal taking cover between the trees.

That's all it is, Lucy. That's all.

Rallying her courage, she forced herself to go on. Then stopped again, almost immediately.

She *hadn't* imagined it—she was sure this time!

A dark silhouette through the foggy rain, just a glimpse as it glided up the incline about twenty yards away, then vanished behind some rocks.

Lucy's heart ricocheted into her throat. A

bear? Yet it seemed too graceful, too fast to be a bear. And the vague, unsettling shape of it . . . something so dangerous . . .

So familiar . . .

The low stone wall behind Irene's house . . . the woods, the deserted road at the Fall Festival . . . the large, murky figure darting in front of Byron's van . . .

"Oh God," Lucy whispered. "Oh God, please help me!"

In sheer panic she began to run. Mindless now with terror, exhausted beyond reason, she stumbled deeper and deeper under cover of the forest, never even noticing the sudden glimmer of light just ahead of her. As Lucy plunged through the trees, the ground disappeared without warning.

There was a dreamlike sensation of falling, of floating, before she suddenly slammed back to reality and rolled down the side of the hill. The earth was soft where she landed, but her body screamed on impact. She lay there, too stunned to move, her breath completely jolted out of her. Against her icy cheeks, the flow of blood felt warm and almost comforting.

Cautiously, Lucy tried to lift her head. She was lying in tall dead weeds, and as she moaned softly and squinted through her pain, she imagined she could see a dirt road not five feet away.

Her head fell back again. She closed her eyes against the rain and tasted blood trickling into the corners of her mouth.

And then she heard a sound.

A sound like an engine, like a car.

Tears came to her eyes, and she pinched the skin on her arm, pinched it hard to make herself wake up, because she knew she couldn't bear one more nightmare, one more disappointment.

But the sound was still there.

And it was coming closer.

With her last ounce of strength, Lucy dragged herself onto the road. She tried to lift one arm, tried to give a feeble wave as the car bore down on her. She knew the driver probably couldn't see her through the rain, through the dusk, and as the headlights blinded her, she braced herself for the shock.

There was a loud squeal of brakes, a wet skid of tires.

And then a door opening . . . hands on her shoulders, turning her over, rearranging her jacket, smoothing back her hair.

Arms lifted her. Carried her without the slightest effort, then settled her gently onto the backseat.

And then, as she finally surrendered to blissful unconsciousness, Lucy heard soft words whispered through the dark.

"Remember to look both ways, Lucy. It's a dangerous road you're on."

3

"My meeting will probably run late tonight, Lucy. Will you be all right here alone?"

Startled, Lucy glanced up to see her aunt standing in the living room doorway. With one quick movement, Lucy managed to hide the piece of paper she'd been holding, slipping it underneath some magazines stacked beside her on the couch.

"I'll be fine." Lucy forced a smile, even though her heart gave a sickening clench. *Of course I'll be fine, I'm used to it; even when you are here, I'm still alone.* But still, she couldn't keep from asking, "Are you sure everything's locked?"

"The house is completely secure, I've told you before. And I'll set the alarm on my way out."

But it didn't matter *how* many times Irene had told her, Lucy never felt entirely protected, never entirely safe. She merely *pretended* each time to be reassured by her aunt's promises, because she knew Irene would never believe her if she told the truth. Neither Irene nor anyone else would ever believe that something, or someone, was after Lucy. Sometimes Lucy wasn't even sure she believed it herself, yet the nagging dread was always there, like a shadow over her shoulder.

And anyway, Lucy told herself, *where else could I go?*

Her aunt turned to leave, hesitated, then faced her again. *Like a robot*, Lucy thought, *more cold and withdrawn than ever*. As though Angela's disappearance had added a final layer of distance to those steel barriers around Irene's heart. Lucy couldn't help wondering how differently things might have turned out if that relationship between stepmother and stepdaughter hadn't been so strained. But speculations were pointless, and now she watched curiously as her aunt's lips twisted into a tight semblance of a smile.

"Did Dr. Fielding mention your going back to school?" she asked, and Lucy nodded.

"Yes. On Monday."

"He feels it's best for you to get back into a normal routine. I agree with him."

Of course you do. Out of sight, out of mind.

"He called me this afternoon." Irene seemed to be struggling for conversation. "He says you're doing well. He says you're coming to terms." Another uncomfortable pause, and then she straightened. "You should eat. Fix yourself something in the microwave. There's pizza. Angela always . . ."

Abruptly her aunt walked away. Lucy waited for the sound of the back door to close, then jumped up and went systematically around the house, checking windows, double-checking that shades were drawn and curtains were closed, inspecting locks and deadbolts and the security system. Then, as satisfied as she could be that the house was impregnable, she sat down again and pulled out the paper she'd hidden.

Angela, Lucy thought miserably, *where are you?*

She stared down at the crumpled poster. A

poster of Angela, just like the ones she'd seen plastered all over town.

With a weary sigh, Lucy snuggled deep into the couch and leaned her head back against the cushions. No one had seen or heard from Angela since that Saturday night of the festival, the night of Lucy and Byron's accident, that strange and fatal night just over a week ago.

Things like this don't happen. How many times had Lucy told herself that in the days following the tragedies? *Things like this happen only in movies. Happen only to strangers. Things like this don't happen in real life, not to normal people.*

But I'm not normal anymore, she had to remind herself now for at least the hundredth time. Not since she'd wandered into the cemetery that night and found Katherine. No matter how much she tried to pretend, nothing would ever be the same again, and it had taken Byron to convince her of that.

Byron . . .

She'd cried buckets of tears, cried until she couldn't cry anymore. The guilt was more than she could bear—the doubts, the regrets, replaying those last moments of Byron's life.

Her heart and soul felt empty. So empty, in fact, that she often found herself wondering if maybe *she* had died, too, and that this strange half existence was but a lingering dream. Her salvation had become a cold sort of numbness, a distancing of herself from both memories and emotions. This was the only way she'd been able to survive.

The only way she would *ever* be able to survive.

Reaching over, Lucy lifted a mug of cocoa from the end table, then tested the foamy marshmallows with her tongue. The chocolate was sweet and hot, but did little to warm the chill inside her. As she took a cautious sip, her gaze returned to the small poster she'd placed in her lap.

MISSING: HAVE YOU SEEN ANGELA?

Looking back at her was a color-copy image of Angela's face, taken from her senior class photo. Those perfect cheekbones and flowing black hair, that model-perfect smile. *I wonder where that smile is now? I wonder if she even* can *smile?*

Lucy fought off the familiar waves of guilt and set her mug back on the table. Then she put the poster aside, drew both knees up to her chin, and wrapped her arms tight around them.

"Not your fault," Dr. Fielding would say if he could share her thoughts now. "Circumstances beyond your control," he'd remind her, and "You can't keep torturing yourself."

Good old Dr. Fielding. Aunt Irene's personal choice of prominent friends, who was supposed to be helping Lucy through the nightmares, helping her to readjust, helping her to come to terms with all that had happened.

Except Dr. Fielding didn't know the half of it.

And Lucy knew she could never tell him.

"It's only been a week, Lucy," the doctor had reminded her in their session just that afternoon. "These things take time. Often, quite a lot of time."

And Lucy had given her dutiful nod and tried to listen politely. Because how could Dr. Fielding even *begin* to have a clue as to what she was going through? How could she even *begin* to tell him everything that had happened to her since she'd first come to Pine Ridge?

"Like I explained to you in the hospital, you

might experience dizziness or light-headedness—possibly fainting spells. You may become disoriented or suffer memory lapses. There could be flashbacks pertaining to the accident, or you might even experience panic attacks."

"Great," Lucy had responded. "That certainly gives me something to look forward to."

But Dr. Fielding had smiled his kind smile and patted her on the shoulder. "These occurrences are all very common with a head injury, Lucy—nothing to be overly concerned about. The important thing is to accept the fact that even if they *do* happen, you really are okay. And you really *are* going to get better."

"But you still think I made everything up."

She'd watched his face, that carefully controlled doctor face, as he'd steepled his fingers beneath his chin and studied her from his leather chair.

"I think that trauma-induced memories are very tricky things," he'd answered, as she'd known he would.

"I'm not lying about what happened."

"I know you're not lying. I believe that *you* believe everything you've told me. And it's still

35

amazing to *everyone* how you could have survived that accident, much less survived for three days afterward."

Lucy's hands had twisted in her lap. "I told you. I was in a cave. But I don't know how I got there."

"And those are three days and nights still unaccounted for," he'd sighed. "The police didn't even know you'd been with Byron until your aunt came home the next day and reported you and Angela missing. And even then, it took time to track down witnesses at the Festival who saw you and Byron leave together. After that, search parties combed that entire area around the accident site. Hundreds of people, even scent dogs, spread out for miles. No one discovered a cave. There wasn't a house or a trail or a single clue. But you must have found shelter somehow, somewhere. It's a total mystery. And nothing short of a miracle."

Lucy had heard it all before. She'd told the police everything she could remember about her ordeal—the muffled sounds and shadows, the pools of blood, the dead rabbit, how someone had tried to camouflage the entrance to the cave, and how she'd finally escaped in spite of it. She'd told the doctors, too, and Aunt Irene, and even the private investigator her aunt had hired to search for Angela. But she knew they didn't believe her. Like Dr. Fielding, they all thought she suffered from delusions, the results of her head injury, exposure, and shock.

"But someone found me and brought me to the hospital," she couldn't help reminding him. "And that was real."

Dr. Fielding had conceded with a smile. "Yes. That was definitely real. Three days after the accident, someone left you outside the door of the emergency room. No one saw this person come or go, and no one's been able to find out who it was. If they could, it might help enormously in solving your disappearance."

"I just wish I could thank him. I think of him every day, and I try so hard to remember something about him . . . *anything* about him."

"Maybe you're trying too hard."

"All I know is, he wasn't the one in the cave."

"And how can you be so sure?"

"I can't explain it, but I just know. His voice was different."

"Hallucinations can seem very, very real."

Hallucinations? Well, maybe she really *had* imagined it. Maybe she really *was* going insane.

"You remembered drifting in and out of consciousness," Dr. Fielding had said, going over his notes once more. "And the will to survive is an incredible thing. It gives us the endurance we might never have under normal circumstances."

"But what if I'm right? What if I'm right, and whoever I escaped from comes after me again?"

"You're catastrophizing, Lucy. Even if this person *were* real, how could you be any safer than you are right now, with all this attention being focused on you? No one would dare try to kidnap you twice."

Lucy had bitten her lip in frustration. Twisted her hands even tighter in her lap.

"So if I wasn't kidnapped, then what did I do after the wreck? Just wander around for miles and miles? Find shelter in some place that doesn't even exist?"

"There was no serious frostbite on your feet; the hypothermia you suffered was relatively mild. Not nearly severe enough to suggest your wandering outdoors for any extended length of time. Your other injuries were consistent with those from a car accident, or from falling down a hill, as you described—scrapes, bruises, mild concussion, those nasty gashes on your head. No broken bones, incredibly. And the rest of the examination showed no evidence what-soever of any sexual molestation."

Lucy had turned her head away, and stared out the office window. *But someone took my clothes. And someone touched me. And something stung like fire, something I've never felt before . . .*

She still remembered the sensation. Remem-bered it all too clearly, though she hadn't been able to find any unusual marks on her skin; no tell-tale punctures, no secret scars, nothing intimate or the least bit intrusive. Yet a few times it had come back to her in the middle of the night, in writhing dreams, flushing her entire body with heat and a sense of perpetual emptiness.

Just remembering it in Dr. Fielding's office today had caused that strange, unsettling ache deep, deep within her. An untreatable ache that made her squirm restlessly in her chair.

"I'm very pleased with your test results," the

doctor had continued, not seeming to notice her sudden uneasiness. "Your stitches can come out in a week or two; your soreness, I'm afraid, will take a little longer. And I expect you to make even more progress in the days to come. But injuries take time to heal, you know." His gaze was one of genuine sympathy. "Not just the physical ones, but the emotional ones, as well."

The ache inside her had suddenly focused on her heart.

"You want me to talk about Byron," she said quietly.

"I understand his funeral is this weekend."

Lucy had swallowed tears, barely able to answer. "Tomorrow."

"Are you going to attend?"

But the tears had only thickened as she shook her head. "I can't. There's no way I can do it."

"Do you think it might help give you some sort of closure?"

"How can there ever be closure? I can't stop thinking about him. I can't stop thinking about his grandmother, and how she's going to manage now that he's gone."

"Do you know his grandmother?"

"I've only heard about her. I know she's sick and that Byron took care of her. And I feel so responsible, and I keep thinking how can I possibly help her—"

"Lucy," he'd said, cutting her off gently, "right now you're in no condition to take care of anyone. Right now you need to concentrate on yourself and—"

"Can we just not talk about it anymore?"

There'd been that uncomfortable silence between them then; that silence, Lucy knew, that always preceded some sort of lecture.

At last Dr. Fielding spoke. "I think there are certain things that each of us must work through in our own time, in our own way. Loss and grief are just two of those things. You know I'm always here to help you. Whenever you're ready."

For one split second she'd almost given in. He'd looked so wise, so sincere, that the need to unburden herself had almost been more than she could bear. *Since you're so interested in knowing, Doctor, it all started when I went into the cemetery, found a murdered girl, was touched with a supernatural power, met Byron, and then found myself having weird visions and being watched and followed by some dark shadowy thing* . . .

She'd actually leaned forward. She'd stared into Dr. Fielding's eyes, and her fingers had gripped the arms of her chair.

"When I'm ready," she'd finally answered.

She could tell he'd been disappointed. Yet he'd reached over and given her hand an encouraging squeeze. "With that said, I see no reason why you can't start back to school. I think a normal routine would be very beneficial at this juncture, offer some stability. People your own age . . . fun activities . . . anything to distract you from the terrible ordeal you've just experienced."

"Byron's dead. Angela's missing." These were the words she'd repeated so many, many times that she'd lost count. "It's all my fault."

And once more, Dr. Fielding had given his tireless response. "None of this is your fault, Lucy. None of this was *ever* your fault. Life has its own agenda; it never asks our permission or approval. You're alive, and you're safe. And, believe me . . . that's nothing to feel guilty about."

How simple he made it sound, Lucy thought

now, shifting positions, slumping down on the couch. Had it been only six days since Angela slipped away from the Fall Festival with her invisible boyfriend—generating search parties and volunteers, police investigations and nationwide alerts, false leads and dead-end tips? Lucy could still recall her cousin's behavior that Saturday night—rebellious and excited, mysterious and hopeful with thoughts of love. Now Angela was just another teenage runaway, just another statistic, like millions of other girls that vanished every year.

Except there was nothing typical about Angela's disappearance—Lucy was sure of it. And there was no one—no one at all—whom she could share her suspicions with.

Only Byron.

Byron whose funeral was tomorrow.

Guilt slammed into her with merciless force—the same guilt that battered her day after day, ripping her heart, wearing her down.

"*If you want to live,*" Katherine had told her, "*you mustn't tell anyone what you've seen here tonight.*"

The words of the murdered girl echoed

through Lucy's brain. Katherine had warned her that night, and Lucy had chosen to ignore it; Katherine had warned her and died, yet Lucy hadn't really believed.

My fault. I told Byron, I told Byron everything, and now he's dead.

How could she have been so stupid? So irresponsible? How could she have dismissed Katherine's warning so easily?

Because Byron already knew what was happening . . . because Byron already understood the danger . . . because Byron was strong and brave and determined to take a chance . . .

Lucy buried her face in her hands.

She would never escape the guilt. It would never stop tormenting her. And no amount of prayers or tears, no well-meant platitudes or rationalizations, could ever bring Byron back.

She'd felt so horribly alone before.

But that was nothing compared to now.

4

The whole world seemed to be weeping for Byron.

As if in keeping with Lucy's mood, the day dawned gray and bitterly cold. Mist hung thick in the air, and after several feeble attempts to break through, the sun sank despondently behind a mourning veil of clouds.

Lucy closed the sliding glass doors to the balcony. In spite of her warm room and layers of clothes, she dug through her closet and put on another sweatshirt. She hadn't been able to stop shivering since she'd woken up. She'd hardly been able to keep her thoughts straight.

"Are you certain you don't want to go to the funeral?"

Lucy spun around. She hadn't heard Irene in

the hall, and now, as her aunt peered at her from the threshold, Lucy's stomach went queasy. Irene was dressed in conservative black, and her face was completely expressionless.

"I understand he's being buried in the old cemetery, but you needn't go if you feel uncomfortable," the woman went on. "You don't even have to stay for the entire service. Apparently his grandmother requested a casket, but it won't be open, of course, and—"

She broke off, looking uncomfortable.

No open casket, no body, Lucy's guilt taunted her. *Just charred remains.*

"I'm going to be sick," Lucy whispered, and bolted for the bathroom. When she finally came out again, Irene had gone, and a morbid silence settled throughout the house.

For a long while Lucy sat on the edge of her bed. She stared at the clock on her bedside table and watched the slow, torturous passing of time. Less than an hour till Byron's final farewell. Her heartbeat kept time to the tick of the clock. Her chest was so tight, she could hardly breathe. On unsteady legs she went back into the bathroom and stood at the sink, running a cold, wet washcloth over her face.

She looked so pale. Empty and haunted. The way her reflection had looked when Mom died. As though this might be the way she was going to look from now on.

She ran one hand slowly through her long blond hair, wincing at the tiny stitches near her scalp and the ones high up on her forehead. No point using makeup, she decided—nothing could hide the dark smudges beneath her eyes or the hollow expression gazing back at her, and her face would be covered anyway. She wove her hair into a single braid and tucked it down the back of her shirt. Then, returning to her room, she opened the top dresser drawer and took out her jewelry box.

Sadly she gazed down into the jumbled contents. She sifted some tangled necklaces between her fingers, and she sorted through a clump of earrings and silver bracelets. And then she found what she was looking for.

A pin.

A tiny, gold, heart-shaped pin that her mother had given her on her thirteenth birthday.

It had always been special to her, something she'd loved and cherished.

And that's why she wanted Byron to have it now.

Tucking it into her pocket, Lucy hurried downstairs. She went straight to the coat closet in the front hall, where she pulled on an oversized jacket and a pair of thick raglan gloves. She wound a knitted scarf around her neck and up over her chin; she stuck a wool cap on her head and worked it down as far as it would go.

Lucy felt satisfied with her disguise. She wasn't exactly sure when she'd changed her mind about the funeral, but now that she had, she felt an urgency to get the whole thing over with. She was sure no one would recognize her, and especially at a distance. She didn't plan on staying long anyway, just long enough for everyone to leave the gravesite, so she could have one last moment with Byron.

Turning abruptly, she headed for the garage. Yesterday morning she'd found Angela's car key lying on her nightstand, along with a brand-new cell phone—emergencies only—and a note from Irene encouraging her to use the Corvette. It made her uncomfortable, remembering how Irene had confiscated that same key the night Angela disappeared. There was something about using Angela's car that stirred Lucy's guilt all over again—almost as though she were *betraying* her cousin—but the truth was, she needed a car, and Irene was seldom around to offer transportation.

So as she drove slowly through the wet streets, her thoughts were focused on how ironic fate could be. The fact that she was using Angela's precious car only because Angela was missing. And the fact that she was going to the cemetery, where so many things in life ended—but where so many things in her life had begun.

The place where she'd first met Byron.

And now, the place where she would tell him good-bye.

Lucy had no trouble finding the old church that adjoined the town's even older burial grounds. By the time she arrived, the solemn cortege had wound its way along a narrow dirt lane through the graveyard and come to a respectful stop behind the hearse. Parking her car around the block where it wouldn't be noticed, she ducked her head and slipped in the back way.

The funeral was not far. The low drone of a solitary voice told her the service had already begun. To her surprise, there was a stone mausoleum instead of a grave, and like several other structures she'd noticed throughout this neglected part of the cemetery, Byron's family crypt reminded her of a miniature house for the dead. Dreary and decayed, with roof and walls draped in withered ivy, each corner was guarded by a faceless angel cradling a skull beneath its wings. Two broken urns flanked the gated doorway; the wrought-iron gates were flaked with rust. And the name WETHERLY, carved above the entrance, was nearly invisible, worn smooth by the ceaseless passing of time.

Suppressing a shiver, Lucy spotted a small grove of elm trees a safe distance behind the gathering, and hid herself deep in its shadows.

The mist had turned to light rain. Rainlike tears, wept from cold, gray sorrow. She could see the large crowd of mourners huddled together, sharing umbrellas and hugs and grief. She could hear the echo of muffled sobs. Byron might have been a loner, Lucy realized, but there was something about losing one of its own that bonded a community. Students, teachers, neighbors, strangers, old and young alike, she guessed, but especially the young people of Pine Ridge. They watched with pale, stricken faces and tragic disbelief.

Lucy shut her eyes, clamped her arms tight around her chest. A desperate wail rose up inside her and exploded in her mind, and as her eyes opened once more, she braced herself against one of the trees, not trusting her legs to hold her. She thought of Byron's grandmother, so frail and all alone. Tears streamed down her cheeks. Through the dim blur of autumn she could see Byron's coffin banked with flowers; she could see the vague figure of a priest. Words of comfort were being spoken—stories related and memories recalled—and prayers that held no meaning drifted back to her on the sad sigh of the wind.

And then it was over.

With hushed finality, people walked slowly

past Byron's casket, some adding more flowers and special mementos, some reaching out with one last touch, before wandering back to their cars. The hearse, empty now of its burden, led the procession of mourners away.

Lucy stood still for a moment as bitter reality sank in. She could see several men in work coveralls lounging across the lane, talking and laughing among buckets and tools, acting as though this were just any other ordinary day. It suddenly occurred to her that theirs was the most final job of all—that of interring Byron's coffin inside his family tomb.

With an effort, Lucy roused herself from her sorrow. She'd wanted some time alone with Byron, a private good-bye—but now she'd have to hurry before the workmen came over. Swiping a gloved hand across her cheeks, she eased from her hiding place and started toward the casket.

The feeling came without warning.

That cold prickly feeling of being watched.

Lucy froze in midstride. As her heart quickened, she turned and peered off through the drizzle, seeing nothing but headstones and crosses and statues, faint blurs beyond the rain.

Get a grip—you're imagining things.

Of course that was it, Lucy told herself firmly. Just the culmination of stress and fear, and everything else she'd endured over the past week, playing tricks with her mind.

You're just upset—not thinking straight. Hurry and do what you have to do.

Burrowing deep in her jacket, Lucy slowly approached the mausoleum. The workmen in the distance had noticed her now; she could see them shifting restlessly, anxious to finish their job, but allowing her some time. She kept her back to them and pretended they weren't there. She bent low over the coffin and ran her hands along its surface, breathing in the warm scent of the flowers, letting her sobs come at last, quiet and soul-wrenching cries of despair.

"I'm sorry, Byron," she wept. "I'm so, so sorry . . ."

She truly hadn't thought she could cry any more. But at last, empty and exhausted, she straightened up, reached into her pocket, and withdrew the heart-shaped pin. For a long moment she stared at the bouquets and personal tributes heaped upon the casket, wondering what she should do. If she left the pin on the coffin, it could so easily slide off. Become lost. Get stolen or thrown away.

She felt her eyes shifting to the family crypt.

Maybe there was another place she could put it—a hidden place no one else would ever know about. An eternal secret between Byron and her.

Squaring her shoulders, Lucy pretended to leave. She walked briskly off through the cemetery, then doubled back through the trees. From behind the mausoleum she watched the workmen gathering up their tools and strolling leisurely across the lane. She was certain they hadn't seen her—if she hurried, she'd be gone again before they even reached the tomb.

She glanced around quickly, the pin clutched tight in her glove. Beside her on a corner pedestal knelt one of the four angels, holding a ghoulish skull beneath its wings. On impulse, Lucy reached over and tried to lift the statue, surprised when it moved slightly off center. With a little effort, she managed to tip it sideways, just high enough to slide the pin under its base. Then she lowered it, gazed at where the angel's face should have been, and whispered a silent prayer.

Goose bumps crawled over her skin.

With a gasp, Lucy whirled around, her eyes probing the mist and the shadows, her heart stuck in her throat.

She was sure she hadn't imagined it this time.

Someone was watching her.

And it's someone I know . . .

Frantically she pushed the thought from her mind. It wasn't possible. She knew hardly anyone in Pine Ridge, the funeral was over, the mourners had gone, and except for the workmen she was all alone.

And yet her blood felt cold in her veins.

Because for one brief second, she could have sworn she'd seen a figure in the distance, standing still and silent among the graves.

A human figure that vanished just as soon as she'd turned to look.

5

School was even worse than before.

Lucy knew she must look like something straight from a horror movie, with her cuts and bruises and stiff, jerky movements. As she went slowly from class to class, she fought off fatigue and depression and kept her eyes averted from the other students. Since Byron's funeral she'd slept little, and even the medication Dr. Fielding had prescribed hadn't prevented the nightmares and sudden awakenings, the chills and sweats and frantic heartbeats as her mind endlessly replayed the car accident, her ordeal at the cave, her unknown rescuer, the shadowy figure at the cemetery.

After she'd returned home on Saturday she'd made up her mind not to discuss any more fears with Dr. Fielding. She knew he meant well, but she also knew he'd never believe her. Confiding in Irene was out of the question. And still being an outsider at school, there was no one Lucy could trust. If there were problems to be fixed and mysteries to be solved, it was totally up to her. She was on her own.

So she'd resigned herself to school today as Irene and Dr. Fielding had insisted, but she'd avoided any contact with her classmates. Not hard to do, Lucy thought ruefully as she made her way through the halls, all too aware of the anger and hatred aimed in her direction. She could feel the open hostility like knives in her back.

Testaments to Byron were everywhere. From the black armbands students wore, to his photographs watching her from lockers, corridors, bulletin boards, the walls of every classroom. A shrine had been set up outside the library—notes and letters, signs and posters, flowers and stuffed animals, and personal gifts. In every one of his classes, his desk remained empty, adorned with flowers and presents.

Lucy felt sick to her stomach and sick at heart. She didn't know how she was ever going to survive the day.

But besides the tributes to Byron, there were reminders of Angela, too. MISSING posters in every building, lining the halls, tucked among teddy bears, bouquets, and cards in makeshift memorials. Across the entire campus, yellow ribbons fluttered from every tree. No matter where Lucy went, she couldn't escape the guilt or the sorrow. Even the teachers seemed strangely uneasy around her, and when Principal Howser called her to his office to express sympathy and inform her she'd be meeting with a grief counselor, he kept the talk brief, as though she might be bad luck and highly contagious. By study hall, she felt like a leper.

Eager to escape, Lucy dumped her purse and books in her locker and slipped out a side door. Despite the overnight drop in temperature and the warning of possible snow, she found a bench at the far end of campus near the athletic field and sat down with her back against the fence. Irene had bought her a new coat that was fleecy and warm, and new boots perfect for winter. Lucy huddled into a snug ball and wrapped her wool scarf high around her cheeks, thrusting her mittened hands deep in her pockets. She seriously doubted she'd freeze to death out here, but even *that* prospect was more appealing than going back in to endure those accusing faces.

She let her eyes do a slow sweep of the school yard. A few kids were straggling in and out of the gym; a maintenance man on a riding mower was clearing leaves from the lawn. Several students had decided to brave the cold and were sharing notes at one of the picnic tables in the courtyard. Lucy sighed and began to tick off a mental list in her head. Her favorite purse and everything in it had been destroyed in the crash, and though she'd gotten her student ID this morning, and—thanks to Irene (who had friends in high places)—her driver's license had been reissued in no time at all, there were still some items she needed to replace. Funny how you took those little things for granted, didn't even notice them, in fact, till they were gone. Like her pen with the fuzzy top and her lucky pink stone. Chewing gum and breath mints and chocolate-covered raisins. Her mini-mirror and matching comb, the little green notepad, a tiny vial of spray perfume. Her leather key ring, with the key to her old apartment still attached.

Lucy closed her eyes and swallowed a lump in her throat.

Her red wallet and her address book, and all the pictures of the friends she'd left behind. Symbolic, somehow, she thought bitterly. Her life was different now—her *world* was different now. There was nothing and no one she could ever go back to.

She swallowed harder as tears welled behind her eyelids. Maybe it was time to fix up that bedroom she hated so much, unpack her boxes stored up in the attic, make the room her own. Maybe she should try to get a job. Buy some new clothes like Irene had been encouraging her to do. Resign herself to reality.

Reality . . . right. Being a freak and being alone.

She was so intent on her misery that she didn't even notice someone had stopped beside the bench. As she heard the sound of twigs snapping, she opened her eyes and saw a pair of raggedy sneakers planted firmly on the ground in front of her.

Lucy stared up in surprise.

"You know," the girl said somberly, "death by freezing isn't quite as painless as you might think. Even though you probably don't care much about that fact right now."

There was something vaguely familiar about this person, something Lucy couldn't quite put her finger on. So instead she returned the comment with a frown.

"I'd like to be alone, if you don't mind."

"That's probably a bad idea." The soft-spoken girl gestured toward the bench. "How about if I join you for a while?"

It was obvious she wasn't going away. Lucy considered her options, frowned harder, then grudgingly scooted over. The girl promptly sat, her legs splayed out in front of her, both arms wrapped around a beat-up knapsack. Lucy continued to frown, then felt a small stir of recognition.

"I know you. You're the girl at the Festival—the one working with Angela."

"One and the same. I'm also in homeroom and three other classes with you, but I doubt that you've noticed."

"I . . . sorry. I guess I haven't."

"Well, it's hard to notice much of anything when you're staring at your desk all the time.

And anyway, when you saw me at the Festival, I was pretty rude."

Lucy recalled her clearly now. The girl at the entrance to Pin the Nose on the Scarecrow, the one with the serious face. "You look different."

"Because I no longer have a bunch of wild brats hanging all over me." The girl gave a mock shudder. "What was I thinking anyway, volunteering for that stupid game? I don't even like kids."

Lucy's resistance melted. She could feel a hesitant smile coming on.

"Dakota." The girl held out a small, wind-chapped hand. "Dakota Montana. I swear I'm not making it up."

This time Lucy did smile. And as the two shared a handshake, she managed a quick, head-to-toe appraisal of her new acquaintance.

The girl had been frazzled and distracted at the Fall Festival, surrounded by children and distorted by colored lights—but now Lucy could see the waist-length red hair; the large, solemn, pale blue eyes; the thick straight brows; the sprinkling of tiny freckles across the fair skin of her cheekbones. Her nose was delicate; her mouth too wide for her heart-shaped face. A good three inches shorter than Lucy, she was wearing faded overalls with ripped knees, a dingy sweater that might once have been white, and the most ridiculous scarf Lucy had ever seen—at least twenty feet of it—knitted in every color of the rainbow. It was wrapped not only several times around Dakota's neck, but also draped down her chest and back, hanging all the way to her sneakers—one pink and one green—both laced with orange ribbon. Despite the unique fashion statement, there was an almost ethereal quality about her, Lucy realized—like a woodland elf or a fairy queen from some fantasy bedtime story. And as she met Dakota's eyes, the girl gave a faint smile, a smile that hinted of wisdom and experience far too old for such a young face.

"They won't act like jerks forever, you know," Dakota said quietly. "It's just because of Byron."

Lucy was taken aback. Her mouth opened, then closed again, with no words of defense. Dakota shot her a glance of sympathy, leaned back, and tucked both hands beneath the bib of her overalls.

"Everyone knows you were with him in the accident," she went on matter-of-factly. "They don't care about knowing anything else."

Lucy could barely choke out the words. "They hate me because he died and I didn't."

"Well . . ." Dakota seemed to be thinking, rocking slowly back and forth in her seat. "It's more complicated than that. They hate you because the two of you got together. And Byron never got together with anyone."

"We . . . we were just friends, if that's what you mean."

"That's *not* what I mean. And it's none of my business anyway. It's just that Byron was here for so long—in this town, in this school—and no one really *knew* him. Then *you* come to school for one day, and he actually spends time with you. You make some sort of connection with him that no one's ever made."

Lucy said nothing, only stared miserably down at her feet. *If only you knew the truth . . . if only you knew the whole story . . .*

Dakota stopped rocking, her brow creased in a puzzled frown.

"Guilt's such a weird power," she mused. "It makes people do crazy things. Mean, hateful things sometimes. And right now everyone's closing ranks, trying to figure stuff out, trying to pretend they were all Byron's friends." She paused for a moment, her voice growing hard. "Now that he's gone, they're upset and they're missing him. The school's brought in grief counselors to help them deal with it. They've put Byron's pictures all over the place. I mean . . . I didn't know Byron very well either. But I think he'd *hate* all this, all this attention from a bunch of hypocrites."

For some strange reason, Lucy felt comforted by these words. She watched as Dakota started rocking again, as the girl plucked up one end of her knitted scarf and twirled it between her fingers.

"I think you're right," Lucy said at last. "I think he *would* hate it."

Once again, Dakota went still. For a long moment the two girls stared at each other. And then they both smiled.

"You *really* didn't want to freeze to death, did you?" Dakota asked, standing up, holding out both her hands.

Still smiling, Lucy shook her head. She let Dakota pull her off the bench, then fell into step beside her as they headed back across the grounds.

"Do you know Byron's grandmother?" Lucy asked, trying not to stumble over Dakota's trailing muffler.

"I know *about* her—but no, I've never met her. To tell you the truth, I don't really know anyone who's ever been to their house."

"I heard about his sister. The rumors, I mean."

"Well," Dakota shrugged philosophically, "what does *crazy* mean anyway? I saw her around town sometimes, she and Byron—but she's been gone for quite a while. She was beautiful . . . always seemed kind of shy. And you can't believe everything you hear— especially in *this* town."

"Well . . . actually I heard it from Angela."

"Even more reason not to believe it." Dakota stopped in her tracks and looked embarrassed.

"Sorry. I shouldn't have said that. I keep for-getting you're her cousin."

"Not really. More like her stepcousin."

"Well . . . still . . ."

"We weren't that close," Lucy admitted regretfully as they started walking again.

"Hmmm. Big surprise there."

"I mean . . . *aren't* that close," she corrected herself quickly, as if speaking of Angela in the past tense would guarantee a bad ending.

Dakota threw her a knowing look. "It's okay. You're not jinxing anything by being honest."

"It's just that . . ." Lucy's voice faltered, "it's bad enough that everyone blames me for Byron. But they blame me for Angela, too."

"Not all of them, Lucy. Maybe not even *most* of them, in fact. And how could you ever think that anyway?" But at the pained expression on Lucy's face, Dakota's tone softened even more. "Oh. So I guess you *don't* know."

"Know what?"

"That this isn't the first time Angela's disappeared."

Now it was Lucy who stopped. "Wait . . . I don't understand."

"I mean she's run away from home before. *Three* times, in fact—at least that I know of. And each time there's a big search and a big investigation because her mom has a lot of clout in this community. And each time her mom hires some private detective who ends up finding Angela and bringing her back home."

Lucy felt stunned, her thoughts whirling in confusion. So was *this* all there was to the mystery? Just another of Angela's normal escapes? Another routine act of rebellion— another cry for attention? A selfish game to cause worry and fear—*and the accident—and Byron's death*—

"No," Lucy whispered, not even realizing she'd spoken aloud. *No, this time there's more to it. The mysterious stranger at the Festival . . . and the green necklace . . . and stalking shapes and bloodred moons . . .*

Every instinct had told her so then, and every instinct told her so now. This time was different. Dangerous . . . and potentially deadly.

"Deadly," she whispered again.

"What?" Dakota leaned forward, but Lucy shook her head and took a step back.

"Nothing. I just . . . nothing."

"Look, I don't mean that something bad couldn't really happen to Angela," Dakota explained, resting her hands on Lucy's shoulders. "It only takes *one* time to be the *wrong* time. And people can never be too careful." She thought a moment, then added, "But when I saw Angela at the Festival that night, it wasn't like she was being carried off against her will. She didn't act the least bit scared or upset. When she left me the envelope to give you, she seemed happier than I've ever seen her."

"So you actually saw the guy who took her away?"

"I was too busy with the kids to really notice. I saw her go off with someone, but it was from the back, and they disappeared into the crowds. The only thing I could tell the police was that he was taller than her, and he had dark hair."

Lucy shivered, remembering the deep voice, the mysterious presence, that she herself had encountered behind the scarecrow tent. "Do you think it was the same guy Angela met the night before?"

"I have absolutely no idea. Angela would flirt with anybody. I'm not surprised she'd go off with a total stranger."

"That evening before we left the house, she actually dropped some hints about running away. But I didn't catch on. It didn't hit me till later."

Dakota nodded understandingly, her hands sliding from Lucy's shoulders. The two of them picked up their pace as the bell rang for class.

"I have to help out at the bookstore tonight," Dakota told her as they approached the side entrance. "My family's bookstore, actually— Candlewick Shop. It's kind of a dumpy little place in the old part of town—but you can drink coffee there and probably find every used book in the universe. So, if you feel like company later on, why don't you come over?" She dug into one of her pockets and pulled out a card. "Here's the store number; my home number's on the back. My dad doesn't believe in cell phones. He says they're just an expensive way to annoy the people around you, and he can do that for free. Anyway, if you need a ride, just call me, and I'll come get you."

"Thanks. I just might."

They jogged the last few feet to the building. Before Dakota could reach for the door, however, it burst open, and a giggling trio of cheerleaders pushed past them. As one of them jarred Lucy's arm, Lucy immediately froze.

The girl with her friends didn't notice. She hurried with the others toward the gym, but Dakota turned and stared at the stricken expression on Lucy's pale face.

"Lucy? What is it?"

Lucy didn't answer. As she gazed after the cheerleaders, Dakota followed the direction of her shocked stare.

"Lucy?"

"That girl . . ." Lucy's voice was scarcely a breath, and Dakota moved closer to hear.

"Lucy, what's wrong?"

Lucy pointed to the girl in the middle of the threesome. "That girl . . . there . . ."

"Who? The one with the really short hair? Wanda Carver?"

"She's going to die on Thursday."

6

For a second the world went dark.

It was as though a thick black cloud had settled in Lucy's line of vision, blotting out the entire rest of the world.

And then slowly, a glimmer came through. It parted the shadows in her brain and began to glow, sending light and sensation into her body once more. With a gasp, she blinked her eyes and saw Dakota peering anxiously back at her.

"What did you just say?" Dakota murmured.

Lucy gave herself a mental shake. Her head hurt, and her legs felt as though they might crumple at any second. "I . . . I said . . ."

Sweat dripped from her forehead, though her whole body was chilled. She stared back at Dakota with a blank frown.

"I said . . ." What *had* she said? *Something about a girl . . . something about dying . . .* Lucy put a trembling hand to her temple and pressed gently.

"You're white as a sheet," Dakota informed her. "Are you going to be sick? Do you need to see the nurse?"

Lucy managed a nod. She felt Dakota take her arm and steer her through the door, and as they walked together down the hall, she tried desperately to replay what had just happened outside. *Dakota and I were talking . . . someone bumped my arm . . . and then . . .*

And then . . . what?

A vision? Yet she didn't recall actually *seeing* anything in her mind, no flashes, no pictures, only a frightening sense of . . . *of what?*

"Falling," she whispered, and Dakota tightened her hold on Lucy's arm.

"You feel like you're going to fall?" the girl asked worriedly.

And Lucy nodded again, because she didn't know what else to do, or why *falling* had swept through her brain, or what she could possibly do to understand it or stop it or make it go away—*falling . . . a rush of breathless surprise . . . a slow-motion horror of no escape . . .*

"—lie down for a while?" a nurse was asking, and in total confusion Lucy stared up at her from the edge of a cot. She could see Dakota next to her, could see the girl's lips moving, forming soundless words that Lucy could somehow hear—*"Do you want me to stay with you?"*—but the nurse said no, that Lucy would be fine, that she had specific instructions from Lucy's doctor and that Dakota should go on to class.

"I'll see you later then." Dakota's voice was normal now, as real as the concern in her eyes. "I hope you feel better, Lucy."

Lucy didn't answer. She lay on the cot and gazed at the ceiling, her body numb, her mind vacant. As though the emotions she'd experienced only minutes ago had shorted out and entirely disconnected. *Something about falling . . . something bad . . . a girl is going to fall . . . going to die . . .*

"Are you feeling any better, Lucy?" The nurse was there again, her manner efficient but kind. "I tried to call your aunt, but she's out of her office at the moment."

"You don't need to bother her. Maybe I could just lie here a few more seconds?"

"Rest as long as you'd like. Dr. Fielding has already talked with us, so don't be afraid to stop in here anytime you need to. It's very important not to rush your recovery."

Lucy watched as a curtain was drawn around her cubicle. She closed her eyes and tried to relax, but the message in her head began to filter through at last, crystal clear and knife-sharp. *"She's going to die . . . She's going to die on Thursday."*

My God, where had that *come* from?

Dakota had given her such a strange look when it happened. *Did she hear what I said?* Lucy honestly couldn't be sure—but then again, she wasn't even sure now if she'd actually spoken the words out loud. *Maybe I didn't say anything . . . or maybe I said something different, something I don't even remember.*

"Memory lapses," she reminded herself, fighting for calm. "The doctor said I might have memory lapses. He said they were perfectly normal."

But *Byron* had said things to her, too—*proved*

75

things to her, too; warned her about feelings and powers and circumstances she'd be helpless to control.

So what if those powers were getting stronger? What if she was starting to turn into Katherine?

Oh, Byron, I'd give anything to talk to you now.

Exhausted, Lucy took a deep breath and slowly let it out. She could hear someone coughing in the next cot. She could hear the distant rumble of the marching band as they practiced on the athletic field. And then she heard a low exchange of voices just outside the curtain to her cubicle.

"Would it be possible to see her?" someone was asking in a hushed voice, definitely male. A familiar voice, too, Lucy thought. One she'd heard before and not so long ago.

"Of course," the nurse replied. "Principal Howser told me Lucy was scheduled to meet with you this afternoon."

Lucy gave an inward groan. *Oh, great. Just what I need right now. A stupid grief counselor.*

"She's right in here," the nurse directed.

"Thanks."

Lucy thought about feigning sleep. But at the last instant her curiosity got the better of her, and she opened her eyes just as the curtain drew back. She caught a glimpse of tousled brown hair . . . black clothes . . . a priest's collar . . .

"Welcome back, Lucy," Matt said. "It's so good to see you again."

7

He'd been disappointed that she wanted to leave.

Deeply disappointed, but not at all surprised.

He had known he couldn't keep her there forever, that eventually she would wake within the shadows, that awareness would begin to rouse her senses once again.

She would realize then that things were not as they should be in her world.

And then she would find strength she never knew she had.

And she would flee from him.

Believing that she truly had escaped.

Now, every time he thought of it, the irony made him smile.

Her wild, desperate flight through the woods—and how he'd always been just one step ahead of her, one step behind her, so close that he could smell her wild, delicious fear and the blood throbbing madly through her veins.

The blood that was partly his own . . .

The blood he had given her from his own lips . . .

She'd been practically dead by the time he got her to the cave.

Cold and motionless, yet still beautiful.

He had undressed her so carefully and tended her wounds. Licking her blood away . . . loving the taste of it.

At times she had moaned, moving instinctively beneath his mouth.

And he had stood there for hours in the dark, gazing down on her, his mind filled with an eternity of possibilities and desires.

Undiluted, his own blood would have killed her. So rich and pure and ageless, that the shock of it to her system would have been more than her mortality could bear.

So he had done the next best thing.

After all, he'd had no time for hunting—not for the prey he preferred and was accustomed to. So he had contented himself with smaller

game instead—rabbits and squirrels and foxes—
and after feeding on them, he had mixed their
blood with his own and coaxed it between her
pale, pale lips. And after a while, when her heart
beat stronger, only then had he sunk his teeth
into her flesh, forcing himself to hold back,
injecting only warmth and bloody spittle straight
into her artery. A place no one would think to
look, and a place she would never suspect.

Not that it mattered anyway.

His mark would vanish within twenty-four
hours, just as it had for hundreds of years.

Leaving his victim oblivious and unscathed.

So Lucy would not know, of course, that he
had saved her life.

A life so sad and lonely, that it longed to be
filled with his blood and his passion.

Yes, he had touched her.

Tasted her, but not *taken* her.

A noble—and most uncommon—sacrifice on
his part.

A sacrifice that left him wanting her all the
more . . .

He had seen The One who rescued her.

He had stood by and watched as Lucy was lifted from the road and placed inside the car and driven far away.

And he could have resolved it then and there, but it was neither the time nor the place for confrontation.

Not the moment for settling old scores.

So he had merely suffered the anger building inside him, the hatred boiling in his veins—reminding himself it was inevitable, that he should have expected it to happen.

Truth be told, it might make the Game more interesting, this vying for Lucy's surrender.

A surrender that must be willing and complete.

A surrender that must be gradual . . . so gradual that even Lucy herself would never see it coming.

For hers was a soul to be nurtured.

Hers was a soul to be understood.

And right now, more than anything else, hers was a soul that yearned to be loved.

Loved . . .

A rare and somewhat disturbing challenge, but not altogether impossible.

He had managed it before in his lifetime, and he was *nothing* if not a Master at deception.

So he would give Lucy what she most wanted. And appear as the faces she would trust. And be exactly what she *needed* him to be.

Soon, Lucy.

Soon I'll be the only one who matters in your life.

He ached with anticipation.

And he remembered fondly all the countless hearts he'd ever stolen, knowing *hers* would be the most precious one of all.

But for now he'd let her keep it . . .

At least for a while.

8

"Matt," Lucy murmured. "What are you doing here?"

"I was just going to ask you the same thing." The young priest eased down onto the side of her cot. "You didn't have to do this to get out of our counseling session, you know. You could've just asked."

Lucy ignored the mild attempt at a joke. "I didn't know it was going to be you."

"I've been here all week. A lot of kids have needed to talk, to work through their feelings. To just . . ."

His voiced trailed off. He leaned slightly forward, hands clasped between his knees.

"Lucy . . ."

"So am I supposed to call you Father Matthew

today?" Lucy interrupted, needing to change the subject.

"Whatever you like. Whatever makes you feel comfortable."

Comfortable? She recalled the few brief encounters she'd had with Matt before her accident—when she'd escaped in terror from the confessional . . . when he'd found the necklace that was missing from Byron's pocket . . . and when he'd given out the information that had sent her and Byron on their wild-goose chase after Angela. He looked like a symbol of death sitting here, Lucy thought now—dressed in his official black, with his face so grave and composed. Just another reminder of doom and loss, and things that made no sense.

"So." Matt's eyes locked gently with hers. "How are you? Really?"

As much as Lucy wanted to avoid this conversation, she couldn't look away. She noticed the pale streaks of sunlight through his hair . . . those long dark lashes . . . that boyishly handsome face . . . everything just as she remembered. Yet *something* in Matt had changed, she realized suddenly. Some secret inner sadness? Some profound hidden pain? Whatever it was, it had darkened the deep, deep blue of his eyes and tempered his smile.

For a moment it caught her off balance. As though in some strange way she should be comforting *him*. Then her defenses rallied once more.

"How am I *doing*?" she echoed mockingly. "I'm here. That's about it."

"That's a beginning."

In a gesture that seemed professionally instinctive, his hand covered her own. Yet as an unexpected warmth touched the cold places inside her, Lucy pulled free from him and quickly sat up.

"Is this where I get the lecture?" she challenged.

"And what lecture is that?"

"The one about Byron being in a better place, and how God had some very perfect reason for killing him? And how I should just accept it and go on with my life?"

"I don't know that lecture," Matt replied seriously. "And I think the issue here is that *you* still have a life."

"Right. Lucky me."

"I'm glad you were the one with Byron at the end, Lucy. I'm glad you were the last beautiful thing he saw in this world, and maybe *that* was God's plan. Byron was a wonderful person."

"How would you know?" Lucy couldn't keep the sarcasm from her tone. "You met him one time. You didn't know him."

"You're right, I didn't know him personally. But I've heard what his classmates say about him; I know he had friends he wasn't even aware of. I know he was close to his family, looked out for his older sister, took care of his grandmother. I know he shouldn't have died so young."

Lucy's eyes filled. She barely managed a nod.

"But there's something else I know." Matt stared down at the floor, his voice low and calm. "I know that as hard as it is to lose people we care about, sometimes it's even worse being the ones left behind."

Silence stretched between them. When Lucy finally spoke, her words were bitter.

"How about being the one everyone blames?"

"You know better than that."

"If I hadn't come to Pine Ridge, none of this would have happened."

"But *something* would've happened, Lucy. Things *always* happen. They would've just happened in different ways. That's called *life*."

Lucy hesitated. Her voice came out a broken whisper. "But I keep thinking about his grandmother. Who's going to take care of Byron's grandmother?"

"She has a nurse who comes through the week. And Mrs. Dempsey, who cleans at the church, is staying nights with her temporarily. Just till other arrangements can be made."

"What other arrangements?"

"Right now we're trying to find family members we can contact. Byron's sister—Katherine—moved away about a year ago, and no one seems to know where."

Lucy felt her heart skip a beat. Without even realizing it, she clenched her right hand, as though she could squeeze away the tiny half-moon scar. "There *must* be other relatives."

"Father Paul and I are working on it," Matt replied, but Lucy could tell he was discouraged.

"And what if you can't find anyone else?"

"Then I don't think we'll have a choice. She'll have to be moved to some sort of long-term care."

The ache in Lucy's heart grew worse. "Have you been to see her yet? Does she actually realize what's happened?"

She watched as Matt shifted positions. He leaned toward her slightly, his expression puzzled.

"The sheriff asked Father Paul and Mrs. Wetherly's doctor to be there with him when he told her about the accident. So Father Paul and I rode over with the sheriff that night, and the doctor drove up the same time we did."

While Lucy remained quiet, Matt cleared his throat and stared past her, frowning at a spot on the wall.

"It was so strange," he finally said. "I don't know what I was expecting, really. But when we all got there, the front door was unlocked and the porch light was on. And Mrs. Wetherly was propped up in bed, almost as if she'd been waiting for us. She didn't even look surprised. Just so sad . . . calm . . . resigned, almost."

A shiver went up Lucy's spine. Byron had told her how his grandmother *knew* things—how she'd even warned him that he'd never see Katherine alive again. *Did she see something the night of the accident, too? Did she know about me? Did she already know Byron was dead?*

"I have to get to class," Lucy said suddenly.

Matt stood as she swung her legs over the side of the cot. He watched her take several deep breaths, then he reached down for her elbows, drawing her slowly to her feet. As Lucy swayed a little, Matt's arms went around her, steadying her against his chest.

"Are you sure you feel like staying at school?" His smile was uncertain. "I'd be glad to take you home instead."

Flustered, but not exactly sure why, Lucy pulled herself from his grasp. "Of course I'll stay. I'm fine."

The thought of being alone again in Irene's house was unsettling. But staying here at school, even for two more hours, made Lucy feel even worse. Opening the curtain wider, she suddenly turned to face him.

"I drove Angela's car today."

"I'll bring it over later. I'm sure I can get Mrs. Dempsey to follow me."

"But will the office let me leave with you?"

"Hey," Matt deadpanned, more like his old self, "I'm on official business for the Big Guy—they wouldn't dare mess with me."

The temptation was just too great. After a quick stop at her locker while Matt got his things from the office and checked in with Principal Howser, Lucy joined him by the main entrance and followed him to the visitors' parking lot.

"My aunt lives on Lakeshore Drive," Lucy told him as they headed through town. "Do you know where that is?"

"I do. And I think you should be very impressed with how well I've learned my way around."

She knew he was trying to keep the mood light. She wished she could join in, wished she could rid herself of the terrible burden in her heart, but neither seemed possible to her now. So instead she stared out her window, so that he couldn't see her face when she finally spoke.

"Matt . . . I'm really sorry."

His voice was genuinely surprised. "For what?"

"For the things I said. How angry I got."

"You have every right to be angry."

"I know I'm feeling sorry for myself. I know how pathetic that is . . . how self-destructive. And I know I should be thankful that I'm . . ." Her thoughts stumbled over sudden bad memories. She closed her eyes and forced herself to finish. ". . . that I got through it okay."

She opened her eyes again and bit down on her lower lip. She waited for Matt to answer, but when he didn't, she turned in the seat to look at him.

"Aren't you going to ask me?" she burst out.

Matt kept his eyes on the road. "Ask you what?"

"What everyone's probably heard about—at least heard *rumors* about. Where I was—what happened to me—after Byron's car went off the road."

"I think this is your street," Matt replied.

He turned into the exclusive neighborhood, following Lucy's directions to the house. As he pulled into the driveway, he let out a soft whistle.

"Wow. I can see why your aunt's one of All Souls' most beloved benefactors."

"Nobody loves my aunt. And don't change the subject."

"You know, a lot of our parishioners live in this neighborhood. They don't attend mass either, but I'm pretty sure their tax deductions include very generous donations to the church."

Lucy stared at him. He tapped his fingers slowly on the steering wheel, then turned off the engine. His expression was thoughtful as he faced her.

"Yes, I've heard rumors, Lucy. *And* questions. *And* lots of theories and speculations. But until I hear it straight from you, I won't believe anything. And I'd never just *assume* that you'd choose to tell me anyway."

Before she could answer, Matt was out of the car. He tapped on her window, and she opened the passenger door.

"You have a key?" he asked, and Lucy nodded.

"But you don't have to come with me."

"Oh yes, I do. I always walk ladies to their doors and make sure they're safe."

In spite of herself, Lucy almost smiled. "Is that a church rule?"

"No, it's my mom's rule," he corrected her,

helping her out. "Which is even *more* sacred than a church rule. And there's no absolution when you break a mom's rule, didn't you know that? Break a mom's rule, and you suffer damnation for all eternity."

"You can walk me to the front, then—it's shorter. But you don't have to check the house. Irene just got a new security system—she swears not even a fly could get in."

The two of them went up the walkway to the wide, columned porch. Matt waited patiently while she fumbled the key into the lock, got the door open, and disengaged the alarm.

"Are you sure you're going to be okay here?" he persisted, his gaze sweeping the entry hall behind her.

"I'm sure. My aunt will be coming home . . . sometime." Then as Matt frowned, Lucy quickly added, "And a friend might be picking me up later."

"I'm glad, Lucy. You need to get out and be with people. It's okay to have some fun, you know."

Despite his good intentions, Lucy felt that familiar stab of guilt. "And here's the key to . . .

to Angela's car. It's a red Corvette. On the far side of the student lot, near the Dumpsters."

"Don't worry. I'll take care of it."

"Thanks. I really appreciate this. And I really appreciate the ride home."

"Anytime. I don't just keep office hours at school and church, you know. I'm on call twenty-four/seven."

Lucy watched him walk to his car. She watched as he backed down the driveway, and she kept on watching, long after the black Jeep had disappeared.

The wind was growing restless. Just as the weatherman had predicted, a powdery snow was beginning to fall.

She wished she'd let Matt come inside with her.

Gripping the edge of the doorway, she fought down a sudden wild urge to call him back.

You're fine. You're strong. And you're absolutely safe.

But as Lucy shut the door and locked it, she couldn't help thinking that the house felt even colder than the raw November air.

9

She hadn't planned on falling asleep.

With thoughts to sort out and homework to catch up on, taking a nap was the last thing she could afford to do.

But she'd been exhausted after Matt dropped her off. Exhausted and completely drained. So once she'd changed clothes and lain down across the bed, she'd fallen asleep so fast, she didn't even remember closing her eyes.

But the nightmares told her.

The nightmares always told her.

Nightmares like this one, that trapped her in Byron's van and in hidden caves, abandoned in the darkness and surrounded by dangers too terrible to imagine. Something was holding her down, something was making her burn, and through it all, someone in the background kept sobbing, *"She's going to die on Thursday . . . on Thursday."*

A frightened cry woke her. As Lucy lay there, groggy and disoriented, she tried to figure out where the sound had come from, then decided she must have made it herself. Bad enough to suffer the nightmares . . . even worse when they encroached upon reality.

She wasn't even sure what reality *was* anymore.

Her mind drifted back to school. To the girl coming out of the building, to the image of someone falling. Was she meant to give Wanda Carver a warning? How could she possibly approach a complete stranger like that? Offer some dire prediction that might be nothing more than the result of a head injury?

Just thinking about the consequences made Lucy shudder. Popular cheerleader Wanda Carver would tell the entire school. As low as Lucy's status already was, this bit of gossip would annihilate it completely.

Feeling depressed and defeated, Lucy sat up in bed. Why even bother telling anyone *anything*? She'd *tried* to tell people about the cave. About her escape through the woods, about the unknown stranger who'd rescued her. She knew how much people doubted her; even worse, she'd started doubting herself. She knew she couldn't prove anything about her terrifying experience, but that didn't make it less real. As real as these stitches on her head, these bruises fading from her face, the cuts and scratches healing along her arms and legs.

As real as seeing things without warning . . . as real as knowing things I can't explain.

Somewhere along the way, the fragile boundaries between Real and Unreal had shifted. Somewhere along the way, the boundaries between Seen and Unseen had begun to unravel and disappear.

Frowning, Lucy reached over to the nightstand. *That's funny . . . I could have sworn that lamp was on.*

In fact, she distinctly remembered turning it on when she'd come in earlier, right before she'd changed clothes. And she'd been staring at the lampshade, too, right after she'd stretched out on the bed.

She jiggled the switch back and forth. But when no light came on, she swore under her breath and fiddled with the lightbulb. Still no luck.

She realized then that dusk had fallen. She could see snow outside the sliding glass doors, drifting onto the little balcony. The house was very quiet. A vast, empty quiet that told Lucy she was still alone. Nervously she got up, closed the curtains, and went out into the hall, rubbing her arms against the chill. The house felt even colder now than it had that afternoon.

The light in the hall didn't work either. As Lucy felt her way to the top of the stairs, she could see only darkness below. Irene had had automatic timers installed in every room—the whole first floor should be glowing with lamps by now.

Wonderful. The electricity must be off.

Lucy stood on the landing, trying to think. It wasn't the first time the house had lost power, but it usually happened only during storms. Maybe it was something simple, like a fuse in the circuit breaker. Maybe that's why the house felt so cold.

Cautiously she reached out to grip the bannister. She'd have to go down and check the fuse box. She'd have to go all the way down to the basement. Anger flared inside her, mixed with fear. Why did Irene always have to work so late? Why couldn't she stay home and care even a little bit about Lucy's feelings?

I need a flashlight. I need to find a flashlight before I do anything else.

Lucy forced her thoughts into a more positive direction. No need to panic. She'd reset the security system after Matt left; she was completely safe. Not even a fly could get in; isn't that what Irene had promised her? Everything was fine. Everything was normal. She'd fix the circuit breaker, and then she'd turn on every single light in the house.

Taking a deep breath, she turned and headed for her bedroom. There was a flashlight in her nightstand drawer, one Irene had insisted she keep there for emergencies. In fact, Irene had flashlights stored all over the house, if Lucy could only remember now where they were. She could always call 911 if she got really scared. *Quit being such a wimp—it's not like this is any big deal.*

Yet Lucy's heart was pounding as she groped her way back along the corridor. And this time, her hand just happened to touch the door of Angela's room.

It was like receiving a shock.

The wooden panel was so icy cold that Lucy gasped and jumped back, pressing her hand to her chest.

For a second all she could do was stand there in the dark. The chill in her fingers shot all the way up through her arm, all the way into her head. She was too stunned to move; it was too black to see. Yet her eyes stared straight ahead, straight at Angela's door.

Irene had kept it shut ever since Angela's disappearance.

As though Angela and everything about her must be sealed away from Irene's disapproval and the constant demands of Irene's busy life.

Holding her breath, Lucy reached out for the door.

And felt it move slowly inward.

Angela's window was open. Lucy could see it from where she stood on the threshold, though the room was thick with shadows. The curtains fluttered like restless ghosts, and snow had swirled in through the screen, lying still unmelted upon the carpet.

Oh my God . . . someone's broken in!

Yet through a surge of panic, Lucy could see that the screen hadn't been cut, the glass was still intact.

It didn't make sense. She couldn't imagine that Irene had come in here and opened that window. And Florence came to clean only on Fridays. But maybe Florence had done it—opened the window to air out Angela's room and then forgotten to close it again. *Yes, that's it*, Lucy told herself firmly. *That must be it—what else could it be?*

But as rationalizations swept through her mind, she began to be aware of something else. It came through to her slowly and faintly, and it took her several moments even to realize what it was.

A sound. A soft, muffled sound . . . like . . . ringing?

Lucy couldn't move. With mounting fear, she strained to listen, and her brain struggled to compute. *Yes . . . definitely a ringing sound . . .*

A telephone.

Goose bumps crept along her spine. Angela's telephone was ringing, and as Lucy turned reluctantly toward the sound, she heard Angela's answering machine kick on. "Hi," purred the sultry voice. "This is Angela. If you think you can handle me, leave a message."

Nobody spoke.

Lucy heard only silence on the other end of the line.

Terrible, frightening silence . . . as someone waited.

Wrong number, Lucy thought frantically— *everyone knows Angela's missing—no one who knows her would be doing this!*

Yet she felt herself walking toward the phone. Maneuvering through the darkness, as the silence on the answering machine stretched on and on and on . . .

In slow motion, Lucy picked up the receiver.

"Hello?" she whispered.

And the voice that answered turned her blood to ice.

"It's so dark here," Angela sobbed, "I can't get back!"

"*Angela!*" Lucy screamed.

She pressed the receiver hard against her ear, her voice rising in panic, her heart racing out of control.

"Angela! It's Lucy! Where are you? Are you okay?"

But there was nothing but static now.

"*Angela!*"

Frantically, Lucy began pushing buttons, but there was no voice, no dial tone, and after several more seconds, no noise at all.

"Hello?" she cried. "Hello? *Angela!* Angela, don't hang up—please talk to me!"

In desperation Lucy jerked the telephone from Angela's desk.

And that's when the truth finally hit her.

The cord was plugged into the wall.

But the electricity was still out.

10

It's a trick—it has to be some kind of trick!

Dropping everything, Lucy ran into the hallway and stumbled the last few feet to her room.

A cruel, sick joke! Kids from school tormenting me, because of Byron, because of Angela—

She locked her door and braced her back against it. Blood pounded in her ears, and her body jolted with every terrified heartbeat.

"Guilt's such a weird power . . . It makes people do crazy things . . . Mean, hateful things sometimes . . ."

Hadn't Dakota tried to warn her? Hadn't Dakota tried to warn her just today?

Lucy's head spun wildly. Maybe Dakota wasn't really who she seemed to be; maybe she wasn't a friend at all. Maybe her warning had all been part of this huge, sick joke she and her *real* friends had already been planning to spring on Lucy . . .

Calm down. Breathe. Think.

Lucy's palms pressed flat against the door. Her spine was rigid. Her vision blurred, then focused. Her eyes made a slow, thorough sweep of the shadows. The sliding glass doors were still shut; no invisible presence alerted her instincts to danger. Long minutes crept by. Finally she forced herself over to the nightstand and took the flashlight from the drawer.

The bright beam of light was a lifeline.

Still shaking, Lucy went into the bathroom and locked the connecting door to Angela's room. Then she sat down on the edge of her bed and gripped the flashlight to her chest.

Damn them! How could anyone be so mean, so heartless? Hadn't she been through enough? Would guilt and blame cling to her for the rest of her life?

Yet she couldn't figure out how they'd done it, how they'd managed to rig the whole scenario. Even with high-tech knowledge, wouldn't someone have had to get into the house to pull it off? Maybe they'd caused the power outage, too. But how had they managed to bypass such a sophisticated security system? It just didn't make any sense.

Unless . . .

Lucy's breath caught in her throat. She squeezed the flashlight tighter, so tight that her fingers ached.

No! No, what happened back there in Angela's room *couldn't* have had anything to do with psychic powers or gifts or curses. Her body hadn't signaled her like it so often had in the past. She hadn't seen visions; there hadn't been a feeling or impression or a warning too overwhelming to ignore. What had happened just now wasn't like anything she'd ever experienced. *So, no. No! It couldn't have been just me.*

Yet no matter how much she argued with herself, she couldn't quite shut out the whisper in her mind. The persistent little whisper that kept nagging her, trying to get through. *What if it's not a joke? What if it's real? What are you going to do?*

Moaning softly, Lucy lowered her head and cradled it in her arms. *No, no, there's a logical explanation, it's a horrible trick, and Florence just forgot and left the window open!* Because she couldn't bear to think otherwise. Because the sound of Angela's voice and the prospects of Angela's fate were just too chilling to imagine.

Imagine? Maybe I did imagine it. Maybe I had a memory lapse or blacked out or hallucinated. One of those things that people with head injuries are supposed to do.

Helplessness engulfed her. She couldn't call the police—they'd never believe her. She couldn't tell Irene—her aunt would put her straight into the hospital. So who? Dr. Fielding with his comfort-coated skepticism? All Lucy knew for sure was that she couldn't stay here a minute longer. She had to leave, and she had to leave *now*.

Leading with the flashlight, she hurried downstairs, yanked her coat from the closet, and stopped to check the battery backup on the security system.

And that's when she remembered she didn't have a car.

What time is it anyway?

She looked at her watch, surprised to see that

it was after seven. Surely Matt should have been here by now—surely he would have rung the doorbell when he dropped off the car.

Lucy pulled aside the front curtains and peered out at the driveway. The red Corvette was sitting there, parked about halfway down, covered with a thin layer of snow.

That's strange . . .

Grabbing her purse, she slammed the door behind her. But as she cut across the lawn and got closer to the car, she began to slow down.

The last thing in the world she wanted to do right now was drive that thing. Not after what had just happened upstairs. Not after what she'd just heard.

Lucy stopped. She stared at the Corvette and felt tiny prickles of apprehension creep along her spine. Maybe she should call a cab. She had no clue about taxi service here in Pine Ridge— *or* the drivers. And right now she didn't trust anybody. *Not anybody. Not even myself.*

She took her time going around the sports car, brushing off the feathery snow, shining her flashlight in all the windows. She told herself she was being silly; she told herself she was being safe. When she tried the handle, the door came open, unnerving her even more.

Why didn't Matt lock it? Why didn't he at least tell me he was here?

Climbing inside, she noticed the air was slightly warm, as though the heater had only recently been shut off. She closed the door and began hunting for the key.

Both visors were empty. Lucy ran her hands along the floor mats, then rummaged nervously through the glove box. She searched the backseat area but found nothing. Maybe it wasn't here at all. Maybe Matt had forgotten to leave it. Leaning her forehead on the steering wheel, she tried to stay calm. Snow was thickening on the windshield, and the car was getting cold.

On a whim, Lucy bent down and began groping beneath the seats. Far back under the driver's side, her fingers made contact with something soft and bulky, like thick cloth. It had been wedged in so tight, it took several minutes of intense pulling to finally work it free.

Lucy stared down at the bundle in her hands.

By the glow of her flashlight, she began to open the heavy folds of fabric. A blanket of some kind . . . a blanket that seemed familiar . . . covered with dead leaves and pine needles and stained with mud . . .

And with something wrapped inside it . . .

"No," Lucy whispered. "Oh God . . ."

Most of the jacket was burned away—just charred holes and black tatters—yet Lucy recognized it at once. Remembered the way it had looked on Byron the very first time she'd met him . . . and in that last split second before the crash.

She needed air. She couldn't breathe. The car was too small, too suffocating, and she clawed at the door, but it wouldn't open.

She didn't even notice the car key as it fell out of the blanket. Or when it landed on the floor at her feet.

She only saw the snowflakes turning to ashes as she slumped forward over the steering wheel.

11

"Lucy," the voice was saying. "I've got you, Lucy—you're safe."

Someone was holding her.

She could feel strong arms around her, and her head was tilted sideways, resting on somebody's chest.

"Let's get you inside," the voice murmured.

I know that voice.

"Lucy? Just relax . . . just lean against me."

Yes . . . yes . . . I know that voice, but I can't quite place it . . .

For a split second of panic, Lucy thought she might be back again, back in the places of her nightmares, back in the shadowy cave, the cold wet woods, the deserted road. But then, as her eyes began to open, she could see a world of pure white, and a door with a large brass knocker that looked vaguely familiar.

"Nobody's answering," the voice was telling her now. "Where the hell's your aunt?"

Lucy barely managed to shake her head.

"Then what's the code?" the voice asked. "Lucy, can you give me the code?"

The code . . .

Weakly, she squinted up into a face. A worried face, but calmly reassuring as well. His hair was sifted with snowflakes, and as a gust of wind hit the two of them, he drew Lucy closer into his warmth.

"Matt?" she whispered.

"Do you remember the security code, Lucy?" he asked her again. "I need to get you inside."

Her head was beginning to clear. She realized they were on the front porch, and that she was shivering from head to toe. With sudden clarity, images of the blanket and burned jacket burst into her mind, and she immediately began to struggle.

"Hey, calm down," Matt held her tighter. "I told you, everything's okay—"

"No, those things in the car!"

"What things?"

"In the car—the blanket, Byron's jacket— you must have seen them—"

"Lucy, I didn't see anything but you. What are you talking about?"

"He put them there! He must know where I live—how can he *know* that?"

"Ssh . . . Listen to me—"

"Why did you leave the car unlocked? Why didn't you make sure no one was following you? You must have led him straight here!"

"Stop it, Lucy, you're not making any sense." The shake he gave her was gentle, but firm. "Whatever this is about, we'll *discuss* it. I *promise*. But right now we need to go inside without setting off the alarm and looking like two half-wit burglars."

"But I *want* the police to come! They need to get fingerprints and DNA—"

"Lucy. Tell me the code."

The tone of his voice got through to her at last. It took her several minutes, but she was finally able to recite the correct numbers in their proper sequence. Then Matt turned the key, stepped into the house, and—following

Lucy's garbled directions—disarmed the system.

"Where's the couch?" Pausing at the foot of the stairs, he raised a quizzical eyebrow and looked for a place to set her down. "Couch, chair, or bed. Your choice."

But Lucy was babbling again. "The blanket? It was the one I took when I was trying to escape. The police will *have* to believe me now."

"Where would you be the most comfortable?"

"No, no, I can walk."

"Don't argue with me."

Seeing the determination on his face, Lucy pointed to a doorway. "The den's through there. But you've *got* to call the police, Matt. He had Byron's jacket, don't you understand? The same one Byron was wearing when we crashed! How could he have Byron's jacket? And I lost that blanket in the woods, so how did he find it? Why is he doing this to me?"

"Hush, Lucy." Carefully Matt lowered her to the couch, then began unbuttoning her coat. "Take this off and wrap up in something warm." He pulled the wool afghan from one end of the sofa and tucked it snugly around her. "I should probably take you to the emergency room. You're half frozen."

"Don't call a doctor—call the *police*! Haven't you heard a single word I've said?"

"What about tea? Do you like tea?"

Frustrated, Lucy grabbed his sleeve. "Listen to me. You've *got* to get that stuff from the car. I didn't have any evidence before, but now I do, and if he's out there right now watching us, the police might be able to catch him!"

"If *who's* out there watching us?" Matt demanded, easing himself from her grip. But as Lucy grew more agitated, he knelt down in front of her and took both her hands in his. "Yes, okay, I'll go out to the car. And if it's necessary, I promise I'll call the police. But first I'm going to fix you something hot to drink so we can get your blood flowing again."

"You're wasting time!"

"Time? Well, speaking of time, just how long were you lying out there unconscious in the car?"

"I don't know. What time is it now?"

Matt glanced at the clock on the fireplace

115

mantel, then double-checked his watch. "Your clock's wrong. Mine says about eight-thirty."

"That can't be right." Lucy stared at him in amazement. "I couldn't have been out there for nearly an hour."

"An hour? People have frozen to death in *half* that time!"

"It wasn't *that* cold. In fact, the car was still warm inside."

Now it was Matt's turn to look surprised. "That's impossible. I brought it over about five o'clock."

"But I'm sure it was . . ." Her voice trailed off as something began to dawn on her. "Matt, the electricity's on."

For the first time since they'd come in, she noticed the glare of the foyer light, the glow from surrounding lamps, the stuffy heat and muted hum of the furnace. Matt was staring at her as if she might clarify her remark with some earth-shattering revelation.

"It wasn't on before," she murmured.

"So that explains why your clock's wrong."

"Someone *shut* it off."

His expression grew more puzzled. "Shut your *clock* off?"

Before he could question her further, Lucy threw the afghan aside and stood up, only to feel Matt's hands on her shoulders, pushing her down again.

"Where do you think you're going?"

"To the car. I'm telling you, someone shut off the electricity in this house tonight. And someone deliberately put stuff in the car. And if you're not going to help me, then I'll do it myself."

"Okay, okay. Hold on." Sighing in defeat, Matt turned toward the hall. "I'll go."

"A blanket. And a jacket. They're both in the front seat."

"Right. But in the meantime, I want you to stay here and cover up again."

Lucy did as she was told. She sat huddled beneath the afghan, her mind spinning in a dozen different directions. Questions pounded at her brain. She could feel her body beginning to thaw, but fears and suspicions sent a different kind of chill to her heart.

She heard a door slam and looked up to see

Matt poised in the threshold. He was holding the car key in his hand.

The car key and nothing else.

"Where are they?" Lucy's voice rose hopefully. "You found them, didn't you? In the front, like I said?"

But when Matt didn't answer, the chill deepened inside her.

"No," Lucy whispered.

She saw him hesitate . . . saw the concern and sympathy in his eyes.

"Lucy—" he began, but she cut him off with an angry shout.

"*No!* Those things were *there*! I didn't imagine them—I'm *not* crazy!"

"Of course you're not crazy." Matt spread his hands in a conciliatory gesture. "I don't think that, Lucy. Nobody thinks that—"

"*Everybody* thinks that!"

"You're wrong. Please don't get upset. Just tell me what's going—"

"Maybe he did it at school! He could have broken in, right? In the student parking lot, when no one was looking? Can you tell if anybody broke in?"

"Who are you talking about? Nobody broke into your car at school—"

"How can you be sure? Did you check?"

"Lucy—"

"Then why did you just leave the car out there in the driveway where anyone could get in? Why didn't you come to the door and tell me you were here?"

"I *did* go to the door. I rang the bell over and over, but nobody answered. You said you might be with a friend tonight. I figured you'd gone out."

Was he telling the truth? Maybe the power outage had affected the doorbell. Had she been asleep?

"And I tried to call, too," Matt went on, "but nobody ever picked up. So I decided to drive by again, just to see if you'd gotten home." When Lucy didn't comment, he took a step toward her. "What's going on, Lucy? What's this all about?"

Lucy kept silent. She *wasn't* delusional! She could still see the scorched remains of Byron's jacket; she could still see the blanket with its crumbled, dead leaves. She'd *used* that

119

blanket—she'd *touched* that jacket. No delusion could ever be that real!

"I'll get them myself," she muttered.

Before he could answer, she marched determinedly toward the hall. But halfway across the room, as a thought suddenly hit her, Lucy stopped and turned back to face him.

"Where was the key?" she asked.

Matt's frown was puzzled. "On the floor of the driver's seat."

"No," Lucy corrected. "I mean, where did you leave it when you brought the car over?"

He didn't even hesitate. "On the front porch. Under the mat."

12

It was strange, he thought, how a person's possessions could still retain such a part of them after death.

Like Angela's car, for instance.

It still smelled of her, even now. A smell so ripe and reckless, he could have found it anywhere in the world without any effort at all.

Expensive perfume . . . cigarette smoke . . . strawberry lip gloss and nail polish. Sex and desperation. Longing and sheer bad luck.

Smells that wafted so strong on the wind, even the snow couldn't dull them.

Sometimes he could still taste her eagerness.

But those memories were becoming more and more of an irritation to him. Taunting him when he yearned to be filled. Tormenting him when he ached to be satisfied.

Perhaps he shouldn't have been so hasty.

Perhaps he should have kept her longer . . . drawn out the deception more slowly . . . built the suspense to a more shocking and shattering climax.

At least . . . until Lucy was his.

His and his alone.

Ah, Lucy . . .

She was rarely out of his sight anymore . . . *never* out of his thoughts.

And she so innocently, so sweetly, unaware.

Believing him to be merely an errant breeze, blowing cold across her cheek.

Or the subtle stirring of a shadow coupling with her own.

Or the deep, impenetrable night gazing back at her beyond her sliding glass doors.

How could she know that *he* was the reason for her emptiness? The longing and restlessness she couldn't seem to absolve or understand?

So making use of Angela's car tonight had been gratifying to him in many ways.

Reminding Lucy of their special bond. Their past together that she so wished to forget . . .

their inevitable future she could not yet begin to imagine.

And dispelling those last lingering scents of Angela, once and for all. The car belonged to Lucy now, and it should *smell* like Lucy.

And there was no smell stronger than fear.

He preferred to think of it as a sort of exorcism.

One more move in his Game.

The Game Lucy would never win, no matter how many clues she might unravel, no matter how far ahead she believed herself to be.

The Game with Lucy as his prize.

But that wouldn't happen for a while yet.

Not when the mere *playing* of the Game was so much fun.

Especially when one played without rules.

13

"How could that key have ended up in the car if I didn't even know where it was?" Lucy's eyes were wide and fearful. "Doesn't that prove *anything* to you?"

"Lucy—"

"How did he find me, Matt? Why is he doing this?"

But before Matt could answer, Lucy pushed past him and ran outside.

"Lucy, wait!"

She was already halfway across the lawn. Even though she knew in her heart it was useless; even though she knew that when she looked inside the car, there would be no evidence whatsoever of her ordeal in the cave, not a single trace of Byron's untimely death.

Lucy yanked open the door. Her eyes made a

desperate sweep of the empty front seat, the empty floor. With a choked cry, she fell inside and started rummaging beneath the seats. Then she popped the latch and stumbled around to the trunk, lifting the cover, staring stupidly into one more empty space.

She should have known. Of course she should have.

"It's a trick," she mumbled. She wasn't even aware of Matt standing there now, reaching for her shoulder, trying to pull her away. "A trick," she kept mumbling. "A trick . . . a trick . . . how could anyone be so mean . . ."

"Come back to the house," Matt urged quietly. "Come back and get warm."

"But it couldn't be a trick, could it? No one else would know these things . . . no one else would have these things . . . so it must be real . . . somehow . . . it must be real—"

"Come on, Lucy. Please."

Lucy stepped back from the car. Through misty eyes she watched Matt close the trunk and slip out of his jacket. He threw it around her shoulders and led her back inside.

"Is the kitchen this way?" he asked her.

She wasn't even sure if she nodded. Every inch of her—body, mind, soul—had gone numb. She tried to think of Byron. Tried to remember all the things he'd told her, all the things he'd warned her about. Things about Katherine . . . powers and visions . . . the green necklace. Things about death and evil, and being stalked. Things about her life never being the same . . .

"I'm not crazy," Lucy whispered.

She realized they were in the kitchen now, that she was being pushed into a chair. Had the light been on in here before? She couldn't remember. Had the person who'd been in the car also been in the house tonight? Turning off the electricity, creeping through the halls? Leaving his mark on Angela's answering machine . . . watching Lucy while she slept?

"I'm . . . not . . . crazy."

But she felt like she was drowning. In a bottomless sea of darkness. Beneath crushing waves of despair. As though the entire world had gone black and swallowed her alive.

"Lucy," Matt said softly.

When had he crouched down beside her?

When had he eased his coat from her shoulders and draped it over the back of her chair? And when had he taken both her hands between his, rubbing them gently, trying to warm them? She could see his lips moving ever so slightly. Speaking silent words, with his head bowed and his hair windblown in long thick strands across his forehead.

"What do you do," Lucy murmured, "when nothing in your life makes sense anymore?"

Matt made a perfunctory sign of the cross. Then his eyes lifted calmly and settled on hers.

"Why don't you tell me what's wrong."

"And I don't mean just *make sense*," Lucy went on, as if he hadn't spoken. "It's more than that. Things that can't be explained. Things that are so bizarre and so unbelievable, they actually *defy* reality. Except they *are* real. They *are* happening. And there you are. You're . . . you're just *trapped* there, in the middle of it. With no one who can understand. With no one who could possibly help."

Matt's gaze never wavered. "I'm not here to push you, Lucy. And the last thing I'd *ever* want to do is interfere where I'm not wanted. But I *would* like to help you. Whatever this is, you don't have to face it alone."

"You can't," Lucy whispered even lower than before.

"Why not?"

"You just can't help me."

"Then if *I* can't, I'll find someone who *can*. But you've got to tell me what's wrong."

I have powers, she longed to tell him. *And my world isn't like everyone else's, and nothing will ever be the same again, and I'm not even sure what's real anymore, I'm afraid I'm losing my mind.*

But instead she told him, "Even if I could . . . you wouldn't understand."

"Try me. You might be surprised."

"I don't want any more surprises tonight."

Matt hesitated, seemed to consider a moment, then slowly released her hands. "Where's the tea?" he asked.

"The thing is," Lucy went on, oblivious, "if I could only have taken those things to the police, maybe then they would have taken me seriously. But I can't tell them about it now. If I do, I'll look less credible than ever."

"Am I close?" Matt was rummaging his way

through every door and drawer in the kitchen. "Am I in the general vicinity? Can you at least give me a clue?"

"Sometimes, when things like this happen, then I start thinking maybe they're right. The police and the doctors and even my aunt . . . then I start thinking maybe I really *am* crazy."

"You're not crazy."

"How do you know?"

"Ah!" Matt sounded pleased with himself. "Orange spice tea. Smells good, too. Now, let's see . . . cups."

"But I know what I saw in the car. I didn't imagine what I saw."

"I'll just zap these in the microwave."

"It couldn't have been a flashback, could it? I mean . . . Dr. Fielding said things can come back to you when you've gone through a trauma."

"Done," Matt announced. "Sugar? Lemon? Cream?"

"Sugar and lemon."

"Ah, a woman after my own heart."

Another patient exploration, this time through canisters, the refrigerator, the silverware drawer. Finally Matt set her hot tea in front of her—

complete with spoon, sliced lemon, and sugar bowl—and took a seat directly across the table.

The silence went on for minutes. Lucy stared morosely at her steaming cup.

"If you can't tell me everything," Matt suggested at last, "then tell me what happened with the car tonight. At least just that."

After another lengthy pause, Lucy nodded. Slowly stirring her tea, she related the whole incident to him without once looking up. When she was finished, silence fell between them again.

"You don't believe me," she finally whispered.

Frowning slightly, Matt leaned toward her across the table. "I didn't say that. The thing is . . . why would someone have Byron's jacket? You said Byron was wearing it when you crashed, so it was obviously . . . destroyed."

Lucy winced at the thought, and his expression softened.

"And even if it hadn't been, I can't imagine anyone taking it from the scene of the accident. There were only emergency people there, right? Police, firemen, paramedics?"

Lucy gave a reluctant nod. She knew Matt

was right—it was next to impossible that Byron's jacket could have survived the fire in any way, shape, or form.

"And what about this blanket?" Matt persisted.

Lucy paused, frowning. She hadn't told Matt any details of her horrific ordeal; she'd kept her account to the barest minimum. For just an instant she actually considered confiding everything to him. But then, taking a deep breath, she opted to keep quiet. And tell a white lie.

"The heater was broken in Byron's van so he gave me a blanket to keep warm. When I woke up after the accident, I didn't know where I was, and I tried to find help. And then I lost the blanket when I was running."

"Oh. I see."

Lucy's heart fluttered. Matt's face was carefully composed, but she had an uneasy feeling that he hadn't believed a word of her story.

"So what was all that panic about earlier?" Matt asked her now. "You wanting the police to find fingerprints and DNA?"

Lucy hedged. "Is that what I said?"

He continued to watch her. Lucy quickly took a sip of her tea, relieved when he let the subject drop.

"So who knew about the blanket?" he asked instead.

"The police. The doctors. Irene, of course."

"Well, there you go," Matt said reasonably. "You've got to remember, Pine Ridge is a small town. From what I've been told—and am *definitely* starting to witness firsthand—*everyone* eventually ends up knowing everyone else's business."

Lounging back, he rested one foot on his opposite knee, and settled himself more comfortably in his chair. He didn't look at all like a priest tonight, Lucy noted, not in his faded jeans and flannel shirt and scuffed hiking boots. She waited while he placed both hands around his cup and stared down into the steam, his expression thoughtful.

"Dozens of people could've talked about that blanket—or overheard someone else talking about it."

Lucy pondered this. "So . . . what are you getting at?"

"Have you ever considered that someone's just trying to scare you?" Matt asked. "Deliberately upset you? Just plain mess around with your head?"

"Guilt's such a weird power . . . It makes people do crazy things . . . Mean, hateful things sometimes . . ."

Once again, Dakota's warning came back to her. As Lucy listened to Matt repeating the very same theory, she didn't know whether to laugh or cry.

"Kids at school?" she managed at last. "Is that what you mean?"

"Well . . . I just know how cruel kids can be. Especially at an overly emotional time like this."

Lucy wanted to believe him—wanted *so much* to believe him. It made perfect sense that anyone in town could have overheard specific details of her post-accident experience. And of course it was entirely possible—and probable—that some of those who blamed her for Byron's death could have staged something simply to frighten her.

"But why the car?" she asked. "And why tonight?"

Matt shrugged. "Convenience? Maybe they've

been waiting for a chance, and opportunity finally presented itself. Everybody knows Angela's car—and it was the only one in the parking lot this afternoon. Maybe they tried to break in then, but couldn't. Anyone could've followed me here. Watched where I put the key. Planted the blanket and jacket, then taken them out again after you went inside."

"But it *was* Byron's jacket. It *was* the same blanket."

"Lucy, you had a flashlight and that little dome light in the top of the car. There's no way you could've seen anything clearly. And you panicked. And I'm sure whoever did this was counting on exactly that."

Should she tell him about the telephone call, too? About the terrified voice—*Angela's voice*—that couldn't possibly have come through during the power outage? While Matt continued his speculations, Lucy debated what to do. She opened her mouth, then shut it again, and realized she was afraid. Afraid of the answer. Afraid she'd only imagined it. And even more afraid that she hadn't.

"Lucy?"

Matt's voice pulled her back again. Taking another sip of tea, Lucy tried to focus.

"Look," Matt was explaining, "I'm not saying that any of those kids really did anything. I'm just saying they *could* have. You're in a very fragile state right now, and the worst thing you could do is jump to conclusions."

Lucy squeezed more lemon into her cup. *No, I have to bring it up*, she decided. *I have to ask him*.

"Do you think—" she began, but Matt had stood up and pushed back his chair, the scraping sound on the hardwood floor drowning out her attempted question.

"When will your aunt be home?" he asked, rinsing out his cup in the sink.

"I don't know. She works a lot."

"So you're here by yourself most of the time?"

She nodded, though his back was still to her.

"Well, you may be by yourself, but you're never alone."

His reply startled her, caught her off guard. "What do you mean?"

Matt turned around, drying his hands on a dish towel. A faint smile touched his lips. "What do you think I mean? You always have the power with you."

Lucy's heart skipped a beat. *Power?* No one knew about her power—*only Katherine, only Byron—nobody else—how could Matt possibly—*

"His power's always with you," Matt said, tossing aside the dish towel, leaning against the counter, folding his arms casually across his chest.

"Oh." Lucy could hardly swallow. "You mean God."

Matt shrugged, still smiling that faint smile.

"To tell you the truth, I don't think God's been around for a while." The bitter words were out before she could stop them. She saw Matt raise an eyebrow, and she added quickly, "If God were here, He'd make things better, right? If God were here, He'd . . . He'd make things not hurt so much."

Matt lifted one hand, thoughtfully stroked his chin. "Yeah," he finally told her. "Hurting really sucks."

They stared at each other for several long moments. In spite of herself, Lucy almost smiled. "Did they teach you that at priest school?"

"Actually, I figured it out all on my own."

Grinning, Matt picked up his jacket and walked over. He reached out and playfully ruffled her hair.

"I've got church stuff to do, Lucy. But I don't feel right about leaving you just now."

"It's okay," she assured him. "I'm fine."

As Matt looked deep into her eyes, she could read the reluctance in his own. He seemed to be waging a fierce battle with his conscience.

"Go," Lucy insisted. "Irene's bound to be home before too much longer. And I'll lock up the minute you're out the door."

"Swear?"

"Swear."

But deep down Lucy wished he wouldn't go. She *wasn't* fine, and she was afraid to be alone after all that had happened tonight.

She told Matt good-bye at the door. She watched from the window as he got in his Jeep and drove away. Then, telling herself not to be such a coward, Lucy marched upstairs and went straight to Angela's bedroom.

Matt's right. I couldn't see clearly in the car.

She turned on all the lights. She closed the window and locked it.

Everything Matt said makes perfect sense.

She forced herself to take the telephone from the desk. She lifted the receiver and listened to the dial tone. She checked for messages, but there were none at all.

But I answered the phone, so of course the call wouldn't have recorded anyway.

Lucy replaced the receiver and stepped back.

The room was still cold, neat as a pin, everything organized and perfectly in place. *Not like Angela's room at all.*

And it struck Lucy then. How vacant it felt in here, despite all the furniture. How impersonal and abandoned.

Like an empty shell.

Or a body without a soul.

As if Angela would never come back to it again.

14

"She told you to take a cab home?" Dakota was clearly puzzled. "No one ever takes cabs in Pine Ridge, except for really old people. And we only have two cabs."

Wincing slightly, Lucy shifted her backpack to her other shoulder. "She said she couldn't leave work to pick me up. And I think she was upset that I asked her to drive me this morning. But the thing is, I've never driven in snow before."

"Two inches? Believe me, this is nothing—it's already starting to melt. You haven't even *begun* to see snow yet. Just wait a few weeks."

"Does it snow a lot here?"

"Not nearly as much as I'd like it to. And it's not that hard to drive in. They're pretty good about keeping the streets plowed, and I could help you practice. And till you feel more confident, you can just ride with me when it snows."

"That's really nice of you. Thanks."

Dakota watched closely as Lucy drank from the water fountain. "You still seem a little unsteady. Are you sure you should even be here today?"

"Doctor's orders." Lucy gave a wan smile. "And Irene's. Anyway, I'm behind enough in my classes as it is."

"If you don't mind coming to the bookstore, we could study together."

Before Lucy could answer, the first bell rang. There was an immediate chorus of voices yelling, locker doors slamming, and feet pounding up and down the nearby stairs.

"I meant to stop by last night." Lucy tried to speak over the commotion. "But I fell asleep. I guess I was more tired than I thought."

"Well, after what you've been through, who wouldn't be?"

The two of them started down the hall, shouldering bravely through a surge of fellow students. Lucy tried to convince herself that no one was pointing or staring at her today, but her senses told her otherwise.

"What exactly are people saying I've been through?" she asked Dakota cautiously.

Dakota shrugged. The knitted cap she was wearing this morning matched her long, trailing scarf and was at least three sizes too big for her head.

"That you were in an accident and then disappeared for three days. And that some good samaritan found you and left you at the emergency room, but you can't remember what happened in between."

"Well," Lucy gave a thin smile, "that about sums it up." She waited for Dakota to grill her for more details, but the girl merely pointed at a series of large colorful posters hanging along the corridor.

"I don't suppose you'd be interested in being on my team?" Dakota asked.

Lucy drew a blank. "What team?"

"The Holiday Treasure Hunt. It's a scavenger hunt, really. The whole senior class divides into teams, and we all compete for prizes. Very big tradition here at Pine Ridge High."

"And is this tradition as important as the Fall Festival?"

"Well, it depends on what you're into, doesn't it?" Dakota proceeded to wrap her muffler numerous times around her neck as Lucy followed her into homeroom. The two took their desks near the window, and Lucy turned her attention to the snowy landscape outside.

It had taken herculean effort to shut off her mind, to not rehash again and again the disturbing events of last night. Luckily, Irene had gotten home within twenty minutes of Matt's departure, but Lucy still hadn't been able to sleep. She'd tossed and turned for hours, trapped in answerless questions and startled at every sound. When she'd finally gotten up and seen herself in the mirror—ghost-white skin and tired hollow eyes—she'd actually found herself wondering if she'd been in another wreck.

Dakota had been tactful enough not to even mention Lucy's haggard appearance. She'd merely stopped by Lucy's locker to ask if she felt better this morning, making casual small talk, putting Lucy at ease, smiling that Mona Lisa smile of hers. At least that's how Lucy had begun to think of it—that slight, mysterious curve to Dakota's lips that hinted of secrets known but never shared. Now, as Mr. Parkin took attendance, Lucy turned and shifted her attention to the desk behind her. Dakota was wearing knee-patched overalls again, fuzzy socks with beat-up sandals, and a leather bombadier's jacket. Between the layers of scarf and the droopy hat, Lucy couldn't even see the girl's eyes.

Like most of the class, Lucy drifted through the morning announcements. Despite her best intentions, she could feel paranoia creeping in again, as her eyes darted around the room, as she wondered how many of her classmates might have conspired against her to set up last night's charade. Was it just her imagination or was everyone trying not to look at her? Were kids smirking at each other, trying not to laugh? And had Dakota been telling the truth about what people really knew? The girl seemed to have a handle on things here at Pine Ridge High—if there were any other rumors going around, Lucy sensed that Dakota would be honest about them.

The bell rang again, signaling first period. As everyone spilled out into the hallway, Dakota tugged on Lucy's sleeve.

"See there?" she mumbled.

Lucy saw. Matt was standing just outside the administration office, jotting in a notebook, and talking earnestly with a small cluster of female students.

Dakota tugged her arm again. "There hasn't been this much sexual excitement around here since Mr. Enright took over the chemistry lab."

"Are you talking about Matt? I mean . . . *Father* Matt?" she quickly corrected herself.

Dakota's tone was solemn. "I have to admit—he's very hot."

"He's also a priest."

"That doesn't mean he's dead."

Lucy opted for another look. Matt was all business again today—properly religious from head to toe. Yet those faint streaks of sunlight still showed in his hair, and his grin was still easy and warm, and his eyelashes still lay long and thick against the fading tan of his cheeks.

For the first time Lucy really noticed the vast number of girls in the hall, moving at a snail's pace despite the sound of the bell. It was obvious from their faces that holy vows of any kind were not uppermost in their thoughts at the moment.

"So are you trying to tell me he's your type?" Lucy couldn't help teasing.

"No. I'm just trying to tell you that's he's too hot to be a priest."

"As hot as Mr. Enright?"

"Hotter. Mr. Enright's gay."

As the girls continued to watch him, Matt suddenly glanced up, recognized Lucy, and waved. Immediately heads began to swivel in her direction. Embarrassed, Lucy took Dakota's arm and moved her rapidly down the hall.

"He's nice, though," Dakota observed. "And he looked kind of worried about you."

"I . . . he's just trying to help me through some stuff. You know . . . like he's trying to help everyone else."

"Well, I'm glad he took you home yesterday. You shouldn't have tried to drive by yourself."

Lucy felt a tiny ripple of uneasiness. "How'd you know he took me home?"

They'd reached their classroom by now. Dakota paused outside the door and began unwinding her scarf.

"Come on, this school can't be *that* different from your old one. You know how information gets around. And besides"—she leaned forward with a conspiratorial whisper—"you can't expect to keep something a secret when Father Matt announces it to the whole office."

"It's not a secret," Lucy insisted. But it *did* help explain all the weird looks she'd been getting this morning. And maybe it explained something else, as well . . .

The whole office . . . the whole school. Which means anyone *could have found out I was alone yesterday.* Anyone *could have planned to scare me,* anyone *could have put that stuff in the car. Just a cruel joke. Just a mean trick, like Matt said.*

But what about the call from Angela? Could someone have managed to sneak into the house? Tamper with the fuse box? Rig the telephone somehow? Imitate Angela's voice?

Please let it be that. Please let it all be just a trick.

"Ladies, you're not going to learn anything lounging out here in the hall. Except, perhaps, bad posture."

As the teacher's voice broke into her thoughts, Lucy jerked back to the present. Dakota was already halfway through the door, and Mr. Timms was motioning Lucy to follow.

"Sorry," Lucy mumbled. She slid quickly into her seat, trying to figure out what the biology assignment had been for today. She couldn't even remember now if there'd been homework last night, much less if she'd done it.

She watched as Mr. Timms began listing various body parts on the board. At the next table over, Dakota was digging through her knapsack, the brim of her baggy hat practically obscuring her eyes.

Lucy took out her notebook. She hadn't even begun to catch up on all the schoolwork she'd missed so far; she didn't have the slightest idea how she was ever going to manage it. Not with so many tests looming on the horizon, and definitely not in her current state of mind. Sighing deeply, she clicked her pen, opened her notebook, and flipped to the next blank page.

And that's when her heart stopped.

For an endless moment her heart stopped beating, and the blood chilled solid in her veins.

She could see the words scrawled there, in large messy letters.

In strokes that had dried to a dark reddish brown.

Words meant for her . . .

And for her alone.

VERY SOON, LUCY

15

"Please—isn't there *any* way I can get in to see him?"

Lucy stood in the office, shifting anxiously from one foot to the other. She watched as the secretary consulted a schedule. Lucy clutched her notebook tight against her chest.

The woman looked up with a regretful smile. "I'm sorry, but—"

"It's very important. *Please*. *Very* important."

"What I'm trying to tell you is that Father Matt's left for the day. But the other grief counselors are still here. Perhaps you'd like to speak with Father Paul? Or Dr. Kauffman?"

"No. No . . . I . . ." Lucy stood for a moment, unsure what to do. Her mind felt blank. The notebook felt heavy in her arms. "Thanks anyway," she mumbled.

"I can schedule you for tomorrow," the secretary offered, but Lucy was already out in the hall.

Maybe this was a bad idea after all, showing this to Matt. Because what could Matt do about it anyway? Calm her down again? Try to convince her it was just another spiteful joke? And maybe it was, Lucy argued with herself. Maybe it *was* just another vicious prank. If she freaked out about it, then whoever had done this awful thing would win—again.

But what if it's not?

And what does it mean?

Had she been right about her unknown captor following her back to Pine Ridge? Knowing where she lived? Taunting her with those things in Angela's car? He could have found her notebook in the house last night and written his message then. And if she *was* right, who was going to help her? Who was going to protect her? If the police and the doctors hadn't believed her before, they *certainly* weren't going to believe her now.

How she longed for someone—*anyone*—to believe her.

Her resolve to keep silent had weakened with last night's incident. Her determination to handle things on her own had become shaky. Matt had listened to her, stayed with her, offered halfway sensible explanations—and though she'd been thoroughly frustrated at the time, it had felt so wonderful to have the burden lifted and shared, if even for just an hour or so.

She wasn't sure how much longer she could go on like this. Recalling the real-life nightmares. Struggling to stay sane. Feeling so terrified.

Being so alone.

But if she broke down and confided in Matt, would *he* die, too? Like Katherine? Like Byron? And what could she tell Matt, really? What could she expect from him if she didn't even know what she was dealing with?

Oh, Byron, I'd give anything to have you back again.

More depressed than ever, Lucy stopped at her locker. There wasn't anything she could do about the notebook now. She'd have to deal with it later—decide in the meantime whether or not to show it to Matt. She was late for class as it was. The bell for second period had already rung, and the corridor was deserted. She threw her notebook inside and was fumbling with the combination lock, when she heard laughter and running on the stairs.

The cheerleaders were late for practice, Lucy supposed. The whole uniformed group of them, with pom-poms in hand, making a beeline for the door at the end of the hall. Lucy drew back as they passed, and her eyes immediately landed on the girl with the short-cropped hair.

Wanda Carver.

She's going to die on Thursday.

Lucy's heart pounded. She felt herself step forward. Lift her arm to wave. Open her mouth to speak.

On Thursday.

She stood and watched the cheerleaders head off toward the gym. Her hands were shaky as she rechecked the door of her locker, tested the lock just one more time to make certain it was secure.

What am I thinking? I must *be crazy.*

Trying hard to compose herself, Lucy walked

slowly to class. She got a lecture for being tardy and flunked a test she'd completely forgotten to study for.

She didn't know if she could survive school until the weekend.

And it was only Tuesday.

16

I'm going to show Matt the notebook.

Lucy sat in the kitchen, both elbows on the table, chin propped in her hands.

No, I'm not.

Yes, I am.

She'd struggled with the decision all day. She hadn't been able to concentrate on anything else. And when school was finally over, she'd half expected the notebook to be missing from her locker, just like the jacket and blanket from Angela's car.

But it was still there, right where she'd left it. She'd shoved it down in her backpack, wedged it in tight, as though by trapping it there, she could end all the torture once and for all.

It was after six now. Irene hadn't come home yet, and as Lucy hunted for a memo pad, she kept glancing over at her backpack by the door. She didn't want to touch that notebook again, at least not till Matt had seen it. She didn't even want it in her room. As soon as Matt read the ominous message, she planned on throwing the notebook away. She could always copy Dakota's notes later.

In fact, that's where she was going tonight—to the bookstore to study with Dakota . . .

"I can't believe your aunt leaves you alone so much," Dakota had told her that afternoon. She'd insisted on giving Lucy a ride home, and they'd been on their way to the parking lot. "Don't you two ever do anything together?"

Lucy's laugh had been humorless. "She hardly even talks to me. And since Angela's been gone, she's been more distant than ever. She keeps Angela's room closed up. And all she does is work."

"Aren't you scared to be there by yourself?"

"Sometimes." But then, as Dakota's eyes had searched hers, Lucy had given in. "Actually . . . most of the time."

"I'm sorry."

Lucy had tried to smile. "The weird thing is, I was never afraid before. We lived in the city, in a walk-up apartment, and there were lots of times I stayed alone. My mom was a teacher. Sometimes she had school things to do at night, or meetings kept her late. It just never bothered me."

"There's my truck," Dakota had said.

It was big and old and clunky and even more beat-up than Dakota's knapsack. It had probably been cherry-red once, beneath all the dents and rust and scratches. And there was an odd assortment stowed in the back—a toolbox without a lid, two fishing poles, a laundry basket full of books, a gasoline can, and a small wicker rocking chair tied down with rope.

When Lucy tugged on the passenger door, Dakota had given it a hard shove from inside.

"Tragedies change us, don't they?" The girl's look had been intense as Lucy settled beside her. "We're never the same people we were before."

How true, Lucy thought now, climbing into Angela's car. She mentally reviewed the directions Dakota had given her and headed into town.

As her friend had predicted, the snow had all but disappeared, leaving streets and sidewalks a wet, muddy mess. Lucy drove slowly, watching for landmarks and street signs on the way. She'd never actually visited Pine Corners—the old section of Pine Ridge—and though a lot of places were open tonight, they didn't appear very busy. The four-block area allowed only foot traffic; there were parking lots at each end and curb parking in nearby neighborhoods. After several trips around the perimeter, Lucy finally found a spot on one of the adjacent streets, then set off briskly to find the bookstore.

Souvenir shops . . . art galleries and local crafts stores . . . cafés and coffee shops and an all-night diner—Lucy passed row after row of charmingly restored buildings, keeping a lookout for the alley she was supposed to take. There were a lot of alleyways, in fact, each of them quaintly named and squeezed inconspicuously between shops, where Lucy could glimpse tiny courtyards and miniature gardens beyond. After making a turn onto Candlewick Lane, she finally found the bookstore. It looked older than the other buildings—narrow, two stories high, and not nearly as well kept—but the door and windows and droopy awnings sparkled with strands of tiny white fairy lights, giving the place an almost magical quality. A curious assortment of lawn furniture and statues filled the small enclosure—stone elves and birdbaths, gargoyles and angels, all adorned with the same twinkling decor. And hanging from a clothesline were thirteen wind chimes, clanging out the most discordant harmony she'd ever heard.

Opening the door, Lucy went in. The first thing that struck her was the smell. A warm, musty smell of worn bindings and brittle pages, old leather and aged wood, damp wool coats and wet shoes, dust, a hint of mildew, and the strong rich smell of coffee.

The second thing she noticed were the books. Books everywhere. Shelves of books, tables of books, books stacked in corners, piled carelessly on the floor. Overstuffed chairs holding books instead of people. Books on the front counter and the rolltop desk behind it, and books on the staircase at the back of the room.

"Welcome to the eighth wonder of the world," said a familiar voice.

Turning, Lucy saw Dakota standing beside her, balancing a stack of books in her arms.

"I've never seen anything quite like it," Lucy agreed.

"Yes. We work very hard to maintain our reputation for clutter. Oh—Lucy, this is my dad."

Lucy instantly saw the resemblance. Though very tall and lanky, with wire-rimmed glasses and an absentminded smile, Mr. Montana had the same red hair and blue eyes as his daughter. He welcomed her to the store, encouraged her to get some coffee, and made her promise to come back again. Then, as a telephone rang, he obligingly transferred Dakota's books, excused himself, and hurried away.

Dakota raised an eyebrow at Lucy. "He'll tell you the exact same things next time you come, so don't be offended. He never remembers anybody."

"I like him. He seems really sweet."

"He is, but he makes me crazy. Come on— I'll give you the grand tour."

Dumping her coat and backpack behind the counter, Lucy followed Dakota through the rest of the shop. There were two more equally cramped rooms downstairs, and Dakota kept up a running dialogue as the two of them tried to maneuver their way around browsing customers and through tightly packed aisles.

"We try to categorize everything," Dakota explained, pointing things out as they went. "Keep all the genres together, make things easy for customers to find. But we just don't have enough space."

Lucy could see what she meant. Shelves bowed beneath their heavy loads, and baseboards were lined with boxes overflowing their contents.

"We're already double-shelving, so the rows are two books deep. And people hardly ever put stuff back where it belongs. So lots of titles end up in the wrong places."

"How do you keep track of everything?" Lucy asked in amazement.

"We don't. If we ever tried to clean behind those shelves, I bet we'd find books that have been missing for years."

The second-floor rooms, though every bit as crammed with books, were far less occupied with people. The light seemed dimmer up here; the rooms more stale and cold. There wasn't space enough for even one chair.

"What's that?" Lucy asked, pointing to a door with a KEEP OUT sign.

"Oh, that goes to the attic. We have a little office up there, but mostly it's just more books."

"Impossible."

"My mom keeps talking about moving to a bigger place. A newer store." Tilting her head, Dakota straightened the lopsided sign. "My dad keeps holding out for character and atmosphere."

"Do they both work here?"

"My dad, full-time. He's a writer, so this is perfect for him when business is slow. My mom's an artist. In fact you probably passed her gallery on your way. It's about five doors down."

Lucy was impressed. "It must be great to have such a creative family."

"Not if you're the only one who's not creative."

"Come on, I don't believe that."

"It's true. My sister's an awesome photographer; my brother's in a rock band and writes his own music. I'm the middle sibling who got *completely* passed over when it came to talent."

"There must be something you like. Something you're passionate about."

Dakota nodded. One corner of her mouth tugged down, and her pale eyes narrowed in thought.

"There is something," she admitted.

"Well, tell me. What is it?"

"You'll think I'm strange." Dakota hesitated, then sighed. "But then, of course, I *am* a bit strange, so you would be right."

Lucy couldn't help smiling. "Just tell me."

"In here."

Abruptly the girl turned and led Lucy into the last of the upstairs rooms. This room was easily the smallest of them all, with an odd configuration of shelving much like a maze, reaching from floor to ceiling and completely obscuring the windows, with unexpected turns and dead ends, and no rhyme or reason whatsoever.

"This is my favorite place," Dakota said quietly. "This is my passion."

She leaned against the door frame as Lucy took a cautious step into the room. For several long minutes Lucy was silent, her eyes sweeping back and forth over the hundreds of titles around her.

"Do all these deal with the supernatural?" Lucy finally asked. A tiny chill crept through her, raising goose bumps on her arms.

"Some people call it supernatural. Some call it real."

"What do *you* call it?"

Dakota moved slowly into the room. Her expression was thoughtful as she ran one hand along a row of old books.

"Lucy, there are just so many things out there that can't be explained or understood—not by our limited human perceptions, anyway. But those things still exist. They still happen. People are still affected by them . . . destinies are still controlled by them."

"Is that what you believe, then—that our destinies are predetermined?"

"I believe in everything." A thin smile flitted over Dakota's face. "But the question is . . . what do *you* believe in?"

"I . . . I guess I never thought about it."

"Witches? Zombies? Ghosts?"

Lucy pretended to be studying some titles. Adamantly she shook her head. "I really don't know much about any of that stuff."

"But you must have wondered about *something* in your life, right? Hasn't anything ever happened to you that was just too bizarre for this world?"

Lucy's eyes shot to the girl's face. "Why would you say that?"

"Vampires? Werewolves? Spells and curses? Just because you can't see what's in front of you doesn't mean it's not there."

The chill spread to Lucy's heart. She was wearing warm clothes, but she was beginning to shiver.

"No," she heard herself say. "No, I guess nothing like that's ever happened to me."

"Oh, well." Dakota seemed totally comfortable

with Lucy's reaction. "I warned you, you'd think I'm strange."

"I don't. I don't think that."

"This is the problem I face with my particular passion, you see. It doesn't involve any sort of creative talent, and I happen to be the only one who believes in it."

Still stunned by Dakota's revelations, Lucy watched her leave the room. *Tell her. Tell her the truth. Maybe she'll believe you. Maybe she'll have some insights . . . maybe she'll know how to help.* But Lucy couldn't say a word. Instead she could only stand there, trapped in a curious web of longing and denial.

"Lucy, are you coming?" Dakota was poised in the doorway, watching her. "I guess we've put off studying long enough."

The two went back downstairs. Dakota cleared off a lumpy, well-worn couch by the front window while Lucy poured each of them a cup of strong coffee from the pot on the counter. Then the girls settled themselves at opposite ends of the sofa, with their notes and textbooks spread out between them.

Somewhere between lists of required book

reports and unsolvable math problems, Lucy's attention began to wander. From time to time, she caught herself glancing over at Mr. Montana scribbling at his desk, or at the big round wall clock creeping interminably toward nine, or at Dakota's head bent low over yet another school project. The shop was practically empty now. Through the half-fogged window, she had a clear view of the courtyard beyond.

"You're drifting," Dakota mumbled, without looking up. "Only two more pages, I promise. Pay attention."

"Sorry."

"Don't be. It's incredibly boring."

Amused, Lucy tried her hardest to focus on the subject at hand. Dakota kept up a monotonous translation of French verbs. The bookstore was quiet now, and despite her megadose of caffeine, Lucy could feel herself getting drowsy. Her eyelids were heavy. With a halfhearted effort, she forced them open again and stared sleepily out the window.

Night lay deep within the courtyard walls. Like diminutive candle flames, the fairy lights glimmered softly through the shadows. The shadows where someone stood watching.

His face was near the glass.

Staring in at her.

And he looked just as she remembered, just as he had the last time she'd seen him, except for the bloodless pallor of his skin and his blank, hollow eyes.

"Oh God . . ."

She felt herself trying to stand. Trying to rise from the couch, trying to hold herself up and lean forward on shaky, unsteady legs . . .

"Lucy?" Dakota broke off in the middle of a sentence, looking up at her with a quizzical frown. "Lucy, what is it?"

And Lucy's voice trembled out, no more than a whisper.

"It's Byron."

17

"What?"

The book fell from Dakota's hands. As she jumped off the couch and reached out for Lucy, her eyes shot straight to the window.

"What! Where?"

But Lucy didn't hear. She was frozen helplessly in place, unaware of anything now but a misty pane of glass and shimmering pinpricks of light and a blanket of nighttime shadows in the courtyard just outside . . .

The deserted courtyard outside.

"I—" From some dreamlike place, she felt Dakota trying to pull her down again. "Didn't you see him?"

"Lucy, there's nobody out there."

"No, there *is. Was!* I *saw* him!"

"Lucy?" Dakota tugged at her again. "Come

on, sit down. Let me get you some fresh coffee."

But Lucy brushed her aside and ran for the door. Ignoring a startled glance from Mr. Montana, she hurried out to make a hasty search of the courtyard. A raw breeze swept down the alley, stinging through her clothes. It snaked through the wind chimes and played a macabre melody.

"Byron?" Lucy called.

You're losing your mind; you know Byron's dead.

Yet she'd seen someone there.

She'd seen *Byron* there.

Lucy rushed from the courtyard and back out through the alley. She looked frantically in every direction, but the shops were all closed, as still and deserted as the sidewalks.

And then she saw him.

He was at least fifty feet ahead of her, head bowed, walking rapidly toward the corner. She could see his dark hair blowing wild across his shoulders, and the long, easy stride of his legs . . .

"Byron!"

Before she even realized it, she was following

169

him, racing along the pavement, oblivious to the cold.

He was turning the corner now.

For one split second Lucy saw him hesitate, as though he might look back at her. He seemed to be listening to the pounding of her footsteps. Then he lowered his head again and disappeared.

"Byron!"

Lucy ran faster.

As she came around the corner, she could see that Byron was moving faster, as well. His shoulders were hunched against the wind, his collar turned high around his neck. He cut across a parking lot, then headed for a gap between two buildings. It was all Lucy could do to keep up.

Her breathing was ragged; her chest burned from the cold. As she entered the narrow opening, she caught a shadowy glimpse of Byron at the other end of the alley. Once more he paused, but just for an instant, before stepping out into the dim light of a streetlamp beyond.

"Byron! Wait!"

Lucy burst from the passageway, her heart ready to explode.

And then she stood there, staring in disbelief. The figure had vanished.

From end to end, as far as she could see, the area was completely deserted.

"No . . . no . . . it's impossible . . ."

She seemed to be in some sort of delivery zone. To her left stood a row of identical buildings, small loading docks, and Dumpsters, obviously back entrances to shops and restaurants. To her right was a fenced-in wooded area, which she guessed to be a park. The high spiked gates were chained with a padlock; there were benches and overgrown pathways inside.

Maybe he climbed the fence. Maybe he left through the park. Yet Lucy doubted he'd had enough time to cover that much distance before she'd come out of the alley.

My God, just listen to yourself.

She was talking about Byron as if he'd deliberately led her here. As if he'd deliberately eluded her.

She was talking about Byron as if he were still alive.

But I saw him. I saw him!

Lucy strained her ears through the darkness. The wind had gone still. It was so unnervingly quiet, she could hear the echo of her own heartbeat.

So quiet . . .

Too quiet.

Suddenly she wanted to get away from here. For the first time it dawned on her just how foolish she'd been to follow some shadowy figure into an isolated part of town. He wasn't Byron—of *course* he wasn't Byron! And now he could be anywhere—*close* to her—*watching* her. The one in the cave . . . the one in her nightmares . . . the one nobody ever believed existed . . .

Lucy turned and ran back.

Back through the alley, back to the sidewalk, where she saw Dakota standing on the corner and looking frantic, trying to figure out where Lucy had gone.

"Lucy! Thank God!"

There was relief in Dakota's voice. Relief and fear mixed together, as the girl ran up to her and caught her in a hug. "Are you okay?"

"I saw him, Dakota. I'm not crazy."

"No, but you're frozen. Come back inside."

"It was Byron."

"We'll talk about it."

Reluctantly, Lucy allowed Dakota to lead her to the bookshop, where Mr. Montana was waiting for them at the door. He handed each of the girls a refill of hot coffee, then tactfully retreated to his desk.

"Sit down." Dakota steered her firmly to the couch. "Drink this. And don't try to tell me anything till you stop shaking."

But Lucy was too upset to follow orders. "I'm sorry," she blurted out. "I . . . I know it sounds impossible—"

"No. It doesn't."

"I know it sounds *insane*, but I really think it was him."

"It doesn't sound insane."

"Well, of *course*, it sounds insane, Dakota. *Byron's dead!*"

Dakota sat beside her. She propped her elbows on her knees and wrapped both hands around her cup. She blew gently on her coffee. She stared thoughtfully at the floor. "If you believe it's real," she said at last, "then it's real."

Lucy's tone was bitter. "But haven't you heard? I hit my head in the accident. I have flashbacks and I forget things. I'm prone to delusions, and I make things up. Most of the time, I don't even know what I'm talking about."

"That's crap."

Surprised, Lucy watched as Dakota looked up, took a cautious sip of coffee, then turned to face her.

"You are not delusional," Dakota said calmly. "You are brave. And you are gifted. And I am certainly not the person who's going to think you're imagining things."

Lucy hadn't expected this. It was such a shock and such a relief that quick tears sprang to her eyes. For a long moment, she couldn't even speak.

"Weren't you listening to a single thing I said upstairs?" Dakota went on. "I told you, I believe in everything."

"But you told me you didn't see anyone out in the courtyard."

"I didn't. But that doesn't mean *you* didn't." Dakota blew on her coffee again. "Reality's in the eye of the beholder."

"But what if you don't *know* what's real anymore?"

Dakota's gaze was steady and serene. "*You know*, Lucy. You have an aura about you . . . a special kind of energy I've never felt before. Except from one other person."

Mystified, Lucy stared at her. Dakota reached out and squeezed Lucy's hand.

"Byron," Dakota said softly. "I felt it with Byron. He had a gift, and so do you. Only yours is much, much stronger. Maybe even stronger than you realize."

18

"Dakota . . . what are you saying?"

A hint of a smile crossed Dakota's face. She tucked her legs beneath her and settled back against the cushions.

"I remember the first time I saw Byron," Dakota explained. "He came into the bookstore, and the whole atmosphere changed."

"I don't understand."

"I told you . . . it's like this individual energy that every person gives off. I didn't know Byron then, but when he walked through that door, it was like a physical shift in the air. I knew there was something very different . . . very special . . . about him. But I never knew what."

Lucy gave a curt nod. She was fascinated by Dakota's observations and wanted to hear more.

"I'd heard stories about his sister, of course—being psychic, being a witch, being a fortune-teller. But people turn cruel when they don't understand someone. And Byron was really protective of her. So I didn't pay much attention to all the rumors."

Lucy felt tension building inside her. The temptation to blurt everything out, to reveal everything to Dakota was suddenly unbearable. Through sheer willpower, she forced her emotions down again, kept her face impassive, focused on Dakota's narrative.

"But with Byron," Dakota continued, "something was definitely there."

"But . . . you don't know what it was."

"No." Dakota took a sip of coffee. "But I think *you* do."

Lucy looked out the window. She could hear the scrape of Mr. Montana's chair, could hear him going through the shop turning off lights. She felt Dakota lean forward again on the couch.

"Lucy, trust your instincts," Dakota said urgently. "Don't let anyone tell you they're not true."

Without waiting for a reply, Dakota began gathering up their books and papers. It was almost as if nothing out of the ordinary had happened tonight, and Lucy sat for a few minutes longer, letting it all sink in.

"Dad and I are stopping for something to eat," Dakota finally said. "Why don't you come with us?"

"No, I really can't. But thanks."

"Are you going to be okay?"

Still avoiding eye contact, Lucy nodded. "I'm okay."

"Then we'll at least give you a ride to your car."

Lucy was glad for the escort. This old section of Pine Ridge reminded her of a ghost town now, and her car was the only one in the lot.

"Be careful going home," Dakota warned her. "There's a bunch of one-way streets around here, and it's easy to get turned around."

Lucy watched the Montanas drive off. She let the motor idle and waited for the heater to warm up. Her thoughts were clamoring for attention, but she couldn't sort them out. All she could concentrate on was the fact that

Dakota hadn't asked for any explanations, hadn't expected any confidences, hadn't questioned her sanity.

Dakota had believed her.

Hadn't she?

Lucy rested her cheek on the steering wheel. It had been so long since she'd felt validated by anyone that suspicions began creeping in. Maybe Dakota was just pretending. Maybe she was just some weirdo who enjoyed acting out supernatural fantasies. Maybe she was just trying to get close to Lucy so she could play another cruel trick on her.

Yet Lucy didn't think so.

"Trust your instincts . . . don't let anyone tell you they're not true."

And Lucy's instincts were telling her now that Dakota believed her. That Dakota was a friend.

Sitting up straight, Lucy adjusted the heater and switched on her headlights. Then she pulled onto the street and started for home.

It didn't take her long to realize she was lost.

Landmarks started looking way too familiar, and after an endless series of frustrating turns, Lucy saw that she'd been going in a complete circle. *Come on, don't panic—after all, this is a small town . . .*

She tried to recall the exact sequence of street names Dakota had given her. But despite her best efforts, Lucy eventually found herself in a neighborhood of run-down houses and broken streetlights, with no clue as to how she'd gotten there.

Damn! Swearing under her breath, she looked for a place to turn around. The houses were spaced wide apart, the yards neglected and overgrown, with wide patches of shadows in between. As she started into a driveway, a dog suddenly lunged toward the car, barking furiously. Lucy jerked the wheel hard to the left. She felt the car swerve, then bump noisily over something piled along the curb. To her relief, she spotted a cul-de-sac at the end of the street and immediately stepped on the gas.

One house stood alone in the cul-de-sac. An old Victorian surrounded by tall trees and clipped hedges and a picket fence without a gate. Though it had definitely seen better days, it looked more well kept than the other houses on the block, and a porch light cast a welcoming glow over the leaded glass in the front door.

Lucy couldn't help staring at it as she drove into the circle. She was still staring at it, in fact, when she suddenly became aware of the car leaning to one side and the slapping sound coming from underneath the front end.

Oh, no . . . don't tell me . . .

Shifting into park, Lucy jumped out and gazed in dismay at the flat tire.

Great. Now what am I supposed to do?

She didn't know how to change a tire. She didn't have a clue where any gas stations were, or if any were even open at this hour. And a flat tire hardly qualified as a 911 emergency. Grabbing her cell phone, she dialed Irene's number and let it ring. And ring. And ring. When the answering machine finally came on, Lucy left a message. Then she clicked off in disgust.

She couldn't just wait here all night—God only knew when her aunt would get home. She'd left Matt's phone number on her dresser, so that was useless; she'd left the business card Dakota had given her, too. And even if she called Information for the Montanas' home number, Dakota and her dad wouldn't be back yet anyway.

Totally frustrated, Lucy looked over at the isolated house. She didn't have a choice, really—there was only one thing to do.

Shutting off the car, she slammed the door and locked it.

Then she took a deep breath, squared her shoulders, and marched determinedly up the steps to the front porch.

19

There was a black wreath on the door.

Lucy hadn't noticed it from the street, because it was hidden in shadows. But now she could see the black crepe and black ribbons, the dried black flowers and tiny black jewels, all woven together in an intricate, antique design.

She'd seen something like this once before. But it had been a picture in a book—a black wreath hung upon a door, an old-fashioned custom to show that someone in the house had died.

Lucy hesitated. The last thing she wanted to do was intrude on a family's grief. If someone in this house had indeed died recently, maybe she should go somewhere else.

She was still trying to make up her mind when the door swung open.

Startled, Lucy found herself confronted by a tall, bony woman with a sour face, pointed chin, and frizzy gray hair. A starched apron was tied over her shapeless brown dress, and she was drying her hands on a dish towel.

"What is it?" the woman snapped.

Lucy quickly recovered herself. "I'm sorry to bother you, but—"

"I saw you lurking out here—don't you know what time it is? Well, whatever it is you're selling, I don't want it."

"I'm not selling anything. I'm just having car trouble."

The woman eyed her suspiciously. "Look at you. You been in some kind of wreck?"

"I . . ." Lucy's hand went self-consciously to the bruises on her face. "I . . . tripped on the stairs."

The woman considered this. Then she craned her neck and squinted toward the street. "Is that your car?"

"I've got a flat tire—I was wondering if I could use your phone book."

"A flat tire, you say? I don't see any flat tire."

"Yes, it's right there on the passenger side.

There in front." Lucy felt the woman's sharp gaze rake over her, head to foot. "Please. I just need someone to change it."

"Well, *I* can't change it. There's nobody here who can change it."

"I meant, I need to call someone."

"Why don't you call your parents?"

"I tried, but nobody's home."

"That's the trouble with kids these days. Parents never around when they should be."

Keeping respectfully silent, Lucy endured several more minutes of scrutiny. Then, apparently satisfied she wasn't going to be mugged by a desperate teenage girl, the woman motioned Lucy inside.

Despite the well-worn exterior of the house, the hall was clean and shiny. Lucy could smell floor wax and lemon polish and the faint scent of lavender as she was ushered into a small, snug living room. And though the furniture looked antiquated, there wasn't a speck of dust anywhere.

It didn't seem like a house where someone had died, Lucy thought. No flower arrangements, no stacks of sympathy cards, no all-pervasive feelings of sorrow and emptiness and despair. Maybe the people who lived here just liked black wreaths.

"Phone book's over there." The woman jerked her chin toward the far wall. "Phone, too. And don't be leaving any smudges on that desk."

"I won't. Thank you."

"What are you doing out this late anyway? Can't be anything good, young person out this late."

"I was on my way home and got lost. I was just trying to find somewhere to turn around."

"Hmmm. Turn around or scope out the neighborhood?"

Lucy ignored the accusation. "I haven't lived here very long. And I'm really bad with directions."

She walked over and picked up the phone book. The woman stood in the doorway and watched.

"Do you know who I could call?" Lucy asked politely. "A gas station? A garage?"

"What do you think this is, New York City? You're not going to find anyone this time of night. Everything's closed."

Lucy's heart sank. She laid the telephone book on the desk.

"Oh. Well . . . thanks anyway."

"Thanks for what? You didn't call anybody. And your tire's not fixed."

Lucy sighed. "Thanks for . . . letting me in."

But as she reached the front door, the woman stopped her. "Where do you think you're going?"

"My cell phone's in the car. I left a message on my aunt's machine—she might be trying to reach me."

"People talk too loud on those cell phones, act like they're the only ones in the world who have something to say. Well, let me tell you . . . nobody cares about hearing their business."

I should introduce you to Mr. Montana, Lucy thought, but aloud she said, "Well . . . I only use it for emergencies."

"So in the meantime you're just going to sit out there in the cold? Catch pneumonia? Get your purse snatched? Or worse?"

Lucy was getting irritated. It had been a long day, an emotional night, and she wasn't in the mood for any more upsets.

"It's not like I have many options," she replied, more sarcastically than she'd meant to.

The woman's lips pinched tight. "Come into the kitchen. Take off your coat, and put it in that closet. And for heaven's sake, hang it up neat."

Surprised, Lucy did as she was told. When she entered the kitchen, she saw gleaming countertops, a well-scrubbed, though outdated, stove, and a table with a blue flowered cloth. Pots of ivy lined the windowsill over the sink, and a large gray cat peered at her from beneath one of the straight-backed chairs.

"You like pie?" The woman's back was turned away from Lucy, bent inside a pantry, taking out dishes.

"I love pie."

"Then sit down. You don't eat pie very often, I can tell. Home cooking either. You're puny."

Lucy sat. She could feel the cat rubbing against her legs, could hear its loud purr of contentment.

"One more thing wrong with kids today," the woman went on. "Never have a decent meal. Never sit down as a family. Too many divorces."

Since she didn't get the feeling that she was expected to answer, Lucy kept quiet. She leaned down and scratched the cat behind its ears.

"There were ten of us when I was growing up. Dinnertime was nonnegotiable. We all had chores to do. Made us learn responsibility. Made us appreciate what we had."

Lucy watched as a pie was sliced, transferred to a plate, and shoved into the microwave. Within seconds, the warm fragrance of apples and cinnamon and buttery crust filled the room. She heard her stomach rumble. She'd forgotten just how hungry she was.

"Kids today expect handouts. Something for nothing, and right when they want it." Indignantly, the woman set a plate and fork down in front of Lucy. "Use that napkin there. And don't make crumbs all over the table."

It was the best pie Lucy had ever tasted. Flaky and sweet, it melted in her mouth and warmed her all the way down.

"This is wonderful," Lucy sighed, feeling almost as contented as the cat. "Really, this was just so nice of you. I didn't want you to go to any trouble."

"If it was trouble, I wouldn't have done it."

The woman pulled out a chair. She sat down across the table, took a tissue from her apron pocket, and dabbed it over her brow. Lucy swallowed another bite of pie.

"So you haven't lived here very long." The woman had obviously been thinking about this. "*How* long?"

"Just a few weeks."

"You go to church?"

"I . . . really haven't decided on a particular church yet."

"You should go to church. Young people today—no morals. No values. That's what happens when you don't go to church." She leaned toward Lucy with a frown. "There's a new priest at All Souls. He's too young to be a *good* priest, but with Father Paul having problems, we're stuck with him."

Lucy stared at her. "You mean Father Matt?"

"And how can I call him Father? It's like calling my grandson Father."

"I've met Father Matt," Lucy told her. "He's one of the grief counselors at my school."

"And what would he know about counseling

people? He hasn't lived long enough to counsel anybody."

Giving a noncommittal shrug, Lucy casually checked her watch. Where *was* Irene, anyway? What if she'd been home for hours and just hadn't checked her answering machine? *How long will it take her to realize I'm gone? How long will it take her to notice the time and—*

"So you didn't have time to know Byron, I guess."

Lucy's head came up. The woman's eyes were narrowed on her like lasers. The last bite of pie stuck in her throat, and she struggled to choke it down.

"As if his grandmother hasn't been through enough already," the woman added, not giving Lucy a chance to reply. "Well, it's not my place to say anything, is it? I'm just helping out. You've heard what you've heard at school already, so you know how he died in that wreck. But he was a good kid, not like most. Took care of his grandmother, just the two of them. Oh, there was an older girl once—mad as a March hare. But she took off, and no one's heard from her since."

A strange feeling of dread began to creep over Lucy. A feeling of secrets and doom, of being in the wrong place at the worst possible time.

"That's him there," the woman said, pointing. As Lucy's eyes moved to the refrigerator, she noticed for the first time a small photograph stuck to the door with a magnet. "That's Byron. Sad. He was such a good-looking boy."

Oh my God . . .

Lucy's throat was closing. Closing up around that wedged bit of food, so that she couldn't swallow, couldn't breathe. Her chest was squeezing. Her hands were frozen on the tabletop.

"This . . ." She could barely get the words out. "This . . . is his house?"

"Didn't you know?"

The woman got up and walked to the refrigerator. Lucy couldn't move, not even when the photograph was thrust in front of her.

"Well, I guess you *wouldn't* know," the woman concluded, "since you haven't lived here that long."

"You're Mrs. Dempsey," Lucy mumbled, and those flinty eyes bored into her once again.

"Have we met?"

"No. Father Matt told me you were staying with Byron's grandmother."

"She's bedridden. Stroke. Been that way for a long time. Oh, the nurse comes, but Mrs. Wetherly appreciates *little* things the nurse can't make time for. Fresh flowers every so often. Nice music. Being read to. Company when she's not too tired."

Mrs. Dempsey returned the photo to its rightful place. Then she studied Lucy with a pensive frown.

"In fact, maybe you should go back and see her. Since you're from Byron's school. Just to say hello."

The kitchen walls gave a crazy lurch, rocking the chair with them. Lucy held on tighter to the edge of the table.

"I don't want to bother her," she whispered.

"You won't. Come with me."

There was no getting out of it. As Lucy took the long walk down the hall, she felt like a prisoner bound for the execution chamber. She could see an open door at the end of the corridor. A glow of light spilling over the threshold, slanting across throw rugs on the floor.

Please, please, let her be asleep . . . please just let me slip out again without her ever knowing . . .

Lucy wanted to turn, to run—but she had images of Mrs. Dempsey grabbing her by the neck and throttling her into submission.

"In here," Mrs. Dempsey said. She stopped just inside the doorway, and Lucy could see the old-fashioned bed, and the mounds of fluffy white covers, and the soft, stacked pillows trimmed in lace.

"Odelia," Mrs. Dempsey announced, "here's one of Byron's friends to say hello."

The frail figure lying there seemed pitifully lost among the bed linens. As Lucy gripped the edge of the footboard, she could see how small Byron's grandmother was, how pale and still, her face a mass of wrinkles, her long braid of silver hair draped across one shoulder of her cream-colored nightgown.

But to Lucy's distress, Mrs. Wetherly wasn't asleep. In fact, her huge dark eyes, every bit as dark as Byron's had been, were directed toward the end of the bed, resting calmly on Lucy's face.

"She can hear you," Mrs. Dempsey advised Lucy in an undertone. "She can understand you, and she can move her left arm a little. But she can't talk. So she uses those things there."

She indicated a small slate and piece of chalk on the nightstand. Lucy managed a stiff nod.

"Well, go on," Mrs. Dempsey insisted, nudging her. "You can't visit clear across the room. Tell her your name."

But Lucy's feet were rooted to the floor. She tried to open her mouth. Her tongue was like cotton; her lips wouldn't move.

"Well, tell her your name, for heaven's sake. You expect her to read your mind?" As Byron's grandmother made a weak gesture, Mrs. Dempsey pushed Lucy forward. "Give her the chalk, and hold the slate so she can reach it."

Lucy felt sick. She crossed the short distance to the bed, wondering desperately what to do. She couldn't tell the truth—she just couldn't. That Byron had died was devastating enough. But that *she* was still alive, standing here in his grandmother's bedroom—that was just too horrible for anyone to bear.

The old woman's eyes had never left her. Even as Lucy picked up the stub of chalk and placed it in the blue-veined hand, those faded eyes continued to watch her, showing no hint of emotion. She heard the doorbell ring and fought a moment of panic as Mrs. Dempsey marched from the room.

But still the words refused to come. Words of comfort, words of remorse—though they tore at Lucy's heart and welled up into tears, she just couldn't bring herself to speak them aloud.

And then, to her amazement, Mrs. Wetherly's hand began to move.

Slowly . . . painstakingly . . . the old woman's fingers clawed around the chalk . . . motioned at the slate. Lucy lowered it in front of her. Held it tightly as the gnarled hand began to write.

The letters were like a child's letters. Crooked and crude, but clearly readable as they printed across the blank surface of the slate.

Lucy stared at them in silence. Four clumsy letters that she recognized at once.

L U C Y.

20

"Oh God," Lucy whispered. "Oh God . . . how did you know?"

The old woman's eyes looked deep into hers. In the dark fixed stare Lucy saw a sorrow that was endless . . . and a compassion that was immeasurable.

The sheer power of it left her breathless.

Unconsciously she took a step back, but before she could look away, Lucy saw something else.

Something forming in the depths of Mrs. Wetherly's eyes . . . something gazing back at her . . . haunting and achingly familiar . . .

Byron's face.

Byron's face trapped there in the dark . . .

"No," Lucy mumbled, "no, it's not possible . . ."

Somehow she made it out of the room and

down the hall. She snatched her coat from the closet, not even bothering to put it on. Fumbling with the lock on the front door, she didn't hear Mrs. Dempsey calling from the kitchen, wasn't aware of the footsteps approaching, until hands suddenly grabbed her shoulders and turned her around.

"Lucy!" Matt exclaimed. "What are you doing here?"

Lucy's head was throbbing, her eyes blurry with unshed tears. She jerked away from Matt and resumed her struggle with the door.

"Mrs. Dempsey told me someone had a flat tire, but I didn't know it was you." Reaching out, Matt pried her hands from the doorknob and took them in his own. "Lucy, it's not a problem. I'll be glad to give you another ride home."

"I don't want a ride home!" Lucy's thoughts were spinning—she couldn't get the image of Byron's face out of her mind. *It wasn't real—I just thought it was. Their eyes are the same, that's all. Just the eyes are the same, just the eyes, that's all it was, the rest of it was just in my mind.* "I'm sure Irene's called by now. I just need my phone. I need to get my phone from the car."

"I'll get your phone—you stay in here where it's warm. What a coincidence I happened to stop by at the same time you did."

"I didn't stop by. I didn't even *plan* to stop by. I never should have come inside, I never should have stayed. I want to go. I need to go!"

"You mean . . ."

Matt finally seemed to be comprehending the situation. For an instant he looked disconcerted.

"You didn't even know whose house this was, did you?" he asked her at last. "You didn't have a clue it was Byron's grandmother."

Lucy turned back to the door. *She knew me— how could she possibly have known me?* Shaking her head, Lucy kept silent. She heard Matt sigh deeply behind her.

"Right," Matt mumbled under his breath. "What are the odds?"

And I saw Byron . . . Byron in her eyes . . .

"Save that tea for me, will you Mrs. Dempsey?" Matt shrugged into his jacket and ushered Lucy out the front door, leaving the woman to stare after them in bewilderment.

"Lucy, I can't imagine what a shock that must

have been for you. How'd you end up here anyway?"

"I don't know," she answered miserably. "I kept taking wrong turns and hitting dead ends. And then I was on this street, and I saw the porch light."

"Let me take a look at that tire."

Lucy watched impatiently as Matt knelt down by the Corvette. But after a thorough inspection, he shook his head

"It's split wide open; you'll have to get a new one." He stood and brushed off the knees of his jeans. "Okay, two options. I can put your spare on right now, or I can take you home."

"Please. I just want to go."

"Then I'll call a tow truck for you in the morning, and you can pick it up sometime tomorrow. Glen's Repair over on Hawthorne Street. It's the one Father Paul uses, and that antique car of his still runs like a dream. So I figure this Glen guy must be some kind of miracle worker."

Lucy took her backpack from the car and locked the doors. Then she followed Matt to his Jeep and got in.

"How come you're out this late?" Matt asked curiously as they wound their way out of the neighborhood. "Not that this is *late*, of course—but late for Pine Ridge."

Lucy stared at the dashboard. The heater was on, but hadn't had a chance to warm up. Unconsciously, she held her hands out toward the vents.

"I was studying with a friend. Her family has this old bookstore in Pine Corners."

"Dakota Montana, right? Yeah, I've been to that bookstore—it's pretty amazing. You could spend hours poking around and still not see everything."

"I saw Byron," Lucy said.

Her eyes widened slowly as she realized what she'd said. *Oh God . . . why did I do that?*

From the corner of her eye, she caught Matt's quick glance. "You . . . what?"

Should she pursue it? Go into detail? Hadn't she acted crazy enough around Matt for one night?

"I was looking out the window. And I thought I saw Byron," she mumbled at last.

"Oh. You *thought* you saw him."

Lucy shut her eyes. "I *did* see him."

An uncomfortable silence settled between them. Lucy opened her eyes again, and focused on her outstretched hands. When Matt finally spoke, his voice was gentle.

"Where? Where'd you see him?"

"Don't talk to me like that."

Matt was surprised. "Like what?"

"Like you'd talk to some three-year-old with imaginary friends. I'm not making it up. And I'm not crazy."

"Lucy—"

"No. I'm tired of people not believing me. I'm tired of people treating me like I belong in a mental institution. And you know, it's all such bullshit. Everybody says *talk* about it—get it *out* so you can move on with your life. But when I *do* talk about it, everyone says oh dear, she's *hallucinating*. It's the *head* injury, it's the *pain* medication."

"Lucy—"

"Out of all the houses I could have picked to ask for help tonight, why was it *that* house? And do you know what happened when Mrs. Dempsey made me go into that bedroom?

Byron's grandmother *knew* me! She wrote my name on her slate! How could she know me, she's never even seen me before!"

"Well, maybe—"

"No. Just listen to me. If you don't believe when I *tell* you things, then maybe you'll believe something you can *see*. Maybe you'll believe *this*."

Furiously, Lucy dug into her backpack. She found the notebook she'd wedged in there earlier, and yanked it out, spilling papers all over the front seat. As Matt kept one eye on her and the other on the street, she started flipping through the pages.

"So you think it's all just in my mind? Then what do you think about solid proof? What do you think about messages written in blood?"

Matt pulled over to the curb. He put the Jeep in park and gave Lucy his full and silent attention. As Lucy kept turning the pages of the notebook, her movements grew more frantic. She got to the end, and a look of confusion struck her face. Immediately she began flipping backward, then forward again, then back. Jerking up the notebook, she turned it sideways and shook it violently, trying to dislodge any loose papers that might be stuck inside. Confusion turned to disbelief. Disbelief turned to desperation.

"Lucy," Matt said quietly.

"No! It was *here*! Someone put it in my notebook, and it was *here*! I *saw* it! It can't be gone—there's no *way* it could be gone! I had it with me every minute, and then I locked the car!"

But then she remembered.

She remembered placing her backpack behind the counter at the bookstore. Going off with Dakota for a tour. Not checking the backpack again when they'd sat down to study. Not checking again after she'd gone to search for Byron and Dakota had gone in search of her. Just assuming the notebook was still there, exactly where she'd left it.

"Someone must have taken it," she murmured now. "Someone must have taken it at the bookstore. That's the only place it could have happened."

But maybe it had happened while she was inside the Wetherly house. Maybe someone had broken into the car, then locked it up again. Anyone could do that . . . an expert could do that. Someone who enjoyed playing mean, cruel tricks could do that or . . .

Someone who follows me. Someone who watches. Someone who hides in the shadows of a cave . . .

She looked beseechingly at Matt. "It said, 'very soon.'"

And she suddenly realized that Matt had ahold of her hands and was leaning toward her, his brow creased with worry, his eyes full of sadness and sympathy.

"What did, Lucy?" he asked her.

"The message. The warning. It was in my notebook when I opened it this morning. It said, 'Very soon, Lucy.' And it was the color of dried blood. In fact, I'm *sure* it was dried blood—it *looked* like dried blood . . ."

Her voice trailed away. She felt Matt draw her closer, and as all the strength drained out of her, Lucy pressed her head against his chest.

"I don't know how it got there, Matt," she whispered. "And I don't know how it disappeared."

She closed her eyes and kept very still. She

could feel the warmth of his jacket and the strong beat of his heart. She could feel the steady vibration of the car, and the rush of heat from the vents.

She could feel Matt smoothing back her hair.

She could feel his arms starting around her, and his sudden hesitation, and the way he shifted away from her then, ever so slightly.

"Lucy." His voice was low. "I want you to have this."

Lucy drew back. She watched Matt reach up and remove a chain from around his neck. He stared at it for a moment, then eased it carefully over her head.

"What are you doing?" she asked, surprised.

The chain was thin, but sturdy. It slid into place, its small, round medallion resting lightly upon the front of her coat.

"Someone gave me this a long time ago." Matt smiled faintly, as though remembering. "It's helped me through some pretty rough times. Maybe you could give it a try."

"Oh, Matt . . ."

Lucy didn't know what to say. Lifting the medallion, she held it up close, trying to see the design. In the dim interior of the Jeep, it appeared to be carved with some sort of pattern, but one that Lucy didn't recognize.

"It's an ancient holy symbol," Matt explained.

"It's beautiful. But, Matt, I can't keep it."

"Why not?"

"Because it's special to you. You can't just give it to me like this."

"But I just did. And now I hope it'll be special to *you*."

Then, before Lucy could protest, he switched his attention to the steering wheel.

"Better get you home," he said quickly.

And it wasn't till much later, when Lucy was lying awake in bed, that she realized she'd never even asked him what the symbol meant.

21

She dreamed she was back at the tomb.

Back in the old cemetery, standing outside the Wetherly mausoleum.

She was alone.

And someone was following her.

In the nightmare, Lucy looked back over her shoulder, into the pitch-black night, through the wind-lashed trees, beyond the pounding rain. Thunder shook the ground beneath her feet. Thunder loud enough to wake the dead.

She pressed her face against the wrought-iron gates of the family crypt. The gates were locked, but she wrapped her hands tightly around the tall spikes and began to pull. Lightning flashed overhead, throwing the graveyard in and out of shadow. And with every stab of lightning, she caught just a glimpse of the tomb's cold interior, the leaf-littered floor, and the catacombed walls.

Terror rose inside her. The terror of being stalked, the terror of imminent danger.

The rain fell harder.

The air reeked of death.

Without any warning, the gates swung open. Yet Lucy remained on the crumbling steps, powerless to move.

"Byron," she called, "Byron, please help me!"

And then a voice—*his* voice—faint and sad and empty, from somewhere she couldn't see . . .

"Keep away," he warned her. "There's no one in this place."

Lucy shot up in bed.

Her heart was racing, and her nightgown was damp with sweat.

As she tossed back her covers, the last bits and pieces of dreaming clutched at her mind before fading and vanishing altogether.

She was out of breath. She swung her feet to the floor and padded barefoot to the sliding glass doors, parting the curtains and gazing out at the darkness.

Snow flittered against a velvet backdrop of night.

The pane felt icy to her touch, yet her body pulsed with heat.

That ache again.

That deep, insistent ache that made her want to moan, that ache that couldn't be filled.

Slowly she drew her nightgown off over her head.

She pressed her naked body to the glass, savoring the smooth, shocking cold against her skin.

How she longed to be out in that darkness.

Out beyond the backyard wall . . . out beyond those trees shining silver beneath the moon . . .

For some weird, unknown reason, the longing to be outside was suddenly—almost painfully—overwhelming.

Lucy started to unlock the doors, then remembered the security system was on. If only she could step out to the balcony, feel the snowflakes on her cheeks, the wind through her hair. The room was getting warmer; the walls were closing in. She couldn't stand being here one more second. Grabbing her robe from the foot of the bed, she slipped it on and tiptoed through the silence of the house.

She paused to disarm the security system. Her breath was coming faster now, her heart fluttering in anticipation. As though she were bound for some forbidden rendezvous. As though the night were her secret lover.

Without a sound, Lucy crept out the back door.

The wind loosened the sash at her waist, blowing her robe open and easing it down off her shoulders. It whipped around her as she spread her arms wide and embraced the cold.

Stimulating . . . invigorating . . . it made her feel strangely alive.

As though sorrow had never touched her . . .

As though she *belonged* somewhere . . .

"Lucy? What in heaven's name are you doing?"

The voice came from behind her. Startled, Lucy hastily tied her robe together and turned to see Irene hovering in the kitchen doorway.

"Lucy," her aunt asked again, but more puzzled than angry, "*what* are you doing out here?"

"I . . ."

Lucy stared back in confused silence. Irene obviously expected some sort of answer from her, but the longer Lucy stared, the more she began to realize that she didn't actually *know* what she was doing out here. Out here in the cold and the snow, in the middle of the night.

"I . . . needed some air."

It was the only thing her brain could come up with on such short notice. She shivered violently and realized she had nothing on her feet.

"Come back inside." Irene's frown was colder than the temperature. "Honestly, Lucy, this makes me wonder if Dr. Fielding should increase your medication. Instead of acting so foolishly, why didn't you just adjust the thermostat?"

Lucy took the scolding in her stride.

She went back to her room, donned a pair of flannel pajamas, and piled more blankets on the bed.

And then she stood there in the darkness,

peering out through the sliding glass doors, hugging herself against the chill that lingered in her veins.

She stared off across the lawn and past the low stone wall, and she realized that something had changed.

Something about the night.

Something that made it different now . . . different in a way she couldn't quite understand.

Almost as though it had been alive before . . .

But now, it was only a dream.

22

"You haven't said three words since we sat down," Dakota chided gently. "And you haven't touched your lunch."

Startled from her reverie, Lucy gave her friend a guilty look. "Sorry. I just don't have much of an appetite, I guess."

"I guess, too," Dakota echoed. "Lucy, you have to start eating better—you need to keep up your strength." Then, when Lucy didn't respond, she added, "Are you still worried about your notebook? I'll ask my dad about it, but I'm sure he'd have seen it behind the counter if you left it."

She watched as Lucy picked up a napkin, folded it into fourths, then absentmindedly dropped it on the table.

"Is it your aunt?" Dakota tried again.

Lucy looked down at her plastic tray. "You know, it's a sad state of affairs when school cafeteria food looks better than what you get at your own house."

"You didn't answer my question."

"Okay," Lucy sighed. "She caught me by surprise. Even though I should know better by now."

"I can't believe it either. I mean, what kind of mother takes off like that when her daughter's still missing?"

"Dr. Fielding advised her to go. He said it would be therapeutic. He said she couldn't do anything here anyway, except worry and be constantly reminded that Angela's gone. And she can stay in touch with the private investigator anywhere."

"Still . . . I think it's sad. It's like she's already decided that Angela's not coming home."

"It's so dark here . . . I can't get back . . ."

Remembering the ghostly telephone call, Lucy's shoulders stiffened. "Maybe she *has* to decide that. Maybe it's the only way she can cope."

"Maybe." Dakota gave a reluctant nod. "But it

215

sort of makes you understand why Angela's run away so many times, doesn't it?"

But this is the last time. The thought loomed darkly in Lucy's mind, though she tried to push it away. *This is the last time Angela will ever leave . . .*

"Lucy, I'll be leaving for a while. On very important business."

Irene's announcement had come that morning while she was driving Lucy to school. An announcement that was so casual and matter of fact, that at first Lucy hadn't even realized its magnitude.

"We're experiencing some difficulties with one of our foreign-exchange programs. It's necessary that I go to Paris and help with the reorganization."

Lucy had waited, not exactly sure what was coming next. Irene had cast her a pensive sidelong glance.

"It's going to take at least two weeks. Perhaps more. And frankly, I'm not sure what to do with you."

That's when the reality of the situation had

begun to sink in. And though Lucy felt stunned and hurt, she'd managed to shrug it off with a forced smile.

"You don't have to worry about me, Aunt Irene. I'll be fine."

"There's really no one I can think of to leave you with," her aunt had gone on, as though she found this mildly annoying. "And Florence can't be here full-time; she has a family and other clients to take care of."

"You don't have to ask Florence. It's not like I need a babysitter or anything."

A slight frown had settled between Irene's brows. "If you were Angela, I'd have to nag you about being responsible. I'd have to warn you not to let strangers into the house and not to throw wild parties while I was gone."

Lucy hadn't answered. She hadn't known what to say.

"But you're not Angela," Irene had concluded.

A pause had settled between them. And to Lucy's astonishment, Irene's eyes had suddenly glimmered with tears.

"And it's not your fault, Lucy," she'd said softly. "What happened is not your fault. I do not want you blaming yourself for any of Angela's rash behavior."

For one split second, Lucy had almost leaned toward her aunt. Almost touched her. Almost given her a hug.

But then the tears had vanished, leaving Irene's eyes as cold and hard as before.

"She'll come home. Eventually." As the car pulled up in front of the school, Irene's tone had suddenly matched her eyes. "When he breaks her heart . . . when she runs out of money. She'll come home like all the times before."

"Aunt Irene—"

"Don't be late, Lucy."

Crestfallen, Lucy had gotten out of the car.

She'd stood there on the sidewalk, and she'd even waved good-bye.

But Irene had never looked back . . .

". . . till she gets back," Dakota was saying.

Lucy looked up from her lumpy macaroni and cheese. The noise in the cafeteria was deafening, and she hadn't realized till this very minute how much her head was beginning to ache.

"Till *who* gets back?" she asked.

Dakota stopped sucking on her orange. She ran one hand slowly through her hair, her eyes fixed calmly on Lucy's face. "We were talking about your aunt."

"Sorry. I guess I zoned out for a minute."

"Oh, that's good. I thought maybe it was me zoning." Dakota slid her tray to the edge of the table. "I was just saying that you could stay with me while your aunt's gone. My parents would be totally okay with it."

"I couldn't do that. It's really nice of you, and I appreciate it, but . . ."

"But what?"

"But I just couldn't, that's all."

After a second's hesitation, Dakota reached over and squeezed Lucy's hand. "I don't know everything you've been through, Lucy. And I know this is none of my business. But I don't think you should be alone right now. So promise me you'll at least think about staying over."

"Yes." Lucy forced a weak smile. "I promise."

"When's she leaving, anyway?"

"Next week sometime."

"Well, you'd definitely start *eating* at my house," Dakota informed her. "My mom and dad are both great cooks. And I bet you'd sleep, too."

"I sleep now."

But Dakota wasn't fooled. Releasing Lucy's hand, she leaned even closer, a wise sadness in her eyes. "Be honest with me, Lucy—when's the last time you *really* slept? A sleep without nightmares . . . a sleep without pain?"

And Lucy couldn't answer.

Because she truly couldn't remember . . .

She'd stayed awake till morning.

Still restless from her need to be outside, Lucy had paced her bedroom in the dark, and she'd stared out for hours through the sliding glass doors. She'd sat on the bed with her arms wrapped around her, trying to give herself comfort. And she'd rocked back and forth, back and forth, but it hadn't lulled her to sleep.

As if she hadn't had enough on her mind already.

After Matt brought her home, she'd had more than enough to think about, a whole new set of fears to consider. She'd felt numb and strangely distant, as though her emotions belonged to someone else. For a while she'd held the medallion Matt had given her, turning it over and over in her hands. Then she'd put it in the drawer of the nightstand and collapsed on her bed, shutting her eyes and trying desperately to shut out the rest of the world.

A world she no longer trusted or understood.

A world of questions without answers.

The message in her notebook . . . Byron's face at the bookstore window . . . a series of wrong turns leading her straight to the Wetherly house . . .

And Byron's grandmother . . . Byron's reflection in those sad, dark eyes . . .

How did she know my name?

Lucy had lain there, too exhausted to move, and praying for sleep. Deep, senseless, peaceful sleep. Kind sleep . . . sleep without dreams.

But of course she hadn't slept.

Not then.

Not while those questions and conjectures had continued to rush blackly through her mind, like bats swarming at dusk from their cave.

Byron must have mentioned her, she'd decided.

At some point, Byron must have mentioned Lucy's name to his grandmother—or described her, maybe—and that's how his grandmother had known.

Yet how could Lucy explain the rest of it? Like her tire going flat, so conveniently near Byron's house? And Byron's grandmother recognizing her from countless other blond-haired, blue-eyed girls who might have happened to knock on her door?

"Mrs. Wetherly was propped up in bed, almost as if she'd been waiting for us. She didn't even look surprised. Just so sad . . . calm . . . resigned, almost."

Matt's words had come back to her then.

Matt's account of the night Byron died— when Matt and Father Paul and the sheriff and doctor had all gone to tell Byron's grandmother the news.

Could it be true?

Yielding reluctantly to her memories, Lucy had opened her eyes and stared hard at the ceiling. Byron had told her once that his grandmother had psychic powers, the ability to "know" things other people weren't privy to. Could it be that Mrs.

Wetherly had *expected* Lucy to show up there?

Could it be that she led *me there* deliberately?

The idea had been too chilling to contemplate.

So Lucy had gone into the bathroom and run a hot shower. She'd stood there under the steamy spray, but her mind had continued to fret.

Should I go back to Byron's house? Tell his grandmother how much he helped me, how much he meant to me?

Or should I stay away from there forever?

And even beneath the soothing flow of the water, Lucy had felt bruised and battered by indecision.

How much does Byron's grandmother know about me? How much did Byron tell her? Does she know about Katherine's horrible death? And how I found Katherine that night in the cemetery, and how Katherine changed me forever?

Lucy had leaned her head against the shower wall, picturing Byron's house again. The second-floor windows had been dark, she remembered. Windows where Katherine had stared out at an unsympathetic world . . . windows that had become Katherine's prison.

And suddenly her heart had ached for Katherine.

Ached and cried for Katherine.

Not only for the girl's heartless death, but for the life she'd been denied. Denied because of her powers. Denied because of her gift.

"A gift sometimes . . . but also a curse," Byron had called it.

And now it belonged to Lucy.

And as the shower washed away her tears, she'd wondered about her own life and the strange direction it had taken.

And she'd asked herself—as Dakota had asked her in the bookstore that night—just what *did* she believe in?

"Hope," said Dakota, and once again Lucy looked at her friend in total bewilderment.

"What?" Lucy asked.

"The candlelight vigil. As an expression of hope." Dakota was standing up now, closing her knapsack with a tolerant smile. "Lucy, I'll be glad to go over all this again when you're back on the planet."

"I'm sorry. I'm just so out of it today."

"Candlelight vigil," Dakota repeated patiently. "For Angela. Tomorrow night in front of the school."

"Whose idea was this?"

"Some of her friends on the cheerleading squad. At least that's what I heard."

"Does my aunt know about it?"

"I'm sure someone plans on telling her. Do you think she'll come?"

Lucy shrugged. "I've given up thinking what she might or might not do."

The two headed off to class. They were just rounding a corner near the office when Lucy spotted several of the cheerleaders standing together, handing out flyers.

"Those are the notices," Dakota mumbled. "For the vigil tomorrow night."

As they got nearer, Lucy's heart began to quicken. She recognized one of the girls as Wanda Carver, and she stopped uncertainly in the middle of the hall.

"What?" Dakota stopped, too, her expression puzzled. "What is it?"

"Nothing. I'm okay."

"You sure?"

Lucy nodded. But her heart was beating faster now, and she could see Wanda starting toward her, one hand extended, passing Lucy one of the printed announcements.

Lucy stood frozen. Wanda was looking at her strangely, as strangely as Dakota was, and Lucy couldn't move, couldn't move even though she wanted to, even though she wanted to turn and run and never touch that paper that Wanda was touching . . .

But Wanda thrust the flyer into her hand, and Lucy had to take it. Had to take it and pretend nothing was wrong, while the quick, sharp flashes of danger strobed darkly through her brain.

"Lucy? You did this last time—what's wrong?"

And she could hear Dakota's voice so close to her as she whirled around and started away, away from the curious stares and away from the feeling of tragedy . . .

She's going to die on Thursday.

"I have to go back," Lucy said.

Breaking from Dakota's grasp, she pushed her way through the packed corridor. Wanda didn't even see her coming, not till Lucy was right beside her and leaning in close to her ear.

"Be careful," Lucy whispered. "Be careful tomorrow. Please."

The girl jumped back, completely startled and completely annoyed. "Hey, what do you think you are doing?"

"You could get hurt. You could fall and get hurt. Just please be careful."

"Get away from me! Are you *crazy*?"

Lucy pulled back. Wanda and her friends were staring at her with undisguised contempt, and Lucy's cheeks flamed in embarrassment.

"Sorry," she mumbled. "I just . . . It's a mistake. Sorry."

Turning on her heel, she ran to catch up with Dakota. But her heart was still pounding.

And the images in her mind had gone hopelessly black.

23

She and Dakota had almost been late for class.

Which is a good thing, Lucy reminded herself wryly.

There'd been no time for Dakota to question Lucy's strange behavior, no time for Wanda Carver to mortify Lucy more than she already had.

Still, by the end of the day, Lucy couldn't help noticing more curious stares and secretive whispers aimed in her general direction.

Lucy Dennison. Certified Nut Case.

She wished she could just go straight home and hide, but she'd already had to beg a ride from Dakota. Angela's car was waiting at Glen's Repair, and after that, Irene had asked her to pick up some dry cleaning.

"We can do that first," Dakota offered, coaxing

her truck from the school parking lot. "It's right next to the soup kitchen where I volunteer."

Lucy was impressed. "Do you really? I've always wanted to do that. What's it like?"

"Interesting. And humbling. It definitely keeps me grounded."

"Do you feed a big crowd?"

"Not like a lot of places, thank goodness." Dakota raised an eyebrow. "Pine Ridge is pretty affluent. But we have our share of homeless. You get to know the regulars. And then there're the ones just passing through town."

"So when do you work?"

"Saturdays mostly. But around holidays or when it's really cold, I work during the week, too."

"Do you think I could help out sometime?"

Looking genuinely pleased, Dakota nodded. "We'd love to have you. Would you like to stop by now and see it for yourself?"

"That'd be great."

As Dakota continued to drive, Lucy lapsed into silence. Several minutes passed before she cast her friend a troubled look.

"Dakota, I need a job."

She'd halfway expected shock at this announcement. At the very least, reminders about her aunt being one of the richest people in Pine Ridge. Dakota, however, kept her eyes on the road and creased her brow in thought.

"Doing what?" she asked.

"I don't know. Something useful." Shifting in the seat, she gave her friend a hard stare. "The thing is, Irene keeps telling me to use her credit cards. I don't want to ask her for anything. But there's stuff I need. And I don't have any money of my own."

Dakota's voice was quiet. "I understand."

"So do you know of anything?"

"Well . . . shops around here always need part-time help around Christmas. But they usually snap up the college kids first." She paused, fingers tightening on the steering wheel. "My dad might know of something. And I'll ask around, too. There's bound to be someone out there who needs you."

"You mean, they're just waiting for me to come along and walk right through their door?" Lucy couldn't help teasing.

"That's exactly what I mean."

The smile faded from Lucy's face. "You're really serious."

"Of course I am. You should know that by now."

"So you *really* believe that somebody who needs *one* particular job done is waiting *just* for me—out of *all* the other people in the universe."

Dakota's glance was solemn. "Lucy," she said, "there are no coincidences."

Lucy frowned, a sliver of uneasiness shinnying up her spine. Dakota's eyes shifted back to the windshield and stayed there the rest of the way. When they finally pulled up in front of the dry cleaner's, Lucy grabbed Dakota's arm before the girl could get out of the truck.

"Aren't you going to ask me?" she demanded.

Dakota gazed back at her, those pale blue eyes calm on Lucy's face.

"Ask you what?" Dakota murmured.

"You know. About Wanda Carver. About those weird spells I have. About what happened today."

"Do you want me to?" Dakota countered softly.

"Well, don't you think I'm crazy like everybody else does?"

That hint of a smile drifted over Dakota's mouth. She rested her hand on Lucy's.

"You're not crazy. You're a person with many secrets. And secrets should never be told until their time. And when they're ready to be told, then you'll tell me."

Lucy didn't know whether to laugh or to cry.

"Come on," Dakota said, shoving open the door. "Let's go sign you up."

Lucy instantly felt at home.

As Dakota showed her around the soup kitchen and introduced her to the staff, Lucy knew she'd made the right decision about volunteering. She hadn't felt such a warm, welcoming atmosphere since moving to Pine Ridge.

Not since her mother had died.

"See?" Dakota looked almost smug as she guided Lucy through the oversized pantry. "These are wonderful people. You fit right in."

"Thanks for letting me join."

"No. Thank *you*." Taking Lucy's arm, Dakota

led her to the main dining area. "Come on. I'll show you how we do the serving line. Just think of it as your friendly neighborhood buffet."

The room was practically empty. Three elderly women in threadbare coats sat at a table in one corner, chuckling over some shared bit of gossip, their raggedy shopping bags beside them on the floor. They waved to Dakota as she passed them, then went on with their conversation. Behind the serving counter, Dakota pointed out the contents of shelves and explained portion sizes, while Lucy listened attentively. She scarcely even noticed when the front door opened and the disheveled figure slunk in.

"Okay, here's someone," Dakota murmured, glancing toward the approaching stranger. "Perfect time to practice."

"Now?" Lucy asked hesitantly.

"Of course, now. Here. Just do it like I showed you."

Nodding, Lucy picked up a ladle and waited for the man to take a bowl. Dakota walked to the end of the counter where a few pieces of chocolate cake still remained in their baking pan.

"Hi," Lucy smiled, as the man stopped in front of the huge soup kettle.

For a moment he paused there, head lowered.

And then he looked up at her.

Dear God . . .

Lucy's fingers dug into the ladle, the smile frozen on her lips. For one panicky second she wondered if she'd actually been able to keep her face expressionless, if she'd managed to keep the revulsion from showing in her eyes.

His cheeks were scarred, this man standing before her—scarred and festering with sores. Across his forehead and through the matted beard on his chin, Lucy could see pus oozing out beneath big, wet scabs. Long hair lay over his shoulders in greasy strands. His body was rail-thin, his weary shoulders slumped, and the odor emanating from his tattered clothes made the bile rise into Lucy's throat.

She hastily tried to collect herself.

But she couldn't look away from his eyes.

His eyes . . .

At first glance she'd guessed him to be

young—somewhere in his twenties, perhaps. And yet his eyes were old.

The eyes of a very old man.

Eyes of vast experience. Intelligence and cunning.

Tragedy . . . but survival.

And as Lucy peered into their rheumy depths, she felt an unnerving shiver pass through her.

"Hi," she heard herself mumble again.

Beneath his coarse mustache, she thought he might have smiled. Rotten teeth and foul breath.

His eyes flickered dimly . . . some emotion she couldn't read.

Lucy plunged the ladle into the pot. Her hand was trembling, and she glanced up to see the man still watching her.

His hand was trembling like her own.

Trembling as he held out his empty bowl, waiting for her to fill it.

A rush of pity went through her. Pity and an understanding of his soul.

On his face . . . in his eyes . . . through the quivering of his hand, Lucy recognized the depth of isolation. The aching loneliness and despair. The qualities that kept him distant and apart.

Before she even realized what she was doing, she'd reached across the counter, taken his bowl, and in its place, laid her hand in his.

"I'm so glad you came today," she said softly.

He gazed at her in silence.

A penetrating silence as he slowly squeezed her hand.

Lucy's breath caught in her throat. For the space of one heartbeat, the air seemed to swell and split around her, as though something in the very atmosphere had changed.

Her head grew light.

Her skin flushed warm.

And from some very distant place came the burning familiarity of a deep, insistent ache . . .

"Lucy?"

Startled, Lucy turned toward the sound of a voice.

Dakota was standing beside her, easing the ladle from Lucy's clamped fingers.

"I think you've stirred that soup long enough," Dakota teased. "Save some of your strength for next time."

Lucy's eyes quickly scanned the room. Except for the three women still talking in their corner, all the tables were empty.

"Where'd he go?" Lucy asked.

"Who?"

"The man who came in to eat."

"He left about fifteen minutes ago." Dakota gave her a funny look. "Didn't you notice?"

"I . . . I guess not."

"Now, that's what I call being involved in your work." As Lucy stared down at the counter, Dakota stepped back, studying her with a thoughtful frown. "But you're upset, aren't you? About that man."

Lucy didn't answer. Her hands felt cold now, her mind hazy—as though she'd just awakened from a dream.

"I know how you feel," Dakota said, trying to comfort her. "It was hard for me, too, at first. Seeing people like that, and wanting so much to help them. But we *are* helping. Just for the time they're here, we *are* making a difference in their lives."

"Who was he?" Lucy's voice was tight. "Do you know?"

"That's odd, isn't it? He must be one of those transients I was telling you about. I've never seen him around here before."

With a sigh, Dakota gazed out the front window, out at the people and shadows mingling together in the dusk.

"You were so kind to him, Lucy. He'll probably never forget you."

24

Her touch still clung to him.

He could still feel the pressure of her hand in his . . . the softness of her skin . . . the length and slender shape of every finger.

Her warmth had flowed into him, a surge of emotions that had shocked each one of his senses into wonder.

Her concern and compassion . . . her undisguised pity . . .

And the sorrowful understanding in her eyes.

It had left him stunned and seriously shaken, a wound within the nether regions of his soul, for seldom in his lifetime had he ever known understanding.

Understanding made one vulnerable.

A lesson he'd learned well, and long ago.

So now he paced, gripped by a strange,

trembling restlessness, his skin too tight, his face transforming into another. He paced like an animal in a cage, stopping only long enough to gaze out through the darkness—the deep, deceptive darkness that was his only friend.

This was his domain, as it had always been, as it would always be.

This kingdom of the night, as black and impenetrable as his soul.

"Damn her."

How could his plan have gone so completely awry?

"Damn her!"

What had he expected? Another ruse to get close to her, to hide behind the essence of his nature and see himself reflected in her eyes.

And for a single moment, he had watched her hovering there on the brink of disgust and aversion, startled by his ugliness and trying not to show it, drowning in the poison of his stare.

But then, without warning, she'd changed.

He had not expected it—not even seen it coming—when suddenly he'd *felt* it. *Felt* it like warm, soothing waves; like gentle arms reaching out to take him in, into a place of comfort and acceptance. He felt it a thousand times stronger than *anything* he'd felt from her before.

He had been so fascinated, so dismayed, he'd simply stood frozen there in place and squeezed her hand.

It had been all he could do not to moan out loud.

Moan with the desire for her, the *need* for her, the wild and desperate hunger for her.

For he had felt *her* longing, as well.

Her ache as strong as his, as deep and un-fulfilled, the frantic throbbing of her pulse, and their connection so strong, so overwhelming, it had sucked his breath away . . .

Distracted his instincts . . . driven him mad.

Since he'd left the soup kitchen, he'd thought of nothing else.

He had no choice but to go to her.

Force her if he had to, take her *now* if he had to—he would *not* wait for willingness or surrender or the right and perfect time.

But even as he crouched upon her balcony, where he'd spent so many nights before, he knew that he must hold himself in check. Remain anonymous and watchful. Infinitely patient. Disguised as whomever she needed him to be.

Like fine gray mist, he slipped inside her room.

Gazed upon her silently as she slept.

Damn her for making him feel!

For touching him like that . . . with her hand and with her heart!

For making him remember another life in another time, times of understanding . . . times of sharing love . . .

No, he would *not* feel—he would *not* remember!

He would feed.

And he would kill.

And he would survive.

For these were the only things that mattered to him now.

The only things he loved and understood.

25

Lucy still couldn't understand what had happened.

Everything had been so normal, everything had been going so well—spending the afternoon with Dakota, and meeting the people at the soup kitchen, and volunteering for something that really mattered.

And then that stranger had come in.

That pathetic young man with the festering sores and the hunger in his very old eyes.

She hadn't been able to stop herself.

She'd reached out her hand and she'd touched him, and slowly she'd begun to recognize something.

Something that had touched her before.

Impossible.

Absolutely impossible.

But now she was lying in bed and thinking back on the whole unsettling experience, trying to tell herself it was only one of those blackouts Dr. Fielding had warned her about, one of those memory lapses.

After all . . . hadn't she lost fifteen whole minutes?

Fifteen minutes unaccounted for, while the stranger had sat down at a table and eaten his meal and left again by the front door?

Of course it had been just memory loss.

How else could she ever explain it?

Yet a doubt still persisted in the back of her mind . . . a nagging doubt and a lingering nightmare . . .

A nightmare swift and needle-sharp—stabbing like fire, piercing hot through my skin, sinking deep through my flesh, clamping down and holding on, suspended there . . .

Lucy turned restlessly, unable to sleep.

Shadows pressed around the bed and shrouded her in black.

Suspended there on boiling waves of panic and burning pleasure . . .

The room seemed to be holding its breath as her fingertips stroked the darkness.

Burning pleasure . . . waves rushing over me . . . through me . . .

Once again Lucy pictured the stranger's face.

She pulled the covers over her head and hid beneath them till morning.

26

He had felt her fingertips caressing his cheek . . .
gliding over his throat . . . down the front of his
chest.

She hadn't even known what she'd done.

Hadn't even realized how close he'd been
standing, only inches away from her bed.

But now it was one stroke past midnight.

He'd been watching the hands of the clock
on her nightstand, the minutes creeping by like
hours, the hours stretching out like the endless
decades of his life.

Lucy's restlessness was nothing, compared to
his own.

His growing frustration, his need to be filled.

There was only one thing that could satisfy
him.

And he would be no gentleman tonight.

He ran through the woods and on through the town, his midnight senses keen and alert, the darkness flowing over him like wind.

It was in the park where he finally caught the girl's scent.

Not virginal blood, but deliciously seasoned all the same.

She was small and well built, athletic and strong, with very short hair, like a boy's. She had books under one arm and she smelled of sweet powder, strained peaches, and soft, fluffy blankets.

She had been babysitting.

And now she was on her way home.

He trailed her over a footbridge, then slunk out of sight behind the trees and the bushes, just one more shadow among many. He kept pace with her and wondered how long it would be until she sensed she was being followed.

Not so long, after all.

Like countless times before, he recognized that first dawning hint of awareness, that first wary glance back over the shoulder, that first startled quickening of the feet.

He always enjoyed that initial shock. That

primal instinct of approaching death, innate to every species.

For a while she walked faster, and so did he.

Then suddenly she stopped and turned to face him.

"Who's there?" she called in a quivering voice, trying so hard to be brave. "I know you're there; you're not scaring me."

And so he let her see him.

He watched her eyes go wide; he smelled her helpless terror. The thrill of the hunt surged through him—that heady anticipation of the kill, that stamina and speed no mortal could ever hope to match.

Just for fun, he gave her a head start.

She screamed, but no one heard.

And for one desperate minute of her tragically young life, he let her think she might actually get away.

But he had no patience for the chase tonight.

And he was upon her so quickly, she didn't even struggle.

Afterward he lay there on the cold, wet ground, feeling empty and disappointed . . . gorged but unfulfilled.

The dead girl's eyes stared up at him. There was no malice there, no accusation—but rather a look of blank and sad surprise.

He took her to the footbridge that spanned the concrete drainage ditch.

With one swift motion he broke her neck for good measure, then tossed her over the railing.

New power for every life . . .

A new century for every soul.

With a bitter smile, he went back into the night . . . as silently and stealthily as he had come.

27

"You can't do this, Matt," Lucy said. "There's got to be another way. You *can't* just put her in some nursing home."

Startled, Matt glanced up from his desk. Lucy was standing rigidly in the doorway of the office, looking close to tears.

"Do we have an appointment?" Hurriedly he pretended to search through his calendar. Lucy was not amused.

"Matt, this is serious. How could you do such a terrible thing?"

"Lucy, *I'm* not doing it. And who told *you* about it?"

"Dakota heard some people talking in the bookstore last night. Some of Byron's neighbors, I guess."

Matt leaned back in his chair. He steepled his fingers beneath his chin and slowly shook his head.

"Mrs. Dempsey can't stay forever, and we can't expect her to. It was always understood that the arrangement was temporary."

"Yes," Lucy reminded him. "Till you could find someone else. But you *haven't* found anyone else yet."

"And it doesn't look like we're going to. Look, I'm as sorry about it as you are, Lucy, but we don't have a choice. Even with the nurse and with neighbors being kind enough to drop in, Byron's grandmother can't be alone at night."

"Then I'll do it."

Lifting an eyebrow, Matt stared at her. "What do you mean, you'll do it?"

"My aunt's going on a trip to Paris. She'll be gone at least two weeks and—"

"The woman's compassion knows no bounds," he groaned. "Are you serious?"

"She told me yesterday. Some sort of exchange program at the university. And I really don't want to stay in that house by myself."

"Well, you *shouldn't*. I'm really sorry, Lucy—"

"The thing is," Lucy interrupted, not feeling up to sympathy at the moment, "do you think Byron's grandmother would even *want* me there?"

"Why wouldn't she?"

"You know why. Maybe she couldn't even stand to look at me. And I wouldn't blame her."

"She's not like that. She's very sweet. Even Mrs. Dempsey says so." Folding his arms behind his head, Matt leaned back even farther. "And if anyone can manage to stay sweet around Mrs. Dempsey, they qualify for sainthood in my opinion."

"Can you arrange it?" Lucy pleaded, but Matt hedged.

"Lucy . . . are you sure you want to do this for the right reasons?"

"I have good reasons."

"Yeah, but . . . maybe you're thinking more about how bad *you* feel, than about how bad *Mrs. Wetherly* feels." Pausing, he added, "It won't work as penance, you know."

Lucy's voice lowered. "But won't my being there help *both* of us?"

For a long moment Matt said nothing. Then finally he gave a deep sigh.

"And I suppose you want me to talk to your aunt about it, too?"

"Would you? If anyone can convince her, you can."

"Thanks. I think." Matt's smile was dubious. "There's the bell. You better get to class."

But Lucy didn't move. "Are you going to the vigil tonight?"

"Actually, I've been asked to say a few words. What about you?"

"I'm coming with Irene."

There was another lengthy hesitation before he spoke. "You think you're up to this?"

"Do I really have a choice?"

With a grim expression she turned to leave, then promptly faced him again.

"Matt?"

"Yes?"

"That medallion you gave me? You never told me anything about—"

"Bell." He pointed sternly toward the hallway. "Late. Go."

Lucy made it to homeroom just in time. Sliding into her seat, she rested one cheek on her pile of books and gazed out the window as

253

the morning's announcements came over the intercom.

In the distance she could see a large group heading off toward the athletic field—coaches, cheerleaders, band members, even some football players, it looked like. And though they were too far away to distinguish each face individually, it was obvious they were all in high spirits—laughing, jostling, joking around.

Lucy's heart melted in relief.

Everyone was happy. Everything was fine. It was Thursday and no one had died . . .

"And no one's *going* to die. And whatever I saw in my mind was a *mistake*. And I'm *not* turning into Katherine."

But she realized she was whispering to herself, and that her hands were clamped tightly over her ears, trying to drown out *another* voice—a sad, empty voice whispering far back in the darkness of her mind . . .

Everything's not *fine, Lucy* . . .

And it's only morning.

The candlelight vigil was scheduled for seven-thirty.

As Lucy let herself into the house that afternoon, it was obvious Irene wasn't there yet. No messages on the answering machine. No notes beside the phone.

She hoped Irene remembered.

How would it look if Angela's own mother didn't attend the service?

Lucy wished she could miss it herself. She dreaded the emotional impact of the ceremony—it had been looming over her like a dark cloud all day. Now she just wanted to get it over with.

Peeling off her coat and gloves, she threw them over the bannister and went up to her room. She was dressed and ready by six o'clock. Dressed for the weather and feeling edgy because Irene still wasn't home.

Darkness had already fallen, and as lights began coming on throughout the house, Lucy went downstairs to turn on more.

By seven, she was really getting worried. Pacing around the kitchen, she nearly jumped out of her skin when the telephone rang. She hesitated, suddenly afraid to pick it up, then heard Irene's voice on the machine.

"Lucy, are you there? I'm running late. Just go on without me, and I'll meet you at the school."

Relieved, Lucy started back to her room to grab another sweater.

But the doorbell stopped her halfway.

She hurried down again, then looked nervously out through the peephole. Within the distorted angle of the lens, she could see a tall figure standing on the porch, his back to her, a clipboard dangling from one hand.

Cautiously, Lucy cracked open the front door.

"Special delivery," the man announced. But he didn't turn around, and Lucy stood there on the threshold, watching him in wary surprise.

"It's kind of late," she said. "What kind of delivery?"

"Are you Lucy Dennison?"

Hesitating, Lucy nodded. "Yes, that's me."

"Then sign here."

She saw him turn around. Saw his pale sharp features and his deep-set eyes as he fixed her with a steady gaze. Both his truck and his uniform were black, but neither of them were printed with a name.

"What is it?" Lucy's voice tightened. "Who's it from?"

His gaze lingered a moment longer. "Well," he said at last, "I imagine that's part of the surprise." He thrust a clipboard at her. It had a pen attached to it, and a sheet of paper that was blank. "Just sign your name. I have other appointments to keep."

Again Lucy hesitated. Then she quickly scribbled her name.

"But what delivery company are you with?" she persisted.

"I told you. A special one."

Before she could ask anything more, the man turned and walked off. Lucy watched him climb into his truck and drive away from the house.

Then she looked down at the box.

It was fairly large—and seemed to weigh a ton. When Lucy couldn't lift it, she finally managed to drag it into the hall, then locked the door and stood there, frowning down at the package.

Who would be sending her a special delivery? And why?

She chewed anxiously on a fingernail. She

stood and tapped her foot, trying to decide what to do.

She didn't have time for packages right now; she had to get to the vigil. She had to meet Irene. She had to be brave and strong.

She glanced at her watch.

If she hurried, she'd still have time to open the box. It wouldn't take that long to drive over to the high school, and since this thing was a special delivery, then it must be something important.

Yet still she stood and stared at it.

Watching as if something might suddenly unwrap itself and jump out at her.

She was being silly—paranoid—but her curiosity was stronger.

Retrieving some scissors from the kitchen, she cut away the mailing tape and lifted the cardboard flaps on top.

It was wrapped very tight, very thickly.

Whatever it was, it had been well protected and packed with great care.

Lucy got a knife from the kitchen drawer. With painstaking caution, she began to work the heavy padding loose.

She was almost there.

She could feel something beneath the filling now . . . something hard and heavy and cold and smooth . . .

No, not quite smooth . . .

Mostly smooth, but with something carved into its surface.

Words? Numbers?

With one final tug, the packing material came away in her hands. Lucy leaned forward into the light and gazed down into the box.

Oh God . . . Oh God, no . . .

The headstone was gray, crowned with a gently rounded arch.

And its design was stark and simple, except for the large black letters engraved deeply across the front.

ANGELA FOSTER

RIP

28

She thought she might have screamed.

Stumbling backward, Lucy heard a distant, anguished cry, the strangled voice of someone she barely even recognized.

She groped for the wall, for something—*anything*—to hold on to. Yet her eyes remained fixed on the headstone and the name that would be on everyone's minds, on everyone's lips, in less than fifteen minutes.

Her knees gave way.

She crumpled on to the floor.

Burying her face in her hands, she tried to think what to do, but her mind wouldn't cooperate. *Call the police? Get out of the house? Go to someone for help?*

Matt would be at the vigil by now. Dakota,

too. Thank God, Irene hadn't come home tonight.

Irene . . .

Lucy's hands slid away from her eyes.

She had to hide the headstone from Irene. No matter what course of action she ultimately decided to take, she couldn't leave the headstone here for Irene to see. She'd have to put it somewhere else. She'd have to *hide* it somewhere else. At least for the time being.

The vigil was just about ready to start. She was already late, and everyone was sure to notice if she didn't show up. There was no way she'd ever lift that box. Maybe she could get Dakota or Matt to help her later, but for now she'd have to hide it somewhere close. Somewhere close enough to drag it.

Frantically she looked around the downstairs. She couldn't focus, couldn't concentrate. *Call the police—I have to call the police! This time I have something real to show them—this time they'll have to believe me!*

But she couldn't call them right now, she couldn't tell them about the deliveryman and the unmarked truck and this horrible, hideous headstone; she had to get to the service for Angela.

Another sick joke?

If it was, someone had gone to an awful lot of trouble and expense just to pull it off. They'd have had to be sure it was delivered here just in time. They'd have had to be sure Lucy was home to receive it.

Would kids at school go to all that effort?

And if they *had* done it, would they be at the vigil tonight, waiting to see her reaction?

But she didn't have time to go over that now. She had to get rid of the headstone.

She could feel her thoughts jumping back and forth, exploding like firecrackers. No matter where she hid the headstone, Irene would be sure to find it. And if Irene didn't, then Florence *certainly* would—the woman was fastidious about cleaning every nook and cranny of this house.

So I can't hide it in here. I'll have to put it outside.

Her watch read seven-thirty now. Irene would be at the vigil, wondering where she was—and Lucy had no idea what she'd tell her.

I'll think of something—I'll worry about that later.

With all the force she could muster, Lucy began dragging the box toward the front door. If she could just get it out on the porch, she might be able to tip it off into the shrubbery. At least the front of the house was landscaped with evergreens—if she worked it underneath some of the branches and piled dead leaves over it, no one was likely to spot it, even if they stood right there and rang the bell.

At least it's worth a try.

At least till Irene's away from the house, so I can report it to the police.

Or at least till I can come up with a better idea . . .

Later she wondered if fear and shock had given her superhuman strength—but for now, all Lucy cared about was wrestling that carton underneath the bushes. As it landed with a dull thud, she hastily camouflaged it, then hurried to the car and drove straight to Pine Ridge High.

She didn't even remember the ride over.

It was as if her mind had detached from the rest of her, and stayed behind with Angela's headstone. She didn't know how she was going to face Irene, knowing what she knew, knowing what she'd just hidden beside the porch. How would she ever be able to act normally? Act as if nothing were wrong?

"But everything's wrong," Lucy whispered.

The sound of her own voice startled her.

Slowly, she began to come back to herself, and she realized she was parked at the school. She could see a huge circle of glowing light on the front lawn of the campus—dozens of tiny, flickering candle flames, and the shadowy figures of those who held them.

Voices were singing softly. Some popular song she felt she should recognize, but couldn't.

Go on. You have to.

Yet still she sat there, watching from a distance. Thinking about the headstone. Wondering what it meant.

She hadn't wanted to admit that Angela might never come home again, even though at times she'd felt it so strongly.

And now . . .

It doesn't mean anything!

Lucy shook her head, fighting back angry

tears. Angela had run away, just like all those times before, and Angela would come home again, just like Irene had predicted.

Lucy wanted to believe that.

Even now . . . she still wanted *so much* to believe that.

Taking in a deep gulp of air, Lucy willed herself to get out of the car. She stood for a moment, trying to empty her mind of bad thoughts, trying to compose her features into some semblance of hope.

She started walking toward the light.

And even before she got there, she sensed that something was wrong.

At first it was the subtle shifting of the crowd . . . the murmurs of curiosity and confusion . . . the gradual fading of voices, one by one.

Uneasy glances and eyes going wide . . .

Then cries of shock and disbelief.

As Lucy approached the circle, the first one she spotted was Matt.

He looked stunned and speechless, and all around him people had frozen in place like statues.

Irene was standing rigidly beside him. Her expression seemed to be caught somewhere between sheer relief and sheer horror.

Above each fluttering candle flame, faces had turned to stiff and bloodless masks.

Lucy saw the police.

She saw Dakota breaking through the circle, pushing her way slowly over to where Lucy had stopped to stare.

She felt her own lips move, though no sound came out.

And she heard Dakota answer her directly, as if Lucy's silent question had been spoken all too clearly.

"It's Wanda Carver." Dakota's face was the color of ash. "They found her in the park tonight. Just about an hour ago."

The world began to shimmer.

The world and Dakota's face and the glowing circle of hope, all shimmering through the swell of Lucy's tears.

"She's dead," Lucy murmured.

Dakota nodded. "She fell off the footbridge over that old drainage ditch in the park. She broke her neck on the concrete."

"When . . . When did it happen?"

"They're saying it happened sometime early this morning." Dakota's gaze was calm and unwavering. "But then . . . you already knew that, didn't you?"

29

She hadn't been able to talk.

She hadn't been able to answer Dakota's quiet accusation, or to defend herself, or to think of anything else except getting out of there and getting away.

She'd turned and run.

Run to the car and driven off.

She'd driven with no idea of where to go or how to get there—simply driven all over town, up one street and down another, till she began to think that Irene might be wondering about her and that she'd probably better get back to the house.

It had actually surprised her to see Irene sitting up, waiting for her. The woman's face had been taut and bewildered, and she'd stared at Lucy for a long, long time, as though her niece were a total stranger.

"When they said they'd found a girl, I thought it was Angela." Irene had finally spoken, though her eyes had been fixed on a place far beyond Lucy. "And then it was someone else. And I was glad."

Irene's numb gaze had turned to Lucy then. And her voice had faltered.

"How cruel of me," she'd mumbled. "To be glad some other girl's dead."

Lucy had felt so helpless. She'd walked over to her aunt's chair, and she'd laid a hand on her aunt's stiff shoulder.

"Aunt Irene . . ."

"She'll be home," Irene had said softly. "It's just a matter of time, you'll see—and Angela will be home."

"Aunt Irene—"

"Go to bed now, Lucy."

But she couldn't stay in bed any longer.

Now Lucy got dressed and slipped quietly from the house. She backed the car down the driveway and headed for Pine Ridge Cemetery.

What little sleep she'd managed to get last night had been fraught with reality and tormented with the truth.

The truth she must finally face.

The truth she must finally accept.

It's real.

Lucy watched the cold, gray dawn creep slowly through the trees. A patina of frost coated the houses and lawns, and a lazy sun continued to slumber behind a thin layer of clouds.

The gift Katherine gave me . . . the powers Katherine gave me . . .

Real.

They're all real.

How could she have ignored it for so long? Been so unwilling to believe?

Because to believe in this gift means believing in other things, too. The dreams and the nightmares, the feelings and visions, the instincts I've never been able to trust before . . .

The existence of unbelievable things . . . unexplainable things . . .

Evil and unseen things.

She felt as if she'd betrayed herself.

And somehow . . . even worse . . . betrayed Byron.

Tears dampened her cheeks. Her heart ached with grief and regret.

When Byron was here, he'd shown her the truth. Shown her a destiny and purpose. Convinced her that her journey, no matter how dangerous or uncertain, was still necesssary and worthwhile.

She'd lost so much in the accident that night.

Byron.

Her faith . . .

Her self.

If only she could have them all back again.

If only she could speak to Byron one more time . . .

So that's why she'd decided to visit the cemetery this morning. To sit beside Byron's resting place and try to sort things out. She wanted to tell him everything, everything that had happened since he'd died. And she wanted to think that somehow he might really hear her . . . help her figure out what to do . . . help her make sense of things.

She wanted to believe that maybe—somehow—she wasn't really as alone as she felt.

But after entering the cemetery, Lucy began to have second thoughts. She hadn't expected it to look so spooky at this hour of the morning. Like wandering phantoms, tatters of soft white mist hovered among the graves, and an unnatural quiet smothered the sound of her footsteps as she made her way to the remote section of the burial grounds. The dead slept deep and undisturbed. Remembered and forgotten alike, they surrounded her on all sides, rotting peacefully to dust.

In the distance, the Wetherly mausoleum came darkly into view, silhouetted against the gloom. As Lucy got nearer, she could see the wrought-iron gates and stone angels that guarded it, and for one unsettling moment, she remembered her dream about Byron and his warning.

"Keep away . . . there's no one in this place."

An icy shudder worked its way up her spine. Hesitating, she dug her hands into her coat pockets and glanced back over her shoulder.

Come on, Lucy, get a grip.

It was easy to imagine eerie whispers and invisible watchers in a creepy place like this— what had she been thinking anyway, coming here so early?

Stop scaring yourself. Nobody here can hurt you.

Giving herself a stern mental shake, she walked over to the front of the tomb. To her surprise, the double gates weren't padlocked as she'd assumed they'd be—in fact, they were standing partway open, one of them creaking rustily as the breeze swung it back and forth.

Heart quickening, Lucy glanced around a second time.

If someone *were* here, they'd be impossible to see, she admitted to herself. Anyone could be hiding close by or far away.

Lucy suppressed another shiver.

Turning in a slow circle, she scanned the graves and headstones, the sepulchres and statues, the trees and shadows and mist. A taste of fear crept into her throat, and she tried to choke it down.

Cautiously, she turned back to the gates.

Taking one in each hand, she eased them open the rest of the way. Cracks had widened along the foundation, and leaves had sifted in over the broken, weathered stones of the floor.

Holding her breath, Lucy walked into the crypt.

She saw the muddy footprints and tufts of clotted hair; the dark, reddish-brown stains smeared along the walls . . .

But she didn't see the figure behind her.

Not till she turned and screamed and stumbled from his arms, trying wildly to fight her way free.

And then she stared up, shocked, into eyes as black and deep as midnight.

"Oh my God," she choked. "Who are you?"

The dark-haired young man gazed coolly back at her.

"Byron's brother," he answered. "Who the hell are *you*?"